"EXHILARATING ...
A sinewy thriller that leaves you wide-eyed ...
top-drawer action and a breathtaking battle
on high steel."
—*Publishers Weekly*

Evan Scott has seen terror up close, but now it is coming closer. When he looks into the young woman's eyes, he sees total fear. She is falling from atop an unfinished Manhattan skyscraper, and her eyes meet his as she plummets past him.

In that instant, Evan's sweet, comfortable life is forever shattered. A successful architect, Evan has led the life men dream of: the coolly beautiful wife, the lovely daughter, and a mistress who fills him with passion. Evan quickly becomes obsessed with the reasons behind the woman's death.

Now, his questions have made Evan the target of a mysterious crime family that even the Mafia fears, and suddenly no one is safe. And as the carnage climbs, Evan realizes it's left to him to track down the enemy. To be a killer of killers. If he lives. . . .

"Action with guns flashing, elevators soaring, . good KARMA."
s

be missed."
uel

"A compulsive page-turner."
—*Library Journal*

KARMA

MITCHELL SMITH

AN ONYX BOOK

ONYX
Published by the Penguin Group
Penguin Books USA Inc., 375 Hudson Street,
New York, New York 10014, U.S.A.
Penguin Books Ltd, 27 Wrights Lane,
London W8 5TZ, England
Penguin Books Australia Ltd, Ringwood,
Victoria, Australia
Penguin Books Canada Ltd, 10 Alcorn Avenue,
Toronto, Ontario, Canada M4V 3B2
Penguin Books (N.Z.) Ltd, 182–190 Wairau Road,
Auckland 10, New Zealand

Penguin Books Ltd, Registered Offices:
Harmondsworth, Middlesex, England

Published by Onyx, an imprint of Dutton Signet,
a division of Penguin Books USA Inc.
Previously published in a Dutton edition.

First Onyx Printing, January, 1996
10 9 8 7 6 5 4 3 2 1

To Linda

prologue

●●

Mr. Feng, used to cheerful service, sat surprised and angry at his usual table for Tuesday's late supper at the Jade Blossom. The boy, Chu, had brought their food with a face of wood. —Hadn't greeted Mr. Feng or his guests; hadn't returned their greetings; had kept his head lowered and refused to smile at all. And only said (in English), "Cook made special dish, sir. Nut dumpling."

"And what would that be, a nut dumpling?"

"Cook make special for you, sir. . . ." Still no smile of courtesy for Mr. Feng or his guests—rather a pale uneasy face, sweating as if the boy were frightened.

Mr. Feng, an officer of the Fortunate Society—not a tong, though some outsiders called it that—was a polite man, easygoing and pleasant to deal with, when those he dealt with were pleasant to him.

When they were not, he was not.

"Set the food down, then, you dirty immigrant creature," he said in Chinese, *"so you do not sweat into it."*

The boy put the dishes quietly down, and backed away from the table as if Mr. Feng might see that harm came to him for his rudeness. —Nonsense, of course. Mr. Feng was a businessman, with many men and women working for him in his painting-and-lacquering company, and in his other companies. These men and women (many newcomers to this country, this city) appreciated his protection, worked their twelve hours each day, and were never discourteous to him.

. . . Still, the cook had cooked well. A wonderful meal, though ill-served. Thrice-shredded pork . . . sweet mushrooms and sesame noodles. The new things, the nut dumplings, were excellent—though his guests refused them, smiling—a soft, sweet boiled dough surrounding a tiny chewy center, rich with ginger, and apparently to be swallowed whole.

A fine meal, if out of a kitchen quieter than usual at the Jade Blossom—silent, in fact, where it was usually noisy with clatter and coarse joking. A fine meal, but from a silent kitchen, and served miserably.

Though his guests didn't seem to mind. The brothers sat smiling as if there'd been no disagreement with him, no question about additional payment for what had proved additional work. Three dissimilar brothers—Hindus, who at least ate with knife and fork in the European fashion and spoke good English. Mr. Feng had been concerned they might eat with their fingers and shame him at the Jade Blossom.

These three brothers had attempted courtesy, except for the fat one, who talked and talked and seemed to believe everything was amusing.

A fat brother, a handsome brother, and a mournful one. The handsome brother seemed bored, and had eaten only a little food. The mournful one, his face long-nosed, dark eyes sad as a clown's, had talked business for them . . . but appeared resigned to the additional payment, to the reasonableness, the justice of it.

A tedious supper, but over at last, and the three Hindus seen to their car, the fat one still smiling, joking.

... Mr. Feng had business that evening in the Bronx—north of the Black Monkeys' neighborhood but reached through their neighborhood—so he drove north with the doors of his green Cadillac locked, and would have been more comfortable·if young Joe Lu had accompanied him, armed.

Mr. Feng drove through dark streets, and at 111th and Amsterdam felt some difficulty with his stomach.

A few minutes later, a few blocks later, this difficulty became more severe, and he cursed the cook at the Jade Blossom. And in mid-curse (as if the curse had been caught by an angry ghost and turned back upon him) Mr. Feng was seized by such a furious cramp that he gasped for breath, doubled forward at the steering wheel, and was barely able to turn out of the avenue's traffic ... turn to the right into a side street. Barely able to bring the car to a stop along the curb.

He imagined his stomach twisting in fury at bad food, at too much ginger—but was mistaken. Ginger was not the cause. The cause was the opening of the first of the little dumpling nuts—not nuts at all, really, but tiny tight coils of slivers of green bamboo. This first sliver, needle-pointed at each end, had been released as the hair-fine threads that bound it dissolved in the acids of digestion.

Those threads dissolved, the sliver had uncoiled, snapped straight, and punctured the wall of Mr. Feng's stomach.

There, the acid had come out.

Mr. Feng, a man of courage and self-control, accepted this severe discomfort and partially mastered it—aided no little by a notion of revenge against the cook at the Jade Blossom.

He sat in his green Cadillac, parked under a streetlight on a street of near darkness, and took deep breaths. He supposed the pain might be getting better.

Then the second tiny coil (smaller than a pea when bound) became unbound, sprang straight—a little green needle—and in his stomach's convulsive churning was caught up and spun, shifted again. Stuck, and at the next spasm pierced the stomach's wall.

Three more opened almost together.

Now, Mr. Feng began to lose control of himself. Lost moment by moment any sense of dignity, of propriety. Now, astonished at what was happening to him, he began to writhe and thrust himself back and forth on his car's rich green leather upholstery. He saw for an instant his own face in the rearview mirror, saw it astonished as a child's at his agony.

Two more bamboo coils snapped open . . . though only one pierced the belly's wall to let a little more acid out. And Mr. Feng began to shout and threw himself this way and that as if to throw himself out of his pain and he scrabbled and plucked at the door locks.

Then he pounded on his belly, as if it were eating him alive and must be beaten to make it stop. He pounded on his belly and arched back almost into his Cadillac's backseat, and shouted something.

Two young black boys and a young black girl had come down to the sidewalk to watch, and they stood under yellow streetlight and watched through the car windows as Mr. Feng heaved and thrashed among his leather seat cushions, and done with shouting, began to scream.

Then blood, at last, was vomited up, called up by screaming—and spattered on the window glass so the children stepped back, startled. Soon, as several older people joined them, they came close again, and watched through stained windows as Mr. Feng, lost to himself, eating himself alive, passed into convulsions, his mouth—difficult for them to see in shadow—stretched wide for screaming, but now making no sound at all. . . .

chapter 1

· ·

The night wind had risen off the Sound, and now sang in the old house's chimneys, hissed like soft surf through the oaks and maples around it.

Evan Scott lay awake in moonlight, listening to Catherine's slow and steady breathing beside him. The wind softly complained down the bedroom chimney—a higher note here than had sounded in his room as a child. His boyhood room, down the hall, was now Beth's—and decorated in peach and gold, crowded with stuffed animals that she, at twelve, still talked to. Evan had heard her one evening as he was walking past her room, gossiping with Baloo, her large and tattered bear. Beth doing the talking (about creepy Susan Clystroop). Baloo only listening.

The wind was increasing, gusting now and then so the trees outside the bedroom's windows, thick with summer foliage, roared softly and leaned away from it.

He heard the big house creak faintly as the wind came again. The house—with its ancient joinery, its timbers pegged and fastened with handmade spikes— sounded like a ship in a moderate sea, running before a variable wind . . . now, he thought, beginning to slacken.

And in a while, as the wind's sound began to slowly

ease down the scale, note by note, Evan drifted ...
drifted, and slept.

He dreamed he was back in-country. He dreamed a
particular day he'd dreamed many times before—and
almost aware it was a dream, began to live it just the
same.

The patrol was down from the foothills, and had lost
seven men—most out of the second squad—in the four
days out and back. Seven dead and airlifted out. Four
very badly hurt and lifted with them.

"A record, Lieutenant," Sergeant Beckwith had said.
"With all due respect, sir—definitely a record fuckup. . . ."

Now, coming back down—one day's march to the
lines—he dreamed the weary route-marching exactly
as it had been. He smelled the spoiled stink of his
sweat and Billy Torrance's sweat as the radioman
walked two meters ahead of him along a narrow peas-
ants' pathway through the paddies. The fields, flooded
shallow, stretched away on either side to distant
treelines of leaning palms. Except for the path's brown
mud, trudged into wet holes by their boots as they
went, everything was colored green in every shade
from almost bright yellow to nearly black, greens so
rich they seemed to seethe and tremble in the heat.

Evan, staggering, weary, dreamed that he was
dreaming. He marched as the others marched, watching
the distant treelines for the first twinkling flashes of
gunfire, listening for a far-off mortar's thump. Watching the path for a punji pit the others had avoided by
luck ... or the faint black line of wire stretched across,
fastened to a surprise.

Evan's remnant squad-and-a-few humped their
weapons and ammo and canteens and equipment along
the narrow way for more than two hours, deeper into
morning and greater and greater heat, until they

marched like dead men marching, and Evan, dreaming, watched it all. Then he saw the path dividing a shallow paddy pond about thirty meters farther on—the trail slightly raised there and tempting as the only solid ground. Evan saw the point man, Diller, step to the right away from that too convenient walkway, and splash instead through the water. . . . Saw Sergeant Beckwith, following at good interval.

In this dream of perfect recollection, Evan tried as he always tried to break the dream and shout a warning to Beckwith. Shout and run past the line of marching men—run past them, shoving them aside, yelling to Beckwith to stay on the path.

But the dream remained too well remembered. And held to silence, Evan watched as he'd watched so many times before. Beckwith ahead . . . stepping to the left off the dubious trail—stepping to the left and taking three strides through very shallow water. To vanish in the white blaze of the blast.

As always—and exactly as it had been—Evan was now allowed to run, shoved the crouching men aside, and found Jack Beckwith sitting and searching through a haze of burned explosive, looking for his left leg—and seeing it lying just out of reach in reddening paddy water still riffled by the shock wave.

"What the fuck *happened*?" The sergeant, sitting half naked, scorched and newly deaf, spoke loud, but not loud enough for the deafened nearest men to hear him. Drenched by fallout water, they crouched in the after-ringing of concussion, and stared at him.

Evan dreamed he did as he had done then—stepped toward his sergeant, moving slowly in silence through a silenced world. And exactly as he had done then, the dreamed Sergeant Beckwith sat squinting through eddying smoke, and put up his right hand, palm out, to stop him.

"Fuckin' mines here, Lieutenant. . . ." the sergeant said. Then, looking exasperated, impatient, Beckwith rocked unsteadily on his limited support and fell face forward with a soft splash the squad could feel, if not quite yet could hear.

"No . . . *no!*" Evan said. The first "no" said there, in the paddy's roasting heat—the last, in the cool present as he woke . . . and lay blinded by memory, his heart pounding.

"What is it?" Catherine beside him, murmuring from sleep. "—Are you all right?" Always her nighttime question, concerned, Evan supposed, about a heart attack.

He caught his breath, then said, ". . . A remodel nightmare," and sat up and slowly slid out from under the covers. "—Total kitchen."

Sid Buchman wasn't on the train. Or Deitner, or Keith Peck. So Evan was free to sit looking out the window, comforted by passing sights he'd seen so often, and able undistracted to notice different laundry out on familiar shanty lines. He saw, gliding by one small gray house, that a child had a new Tonka toy— the big yellow dump truck—parked carefully by the back door just across the switchyard tracks. For rail-road children, toy trains probably held no interest, no imagined possibilities with the actual items squealing softly past every hour or so, or rumbling by like dino-saurs digesting.

He noticed, ghostlike with these sights, the faint and changeable reflection of his face in the window's heavy glass—a caricature, it had always seemed to him, of Wasphood. Dark hair (touched with gray and neatly parted on the left) over a long face slightly seamed with middle age and sunny summers of tennis. An almost horse-faced senior executive type, indefinitely gray eyes ... kept himself in very good shape, running, weight training, polo and tennis. ... A face, a representation, quite misleading, since this one belonged only to a journeyman architect, no creator, no industry leader, no leader of men.

Evan supposed old Clive Breedon had been disappointed this face had not been lived up to. Had not over the past twelve years become a partner's face ... the face of a person accustomed to create important buildings. ...

At Penn Station—and only twenty minutes late— Evan walked out through the structure's crippled arcade, saw a providential taxi, an ancient Chevrolet, and whistled it down.

As always on the streets—particularly when he first came in—the city disappointed him, seemed so much meaner than when he'd been a child and his father had brought him in to his office on occasional Saturdays, then taken him uptown to McGinnis's for lunch. Roast beef sandwiches ... with the restaurant's coarse horseradish.

"Clears the old sinuses," his father had said, perched lanky on the tall counter-chair beside him. His father an unmistakable gentleman, beautifully suited and shod, but with his great-grandfather's large and heavy-knuckled lumberjack's hands emerging from white French cuffs, and resting on the counter before him as if ready for more serious work than corporate law.

"Give me the news, Evvo," his father would say, having a glass of draft beer while Evan had birch. "Give me the news. ..." His father, a Ranger at eighteen, had fought in Italy and won the Silver Star.

Evan got out of the cab on the corner of Wooster and Spring, crossed the street to Ward & Breedon's small brownstone building—built in 1843 as a tobacco warehouse—and paused at the newsstand to buy a *Wall*

Street Journal, an organ just remote enough to be untroubling. The newsstand dealer was Hindu (Indian at any rate) and elderly, nose large over a military mustache, his complexion crumpled bronze, dark eyes dismissive. The old man had nothing to say—had never had anything to say in the year he'd been on the corner since supplanting a black woman named Margaret Hyde, who held constant grievance against her bank. . . .

Evan went through the glass double doors—WARD & BREEDON painted across them in black script—into a narrow tweed-carpeted lobby, and took the small elevator to the second floor.

Ward & Breedon's second floor—the partners' offices were up on the smaller third—was occupied by architects and draftspeople. Two architects, eight draftspeople. As he walked the center aisle back to his office, Evan saw, second in the row on the right, Sanchia's dark cloud of hair just over her partition as she bent to her tilted table.

"Jesus, what a gnome!" Peter Talbot (New Construction) commenting on Sanchia's first office entrance a year earlier. "—Old Clive's double-dipped Equal Opportunity: Hispanic and a woman. And she looks like a little spic hooker."

And she had—still did, since Sanchia took advantage of a draftsperson's noncontact with the public to dress miserably in too-bright Latino outfits, the colors of which always suggested pizza. Too colorful, and badly cut for a young woman so short, lean, plain, and banty-muscular. Her makeup unfortunately orange on a dark blunt little cat's face, beneath a Caribbean explosion of hair.

She looked up as Evan passed, observed him, expressionless, and bent back to her work. Plumbing, wiring, piping, ducting—puzzles she was fond of, and at which she was more than competent.

Following the initial office introductions—the occasion of Talbot's complaint—Evan had said nothing to Sanchia Fuentes except professionally. "—What in God's name are we supposed to do with the gas line? We have a slab house; we have a chimney complex the line cannot enter thanks to Guilford code. We have to have a shutoff, and the only place to put it is into carved mahogany paneling placed in 1857, and worth more than the stove and refrigerator put together."

"Pull the paneling section, Mr. Scott, move it down to the end of the counter, stain a square of birch to match, drill it, and mount the shutoff inside a rosette, the return to the left behind the drywall."

". . . Thank you, Ms. Fuentes."

"You're welcome."

And so he was, or would be, many months later— after he'd met her shopping in Bien Sûr on a rainy fall evening after work. "I can't afford this shit"—Sanchia referring to their curried chicken at $9.47 a pound— "but I gotta have it."

Evan, amused, had shopped with her, then walked her through misting rain across town deep into the East Village, to her shabby and dangerous street. He noticed, as they walked, how small she was, how odd. How plain—not even *jolie laide*.

"Come on up an' get dry," she'd said, then mounted, short and sturdy, up the stairs before him. And, once behind her small apartment's door—painted black, and triple-locked—had put down her purse. Then, still in her green plastic raincoat, she'd reached up on tiptoe, suddenly put thin muscular arms around his neck, and stretched up to kiss him while he stood very surprised, his Burberry damp across his shoulders. A kiss not at all Latin in passion, but rather shy, gentle, and rich with affection. More than affection.

Evan had wondered at himself while getting undressed. Had wondered at himself—contemplating only this second act of adultery in his marriage—as he slid into this odd young woman's rather narrow bed, and was confronted by a body (brown, small, and spare) as different from Catherine's elegant, pale, smoothly padded length as could be assigned to woman.

Expecting some sort of passionate attack, Evan had been startled (as the kiss had startled him) to find that Sanchia—having directed him to bed—had become shy and uncertain. So he was left a task to undertake, to make what love he could to this young woman lying staring up at him out of eyes the shade of hot chocolate.

He began by kissing . . . and, after some time, found himself in a world of kissing, and of love from her so unmistakable it frightened him. So he stopped that and commenced caressing, instead. —Then found that too risky, and hurried to fuck, to get matters over with.

No avoidance worked, and discovering Sanchia to be relatively inexperienced, Evan found himself making love as well as screwing, until, uneasy, he came, kissed her just once more, dressed, thanked her, and left. And, his trench coat still unbelted, trotted swiftly down her three flights of battered stairs and out into cool, rainy, and relieving night . . . free for the time being.

Free, apparently, permanently, since Sanchia made no demands, allowed no hints of affectionate behavior in the office, made no further approaches. Offered no invitations.

But when Evan—very foolishly, he thought as he was doing it—caught up with her on the street at noon one Wednesday, and asked her to lunch, she had instead waved down a taxi, gripped him by the hand and tugged him into it, directed the driver across town— and had taken Evan up to her apartment and into her bed.

It was a lunch hour, rich in affection and tenderness, from which there was no recovery, and Evan had two women in his life. Three, counting Beth.

"What do you have on your plate this afternoon, Evan?" Clive Breedon—perched on a high draftsman's stool behind a major shelf of walnut desk—was aging well, a drop-bottomed pear in a dark-blue summer-weight wool suit, plump and rosy-faced with rimless glasses and thin white hair combed straight back.

Clive had achieved some reputation by arguing very publicly with Lloyd Wright at a reception in the fifties. Clive, then a Young Turk, had accused the Master of building, instead of houses, ego elevations by the yard—and had received Lloyd Wright's reply, a tossed Scotch-and-soda down his front.

Clive had then been mad for the baroque, for Shildraken and Gaudí, but had gradually reformed into Miës van der Rohe spareness and profitably useful space. All interpreted with clever variations by Henry Ward, his partner—younger, very fat, talented, and quite eccentric; also apparently the only member of the firm to have casually gathered that Evan and Sanchia Fuentes were screwing. "The odder the truer," Henry Ward had said to Evan, descending with him in the small elevator one evening some time ago. "Kafka, Charles Lepidus, you and the Fuentes girl. . . ." And had said no more to Evan about it, then or ever.

Evan had looked up Charles Lepidus, found he'd been a barn builder for the most singular sect of Shakers—and had gone mad seeing everything in angles. His last words had been "A curve would save my soul. . . ."

". . . I'm pretty busy, Clive."

"Well then, this evening. Our impossible clients for 366."

"Madison Avenue. . . ."

"Right. The big job, last of the current crop of sky-scrapers on the avenue. —Our impossible clients revealing—painfully revealing—their Midwest origins, have come up with the notion—I suspect Dan Prie-singer—have come up with the notion of our adding a cap to 366. 'Jazz it up a little.' Memorable phrase. One of those postmodern horrors with scrollwork and pillars and an angled roof, and of course—of course—painted *something*. Orange, mauve. Some-thing unacceptable."

"Sounds bad."

"Is bad, Evan. But money talks. And these people, particularly Mr. Priesinger, believe they have taste."

"Really unfortunate."

"Yes. Well, I know that, and you know that. Problem is to convince the partners. Now, they're happy to pay for the addition. No difficulty there. Unfortunately, it would make this firm look like a set of just-behind-the-times jackasses—which 366, uninspired though it may be, will not."

"So . . ."

"So, your task, as our add-on expert, remodels your specialty . . ." Said, it seemed to Evan, with some off-hand malice, out of old disappointment. He'd heard from Peter Talbot that the old man had once said in ca-sual conversation, "I think Evan might have been more comfortable over in Greenwich with Shope, Reno—stayed out of the city altogether."

"—So, add-ons as a specialty, and your being a stranger in the firm to Dan Priesinger and company, your task will be to get uptown this evening and survey the building, which is steel-framed out to the seventy-sixth floor, structural work almost complete. Then tomorrow, if possible, do a sufficiently embarrassing sketch of this requested capital to persuade them to shy off. Provincial, corny, etc."

"Better not 'provincial.' "

"No, you're right. Skip provincial. Say corny. Say expensive. Say already out of date—"

"While the classic—"

"—is timeless. You've got it, Evan; go do it." Clive shifted on his draftsman's stool, and it occurred to Evan that the old man must long since have found the stool uncomfortable, yearned for the ease of a leather executive's chair, but was stuck with this affectation.

"And what if I see that an ornate capital might really work?"

Clive sat looking at him for a moment, rose slightly off his high stool, then settled back onto it, a plump, blue-suited bird. "You would keep that to yourself," he said.

. . . Evan called Catherine from his office—got the answering machine and left a won't-be-up-till-late message—then walked out and down the aisle to check a contractor's change of plans with Abe Swann. Then a discharge routing on the New Jersey job with Sanchia. "I'll be in town late this evening . . . ."

"Good," she said. Sanchia was wearing a blue sweater, maroon skirt. Unusually cool colors. . . . On these occasions she never said she'd be busy. Never said she'd prefer not, not this time. Never said she'd like to talk about their situation, their relationship. She always said, "Good."

It took some time to get a cab—evening rush hour in tumultuous progress up from the law firms, banks, and

brokerage houses downtown. Then took much longer
to ride uptown; the cab driver, a young Israeli with
oddly idiomatic English, not yet having learned to relax into the traffic, battling it in fits of start-and-stop
every few yards.

Evan thought of advising calm, then decided not,
and after almost three quarters of an hour, got out at
the corner of Madison two blocks south of 366—and
could see from there in early sunset's light the building's towering skeletal front of infinitely repeating red-
leaded steel beams, uprights and horizontals. Saw the
faintest web of safety net half furled very high, just below the top three levels. —It was, or shortly would be,
the tallest building within two or three blocks, and
something of an architectural coup for Ward &
Breedon, a major building when few major buildings
were being contracted for. The owners (Dan Priesinger
a partner) being Midwestern businessmen whose
eleven-branch savings bank had avoided the worst of
the eighties' bad loans. Now, armored in plus capitali-
zation, they were advancing on New York real estate,
for which they had high hopes.

Misplaced hopes, it seemed to Evan. . . . He looked
for the tallest building nearby, saw the Midtown across
the side street, and walked up to it. The Midtown
Hotel—a Solvig, Brady & Day building, narrow-
fronted and quite tall—was grimly ugly in bronze
sheathing, bronze window-framing . . . bronze accents
at the entrance, where a bulky Irish doorman peered
anxiously downtown for a cab to whistle in for two
older women and a small blond boy, five or six years
old.

Evan tracked down an assistant maintenance man—a
young Eastern European of some sort—in a subbasement. And, in exchange for a polite request and a
twenty-dollar bill, received a key to the roof-dormer

door above the south fire stairs. He took an elevator to the sixty-eighth floor, and walked up the last two flights from there.

Once out on the roof—pleased with fading auric light, with the huge buildings towering up blocks away on either side—Evan walked a distance over slightly sticky tar (rough with rolled-in pebbles here and there) that tugged gently at his loafers. The Midtown's north parapet, a stocky wall less than three feet high, was weather-battered, dappled with chalky pigeon shit.

Number 366 was right beside, just across the street—a width seeming narrower up here in the air than down below, where its paved space was filled with noise and motion.

Three six-six rose that modest distance away ... rose larger, broader, much higher than this building. Rising, rising up another several structural-steel stories and more toward its eventual eighty floors at completion.

Its beams and uprights gleamed dull red as old blood in the sunset's failing light. Scattered strings of occasional night-light bulbs already shone pale yellow, laced through the structure here and there up to the sixtieth floor.

Up here, hissing softly, a wind blew—enough to flutter Evan's tie, make him squint slightly when he turned to face it. A wind off the river, not the spoiled breeze that turned the corners of the streets below.

Evan thought he heard a sound, and glanced out across the space. Thought someone had called. He looked out over the wall, looked up—expecting some workman waving across the way—looked up and saw through soft, richly golden light, a girl come falling.

She fell from far higher, out from the red steel skeleton of the building in progress—not more than yards away across empty air.

Evan heard her call again ... something. Only a startled exclamation—certainly not a scream, not a shriek as she fell. And he saw her, and she saw him watching as she fell so seemingly slowly, lying spread-eagled in the air, wearing a tool belt, work clothes—jeans, shirt—all softly beaten by the air, and her long black hair bannering out, ruffling in the wind of descent so Evan heard it through the silence.

Their eyes met at almost an even plane. He looked into her eyes—dark eyes, wide, startled at what was happening to her. She saw him and made a wry face, as if he'd just seen her slip, awkward on icy pavement—and Evan had the oddest urge (before even surprise, even horror) to step up on his low barrier wall ... to leap out into the air to keep her company on her swift journey down, so she wouldn't be so alone.

Then she was past—still not screaming—but sailing, sailing slowly then more quickly down, arms and legs gently rowing in the air as if she were swimming a slow breaststroke. Long hair floating, floating up as she fell away from him—falling seventy stories toward the slender crossroads of the streets so far below.

Evan stood frozen, unable to look away—as if that would be the worst cowardice, to let her fall so alone she was not even seen. He stood, bent over the low parapet wall, watching her fall away, diminish ... until she was much smaller, a tiny girl ... then only an object, hard to discern. Then not even that ... and finally ... finally some sudden slight disturbance, hardly visible confusion in the thread of a line of traffic.

Evan said, "No. ... No," and recalled saying that before.

The river wind blew past as it had before, and Evan, as if shoved back from the low parapet by some after-echo of a smacking impact thumping up from so far below, took a staggering step back, and to avoid any more looking down, glanced up—saw another watcher—and felt great relief not to have been the only one.

This observer stood high on the bare steel of 366 across the way—several stories higher than Evan—and was still staring down. An odd figure by dimming evening light—tall, bearded, dressed unseasonably in a long khaki-colored raincoat, the coat's material flapping at his legs in the wind. A watchman just come on duty. . . .

Evan turned away and walked back across the roof as if he waded through dark water, slowly, and with labor.

Once through the access door, going down the two flights of stairs, he moved more easily, as if his muscles, somehow frozen, were now thawing. In the elevator, standing still, avoiding the ignorant eyes of passengers getting on as he descended, he felt much better.

Evan walked out through the lobby, feeling a growing annoyance with the girl—more than annoyance, feeling angry with her for creating such a spectacle, for falling senselessly through his life like a stone. . . . He went through the front doors past the doorman (noticing the man's uniform coat, plum-colored, with yellow lace down its sleeves) and walked out into warm odorous gusting evening breezes, onto a sidewalk busy with passersby.

Far up the block, at the corner, two police officers—both women—had left their squad car parked, its beautiful lights flashing red and blue in sequence. They were stopping crosstown traffic. A crowd stood along the curb there in twilight, looking into that drafty side street. Emergency vehicles were whooping nearer.

Evan walked south half a block . . . feeling he was traveling slightly above the pavement, separate from everyone. Then—with no reason but necessity's hand on his right shoulder (as an adult's on a child's in traffic) that seemed to slowly stop him, then turn him—he walked back the way he'd come. Going back so as not to leave the fallen girl alone, displayed only to strangers now she was destroyed.

Evan walked back, went to the small crowd and shoved his way into it—pushed between a man and a woman, a couple who seemed surprised to be separated—and stood at the curb's edge.

He looked out into the street, and saw the girl lying almost in its black-tarred center. She was lying on her side in the last of daylight, a slight conforming bladder of fluid and fractured bones—though her clothes still almost fit, her tool belt rested around her. Her right foot looked odd . . . but only her skull showed broken, a smashed doll's head resting in spattered red her long black hair couldn't blow to cover, no matter from what quarter came the wind.

chapter 2

· ·

Evan woke with a jolt, and sweating.

He lay still for a few moments until his heart
stopped racing, then eased out from under the covers,
got up, and walked around the big bed in darkness to
the bathroom (like the bedroom, still in old-fashioned
late-fifties style, and except for a walk-in closet, never
altered). As the house itself, a big two-story white
clapboard Colonial built where once a small farmhouse
had stood, had never after been added to or rebuilt, remaining the same for almost two hundred years. —The
same, and a comfort, resting on five wooded acres
sloping to the cove, the small boathouse and dock. All
preserved, and still accompanied by serious money,
thanks to a great-great-great-grandfather rich from
Connecticut lumber and New York's railroads, one of
Jay Gould's dubious partners.

Evan stood in boxer shorts in the small bathroom's
privacy, and found he had no business to do there—
had simply gotten out of bed to be farther from the
dream. Not a dream of the falling girl. A dream of war,
the second in almost a year, and recalling, replaying,
exactly what had happened to Jack Beckwith more
than twenty years ago.

Most of Evan's dreams of the war had been only

odd—finding himself, for example, standing in the mess line at Kan Simang for Thanksgiving dinner, receiving his piece of turkey breast only to find it still alive, trembling in cranberry blood.

In that dream, he'd eaten the turkey anyway, and the bites had moved in his mouth. He'd chewed and swallowed them, afraid to spit them out . . . see them lying twitching in red dust.

The dreams, just after the war, had come to him in the hospital every night, no matter what medication they gave him. The dreams had been so much richer, so much more real than daylight living that he'd been very impatient to get to sleep, dream the next dream, and understand more. . . . In the dreams, he'd learned a great deal about the men he'd lost. He grew to know them better than their parents, better than they knew themselves. In his weeks in the ward, Evan learned to know those dead men as well as God might know them. Collins, Bateman, Reynolds. . . . Eleven of them, each a universe to himself.

Then all that—so much more interesting than life— had gradually diminished, faded after he was out of the hospital, married to Catherine. Faded away year by year, so now the dreams were much less frequent, less important.

The day they'd come in after the fight, Captain Steinbrun had said to Evan, "Well, congratulations, Lieutenant. You apparently are a real war god. I give you the best patrol platoon in the brigade, and you go out for goddamned two days to goddamned Voc An and deliberately tangle assholes with a fucking mainforce unit for Christ's sake, and lose almost a squad! —Not including Beckwith, just the best noncom around. I don't know how you got Jack Beckwith killed. . . . Really great work."

"I didn't know they had more people to come up and reinforce."

"Well, I guess you know now, don't you? I guess those dead guys know for sure. It's called being professional infantry, Lieutenant—you always have a support formation just in case you get your ass caught in a wringer. What the fuck . . . what the *fuck* did they teach you on Okinawa?"

But, a few weeks later, when the citation for the Navy Cross came down, Steinbrun had said, "I suppose, Lieutenant, that killing people is what it's all about. —Theirs, ours, who gives a fuck?" And had poured Evan a cup of Lance Corporal Johnson's brewed raisin brandy. ". . . Let it go. You can miss a dozen ambushes, but sooner or later, if you keep moving, they'll get lucky and you'll get unlucky." Steinbrun had become philosophical by then, pleased with the unit's mention in Evan's citation.

Steinbrun had been in-country too long. Major Peterman came after him, and Peterman sent Evan commanding other deep patrols, left him on a long leash. But by then, Evan found no more pleasure hunting through the Ki Noa hills. . . .

He flushed the toilet so Catherine, if she was still awake, would hear it, not be curious and ask another question. "What's wrong?"—that sort of thing. When there was nothing much wrong except bad memories— which his father must have had about Italy, her dad about Chosin Reservoir. Not unusual—and unbearable to whine about, to join those shaggy aging Viet veterans (a majority having served, after all, in support, transport, and clerical units) who constantly complained, seeking federal handouts, group therapy, any sympathetic ear.

Evan ran water out of the sink faucet for a moment—phantom hand-washing to complement a phantom piss—then turned off the bathroom light and walked out into the bedroom and darkness. Heard Catherine's breathing as she slept, deep and regular always, sounding like the soft sweep of oars through calm water, rowing her through no unpleasant dreams.

"I hate country sausage—it's just ground-up poor piggy! And it's got loads of bad fat." Beth, blue school bag on the window seat behind her, and dressed in a blue dress to match, light-brown hair braided and coiled upon a head seeming too elegantly large for a twelve-year-old's slight body. Her eyes, milky blue, were still soft with sleep.

"Then you don't want your second patty?" Catherine, captain of the morning ship—tall and limber, her short-cropped hair dark blond, which, if not tinted, would have been brushed in the lightest way by gray above her ears. Catherine stood by the stove in her white terry bathrobe, her bright spatula poised above the pan. Her skin in morning light was a polished white, and even whiter at her ankles, revealing traces of pale blue veins above her terry slip-ons. Catherine's eyes were Beth's blue unclouded—almost excessively clear, bright as if she were always very interested—and set beneath a wide forehead as smooth, rounded, glossy as a child's. Her face narrowed swiftly from wide, almost Asiatic cheekbones and a girlish nose to a firm mouth, a small rounded chin.

"Oh, I'll eat it. Poor pig's dead already—at least he'll be *appreciated.*"

"No doubt." Evan sat across the small round table, scarred tough old cherry wood—Catherine's grandmother's, from Maine—and warmed himself with his daughter's presence.

As often after a dire dream, this morning's living present seemed the fable—seemed to Evan fragile, insubstantial, presented in only two dimensions that he might discover if he stepped quickly enough to the side, before whatever object had quite turned to face him fully. . . . Years before, Evan had had this impression (of things being fragile) very strongly after war dreams. That notion once lasting more than a week, when he'd walked carefully through Fairport and New York City, so as not to tear them.

He'd avoided touching Catherine then, avoided touching Beth as well, worried they wouldn't be themselves, but only representations. To make up for that, Evan had smiled at them a good deal, talked quite a bit, asked questions about Catherine's days—and it was true that when Beth, then only two, came to sit in his lap on one occasion he couldn't avoid, she seemed to be lighter than she should be, no burden at all. . . .

He'd put up with this for many days, then decided not to allow it any longer—tested several things and found them solid enough to hurt him (a maple tree, the back bumper of the Mercedes station wagon they'd had then) and gradually found himself living in a corporeal present, actual, physical, and true.

No episode like that in the years since—the dreams in fact less and less frequent, less grim. Evan supposed he was at last outgrowing them. Perhaps was only growing up, becoming less concerned with himself.

"Evan?" Catherine holding out a smoking sausage patty balanced on her spatula—seemed to have been holding it a while.

"No, you have it."

Catherine, never shy about accepting food, turned to neatly tip the patty onto her plate beside another, came over to the table and sat down between them.

As eager to cook breakfast as she was uninterested in making other meals—allowing Mrs. Hooper to do those—Catherine was alert to dangerous diet, but permitted sausage once every week or so, on odd days. (Beth, protesting for murdered pigs, always ate it.) For Catherine, this breakfast duty, or pleasure, seemed sufficient householding to balance the constant tennis at the club, the golf in season. Skeet shooting.

It occurred to Evan this morning—its sunny light frailer after dreaming Vietnam's bright heat—that Catherine often seemed most comfortable some little distance from him—perhaps always had. Six feet away . . . twelve feet. Coming closer for whatever reason, then always retreating back for that space between them, rarely lingering, hugging, or holding. He would, for example, soon feel her slight relief when she'd finished eating breakfast, was once more comfortably a few feet away, at the sink.

A requirement of distance applying not only to him, to her great-aunts, but to Beth as well. Catherine very happy to call her daughter, speak lovingly to her, but then faintly impatient to be free once Beth came to her arms, as if Catherine were a similar animal, but only similar, so distance was an instinct with her.

And, to be fair, not only with her. ". . . You always make love to me as if we'd just met. You always do everything as if we'd just met."

Evan had thought at the time that was a compliment from her (fueled by three Tom and Jerrys at the Howdens' one evening). —But thought that less and less after she said the same phrase again, one morning, when they'd been married years longer. Married for eight years. Then he realized it had been complaint, not compliment . . . or had become complaint.

Evan spread marmalade on his second piece of toast, and regretted the sausage patty. Now, he would have liked it.

* * *

"Do you want coffee, Mr. Scott?"

A special occasion, or perhaps only the early hour. Mrs. Koskovic, formal on the partners' small loft floor, usually didn't offer anything to people from downstairs, architects or not. Short-haired, sturdily plain in a gray suit, Mrs. Koskovic seemed to float in the outer office's white simplicity—calculated to present spareness, businesslike good taste, its white paint glowing beneath two skylights in bright morning light.

"I'd prefer tea, if you have it." Taking advantage of the occasion. "—Sugar and cream."

Mrs. Koskovic seemed surprised, and her mouth, a small lipsticked pout, thinned as she said, "Certainly."

Sanchia, the evening before, had also offered coffee—had insisted on it, rattling around her tiny kitchen, saying "Ah, *Madre* . . . *Madre.*" She hadn't cared who'd fallen, only that Evan had seen it—as if the injury had been to him.

Largely his fault. He'd walked in, blurted it out to her as if he'd been a schoolboy who'd just seen some shocking accident. He'd been only concerned with digesting the girl's death—or concealing it in a way, under words—and hadn't considered that Sanchia needed to be told more carefully.

"Oh, my God . . . oh, my God." She'd stared up at him as if to see the girl falling in his eyes—looked into his eyes as though she might be able to catch that fleeting motion . . . down and down.

"Nothing I could do." His additional absurdity; Sanchia had seemed confused by his saying that. Must have tried to imagine what he thought he might have done. . . . She'd gone into her little kitchen, and set about making coffee the way she was convinced he preferred—all the ceremony of grinding and filtering and so forth. None of which he cared for. He preferred tea, had drunk it even in the service, but had felt at their beginning that such an odd preference might seem strange to Sanchia. He'd asked for coffee, and now was stuck with it—too many praised cups of special brew having been ground and filtered and served to him. . . . If, by some mad circumstance, he ended married to her instead of Catherine, he would have to drink coffee the rest of his life.

Evan had sat in her only comfortable chair—a large shabby armchair (moss green, stained darker along the arms and the top of the backrest) that had belonged to her father. That small hardworking man (a furniture mover for various companies in Brooklyn) had left, after decades, only a meager impression in the seat cushion. —Evan had sat in her father's chair and supposed that Sanchia, in the kitchen, was puzzling over that last remark. "Nothing I could do." Imagining, as the grinder grated and whined, that he might have the power to transform himself somehow—into a comic-book hero, or less pleasantly, into some sort of huge flying creature or machine—perhaps into a half-human half-Huey helicopter. . . . And might have flown out and down, sailing, diving through the air to overtake the girl as she fell sprawling. He would have turned camouflage green-and-yellow . . . the Delta's colors. . . .

Sanchia had come out with the coffee—waited standing, as she usually did, until he smiled and said it was good, then (very agile) had half-turned and slid into his lap, fitting under his raised cup (less a burden than Catherine . . . than a larger woman would have been), and undertook more comforting. "Ohhh, such a terrible thing," kissing him gently, stroking his hair.

After that, she'd talked for a while, apparently trying to get him to say something particular . . . trying to pry something out of him as if she'd found a loose yarn-end on a sweater sleeve, and was determined to tug and tug at it until she unraveled everything. Wanting some statement, some admission, as if it was a secret she had to know—exactly what he felt, was feeling.

But that seemed to Evan something personal between him and the girl who'd fallen. Not something that he had to share, even with Sanchia, simply because she was fond of him. Even more than fond. . . . The sort of acquisitive impulse women seemed to have, to know everything—even though then they might regret the information.

Evan had thanked Sanchia for the coffee, kissed her, and gotten up to go . . . catch the eight-twenty to Connecticut. . . .

Mrs. Koskovic brought him his tea in a white office mug with the firm's logo (an Escher staircase intersection) in black on its side, and set it on the lamp table beside the chair. "I already put the cream and sugar in."

"Thank you." The tea was only warm, but Evan sipped it as he leafed through a back issue of *Architectural Digest*. A grimly unpleasant home was featured; a Philadelphia townhouse improperly restored middle-Victorian, and packed with dubious antiques. . . . Clive had said, "Jesus H. Christ," last night, when Evan called him from Sanchia's apartment—called him at home in Darien.

"Where are you?"

"Still in town, on my way home."

"And it was a woman?"

"In work clothes."

"Jesus H. *Christ*." Clive, upset, had sounded elderly. "The goddamned union. . . ."

"Clive, it isn't our problem, is it? It seems to me the contractor—"

"Evan, for your information, we *and* Harris, diNunzio agreed to an accelerated completion schedule. OK? Makes us a pair, if the union or any other party is looking for culpability. Or just looking for some pockets to pick in court. . . . How in the hell did she fall? They have damn nets up there below the working floor!"

"It was furled, looked as though they'd just brought it in to rerig it. She was probably working with that crew—went up a floor to anchor the cables."

"Incredible . . . so then, *then,* this damn fool woman takes the opportunity to do a Brody. The legal fees on this are going to be—I don't even want to think about it. Where the hell are you, Evan?"

"I'm still in town."

"Oh, right. Well, God *damn* it. . . ."

"She was young. I was up on the Midtown's roof, just across as she fell."

"Dreadful thing to see. . . . I'm sorry, Evan. Terribly sorry. And you'd better come in early tomorrow, come upstairs; I'm sure Nate Springman is going to want to talk to you. We are definitely going to be in the hands of the Chosen People on this one."

"I don't know her name. . . ."

"We can't have had many of them up there—not women. And it must have been after the regular day shift. I'll call Paul and Chet Harris, who will certainly have heard already. I'm not looking forward to those conversations. . . ."

". . . Do you want to go on in, Mr. Scott?" Mrs. Koskovic stared across her desk as if she'd already asked once.

Clive and Nate Springman looked up when Evan walked into Clive's office. Henry Ward—a beached whale (a pilot whale, only relatively small) in blue slacks and shirtsleeves—was lying apparently half asleep at one end of the cream leather sofa. He didn't look up. The cream leather office furniture, chosen by

Alice Breedon, had been an irritation to Janice Ward, who'd already decided on cushioned wicker.

"Come in." Springman, lean in gray sharkskin and russet as a fox, beckoned Evan as if this were Springman's office, not Clive Breedon's. The lawyer examined Evan, watched him sit at the sofa's unoccupied end, then said, "Josephine Fonsecca. Jerry Fonsecca's daughter."

He appeared to pause for comment, and Evan said, "The poor son of a bitch." Then thought that Jerry Fonsecca, the job's foreman—very tough and a driver—must have produced a formidable daughter for her to have persuaded a union card out of him, and dangerous work on high iron. —And must have bitter regrets now for having yielded to her.

"His oldest daughter," Springman said, then corrected for accuracy. "His only daughter—oldest child. I understand you saw her go?" Springman had a light baritone voice, easy to listen to.

"Yes, I saw her falling."

"I see. . . ." Springman waiting for more. Henry Ward hummed softly at the other end of the sofa—perhaps dozing, perhaps not. "Falling" seemed to Evan a limited word, not really describing what the girl . . . what Josephine Fonsecca had done. That was not only falling. It had been descending, sailing down . . . drifting a little sideways in the wind. Descending at increasing speed, but with shifts from side to side as if at any moment she might reverse direction—slow to a halt . . . then heave up and up again, rise and keep rising all the way, until she lifted past Evan on a strong updraft, made a merry face at him, rose farther and kited a few yards sideways to settle on a long red-leaded beam.

"Didn't see her slip, whatever?" Springman had gotten tired of waiting for more.

"No, but someone else might have. A watchman, a couple of floors up—bearded man, tall, in a long raincoat. He saw her fall."

". . . Well, God knows," Springman said, and leafed through a manila folder on his lap. "There was apparently something of a convention being held up on 366, considering it was well after the day shift had quit. What do you call them—riggers?—were up there. Some elevator people. Electricians, placing electric motors. And watchmen—one of whom I suppose might have been your man. We'll check with the contractor, look into it."

"Trouble already," Clive said, looking soft and rumpled on his draftsman's stool.

"Yes, with alacrity"—Springman closed the folder—"with really remarkable alacrity, the electrical equipment company— Roo . . . *Rao* Electric, have notified Harris, diNunzio's attorneys of record—senior partner was called at home—of their intention to file a preemptive suit to cover any and all damages suffered by them in any future action as a result of unsafe working conditions, leading to the death of the young lady—or any other occasion of damages." Springman sighed. "Very cute, and very quick—and no doubt shortly to be followed by every subcontractor working, or who has worked, on 366. Nobody wants to be left holding the bag—and Rao's attorney just moved fastest."

"What about the union?"

"Evan," Clive said, "the girl was Fonsecca's daughter, and he's the union rep on the job. What do *you* think the union will do? Paul diNunzio is worried sick, I can tell you that."

Henry Ward, his eyes closed, shifted on his end of the couch, made cream upholstery dip his way. "We are talking," he said, "about millions of dollars in de-

lays, if nothing else, and major final payments we have
not yet received."

"Still the contractor's grief," Evan said. "Isn't it?"

Springman seemed annoyed by the question.
"No . . ." and had forgotten his name.

"Evan Scott."

"No, Evan. Your firm cosigned an accelerated construction agreement, which Clive thinks is the sore
point—and I agree. But it makes no difference, because if Harris, diNunzio get stuck, they're going to
turn right around and stick you people."

"And I don't know," Clive said. "It's possible the
owners may get involved. Midwest people. . . ."

"They certainly will get involved." Springman
seemed grimly pleased to have more attorneys to deal
with. "At least their legal people will be checking in,
see which way the wind is blowing. *So* . . . what I need
from you, Evan, is a very definite and complete statement of what you saw—the precise time, if possible,
though we'll have the police report, and whether you
saw any possible cause of the accident, saw her trip,
slip, whatever—anything at all. For instance, if she
tripped over her own lunch pail, if she was horsing
around up there, playing hide an' seek—that would be
very helpful."

"Nothing."

". . . That's not helpful."

"Sorry—I just saw her falling. I heard . . . she called
out. She didn't scream. I heard her call out, and I
looked up and saw her falling. She fell right past me.
She looked at me. We looked into each other's eyes as
she fell."

Henry Ward reached out, patted Evan's right hand.
"A bad memory for you, Evan," he said.

* * *

"Are you fucking kidding me?" Peter Talbot, morning's insulated plastic cup of coffee in his left hand,
standing in the doorway of Evan's small office. "You
saw her go? Holy shit. . . ." All in an odd explosion of
profanity, so Evan suddenly saw Talbot, now a burly,
dark, handsome man, as the adolescent he had been,
shaggy-haired, gawky, easily startled.

"I don't think she killed herself. . . ."

"Oh, great, so it was just a slip. That's great. Poor
kid. . . . Before you came in, Clive and Abe said we
had a workman come off 366 yesterday—but I didn't
know you saw it. Shit," and subsided.

"Upsetting," Evan said, thinking Peter would expect
at least that.

"Damn right. . . . Damn *right*. Where the hell was
the net?"

"No net, not under her. I think the crew was there to
rerig it, and she was probably a floor or two above
them when they had it furled in."

"Lord," Talbot said. "Think about that, falling that
distance; it just makes you sick." He paused and
seemed to collect himself, grow older and tougher, better fitted to his summer-weight blue blazer. "Really too
bad," he said, and finished his coffee.

"Someone else was up there, on the upper floor—
odd-looking, bearded—a watchman, I think."

"Well, contractor's going to hear from the union;
you can bet on it. Insurance people are going to be
very unhappy. . . ." Talbot turned, half-waved, and
drifted out into the corridor.

Evan opened his bottom-right desk drawer—took
out the Conners folder—guest room and bath, wing to
be added to a Milford saltbox too small to comfortably accommodate it. "Our grandchildren come to
visit. . . ." The saltbox beautiful as it was.

For years too long at remodeling to consider houses

as conscious—Evan had now been at it even longer, had had time enough to reconsider the matter. It seemed to him now that if the houses didn't know, then the architect knew for them. They spoke in him, through him; the houses spoke through even mediocre architects.

The saltbox was too small for the burden of another wing, its Sound-side lot too narrow. The little house's structure (two hundred and fifty years of tenoned post-and-beam) trembled as it was if anyone weighty stomped into its parlor, went thudding up the stairs to its bedroom. The bath added there in the fifties, a crude addition, was small enough not to disrupt the balance of the house.

Ropewalk, the house was called—incorrectly; the Merryman ropewalk had been a hundred yards north, where a creek (gone now) had run to a lagoon (gone now), then to the Sound.

Evan closed the folder, opened the next-higher desk drawer, and took out an apple set aside from lunch two days before. It was a Red Delicious, looking better than it would taste, a fruit far out of season. He sat half up out of his chair to get his hand into his right trouser pocket, take his small penknife out. Opened its large blade, cut a slice off the apple, ate that—mealy, but sweet—and cut another, the blade's steel point like a tiny shark's fin, cruising an apple-flesh sea.

. . . The apple finished, and first-floor schematic of the Horvath job laid out—to be preliminaried today, if possible—it occurred to Evan that Catherine was bound to hear at the club about the girl falling. Someone certain to mention it—and probably mention that Evan had seen her fall. It would have been less trouble to have told Catherine himself . . . and if not last night, then this morning, after Beth was off down the drive for the school bus. ". . . Really tragic thing in town, last evening."

But then Catherine would have wanted to know more—though probably not his feelings about it—and it had seemed to Evan that would be more sharing than the dead girl would have liked, and too soon.

Which, of course, was exactly the sort of thing Catherine had complained about years ago. Long after he was out of the hospital. "—Your excessive silences. Absences, really." She had, in affectionate moments, called him "Sleeping Beauty." Or "Silent Sam." And she'd had a point—except that each of the so-called "silences" had its reasons.

chapter 3

....

Dodo was a driver.

Stupid, stumpy, sooty black, a fire hydrant among agile shifters, Dodo—cut proud, heavy-shouldered, and always simmering with a near-stallion's temper—loved contact.

Evan, marking Beckermann, followed at his near flank as the man rode his line fast and straight on a long-legged chestnut Argentine, turning in his saddle, whipping a shot, then following on. —Thick-bodied, a seven-goaler and bruiser by reputation, Carlo Beckermann, a banker, had just moved up from Buenos Aires.

Evan heeled left, felt his chunky pony—so inelegant—swerve fast in a rattling gallop, cutting the angle on the chestnut. Beckermann's face, flushed roast-beef red as an Englishman's, contrasted with his helmet's white as he looked right, saw Evan coming, and spurred.

Over the timpani of hooves on turf, creaking tack, the ruffling wind past his helmet smelling of bruised grass, Evan heard the spectators' faint murmur of anticipation. Beckermann, reins slightly slack, leaned and whipped his mallet around to hit the ball just as Dodo thundered into the chestnut and struck it solidly on the left shoulder as Beckermann spurred to avoid. Struck it as it changed leads—so it tripped and went down kicking. Dodo galloped straight over the chestnut as Beckermann rolled away, helmet flying off, mallet whipping on his wrist strap as he went.

Evan saw the ball to the right, turned in his saddle, slacked his rein, and backhanded it down the field—then reined left in a spatter of flung dirt and turf as the blue team's Number One came driving for him.

A hoarse shout from the low stands, from the rows of vans and station wagons along the field's other side.

Dodo—the Little Engine That Could—kept chugging along, difficult to turn, slow to turn, so Mick Pierson had already gotten on the ball and hit it positioned for the blue goal when Evan, galloping back, could take in the game. He rode past the chestnut (the pony already up, apparently not hurt) and saw Jerry Broughton spin his pony and forehand the ball in.

Beckermann was up as well—his helmet off—and was trying to catch his horse amid the rush. He had an Englishman's hair (fair, close, and curling) as well as complexion, and looked displeased.

Meredith, frosted black, elderly, and lame from horse-kicks, spoke with a light-cadenced Virginia accent with no undertone of country black in it, so he'd often—during telephone conversations from the stables—been invited to this club or that, this race box or that, this home for cocktails and so forth, by people who'd never seen him and assumed him white. Dour, strict, and short on humor, Meredith had accepted none of these invitations—though not from any sense of inferiority. Rather from a general contempt for those (the vast majority—white, black, yellow, or brown) who knew less about horses than he did.

"Ignorant Kentucky shit," he'd say in that humming

Tidewater planter's voice, say it particularly when racing burdened young fillies was discussed. Or occasionally, "Ignorant French shit," referring to the French notions of breeding Thoroughbreds. "Ignorant Irish shit. . . ." Though that less frequently, since the Irish, for all their sins of misfeeding, were in love with horses.

"You are beatin' this animal to death. . . ." Referring to Dodo, who stood solid as stone outside his stall, while Meredith, kneeling stiffly, squeezed and fingered at his left fore.

"No, I'm not, Meredith. He loves it."

"Whoa now," addressing Evan as a horse, "just a minute. This here animal is a *child*. He is ignorant and innocent— an' he depends . . . he *depends* on you, Mr. Scott, for higher functions. For sense, for common sense."

Dodo, expressive of brutal motion even standing still, gazed at Scott with a glassy black eye as fearless as a bear's. He was waiting for sugar.

"There's nothing wrong with that leg," Evan said. "I would have felt it, riding him." Race car driver to the pit man.

"There is nothin' wrong with this leg now." Still kneeling, stroking the leg. "But there is somethin' *preparin'* to be wrong with it, if you keep beatin' this animal *up*."

Evan had learned, as everyone who stabled at the club had learned, that arguing with Meredith was wasted breath—and usually mistaken as well. No man knew his own pony string as Meredith learned to know it, stabling, watching workouts and stick-and-ball, watching matches, living with the horses. . . .

"What you need to do, what you should do—"

"I am not buying another couple of ponies right now. I don't play enough; I don't travel to matches."

"You play too much for this pony, Mr. Scott. An' you play this pony too much."

Not only biblically cadenced, but true, and Evan didn't reply. . . . Dodo's headlong ways just suited him, better than Tulip's (named by Beth two years before). Tulip, a tall sorrel, seemed too intelligent, calculating, cool, only quick when she had to be. She was biddable, took her cues and responded, and that was all. . . . So like him that there was no marriage between them, no difference rubbing them into action.

Dodo was another sort of creature.

As Evan was leaving, Meredith came out of his office with a folded note. "Left on my desk with your name on it. . . ."

Evan unfolded the sheet, saw *"Horseman, pass by"* written on it in blue ink in a round accomplished hand. There was nothing else. The phrase from a Yeats poem, he thought. *"Cast a cold eye on life, on death. Horseman, pass by. . . ."* Something close to that. Not the sort of message his polo friends were likely to leave at the stable. Perhaps Henry Ward, driving through . . . intending some comfort.

Evan considered, as he walked back from the stables, that these buildings (the club buildings, and even the buildings in town) were none of them high enough to ensure death in falling from them. As if even in that, Fairport was different from the city—its buildings less strenuous to achieve great heights, less dangerous to fall from. As everything was different here (only an hour's train ride out)—safe, beautiful, its woods rich green behind occasional white houses. So different from the city's seething noise, its grotesqueries and dirt . . . as if not just location were involved, but a different country and a different time.

* * *

"Hey—*you!*"

"Evan Scott," Evan said, walking out of the shower room's pleasant heat and haze. He wrapped his towel around his waist. The banker, Beckermann—standing still dressed in the middle of the locker room—was much shorter than Evan even in his boots, and was built wide and flat as a big-league catcher. His ruddy face was heated as a furnace; blue eyes staring out of it, furious.

"Your pony is a pig—and you don't know this game!" Really upset, and before an interested audience. Interested and amused. Pete Talbot and Pierson by the lockers, Christopher and Mark McNeil coming out of the showers. "—You rode me off at more than forty-five degrees!"

"You're mistaken," Evan said, and Mick Pierson, at his locker, said a soft *"Boo-hoo. . . ."*

"No, I am not mistaken!"

"Beckermann, let's leave it that your chestnut is a first-class pony," Evan said. "Really fast—not shy at all. And I assume that last is true of its rider."

A grunt from Mark McNeil.

"What are you calling me?" Trace of German accent there, almost a *V* beginning "What."

"So far, only a bad sport." Smiles around the locker room, so that Evan began to feel more and more uncomfortable. He saw Beckermann, stocky, foreign, and a stranger, a new boy in school being bullied by the old boys, by Evan as an old boy.

". . . Beckermann . . . I retract that remark about shyness. I've been rude, and I apologize." Tommy Christopher whistled softly as he closed his locker door. "—You're a good player, and you couldn't know about Dodo; he's not handy, but he loves to run on in. We do play a rough game here; club ball, not tournament."

Beckermann, unsettled by the apology, stood still angry but uncertain, and when Evan held out his hand, could only take it or stomp away. He was not the stomp-away type, apparently, so he took Evan's hand and shook it briskly, very European in handshake.

"The pony is still a pig."

"Yes," Evan said, "—and stupid. I'm very fond of him."

The card table was already set up and laid with cloth, silver, and napkins when Evan saw the Range Rover's bulky blue, and walked toward it down the long line of station wagons, four-wheelers, vans, and big horse-trailering pickups ranked on the rich grass along the polo field's forest side. Tailgates were down along the row, cooler lids open as food was unpacked.

"Good match." Tim denBrinck, cocktail in hand, sitting in moccasins, jeans, and blue work shirt by the lowered tailgate of a maroon Mercedes station wagon.

"Thanks, Tim. Would have done better if you could have been with us. . . ."

"Like hell." DenBrinck, a nine-goaler years before, now elderly, unsteady after a stroke. ". . . Like hell." But pleased just the same, as Evan went on his way.

Catherine had the picnic plates out, was spooning portions of potato salad. "—She put egg in it again."

"Good, I like it with eggs." Beth, in white tennis shorts and one of Evan's old Sulka shirts, lay in a lawn chair, reading *Mademoiselle*. "For the bra ads," Catherine had said, mentioning the magazine reading a few days before. "Wishful perusing . . ." Beth's older-girl's head—long brown hair up in a twist, eyes concealed behind Evan's dark glasses—seeming slightly out of proportion balanced on a child's slender neck, a child's slight body and narrow, tanned, unaccomplished legs. Beth was reading while waiting for one of her interchangeable friends and/or enemies to come by, full of chirping hen-sparrow gossip, for which Beth would have to put down her magazine, sigh, get up and retreat to the Rover's other side, for privacy.

"I don't like eggs in potato salad; it's Southern-style, and not healthy." Catherine served more of it, a second spoonful onto Evan's plate. "But this is the way Edith shows her independence. She always includes something I don't like. It's a little message to me. 'Just because you pay Edith Hooper, doesn't mean you own her. . . .' "

"I'd say that's the message. . . ." Evan tugged another lawn chair out of the back of the Rover, unfolded it.

Mrs. Hooper had filled a two-quart plastic keeper with the potato salad, baked a rhubarb pie, and packed sliced smoked ham, half a roasted chicken, sliced tomato, Colman's mustard, a small keeper of her mayonnaise, a jar of her relish, a wedge of Jarlsberg, dill pickles, tangerines, two Granny Smith apples, and a baguette of French bread from Allan's, in town. There was a bottle of ginger beer for Beth, and chilled Riesling (two bottles) in an insulated soft green zippered pack with padded pockets for six small Irish crystal wine goblets.

She'd provided, as usual, more food than they could eat. "—Those Maitlands or those Talbots'll be coming along looking for lunch. Don't know what it is about some poeple can't bring any food for themselves. —Wouldn't do it out in the township. Wouldn't do it at the Firemen's Fundraiser, I'll tell you that. Peggy Cooke would have something to say to them right quick, you better believe it. Send those people straight home again for ice cream or peanut butter sandwiches at least. . . ."

Evan set the lawn chair alongside the table, and sat in it with some relief—still a little surprised at the aches hard riding now left him with. He'd used to play chukkers all afternoon, run three or four ponies out, then

dress for dinner and a dance ... and afterward sometimes take Catherine out in *Spindrift,* sailing the Sound
in the moonlight, reaching over to the sea to ride the
offshore rollers rumbling onto Long Island's beaches.
Listen to them toppling as the yawl hissed past. ...
Then tacking with the sea wind to the land wind to the
sea wind again, and home with Catherine in warm
breezy darkness already lightening to dawn. Then lovemaking, then sleep as the sun rose.

And up again in full morning, and into New York to
work. And thought nothing of it. ...

He was as strong as he had been (rode, if anything,
better), could jog as far, lift the same weights, could
stay out all night if he chose, and the next night, too—
could do anything he wished. But now not without effort. ...

Catherine handed him a bottle of wine and the forked
opener, and Evan peeled the wrapping, worked the thin
steel prongs down alongside the cork, turned and tugged
it free. He poured a glass, and sat back in the lawn
chair, felt the long muscles in his back easing, relaxing
into the chair's soft plastic webbing. He took a sip of
wine, allowed his eyes to close just enough so the
sweep of lawn, the softer greens of the meadow and
woods beyond blurred into backdrop for the people
strolling, visiting friends ... the families picnicking beside their cars.

The cold wine warmed his mouth.

A girl called, shouting to someone, and Evan started
and looked up as if Jerry Fonsecca's daughter was falling again ... falling in that slow swimming way, her
long black hair bannering out. —But falling here, from
an afternoon sky sweetly blue, cushioned at its corners
by sailing clouds. Falling more slowly here than she
had in the city, and through softer air toward grass so
richly green, paced by such handsome leisured people

she might imagine she'd fallen somehow up, and into heaven—and when she struck this ground, find its lawn too welcoming to injure her.

Evan's eyes had caught the sun, and dazzled he looked down again, glanced across the table and saw Beth watching him over her lunch, a shady glance behind dark glasses. Observing him. *What is this father ... this male creature up to? What is it thinking? Why does it look so sad ... ?*

"Sweetheart," Evan said, "you want to grow up to be an independent, empowered, sophisticated woman who's also very beautiful? Then finish your potato salad."

"Oh, really amusing, Daddy."

"And have a tangerine," said Catherine. She was looking away from the table, watching something or someone farther down the row. Leaf-mottled sunlight seemed to stroke Catherine's face, as if displaying her to remind Evan of her loveliness, her importance. The sunshine lit a trace of down along her cheek in front of her ear, as if there and just now, she was beginning to turn to gold.

It seemed to Evan she had changed very little from the summer he'd met her—just before he'd shipped over—he and Doug Mayfield had been up in Kittery, racing, and she'd come down the sea-worn sunbleached dock barefoot in T-shirt and cutoff jeans. Her friend Brenda with her ... coming to crew the *Whitecap* for the coast leg.

Walking barefoot down the dock, Catherine had shone through white noon light. Her hair longer then, tawny yellow—her skin, taffy-brown, as smooth as glass. Her legs were fine, her feet less ladylike—a farm girl's, with sturdy toes. The whole young creature complete enough, it seemed to Evan then, to stand for all girls' beauty.

She'd liked Doug better than Evan, at the start ... but by the race's end in a rainy evening, when she was hauling sheet beside him, she'd looked over and found Evan watching her. He hadn't smiled; just looked. And when they'd docked, and Brenda was going to drive home, Evan had said—very much against his nature, his shyness and quiet—"I'd like Catherine to stay with me," which struck everyone as funny. And Catherine had said, "All right, I'll stay with Evan."

She had dinner with him at the Sand Dollar, and sat and watched the sea with him after that. Then he had driven her home to Brenda's father's place, and come around the car to stop her on the steps and kissed her. ...

Two years later, she'd come out to San Diego and visited him at the hospital. Visited, and read to him, and slowly ... slowly counterbalanced the richness of his dreams by being greater treasure, so that one morning he found her more real, more valuable than even Lance Corporal Chavez—burned to death by friendly napalm dropped along the wrong treeline—whose life in East Los Angeles Evan had been reliving alongside as a sort of powerless guardian angel, who saw and heard every hour of Hector's every day for many years. An angel who hovered but could accomplish nothing, save no one. ...

Catherine, alive in California light, became gradually more valuable than Evan's dead men.

... But since, she and he, year by year, seemed to require more distance from each other. A distance necessarily less at night in their bed, in minimal light. She rested close enough then for Even to see her shady grimace of pleasure, a sort of wincing, as if fucking were a candy too sugary, so it hurt her teeth. Eager for it, though. Still very pleased—at least her loins were—in muscular motion. Her face then belonging to a slightly

different woman, though handsome, interesting in
shadow. Pale, surprised, discomposed by what was happening to her, what her hips insisted on having, heaving, smacking in appetite.

In bed, the closer Catherine seemed a bigger woman
than when at tennis or other sports, as if she grew by lying down, her thighs and buttocks turned massively hor-
izontal, shining subtly in lesser light, her torso longer,
heavier, very smooth, as if a larger younger more familiar sister had just taken her place. . . .

They were still eating—Beth just come back from a
foray with friends to pick at seconds—when Donna
Maitland, handsomely leathery at fifty-five, came over
and said, "I am *not* here to cadge lunch. We've already
eaten. Catherine, I just wondered if you'd heard the
news. . . ."

"No, I don't think so. . . ."

"Lou Bonner has married the Mexican."

"You're kidding me! —Married Dark-an'-oily?"

"Did I ever see him?" Beth said.

"—No, sweetheart. Donna, you are *kidding* me."

"I am not. —That ham looks wonderful. We had
tuna sandwiches."

"But why would she *do* that?"

"Are you serious? Because he's rich; that's why. He
owns all the used-car lots in Mexico—or half of them,
anyway. It's all about money. That's all Lou ever
thought about since Harold died, and now she's got it.
Money money money. Disgusting." Evan felt a light
kick against his right shin. Beth's sandaled foot
commenting beneath the table. —A descendant of
one of Thomas Edison's partners, Donna, loath to
spend on anything else, collected castles: a Norman
keep in Kent, a chateau outside Nancy, and a Schloss
Something-or-other in the hills above Baden. She kept

those baronial properties fully staffed, ready for visits she might choose to make ... this year or another.

"Used-car lots. God. ..."

"Catherine, Lou doesn't care as long as he's rich, *and* he'll spend at least half the year up here, so she can have her dogs. She's afraid the heat would be bad for them down in Guada-whatever."

"Well, she's right." Catherine unwrapped the rhubarb pie. "—English setters can't take heat. ... Why don't you have something, Donna? Really. We have a ton of food just going to waste. Have some of the ham; save us packing it up. Then you can have a piece of pie."

Evan slid the platter of ham over. "Have a sandwich, Donna. I'll get you a chair." He stood and went to the Rover to tug another lawn chair out. "... I've met him—Robbie Ochoa. He seemed to be OK. He's a sailor."

"Evan, please." Donna took two slices of ham, held them in tanned veiny hands, and, still standing, looked for bread. "—Half the kikes in Connecticut are sailors."

"Sue Talbot said you saw a girl falling." Catherine, just come from Beth's room after a bedtime story. Evan was sitting up in bed, sketching an unsatisfactory wing onto the east side of the Conners' saltbox.

Beth, at twelve, had grown too old for bedtime stories—which now had to be so complex they'd become only Saturday night productions, in which a barely adolescent heroine must be involved, as well as a dog—an English sheepdog—and occasionally, peripherally, a boy. The sheepdog an image of Chauncey—put down the year before after over a decade as constant companion to her.

Chauncey's death appeared to have given Beth

frightening notice of her own, however far removed, and disturbed her so Evan saw her shaded by it, no longer so flashing bright. She'd been interested in no new dog—as if its future death might confirm, beyond doubt, all endings.

"—Said she fell off one of the jobs." Catherine went into the walk-in closet.

"That's right. I saw her fall off 366 yesterday evening, when I was surveying the damn thing for a possible addition. Nothing I could do about it—she was there, then she was gone."

"I see." Catherine, out of sight, was sliding hangers, preparing to undress.

"It didn't seem merry news to bring home. . . ."

"I suppose not." Opened a drawer in there, then closed it.

"She was working very high, rigging the safety net."

"Alone?"

"No. Well, the rest of the crew was working on the floors below, apparently."

"Was she a Mohawk?" Catherine came to the closet door palely naked, a rose pajama top in her hand. Her breasts sagged slightly from years and their moderate glossy weight—the nipples and areolas the tenderest pink, as if never treated roughly by Evan (though they had been), never bitten by Beth as a hungry baby (though they had been).

"No, not a Mohawk—an Italian girl. Josephine Fonsecca."

Catherine saw him looking at her breasts, and lifted an arm to cover them. "And it was just an accident. . . ."

"Doesn't take much. Any misstep that high."

" 'Any misstep . . .' " Catherine said, and went back into the walk-in closet.

In bed a few minutes later, in darkness, she turned to

Evan as if surprised to find him there—then slowly began to explore him as if to make certain who he was, be sure he was the person she knew. She put a long left leg over him under the covers, slid her hand over his chest, and slowly stroked his stomach.

He heard her breathing, and for some reason was sure Catherine was imagining the girl falling, seeing her as clearly as Evan had seen her—and now, obscurely jealous, was demonstrating her possession, her being alive.

She worked her hand under the waistband of his boxer shorts. Found his cock, squeezed it as it grew erect, tried gently to bend it back, and when it resisted, rewarded it by slow stroking.

"Suck it," Evan said, as if he hardly knew her, as if they'd met only a short time ago—and Catherine paused, and held him. Then, as if she were such a near-stranger and pleased to obey him, she pushed the covers down, then his shorts, bent to find the swollen head with her mouth and licked it as if to cool its heated skin. She bent farther (barely seen in the darkness), took it in, and deeper, and began to suck as if to hurt him by sucking. . . .

For no reason he understood, Evan grew angry as he drew nearer to coming, feeling that insistent mouth (that might have been any woman's) working at him, wanting whatever it was she wanted, making wet sounds in the bedroom's dark.

He'd had enough before he'd had enough, and reached down to gently push her head away, grip under her arms and pull her to lie alongside him. Then he rolled half onto her—and still angry, felt to find and hook his fingers into the waistband of her pajama pants, and pulled them over her hips, and down her legs and off her.

She wrestled underneath him—to get closer or to get

away, he didn't care which—and he shoved her legs wide and leaned in between them, into the moving framework of warm thighs, shifting, that could have been any woman's. Then reached down to grip his cock, managed it against her fur, then down slightly and found a slippery place, fitted himself there—shoved once, felt warmth opening wetter, then shoved harder and as she moved with him (closer than she'd been all day, gripping him as if he were what she wanted after all)—slid slowly all the way up inside her.

Catherine said nothing, made no noises but liquid pumping as she thrashed beneath him smelling of sweat and bath powder, faintly of fish blood.

Then she said, "Oh, you're fucking me." And a while later, said, "Oh, yes," and shook in his arms, hummed as if she were starting a song, and came as he came into her. Then Evan, as he held her, loved her, and couldn't help but tell her so.

"Evan, we have a problem here with the Martins' loft—the Broome Street loft."

"I know; two bathrooms." Evan still train-weary from a slow, slow ride into town. Several halts . . . delays.

Abe Swann unrolled plans across Evan's desk, and weighted their edges down with the stapler and pencil cup. "Look at this, it's ridiculous. They'll have two bathrooms side by side—and no bathroom anywhere else in a two-thousand-square-foot loft. More than two thousand. It's absurd!"

"And it's just the way they *want* it, Abe. They want separate bathrooms. And they want them entering the master suite."

"You don't think you should talk to them? This is not going to be a viable layout—I can feel how wrong it is on the board! They are not going to be able to live with it."

"In which case, as I've already pointed out to them, we have room alongside the entrance closet for a small half-bath for guests. Galliani's the builder, and he doesn't mind."

"Tony would build anything for a buck. —Evan, that half-bath would cut the closet space, and just to do it we'll need to reroute ten thousand dollars' worth of plumbing. These people are spending over two hundred and fifty thousand dollars to make over a seven-hundred-thousand-dollar penthouse loft—and they are screwing it up!"

"Don't I know it," Evan said, and took a small almond Hershey bar out of his top-left desk drawer. "—And haven't I told them." He unwrapped the Hershey bar and leaned right to drop the paper in the wastebasket. "You understand, Abe, they have signed *off* on this plan, with a paragraph including my objections to this two-bathroom-side-by-side bit. They have signed it *off*. . . ."

"It's a mess."

"Not the first, Abe, and not the last. —Want a piece of chocolate?"

"No," Swann said, "I just had lunch." He scrolled the plans, snapped a blue rubber band around them. "Only once, I'd like to see big money in the hands of sensible people."

"Sensible people don't make big money, Abe."

Swann out of his office (the awkward plans tucked under an angry arm), Evan ate the Hershey bar, kicked his desk chair rolling back to the wall cabinet, slid out a big sheet of drawing paper, and rolled to the side to smooth it across the drafting table and pick a Rapidograph pen out of his beer mug—a chipped souvenir of six years in New Haven, Yale crest and motto in fading gold. LUX ET VERITAS.

He drew a straight line—a minor freehand skill useful in presentations—then doubled that, and drew a short three-step staircase below and to the right. Then joined the two in a very large and pleasant bathroom. . . . Hanging ferns. . . . Then sketched in double sinks and an oversized tub. Added, more carefully, two toilets—each in a separate closet at either end of the bath. Finally, a shower stall beside the long window. Then sketched, as seen through the window, the roofs of Dominick, then Spring, then Vandam Street leading away in succession. . . .

It was possible Sybil Martin might like it—and if she did, Harley would go along. A last chance to avoid the foolish bathrooms side by side.

Evan finished, sat looking at the sketch, then added slight shading here and there, careful not to do too much, preserve the false dashed-off look clients seemed to appreciate—then he got up, walked out of his office and down the draftsmen's aisle.

"Abe . . ."

"Not something new."

"Your fault." Evan handed the sketch over. "Hold off on the loft final for this—last chance for something a little less bizarre. . . . Let's see. The Martins are out of town now. And I have something to do tomorrow morning. . . . Then I have to drive over to Hartford for the next two days, checking the bank site. *Then* I'll stay over at home to take another look at the saltbox—and, I hope, get in some tennis. So—"

"I should have gone on to graduate school," Swann said. "—Become an architect. Then *I* could be staying home in Connecticut and getting in some tennis."

"Abe, Abe . . . envy is very bad for the liver. —So,

I'll try this new bathroom situation on the Martins the end of the week. If not, then the beginning of next."

"We do have a deadline on final plans."

"I know it. Still have thirteen days."

"Well," Swann traced the sketch with a rapid finger, "—it isn't wonderful. . . ."

"Thank you."

"But at least it's not so stupid."

"Thank you, Abe."

Rosealba's—distinguished as a funeral home by its blue canvas marquee—was in a brownstone. An oddity in this section of Queens, where Evan, during the taxi ride, had seen little brownstone used. Almost none, unless it lay concealed behind false stonework on some of the two-story homes.

The drive out had taken more than an hour from Penn Station, since the young woman cabby (fresh, she'd said, from Nigeria) apparently had never driven into the borough and knew no locations in it. Seemed never to have driven the morning rush hour, either.

There was no one out on the sidewalk in front of Rosealba's. Evan paid off the taxi, crossed the street, went up shallow steps and through heavy double doors—oak, stained as mahogany.

"Can I help you?" A handsome young boy—swarthy, fourteen or fifteen, and slightly too plump for his dark-blue suit.

"Josephine Fonsecca," Evan said, and felt as though he were asking for her in some women's residence—that soon she'd come down the staircase, vivid against dark paneling . . . smiling as she saw him waiting.

"The Fonsecca services are at the church at this time," the boy said, very formally. An heir to the business.

"I see. . . . Which church?"

"Catholic." Accompanied by a less formal teenage glance, amazed at adult ignorance.

"And . . . which Catholic church?"

"St. Michael's." Having said that, the boy seemed to think he'd said enough, and stood looking up at Evan as though expecting him to be satisfied.

"Last question—where is St. Michael's?"

Apparently judging Evan an informational cripple, certainly a stranger to the neighborhood, the plump boy said, "OK" and fingered his left shirt cuff back to look at his watch, a businesslike gesture probably learned from his father. "Well, you're goin' to miss the service. Procession will be leavin' St. Michael's before you even get there—you don' know the neighborhood. I was you, sir, I'd go right on out to Green Hills. —Cemetery." Then waited, expecting Evan would require something more.

"May I use your phone to call a taxi?"

"Certainly," the boy said. "You bet." And he led Evan into a side office, where a middle-aged woman, dark and pretty, sat at a computer keyboard.

"Needs to use the phone," the plump boy said. "Call a cab."

Morning sunlight fell harshly on Queens—at least on this commercial avenue—perhaps filtered more gently through trees on the side streets. An interesting borough—Evan doubted he'd ever driven through much of it before.

What should have been ugly—landscapes of small ranch houses and split-levels, two-stories and duplexes, all on tiny wire-fenced lots, all jostling side by side (and many decorated in forthright bad taste)— what should have been ugly was not. They seemed safe and satisfactory homes, small houses given great attention. Mongrel houses—odd, lively, and loved. . . .

Evan supposed Green Hills was a minor cemetery,
by New York standards—a long and gently sweeping
hillside above a thrumming six-lane branch of the
Brooklyn-Queens Expressway.

He saw a funeral group up on the slope, had the
cabby stop just inside the gates, and asked him to park
and wait.

"Be on the meter, pal." The driver—C. Fortunato on
his permit—was a fat pale custard, barely fitting behind his wheel.

"That's all right."

Evan walked up a blacktop access road to the small
crowd—and saw, as he got closer, that this was an improbable funeral for Josephine Fonsecca. Only ten or
fifteen people, most of them elderly, gathered around a
plain coffin. There was only a single bouquet of flowers on the dark wood; its colors seemed stephanotis
and forget-me-not.

Evan stood in the road, looked along the hillside
through a bronze-and-gray forest of markers and
gravestones, and saw a more substantial crowd a distance over and farther up the hill, by a turnaround. The
roadway there was thick with parked cars, work vans,
and pickup trucks.

He walked that way past weather worn stone angels,
blurred inscriptions describing the loss, over a century, of extraordinary men . . . the loss of radiant
women. The loss of children fragile and beautiful as
Christmas decorations. —The enscribed determination
to see these lost people once again was very great. The
likelihood of that, sounding less certain. . . .

And here were Josephine's family and friends—so
many of whom must have imagined her fall. A thick,
silent crowd of families—over two hundred people
dressed in suits too light a blue, or slacks, jackets, and
ties. Most of them working people, the men bulky,

weighty with muscle—or, if young, lean and often handsome. The women, except for a few slender beauties, stood stocky with childbearing and good food. The children all solemn, silent—most with their hands held by their parents as if the angel of death, not quite appeased, might suddenly sweep by to snatch one away.

Evan walked down nearer the crowd—heard clearly spoken Latin over the mourners' heads, over the harmonic hum the traffic made below the hill. He walked near enough, he thought, to be one of the party, a committed onlooker so that Josephine, if she could know he was there, would not be disappointed with him. —But not too near, not standing quite among the crowd, not even along its edge, so people might turn and wonder who he was, what his business was at this funeral.

Evan saw the priest, an elderly man with a long, sour Irish face, his lips hardly moving as the imperial language rang out. No trendy English for this priest; his Latin spoken as if the words had power to protect the dead girl, then be the engine of her journey into paradise—to purgatory, at least.

Evan remembered enough of his classes with Mr. Larramore at Groton to recognize church Latin when he heard it. Syntax too simple ... not quite Cicero's Latin. ...

The priest's voice rolled on, speaking loud enough for several of the closer dead to be affected. Loud enough for Josephine to hear him, even lying beneath a blanket of bright and various flowers ... lying beneath a fine casket's heavy bronze.

Henry Ward was there from the firm, with Janice. Evan saw them standing back between two family groups. They looked like wealthy angels—sleek and smooth, both handsomely dressed in blue nearly dark as black, and flown down from Westchester to monitor the ceremony.

To the right of them, and up front, Evan saw Josephine's mother—looking surprisingly like his memory of her daughter, darkly attractive, strong-featured as one of the Italian actresses popular just after the Second World War.

But the mother had suffered insults her daughter hadn't had time for. Black hair slightly graying, a strong body grown thicker, softer. Josephine's mother looked stricken, surprised as if she'd just seen her daughter die, just come from her daughter's deathbed.

Evan recognized Jerry Fonsecca. He'd met him once or twice when Fonsecca was bossing the riggers and ironworkers for Ward & Breedon's rebuilding of the Blue Line wharf at the Seaport. Fonsecca stood between his wife and his daughter's casket as if to keep them separate—as if his wife, if allowed too close, might rush to the coffin and heave up its heavy lid to see her girl once more.

Jerry Fonsecca didn't look stricken. He wore no expression at all, as if he were only a perfect representation of a very strong, dark, blunt-featured man in an awkward suit—as if he were an example of what a formidable working man (hands so powerfully capable) should look like. But a picture only, a holograph that any breeze might blow through.

The priest had turned to English for his lesson, lowered his voice only a little.

". . . which makes this loss such a particular tragedy. Josephine's love of life—her God-given ability to live her life so very fully, with such humor and grace, makes our loss of her—though God's gain—still a terrible grief to all of us. . . ."

Evan thought the priest was doing very well. He was, in a limited way, describing the Josephine that

Evan had met in passing. He thought the priest was doing very well, but Jerry Fonsecca and his wife were paying no attention.

Their two young sons—twins, and perhaps four years old—also were paying no attention. Very small sturdy versions of their father, they stood side by side in little black suits, staring at the heap of flowers, the bronze lid beneath which, for some reason too difficult to grasp, their smiling sister lay unsmiling. . . . When they went up to kiss her in the church, her face must have been cold as meat from the freezer, and smelling of strange perfume.

Several women, a distance from the family, were crying into black handkerchiefs. And Evan saw two young men—ironworkers, he supposed—also weeping, making no attempt to hide it. . . . Here, of course, no one would mind if he, too, cried a little. He was a stranger, and might be weeping for his own reasons. But though he saw very clearly the falling girl's wry grimace as she passed him—saying in that brief contact her good-byes to everyone—and his eyes began to hurt him and he thought he might cry, he didn't. Didn't, perhaps, out of fear that once he began, he might never stop, having the second squad to cry for, also—all because he'd insisted on patrolling one click more to sunset, up into the hills.

Evan felt he had some message to give her family, felt that so strongly he stepped down to the edge of the crowd. —Then stopped, not certain what his message might be . . . perhaps only that she'd been brave, hadn't screamed in that long long fall. Perhaps some other message. . . . But he saw himself being an unforgivable fool, mumbling something odd to people who'd known her so much longer than a second . . . perhaps two seconds. People who had loved her.

Still he felt this funeral was failing, that so rich a

funeral—with Josephine surrounded by such love and loss, such regret—should wake her, wash the chemicals from her white veins, pour in blood, blood contributed from all of them by wishing, so she shook, then stirred awake in that close dark ... woke and her small fists, hard from hard work, began to hammer ... hammering inside the coffin until they rushed to release her.

Evan hovered there at the edge of the funeral crowd like a haunting ghost—one of last century's Anglo-Saxon-Scots ghosts from the top of the cemetery hill. He lurked at the edge of this group of sturdy darker people, bowed his head and whispered good-bye to Jo Fonsecca—took the opportunity to ask her to say happy birthday to John Haskell as well (his birthday really the day after tomorrow), who'd been shot through by a burst of fire at Mei Kun, and died while Evan held him, waiting for the corpsman, and rounds had thumped and twanged through the air around them, a swarm of furious bees. "Is this weird, or what?" Private Haskell had said, then blown large slow red bubbles—and glanced up inquiring, to see if his lieutenant had noticed the trick.

Evan, when he raised his head, saw Jerry Fonsecca looking at him over the slow stirring heads of mourners.

chapter 4

....

Evan turned the Lexus into the saltbox's narrow drive,
stopped, switched the engine off and got out.

The early-morning air, with the Sound lying just
across the road, had none of the smothering weight that
even early summer had pressed down on Hartford
during two days spent wandering the bank site downtown—sketching finally a front fairly National Social-
ist in style. Massive smooth uprights. Plinths. . . .

The Conners' little house lay crouched like a resting
elderly gray cat, watching Evan walk over to it.

On the ground, it was apparent that an extension
built off the cottage's far side would bring the structure
to only ten feet from the property line. A new and improbable Colonial (painted off-white, with coffee trim)
stood over there through a thin rank of young maples.
—Would take it too close to the line, and would pull
the saltbox lopsided . . . any window treatments only
unbalancing the small house further. . . .

Evan walked around the house's far side—saw that
the stone foundation, reworked every two or three generations, needed attention—and went on around to the
back. A clothesline had been rigged there . . . weather-
whitened cord with three or four worn clothespins
along it, sagging in the sunshine between a leaning fir

post and an eye screwed into the stables' worn gray clapboard.

Looking along the saltbox's plain rear elevation (broken only by kitchen steps), it struck Evan that a small addition might be built from there—so the far side wall was extended to run back single-story about thirty feet, like a Maine barn's cow walk, or an addition to a New York State farmhouse. . . . The Conners then would have their extra space, enough in that extension for two small guest rooms, a half-bath, a utility and storage room—and the little house left almost uninjured by it. That back extension would give them good additional living space—and, with southern exposure, a sheltered backyard L for gardening.

Evan walked on around the rear of the house, and past the stable to the drive. He sat in the Lexus's passenger seat, leaving the car door open, reached back for his briefcase, and took out a drawing tablet and pens. Then he tried for jazz on the radio—found a New Haven station—and began to draw across a shaft of sunlight on his page, listening to what sounded like the Erskine Hawkins band, playing "Raindrops."

In early afternoon's warm breezes sliding down the range, Evan, visiting on his way to the club, stood with two other skeet widowers—Turner Gruen and Bob deYong—on mounded gravel to the left of the firing stations, and watched Catherine waiting for her target. The two other women, cradling guns, stood well behind her. They were practicing, taking turns running ten targets at shooting stations one and two, beside the high house.

Out the first few times, Evan had flinched at the shooting—but not for a long while now. Now the gunshots were only a rhythmic counterpoint to Catherine's concentration.

Fitting her shotgun to her shoulder—the piece one of two heavy rib-barreled Remingtons—Catherine stood ready, a dark-blond Athena wearing tweed jacket and jeans, owl-eyed in amber shooting glasses. A mature goddess, and today without her attendant sprite—Beth (in school till three, then due for a tennis lesson)— usually pleased to stand behind the half-circle, loading the two shotguns in turn for her mother.

Catherine called, "Pull!"—and swung on the released clay target as if she and the weapon were entering the first measure of a dance.

Her shot, as always, came as a surprise within the few seconds' window as the disk went sailing out and away, rising in a swift curve—until the shot—then puffed into dark powder, struck sifting out of the air.

Evan watched Catherine's satisfied step back and away. Practice and pleasure done, until her turn at second station and two targets sailing by, one high, one low. . . .

Turner and Bob deYong stood on either side of him, both attentive, but deYong as usual restless, shifting a little side to side, perhaps uneasy at standing passive, unarmed behind armed wives.

Turner Gruen, a massive developer retired from Arizona's breathless heat, had earned a hound's dark, sad, deeply wrinkled face under desert sun. Relaxed, shambling even standing still, he wore a khaki shooting jacket as if he might be called in a moment to shoot his wife's rounds.

"Look at her elbow," said Bob deYong, referring to Dana deYong's stance as she stepped up in Catherine's place, settled her shotgun's stock, then lowered the piece a little, ready to call her bird.

"—Got her elbow cocked up there in the air like goddamned Daniel Boone!"

"I've known good shooters hold like that," Evan said, and Turner said, "Mmmm."

"Hold a rifle like that—pull a rifle in like that, all right. But not a damn gun!" DeYong, handsomely blond as a male model, observed his wife (equal in blondness, and very slight) and shook his head, disappointed in her. "Had that stock fitted to her in Modena instead of one of those mechanicals—people went to a lot of trouble. And look at that. . . ." Dana deYong had called and now received and took the streaking target on the fall and broke it, the blunt echo of her shot thumping, chugging back across the field, a small invisible locomotive. "—Shoots like a nigger playing golf."

"She hits," Turner said.

"Skeet's only half about hitting—it's also about proper shooting." DeYong, whose people had once owned almost a third of upper New York State, had the silvery dismissive air Evan had noticed in those Argentines, Southerners, and Englishmen whose families had owned grand and ancient properties, from which money still descended to them like green-gold ghosts of lost forests, farmlands, acres, hectares, counties and country rivers. "—About goddamned proper shooting."

Evan and Turner Gruen said, "Bullshit," almost together, and smiled at each other over deYong's handsome head.

"Pull!" A pause not quite long enough for breath . . . then again the shotgun's slamming sound—definite enough for the beginning, or the end, of anything. . . . So unlike the breathless inconclusive pow-pow-pow-powpowpow of automatic weapons fire, that always seemed part of continuous dialogue (tap-tap-tap-taptaptap . . . pow-pow-*pow*), out of which, often, damage had resulted.

At first, the shotguns had bothered Evan. Now, their solid sound meant nothing to him.

Catherine had been runner-up in the state finals for three years—always just behind two tiny ladies, twin sisters in their late fifties, smiling near-midgets wielding heavy Browning twelve-gauges like fairy godmothers' magic wands. One of these women, Claudia Turley, had seemed to Evan the most natural killing shot he'd seen since Lance Corporal Warren. . . . Warren, very young (nineteen), and a West Virginian, had breathed death out of his rifle for several months— then caught the infection himself, and died under mortar fire.

The breeze was slowly becoming a wind, and warmer. Crosscurrents interfered in skeet—the shot, like hurled gravel, hustling slightly to leeward.

"Pull!" . . . The shot, and hit.

"Will you look at that elbow?" said Bob deYong, and the wind brought gunsmoke to them, rich as Cajun cooking.

Evan, sitting alone in tennis whites at an umbrella'd terrace table, was deciding between a sliced chicken sandwich and an avocado salad when one of the waiters, a young black man named Paul, wended to his table through the others.

"Mr. Scott, there's a gentleman asking for you at the reception desk."

"Who is he?"

"He's an Indian gentleman, I think."

"Indian as in from India?"

"I believe so."

"All right. Please tell Robby the man's a guest of mine, and bring him out."

. . . The chicken sandwich was always good: there'd been a comic scandal the year before, accusations that

sliced turkey was being used instead. Chicken was always good—the avocado a little more chancy.

Evan saw two women, sitting at a table nearer the
terrace's French doors, stop eating and raise their
heads to watch Paul coming back, followed by a re-
markably handsome young Indian—very dark—small,
slender, and a little too well dressed in what seemed to
be a cream linen summer suit. The young man's hair,
perfectly black, worn long and artfully combed, appeared to have been oiled—and he stepped along behind Paul in an oddly lively way, as if he might at any
moment break into a dance step and segue along the
terrace between the tables, the watching members—at
this time on weekdays—mostly elderly.

Arrived, and Paul having stepped aside, the young
man displayed an eager smile and an extraordinary tie.

"Mr. Scott—Vijay Bhose," he said, bent smartly at
the waist, and reached across the table to shake hands.

Handshake done, Evan said, "Sit down, Mr.
Bhose—I'm having a very late lunch; would you care
for something?"

"Oh, no. I wouldn't trouble."

"It's no trouble. Please, join me as my guest."

"OK!" and Vijay Bhose, eager as a boy, fell into the
chair opposite. "Being good food, is it?"

"Not wonderful, but you might like the chicken
sandwich"—then thought Bhose might be vegetarian—"or the avocado salad, if you'd prefer."

"Is both a reasonable amount?"

". . . Good deal of food, but certainly within reason."
Evan avoided looking up at Paul. "Paul, Mr. Bhose
will have the chicken sandwich, and the avocado salad.
I think I'll just have the sandwich. —And iced tea for
both?"

"Oh, certainly," said Bhose, and, the waiter gone,
said, "Too soon for business?"

"Not in this country," Evan said, and took the card handed over. " 'Anchor Insurance Company—a Division of Bidwell Group.' "

"British-owned—well, British-controlled—but doing, I assure you, Mr. Scott, a very great amount of business here . . . and in Canada also. Is insuring at the moment the firm of Rao Electric on a particular project—which, speaking frankly, is why I suppose I have been assigned, Hindi speaker and so forth, and sent from Toronto. . . ." Bhose paused, then said, "A very pleasant trip down through Rip Van Winkle country. You know that country?"

"Yes. . . . Charming."

"Such a river. Not the St. Lawrence, mind . . . but such a river."

"Yes. . . ." Evan glanced past Bhose, looking off the terrace out to the tennis courts. Bhose noticed and turned to look as well.

"My daughter," Evan said. "Tennis lesson." Robin Cluen, Bud's assistant, was just beginning the young intermediate class, hitting to five youngsters, each in turn. Beth the slightest, beige-legged and lively, neat in white shorts, white shoes, white T-shirt.

"And which one is . . . ?"

"The youngest."

"Oh, she is so pretty—a young female *sambar*. A little deer, you know—look how she runs!" Evan and Bhose sat watching as the young woman instructing, and her attendant girls—all in white, their legs already darkening in early summer tan—danced an occasional start-and-stop ballet across the farthest court, its deep green relieved into rectangles by lines perfectly straight, perfectly white.

"Lovely," Mr. Bhose said. "Such a scene of safety, such little ladies here so far from trouble." He turned back and smiled at Evan. "Far from age, too, of course. . . ." It seemed to Evan an odd remark from such a young man. "And your daughter the most charming of all."

"We're very fond of her."

"Oh, an understatement surely, Mr. Scott. Westerners are *very* fond of their daughters. I only wish it were so in my country. There, it is everything for the boy-child—nothing for the girl. Scandalous. . . ."

"Well. . . . And how can I help you, Mr. Bhose?"

"Oh, please. 'Vijay,' please."

"Vijay."

"I saw you at the lady's funeral, isn't it? In the Borough of Queens? I was sitting in a parked car to watch. Sitting catty-corner—is that correct, 'catty-corner'?"

"Yes, that's right."

"—Sitting there in line of duty, looking for an oddity. And of course I *did* see an oddity—you. I hope you're not offended, Mr. Scott."

"No offense."

"Line of duty, otherwise I wouldn't have intruded. I had a Dodge car—rented from Budget. They're in Canada as well."

"Yes, it seemed to me . . . I thought someone from the firm should attend."

"Oh, no. No, no. I understand you better than that, Mr. Scott, and we've only just met. Your Mr. Ward, of the firm, was already attending. —So I believe you went for yourself alone, to say a decent good-bye to the young lady. To see her off, isn't it?"

"That too."

"Yes. Oh, my, a dreadful death. You will permit I should say that that poor young lady must have misbehaved in a previous life, been very naughty, to be taken from this one in such a way. Now, though, now she will be fine . . . do very very well. All paid for."

"It would be pleasant to think so, Mr. Bhose."

"Vijay. Please, *Vijay*."

"Vijay." Evan saw Phil Nash coming toward the table, his racquet tucked under his left arm. Phil raised an eyebrow, and Evan shook his head.

"A friend?"

"Tennis."

"You're having a game this afternoon? Perfect. In India, in times gone by, the British were very cruel about clubs. No one of color—not even a rajah—was accepted. Many many hurt feelings. And feelings are what we ride through life, isn't it? A very wise man said that—I didn't say it; I only repeat it."

"It seems true enough."

"Oh, it's true, Mr. Scott. You have my assurance."

Paul arrived, swung his tray to rest at the table's edge, put a chicken sandwich (with potato chips and a slice of sweet pickle) before Bhose, a large bowl of avocado salad beside it. A tall glass of tea.

"Oh, my." Bhose seemed very pleased with the food. "Oh, yes, times have changed. I am now a member of a very fine club—a club for good health in Toronto— and no one gives a damn the color of my skin! No, not a bit."

Evan accepted his chicken sandwich and tea, glanced up as Paul glanced down at him ... left the chit to be signed.

Bhose had careful table manners in the European fashion (fork held reversed, much use of the knife) and took neat swift bites of his sandwich, judicious forkfuls of avocado salad—but drank his tea very oddly. He tipped the glass up high, just clear of his lips, put back his small, handsome head, and poured the tea down his throat, apparently without swallowing. Evan recalled Basques drinking wine from their *botas* in that way.

"... What I need from you, Mr. Scott," a bite of

chicken sandwich chewed and swallowed, "—what I need is some description of the circumstances." Bhose looked up from his food, his dark eyes large and gentle as a woman's. "Those terrible circumstances. . . ."

"I saw her falling. I didn't see the slip or whatever—the cause. I only saw her falling."

"And falling near you." Bhose, eyes down, searched his salad for something. "So near, and you were seeing her."

"Yes," Evan said. And though he hadn't intended to, added: "And she saw me. She looked at me for an instant as she fell past."

"Oh, *Ram*. . . ." Vijay Bhose stopped eating. "Poor girl—and poor Mr. Scott. As if you shared her fall, isn't it?"

"Not that. More that I refused to share it with her."

Bhose sat staring, salad fork poised, then said, "My, oh my," stared at Evan a moment longer, then began to eat.

He finished most of his salad without looking up, then put down his fork, glanced at the remaining half of his chicken sandwich as if to assure it was still waiting there, and said, "Of course, my company would be most pleased to discover that the poor young lady—Miss Fonsecca, Josephine Fonsecca—'Jo' to her friends—that this young lady had committed a suicide. Totally her responsibility—nothing anyone could ever blame on my company's clients, Rao Electric—such as a misplaced electric cord, hurry-hurry on the construction contract so that she was exhausted, poor girl, and therefore fell. Nothing *their* fault—everything *her* fault. Or perhaps the general contractor's fault, or perhaps your firm's fault. . . . Those are precisely the sort of things my company would like to hear." He started on his last half of sandwich, swallowed the first bite. "It is, as I said, why I was chosen to come down, that

Rao Electric is an Indian-American company, and I am Indian, also, speaking the Hindi and Urdu. English too, of course."

"She didn't commit suicide."

"But how do you know that, Mr. Scott? You didn't see the beginning of her fall." Bhose finished his salad.

"I saw her face. She was startled, embarrassed. It was nothing deliberate ... she was full of life."

"An accident, then? A little misstep?"

"Must have been."

"And so, nothing odd? No one's fault, no messing about up so high—skylarking, isn't it?—playing hide and seek, harum-scarum?"

"Nothing I saw, or heard."

"And no foul play?"

"Nothing I saw—you need to talk to the other man."

Vijay Bhose ate the last of his sandwich, and said, "What other man?"

"One of the watchmen, I think—it was evening, sunset. A tall man with a beard. He was wearing a raincoat. I saw him watching from a few floors up as she fell; he may have seen something I didn't."

"Was it raining, Mr. Scott?" Bhose picked up his tea glass, gently shook it to rattle the ice.

"No."

"But this watchman was wearing a raincoat."

"Yes, he was. It looked like a raincoat."

"Goodness gracious," said Vijay Bhose. "A mysterious figure ... !" And business apparently ended with the last of lunch, he threw back his head, poured tea neatly down his throat, then abruptly pushed back his chair and stood up, so Evan stood up as well. ". . . And what a marvelous lunch you've given me. The shame of it I have to hurry away. I will certainly tell my friends what a superior lunch your club provides, how courteously a guest is treated—and I tell *you* that you must come and stay with me every time you come to Toronto. Every single time," and held out his hand to shake again.

"A kind invitation," Evan said.

"And so pretty a little daughter."

"Thank you."

Bhose smiled, said, "Bye-bye," and stepped rapidly away in his near-dancing gait—his shadow, angular and antic, just keeping up—waved merrily to Paul passing with a loaded tray, and went out through the terrace doors.

Phil Nash strolled up. "We're going to lose our court."

Evan bent to sign the chit. "I'm with you. Let's go."

"Who was the raghead?"

"Business. —Insurance."

"Damn their black hearts to hell," Phil said. His father-in-law, an unpleasant man, was CEO of Central Casualty Life.

"You're doing very well, sweetheart. Much sharper serves. And when school's out—"

"Not for weeks, Daddy. Public school will be out a *lot* sooner."

"Well, when school's out, you'll have more time for your tennis. But you're already doing really well."

"Thanks." Beth looking out the passenger-side window as they drove by wide lawns on Woodrow Street. "But Cluen is really gross. I mean, it's OK to be gay, I guess. . . ."

Robin Cluen, the tennis pro's assistant, was a wonderful player and patient teacher—particularly good with children. Lively, sturdy, humorous and plain, Robin was afflicted with occasional crushes at the club—and had, in spring two years before, been caught having sex with a member's wife, Charlotte Pirie, in the massage room.

After what must have commenced as a pleasant rub-down, then gradually turned to richer attendance—stroking, murmuring, slowly to kisses ... then, at last, to devouring—Charlotte's cries had attracted attention. Two other women had hurried in, and reported finding slight Charlotte Pirie (naked but for her athletic socks) arched on the narrow table, her head thrown back, slender legs (still winter-pale) spraddled wide—and Robin, fully dressed in her tennis whites, crouched between in an odor of heated glue, fastened, nodding forceful forever yesses.

In the week's quiet tumult ensuing, Robin's job had been saved only to prevent further scandal (instances with more than one other wife having been suggested) and after the direst warnings.

"Is Robin misbehaving ... ?"

"Not with *kids*. But she's always giving Terry Guild these looks. Really gross ... moony *looks*. And Terry was playing doubles two courts over—and, well, Robin just was staring over there and it was ridiculous. Terry Guild isn't *gay*. She doesn't even know Robin is alive. ..."

"Sad."

"It isn't sad, Daddy. It's ridiculous."

"Ridiculous, and sad," Evan said, and turned right onto Farmer Road. This wound past Steeple ... then Harbor Drive, then along the cove past large houses, clapboard or fieldstone—each set back deep among trees on a four- or five- or six-acre lot.

At Cove Lane, Evan turned right again ... and a hundred yards farther on, past woods on either side, turned left onto his drive. After the first long curve, the house appeared—two-story, multi-gabled white clapboard glowing with the last of afternoon's light, and patterned with clouds of leaf shadow, maple and oak.

Evan parked the Lexus by the front door, and when Beth had taken her racquet and gym bag inside, he walked around to the north side of the house to see how the paint was holding up. They'd painted four years ago, and he'd noticed some chalkiness on the entranceway. . . .

Evan walked along the house's side, reaching up over the evergreen plantings to stroke the paint along the old clapboard. No problem with it here; it was good for another year or two. . . . The side yard was turf the hundred yards to the trees, past Catherine's small greenhouse. There'd been some talk of expanding the garage, on the other side of the house, to a four-car, since Beth would be driving in a few years . . . then later coming home from college. But Evan had preferred not to do that.

"Is there any change you will permit to this old barn?" Catherine had been annoyed about the garage.

"You have the greenhouse."

"Yes, Evan, I have the greenhouse. It would also be nice to have the boathouse repaired, to have the kitchen redone . . . to have a third bath upstairs."

"We could do that, if we need to."

"But you'd rather not. . . ."

And Evan supposed he would rather not—rather not change a present that reminded him so strongly, so sweetly of the past. It seemed to him—and he'd remodeled many for Ward & Breedon—that a house, once changed, was often no longer quite such a home, and couldn't be for some time. . . . This house had stood here two and a half centuries—a farmhouse first—through years of ease as crops and coastal shipping prospered, then through years of want. Had stood through several wars, in the first of which (discounting previous skirmishes with Pequot and various local tribes) British cavalry had killed two men—Scott cousins—at its front steps. The place had stood its dwellers' losses from several wars thereafter, distant killing; those wars leaving the house uninjured, the deaths spoiling none of its serenity.

Catherine, having said that much about the garage, the boathouse, the kitchen . . . a third bath upstairs, wouldn't mention them again for a long while. It was her way to let a single mention ripen, rest unechoed while slowly becoming heavier and heavier—never lightened by repetition. It was a collected and dignified method, and in time often had its effect.

Evan walked down the lawn past the laurels, and on down to the boathouse path's uneven flagstones wending through his grandmother's Chinese garden, its half acre now grown more relaxed, almost medieval in its clumps and stones and tussocks. . . . Then down to the water and in through the boathouse door. The boathouse did need work; the paint hadn't lasted there on the water as well as it had higher, on the house. The boathouse needed work. . . .

Evan walked through the narrow building, past the old mahogany Chris-Craft (hadn't been out yet, this year). He reached up to take the battered portable radio off the supply shelf, then walked on out the dock door and along the planking past the Crealock's glossy white length—at forty-two feet, ketch-rigged to handle more easily than the old Cheoy Lee. The boat's cockpit and cabin were packed with glittering dials and dull red readouts to keep track of depths and shallows, satellite-supported positions, proximities, radio traffic, weather mapping . . . everything. Almost too much for peace of mind, for being left alone to sail. . . . The Crealock was new, an oceangoing far traveler, very sturdy, solidly built.

"Why so much boat?" Catherine on the day of delivery in April, when he and the yard people had brought her over from Long Island.

"She'll go anywhere," Evan had said then, standing on the dock, watching the boat shifting slightly at its moorings.

" 'Anywhere' is nowhere," Catherine had said, and gone back up to the house. So Evan had named the ketch *Anywhere,* and had Cary Jeakle paint that across her stern in gold leaf. ANYWHERE. . . . And, below that, *Fairport, Conn.*

Evan walked down to the skiff ladder and sat there, legs dangling, looking out over dark water.

The Cornishes' house just showed across the cove, across two hundred yards of water—half-timbered stucco and stone, a fairly accurate Tudor. The Whitakers' place was far to the right, deeper into the cove—its red-brick second story half screened by oaks and four tall birches along their lower lawn.

Dave Cornish had bought his house seventeen years ago; the Whitakers had lived at the cove for two hundred and thirty. Fishermen, then. Real estate brokers now. . . . And well-founded rumor that a then Major Scott in the Continental Army had seen to it a Tory Whitaker was hanged, on evidence he'd passed information to a British cutter while fishing the Sound. That Scott, many years later, arrested with Burr—and freed by a jury considering the old man's behavior in the war, his missing right arm, clipped by cannon at Trenton.

Looking across the water, Evan found it easy to recall Josephine Fonsecca's face as she fell. He seemed to see it reflected up out of sunset light on the Sound's shifting surface, where the sea swept into their small cove and out again. He felt a loss so sharp it startled him—a loss of a stranger he might have met. Not loved, not even cared for ... but simply met—and might have, too, any day he'd visited the job at 366. Might have taken the work elevator up to the sixtieth or sixty-fifth floor, and met her while he was walking over the open steelwork, its unstable temporary decking.

She would have hurried past, glanced at him, perhaps. Not a remarkable girl. Dark, sturdy, her black hair tucked under her hard hat. ... The orange hard hat had been gone when he'd seen her falling. Must have fallen away separately, scaled away at an angle through the air ... down and down. Struck the pavement somewhere, or a lower building's roof. Her hair had been whipping free as he watched her fall.

She would have glanced at him as she hurried by, a coil of light cable over her shoulder, hustling, working hard, demonstrating for the others, for her father, that a woman's muscles were useful as a man's.

But—if only in passing—he would have met her when she wasn't dying, and it would not have been so important. ...

Evan slid the radio nearer, switched it on ... searched for the jazz station, and heard a swift run of piano, caught in mid-introduction, pause and step aside for a sax's comment, musically harsh as a jungle bird's. He thought Stan Getz was playing ... and after a while listening to "Stardust," was sure, and knew Kenny Barron was playing the piano.

Evan sat, watched the water, and listened through to "Stardust"'s end in European applause (clapping larded with comments, yodeling calls of approval), and supposed it was one of the old performance sets from Denmark. He sat feeling sleepy from the long day—driving over from Hartford, working at the salt box ... then lunch with what's-his-name, then tennis. ... Had beaten Phil, but not by much.

—The next side was Stan Getz again, playing with a group of people Evan didn't recognize. Scandinavians, probably. They had a very steady style, backed Getz reliably ... didn't get in his way. Didn't seem to contribute much, either.

He felt, or thought he felt under the music's beat, a faint vibration through the planking—looked down to see if wavelets were slapping at the pilings, then glanced back and saw Willie running toward him down the dock. The hugely fat coon cat galloping in his rabbity gait, almost a hop. Willy reached Evan and collapsed panting beside him, golden eyes slightly bugged by effort, breathlessness.

Evan didn't stroke him—the cat didn't like it, though he was fonder of Evan than of Catherine or Beth (even so, Beth was suspected of feeding him secretly). Willie, if not stroked, was usually content to rest alongside Evan—and particularly out on the dock, as if at any moment this man might suddenly begin to fish, catch one, and leave it flapping on the decking at Willie's mercy. That had happened only two or three times since Willie's kittenhood, but hadn't been forgotten.

Evan sat a while longer, watching the surface of the cove turn paler gray, streaked with sunset maroon in places beyond the tall trees' shadows. ... Some children were calling, playing over at the Cornishes, out of sight under oaks.

Insects had come out into the evening, were whirring over the cove here and there—and with them, flickering bats hardly discernible they flew so quickly, irregularly. ... The summer before, tree swallows had nested at the cove, and flown and dipped to the water to leave each time a small series of rings expanding on its surface.

No swallows this year.

Deep into the cove, the white reflection beneath the stern of the Whitakers' big Bertram—which they rarely took out—was fading as if the cruiser itself were a ghost ship dissolving into darkness.

Evan stood, bent to pick up the radio, and walked back through the boathouse to put it away, Willie lumbering along behind. . . . Then they went up the path together through birches to the garden, then the yard, and across to the back porch steps. The siding paint was fine back there, no checking, certainly good for another year.

Going into the pantry room through the screen door, Willie crowding in behind him, Evan could smell dinner cooking, hear Mrs. Hooper in the kitchen, talking to Catherine about the Reeses.

The Reeses had built a forty-room house on Derry Lane, and were in constant battle with their Peruvian servants—a cook, maid, and gardener they'd imported as likely to be cheaper and less troublesome than locals.

It was the town's opinion that the Reeses would soon be found murdered by their employees—the cook (a tiny large-nosed man the color of eggplant) being particularly tired of having to produce classic French cuisine, the odors of which made him ill.

"Those people have gone too far," Mrs. Hooper said at the sink counter, and turned to nod to Evan as he came in. "Really. They've gone too far this time."

The kitchen was scented by odors of leg of lamb and baked potato. The salad would probably be cress and cucumber, a combination which Mrs. Hooper was fond of serving with any red meat. "Cools the meal. . . ." Dressing, spiced tomato purée.

A number of years before, just after she'd come to work for them as cook-housekeeper, Evan had asked Mrs. Hooper (small and scrawny, with slightly bulging bright brown eyes) whether she minded serving dinners. —Then, and thereafter, Catherine had allowed breakfasts and lunches in the kitchen nook, but insisted dinners be more formal, in the dining room and eaten off good china; Saturday nights to be candle-lit. Her grandmother and great aunts, formidable relics of a Maine whaling-fleet fortune, had held that much state, and taught it to her.

"No, I don't mind serving at all." Mrs. Hooper (Edith Hooper), already a widow, had seemed surprised at the question. "Your people have always lived here, and your wife is a lady and she knows what she wants and that's good enough for me. —If I *don't* want to do something around here, you can believe I'll let you know, Mr. Scott." And, having made her position clear, Mrs. Hooper had proceeded to do everything they asked of her, energetic as a terrier. At times, too energetic.

Evan crossed the kitchen—a large room, almost fifteen feet on a side—and slid the old Wostenholm carving knife out of the cutlery block. The other carver was an American stainless, sturdy but inelegant. He drew out the sharpening steel, and passed the slender blade (slightly curved) along it twice and then again, then opened the counter's top drawer to get the serving fork, and took the set down the hall to the dining room.

He recalled his grandfather sitting at the head of the table only a few months before he died—his father just to the right, his mother at the foot. The old man, sweet-tempered and hard of hearing, was preparing to carve with the same Wostenholm—its steel already narrow with metal lost to a century of honing. The long table had been set as it was now, the same silver now lying bright on white linen under the chandelier. —The table's wood was black walnut, and very old, dark, its grain like black coffee running in ripples across it.

While his grandfather had talked (speaking up), Evan had sometimes traced the wood's grain with his fingertip, trying to find an end to it.

The phone rang, and Evan heard Mrs. Hooper answering it in the kitchen. Then heard her footsteps up the hall.

"Mr. Scott—there's a call for you."

"Thank you." Evan took the call in what had been the butler's pantry—no butler in it since the twenties.

"Evan?" Nancy's stony old voice.

"Hello, Aunt Nan. . . ."

"I want to talk to Catherine, but first I want to talk to you."

"And what about?"

"Well, I want to know if you're coming up or not. Rebecca thinks the child is still in school."

"Yes, she is. 'The child' is in school until the end of the month."

Beth, on her way to the kitchen, paused in the dining room's entrance to make a goggling face. Evan made one back.

"That is the most absurd thing I ever heard—for God's sake, it's June; we're deep into summer!"

"Not that deep—"

"—And Beth should be up on the island, playing, getting some sun and sea in her bones, not sitting in a schoolroom. She'll grow up with crooked legs."

"Her legs are fine."

"Well, are you coming up or not?"

"Nan, I doubt it. We wanted to do some sailing down here this summer. I need to work the Crealock in."

"Oh, for God's sake—if you want to sail, then sail *up*. Catherine says your father sailed up to Newfoundland every year."

"Right, he did, and my grandfather did the same—

and it's precisely remembering those trips, the sail back down in autumn, that keeps me from doing it with Catherine and Beth—and in a new boat I don't know yet."

"Lord, how people have shrunk. If anything is any effort at all ..."

"So, I doubt that we'll be coming up—or if we do, just for a week or two."

"And I suppose I'm to pay that fool Fred Pell to clean up on the island for no reason at all. Fix that damn water tank—which John Hollis pretended to fix two years ago."

"I'd tell Fred to leave the tank alone. He won't improve it; it needs a new liner."

"I think—if it's important what I think, Evan—I think that is something you should take care of. You are the man of the family, not just some sort of social wallpaper. I don't understand men these days. When I was a girl, they were always up and doing—running the whole damn world, for God's sake, and enjoying doing it, not just standing back ... always standing back and letting the women handle things."

"Nan, we're about to have dinner."

"You can give me a few minutes—if your dinner was cooked by that impossible Hooper creature, it can damn well wait." Heat apparently still lingering from two instances of severe personality clash between this great-aunt and Mrs. Hooper. "... So, you're not going to use the island place?"

"Maybe for a week or two, later."

"—Because I certainly can't get up there this year. Rebecca would have a fit if I even suggested going up, leaving her *alone*—and by the way, at the risk of sounding painfully like a maiden aunt, though I'm certainly no such thing, not a maiden at any rate, I must tell you that my sister Rebecca has taken to having very feverish and dubious conversations with any male who comes around—and I do include delivery people. Feverish conversations and a revealing lemon-yellow peignoir—though what the poor old bag has to reveal is mighty unappetizing, it seems to me. I think she's going off her rocker, and I just want to let you know. Let Catherine know."

"Nan—she's been going off her rocker for some time."

"Not this far; two or three men, a painter and two pizza-delivery people, have left this house in haste, and looking mighty pale. I think they saw just a little too much of Rebecca, something they'd rather not have seen. Those boys looked as if they needed a drink in the worst way."

"But she's behaving, otherwise?"

"Otherwise—oh, otherwise, butter wouldn't melt in her mouth."

"Well. . . ."

"So, you don't intend to go up?"

"Catherine's not fond enough of sailing to be sailing up to Maine, then sailing down again in autumn weather."

"What a sissy. The pack of you are just sissies. My nephew, Frank, would have sailed up and not thought a thing about it—and if Catherine's mother hadn't wanted to go, he'd have taken the children and just left her behind. You really need to get a little tougher with Catherine, Evan."

"Um-hmm."

Catherine's long cool arm slid over Evan's sleeve for the phone. "Who is it? The gorgon?"

"What did she say?" Nan's voice, strident, being carried away with the receiver.

Evan bent to follow it. "She called you a gorgon," as Catherine tugged the phone away.

"Nan ... ? How are you feeling, dear ... ?"

Evan woke deep in the night, still half in a pleasant dream of flying—in Vietnam, but flying over it just high enough to see no soldiers ... only occasional airbursts, cool gray against green hills. On his right, the China Sea, bright beaten silver, hardly wrinkled as it lay against the land.... Left, the Annamese Hills rose into mountains—and covered in jungle absolutely green, looked like a different ocean, an ocean whose great waves some wizard had frozen at their crests.

Evan rose higher, to lose even geography, and barely heard men laughing ... but well enough to begin to wake. And lying still, listening, thought he heard through the open bedroom windows two young men laughing some distance away.

Then, Willie yowled down in the Chinese garden.

chapter 5

∙∙

The Dond loved riding the subways at night. Their irregular motion reminded him of a mountain pony's uneven trot along high trails.

He often rode the trains for hours into early morning—very tall, bony, and lank, his nose an outsized
beak broken once or twice. His teeth were yellow,
strong as a horse's—and showed like a drowsy dog's
sometimes, as he dozed. The Dond's hair—the same
oily gray-streaked black as his tangled beard—fell almost to his waist, unbound. In this country he wore it
coiled up, held in place by a steel comb under his
brown wool cap. He paid no attention to weather, to
cold or heat, and always wore his ancient camel-wool
coat, grimy brown and draping below his knees.

Most passersby thought him one of the odder
homeless—a probable mental case like so many others
wandering the streets and sleeping in subways. Police
officers thought the same. —They were wrong. Anyone who knew Afghanistan would have known better.
Any elderly British officer who'd served on the old
Northwest Frontier—any young Russian officer who'd
served there much more recently, particularly among
the outlawed mountain tribes—would have known
much better. . . .

The Dond's eyes were a pale amber-brown, their black pupils always wide and staring as a hunter's in sight of game. He'd learned in this country, this city, not to look directly at people. It troubled them.

The Dond had never been disturbed in his nighttime subway riding. He looked too dirty, too poor. It had never even occurred to him he might be molested on the trains—though he would have noticed at once if a Pathan tribesman, an Afridi or Dard, had entered a car. That might have been a matter of feud.

But this had never happened, and it didn't trouble him when well after midnight, still warm, still humid here below the early-summer streets, three young black men in beautifully casual baggy clothes (soft cotton trousers, bright-striped shirts, and light richly colored leather jackets), came into the car, noisily joking. Three young lords of misrule with gold rings in their ears—and pleased with the unease they caused among the few other passengers.

One young black man, the shortest—but very wide across the shoulders—led the others to a bench seat, and stood staring down at an older Hispanic until he got up and moved away.

Then the three of them sat jostling each other, talking loud over the subway's squeal and rumble. But not for long. Restless, more uncomfortable as they got comfortable, they suddenly stood—and the stocky boy, his head shaved gleaming smooth, led them strolling, swaggering down the car. They filled the narrow aisle with color and moving muscle, and balancing nicely against the train's shifting, glanced from side to side at averted eyes, lowered heads, two of the passengers carefully reading.

The Dond sat with his long legs stretched out before him, brown feet bare and bony in rough sandals.

The wide-shouldered boy stopped there, his way almost blocked by those large feet, so he would have to step a little aside to pass.

"You better move outta my way, motherfucka. . . ." The young man said this casually, as good advice. The Dond didn't draw his long legs in.

The boy waited a moment, then kicked the sandaled feet briskly aside. With harder shoes than sneakers, it would have been a painful kick.

The Dond, who came from cruel country, was not offended by roughness. He grunted, drew his long legs in—and the three young men trooped by. But their leader, still annoyed by this weirdo's slow response, suddenly turned, walked back to the Dond, and bent over him. The young man's face, broad, black, and handsome, reflected no anger—only the necessity of teaching respect.

"Nex' time, you fuckin' jump what I tell you to *do,* homeless motherfucka." And he reached down and yanked the Dond's ragged beard.

This was rudeness, much more serious than a casual kick, and the Dond stood up—a stork (but eagle-beaked) unfolding to more than six and a half feet, and biblically robed in the folds of his long brown coat.

It was impressive height, even so bony, and as the wide-shouldered boy and his friends looked up, the Dond—very swiftly—reached down inside his open coat to a wide cracked-leather Bokhariot belt, and drew out a Khyber knife (a short sword really), its blade seventeen inches long, deeply curved, and more than sharp enough to shave with.

—Drew it and in smooth continuous motion set the blade's point at the young man's left hipbone, thrust deep—and sliced suddenly sideways so the boy was opened across his belly.

Blue bowels came bulging through the pretty shirt in

a squirting rinse of red, and the boy, in shock, knelt and put his hands there to hold them in.

The second young man had reached into his jacket and drawn a small stainless automatic—and the Dond, enjoying himself now, swung his heavy blade to chop that hand off, so the black hand and bright pistol flew down the subway car together. Then he killed that boy, while the few other passengers sat still, frozen, eyes tight closed so as to witness nothing.

The third young man turned and ran just as the train slowed and lurched into a station. This boy ran away through two cars, past only seven or eight passengers, so late—then, as the doors opened, sprinted out onto the platform past a man and woman who wouldn't watch.

The Dond, loping in great strides, caught this young man on empty stairs to the street, and dragged him down and off, then under the staircase. There, the boy sat amidst dirt and litter, his face a terrified baby's, wet with tears and snot.

The Dond spoke to him in Pushtu, asking if he wished to pray—and when the boy only sat and cried, the tribesman frowned, clicked his tongue in disapproval, reached down, pulled the boy's head back, and cut his throat.

"Oh, look!" Beth, book bag hanging off her narrow shoulder, come back up the drive and through the front door with Willie, discontented, loaded in her arms.

"Beth, you'll miss the bus!" Catherine, still in her white bathrobe, coming down the hall. The Academy's small bus was briskly scheduled.

"I've got time. —Look!" And fingered at Willie's thick-furred throat to show a slender gold chain, a tiny gold bell hanging off it.

Catherine examined it, said, "Oh, it's gold!" And to

Evan, come down the hall behind her, "Evan, what in the world did you buy this for?" Catherine's voice still slightly yolky from a long night's sleep, an oatmeal breakfast.

"Buy what?"

"Buy the cat a gold necklace or whatever." Outlined by morning light through the open doorway, she stood with her hand at Willie's rich throat.

"It's a little bell," Beth said. "I saw it shining. . . ."

"I didn't buy it."

"It's a little gold bell," Beth said, and reached under Willie's chin to shake it. "But it doesn't ring. It doesn't make any noise at all."

Evan touched the little bell, shook it gently on its slender gold chain. " 'Silence is golden' is what's meant, I suppose."

"Well, who would do a silly thing like this?" Catherine looking down as Willie gazed up from Beth's arms, they exchanged glances, blue to gold. "Beth, you're going to miss the school bus."

"All right . . . OK, OK." Beth leaned to dump Willie out of her arms; he landed with a soft thump, annoyed, and walked off toward the living room as Beth went out the door, swung it closed behind her.

"That was really ridiculous. A gold chain for a *cat*?"

"Not my doing. . . ."

"Oh, Evan, then who did?"

"Someone with a sense of humor, I suppose."

"Um-hmm. Well, please go get Willie and take that thing off him. He'll only lose it. Really ridiculous, Evan. . . ."

The Hartford bank was presenting all the problems that deliberately ugly architecture had to. Things didn't fit together very well—a tribute to Henry Ward's talent for spaces that they fit as well as they did.

Evan had sketched two different entrances for the bank's basement parking garage (a detail Ward hadn't troubled with) and now, during lunchtime, was working on a third. . . .

On the train in, Evan had mentioned Willie's bell to Norm Deitner, and Deitner (supposed to be an extremely successful corporate attorney, though looking too young for it) had immediately said, "Unwarranted attentions."

"I suppose it was."

"Listen, Evan, exactly the same thing if a child comes home with a box of expensive chocolates. Unwarranted attentions, and a source of parental anxiety. 'What does someone want with my child?' "

"Willie's an unlikely subject for molestation, Norm."

"Depends on the tastes of the molester," Deitner had said, and gone back to his paper. . . .

The third sketch seemed to work better, made the entrance at least a respectable-looking entryway, less of a gaping hole in the side of the building. . . .

"Am I intruding? I so often am."

Evan looked up and saw a rumpled man, burly, fairly fat—and very dark, apparently another Hindu—standing in his office doorway.

"There was no one at all in the outer office, so I simply wandered here and there until I was finding you," the fat man said. "—And such a nice office. Everyone else gone to lunch—tiffin later, I suppose. I did wait outside to see if you might come out, but then I thought, 'Oh, he isn't coming out, I shall have to go inside.' And I have." The fat man was wearing a wrinkled brown summer suit.

"I had to stay a while, some work to get through. —How may I be of help, Mr. . . . ?" Second Hindu this week.

"Chand Prasad. And unfortunately it is not simply 'Mr.' " The fat man smiled, reached into his jacket pocket and brought out a badge wallet, opened that to reveal a gold shield. "I know I'm not really looking the part."

"Come in, officer. . . . What can I do for you?"

"Well, that depends, doesn't it?" The fat man, his gait rolling as a sailor's, strolled around Evan's desk as if he were a client, and peered down at the preliminary.

"Oh, *very* elegant. What a perfect drawing. You are a so-talented man! And of what building?"

"It's for a bank in Hartford."

"Handsome. What a handsome bank, and so beautifully rendered. I should certainly give them my money. —Well, perhaps not all of my money." The fat man had a rich smile, that made him squint. "Perhaps just a little of my money. I should want to know, for example, whether they could really be affording such a wonderful, beautifully designed new building—and why the old building was no longer good enough. My money being spent, after all."

"Just so," Evan said. "In fact, their old building is a beauty."

"Ah, out with the old, in with the new. . . ." The fat man ambled back around the desk and stood beside the nearest of the office's sling chairs, apparently waiting for an invitation to sit.

When Evan gestured, the policeman eased himself down into the chair, adjusted himself to it. "I'm here to inquire about sad circumstances . . . the young woman's fall. And by the by, I should identify myself completely. I am, however improbable it may seem, being Detective Sergeant Prasad, NYPD."

"Prasad. . . ."

"P-r-a-s-a-d."

"I see. Excuse me, but ... would this be a joke? Something Pete Talbot thought would be funny?"

The fat man stopped smiling. "Do I seem that odd, that 'funny,' Mr. Scott? Believe me, those who encounter me professionally don't find me amusing at all. . . . And I'm sorry to say I'm not knowing your Mr. Talbot. Is he a friend?"

"I see. . . . Well, I apologize, Sergeant. Foolish of me."

"No, no." Smiling again. "I am the one with silly sensibilities. A foreigner, after all—among the alien corn and so forth. And now you see why I waited outside for you—for your going to lunch, is it? A visit by the police is always an occasion for possible embarrassment; it seemed easy enough to be sparing you that annoyance. But your coworkers all came out, and you did not, so I came in."

"Thank you."

"Well . . . so, to the point. Have you, Mr. Scott, ever heard of the Italian Squad?"

"No, I don't believe so."

"This 'Italian Squad' was formed in the city at the turn of the century—purpose being to use Italian-American officers familiar with the immigrant culture, to combat the criminal organizations that had accompanied those immigrants. The so-called Unione, the Camorra, Black Hand, and so forth. Relatively primitive, actually. *Badmashes*. . . ."

"I see. . . ." Evan glanced down at the elevation. He'd misdrawn the degree of slope.

"Now, I and my partner have been appointed to just such a squad, a very similar unit. The 'Indian Squad,' you might say—Indian as in India, not as in Native Americans. We, and six other officers, speaking Hindi, Hindustani, Urdu, Pushtu and so forth. We have been assigned to deal with the rather more ancient and formidable criminal organizations that may accompany *our* countrymen here, to prey on those decent and hardworking people. To prey on yours, as well." The fat man paused, sat looking past Evan to a pen-and-ink sketch of the Rovere Gymnasium, framed on the office wall. "My, that is such a pretty building. Is it a theater?"

"A gymnasium."

"Really? So pretty, and only to perspire in. Exercise and I, as you can imagine, Mr. Scott, are strangers— except in the line of duty. And our squad's duty, up to now, has been very little work at all; our people here are being such good citizens.... Alas, now it seems the serpent has entered Eden. Is that a correct Christian metaphor?"

"Yes, it is."

"But you are wondering what all this has to do with you."

"Yes, I am."

"Now, you see, here is what happened: two of our people—much thinner than I—looking proper detectives—were surveilling a certain young Sonny Varma, day before yesterday, on a matter related to the matter we are going to discuss. They followed young Sonny to that so-lovely Fairport in Connecticut—please, please don't be informing the Connecticut authorities of our trespassing; your states are as jealous as ours in India." The fat man paused, heaved slightly to the right, reached down into his left jacket pocket and brought out a pack of chewing gum. He slid a stick free, held it out to Evan—"No?"—took off its wrapper, folded it, and tucked it into his mouth. Then began to chew very busily, as if there were a mouthful to deal with. The fat man had good teeth, a coated tongue.

". . . Well, our people were so surprised to see young Sonny—*not* a gentleman, though likable, though personable—go into the Fairport Club, and stay for such a long time."

"To see me."

"Yes! So surprising. . . ."

"The man who saw me was named Bhose."

"Oh, yes. That naughty Sonny. . . . 'Vijay Bhose,' isn't it?"

"Yes."

"That was our Sonny Varma."

"He said he was in insurance."

"And showed you a business card?"

"That's right."

"But no identification otherwise? No picture identification issued by the insurance company?"

"No, nothing like that."

"Oh, you Westerners. You are being trusting as children . . . really. For example—now, only for example—I have shown you a badge. Now, will you call downtown? Will you call Captain Gernsbach at Police Plaza, and check on this plump police officer's *bona fides*? —No, you will not trouble. Very unwise, particularly since just a moment ago you thought I might be part of a practical joke. —Odd phrase; I wonder what an *im*practical joke might be. . . ."

"I see your point, officer, but I'm still not sure why Bhose or whoever—"

"Sonny Varma."

"—why this Varma person went through that particular charade."

"Because you saw the Fonsecca girl *fall,* Mr. Scott. That's why. You saw her fall, and that is why you very shortly after had lunch with a member of the Rao family. A cousin—the so-charming Sonny."

"And not in insurance. . . ."

"Well . . . in a way. The family of Pandit Rao— *daddi-ji,* as they call him—is very much in insurance of a sort, as well as now in electrical contracting. Insurance—'protection,' as you call it here—insurance against accidents of all sorts. And it's very good insurance to be having. . . . Now the Rao family as such is quite small. *Daddi-ji* and three sons—I know them; oh, I know them all very well. Let us see. . . . The sons are Vasud; he is very clever, a very clever fellow, and so charming. And Dev, he is the handsome one. Oh, very good-looking. How the ladies love Dev Rao . . . though he is handicapped socially by a bad temper, a really severely bad temper. And the last—but by no means the least—is Chandra Rao. Chandra is the oldest brother, and very much in charge. No one knows what bad temper Chandra might have. No one has ever cared to try his temper, do you see?"

"Yes, I believe I see."

"Of course, they are all three under their *daddi-ji*, and there are one or two sons-in-law and two or three cousins. Brother-cousins we call them. Not many. One *cha-cha*—an uncle. Only a few people, really. Low overhead. . . . And all blood relatives. No 'button men,' no 'associates' in these families. Only blood relations, though of course the different families are doing business from time to time." Prasad reached up to take out his chewing gum, glanced at it, and put it back in his mouth. "Am I being rude? I see you look as if I am being rude. Taking the gum out, is it?"

"No, of course not."

"Oh, yes, I see that look. That look said, 'God, whatever next?—this creature is sitting in my office examining his *gum*.' What? Is it that once in, it should never come out? That's the improper part? Taking it out again?"

"Officer, I think you should chew your gum however you please. And if I indicated differently, then I was the rude one."

" 'Manners maketh the man.' Do you think that's true?"

"No, I don't. . . . Now, you were saying Rao Electric is just a front for criminals?" Evan glanced down for a moment, made a line of correction to the entrance pass-through.

"Not only a front—a very successful business. But yes, a front as well, a vehicle for other . . . enterprises. But Mr. Scott, don't mistake the Raos for your common gangsters, your clumsy Italian and Irish hoodlums here. No, no, no. They are very much more formidable; they have, after all, two thousand years of criminal history behind them, a very ancient sect. *Goondas* in the cities . . . deceivers—highwaymen—in the countryside. You see, traditionally, they are believing they have been given all the world's roads, all its ways of traveling as theirs, to do with as they please. And this city is the crossroads of all roads."

"I see. And supposedly, as part of some extortion threat, these people were involved in the girl's death?"

"Well . . . do you know what the Raos and families like the Raos do if you don't *buy* their sort of insurance? Or if you might interfere in other business of theirs? Do you know what they do? What they've always done?"

"Something unpleasant, I suppose."

"Oh, yes—and so simple. They don't harm you—oh, no, no, no. You are useful to them; why should they harm you? That's the very last resort—though, of course, occasionally resorted to. No, first they are giving you little hints, cautionary hints—and, if these aren't effective, they simply kill your oldest child." The fat man hitched his bulk to the right again, got his left hand into his coat pocket, and took out another stick of gum. (Juicy Fruit, Evan saw now.) He unwrapped the gum, doubled it, and popped it into his mouth.

"Loses its sweet taste, isn't it, unless you're having more? So ... kill your oldest child. It's a way of getting your attention, do you see? And if you don't have a child—oh, then your wife, a lady friend, a parent ... even, in some cases, a dear pet. Yes, even a little dog. It's a ... wake-up call, you might say. And if you don't wake up, they simply keep calling. Another of your children, perhaps...."

"I see."

"And almost always by what seems an accident." The fat man paused for a moment, apparently to chew his gum more noisily, relishing it. "Not always, but usually. They are using lorries—trucks—and other methods, poisons ... various indigestives."

"Accidental falls...."

"Oh, yes—and best if from very great heights. Do you know the reason for that?"

"No."

"Ah, you're seeing the girl again, isn't it? Seeing her as she fell. Oh, dear.... Well, two reasons: first, time for suffering before the end. Very important—oh, goodness, yes. Persons who love them can imagine that suffering during the fall. Other reason...."

"Other reason?"

"Other reason is pleasure to the lady. Dark lady."

"Lady?" ... This all much too elaborate to be anyone's joke. And the fat man too eccentric to be anything but genuine.

"Do you know Shaktas, Mr. Scott? —No, you don't know Shaktas."

"Afraid not." ... The interior slope of the parking garage was still too steep. And even with a milder slope, daylight lighting would be necessary from the

entrance down . . . and from the exits up to street level
at the back of the block. . . .

"Shaktas are those believers who are worshiping the
lady things. Lady powers. The Mother of the Earth as
the beautiful Durga, and so forth."

"I see. . . ." It occurred to Evan that this odd plump
policeman—speaking near-Victorian English with an
Indian accent—seemed to belong with Evan's dreams
of the war, so much more vivid than life lived between
Fairport and the firm's New York office.

"But the Raos, the other families like them—only a
very few, thank God, and most still in India—they
worship—well, better to say they 'respect.' They are
respecting a certain other avatar, the dear blessed Lady
of Darkness." The policeman seemed lost in his lec-
ture, caught up with his Eastern felons, their ancient
and intricate ways. The dark eyes shone in the broad,
fat face.

" 'Darkness.' . . ."

"Oh, my—now you're thinking I'm a quite mad person. Quite mad. Now, you're thinking you had better
call Captain Gernsbach after all, and inquire about this
mad policeman, this so-odd Third World cop."

"No, not at all. . . ."

"You're very patient; you're very kind—and must be
hungry for lunch. Now, this dark lady, this goddess,
they call Kali—the blackness, that which time con-
ceals. Dark as the past, which is lost forever. Dark as
the future, which is not yet found."

"I see."

"And many arms." The fat detective waved his arms
to illustrate. "Many arms holding this or that, a spear,
a human head. She wears a necklace of skulls . . . and
her tongue is so," sticking his own tongue out, the wad
of gum precariously balanced on it. "Eyes . . . eyes
very angry. Always *angry*." The fat man made a mur-

derous face—almost funny, but not quite. "Her music
is bone flutes and little drums. Her flower, the mari-
gold. Her dancing—oh, my!—spectacular. And they
sing." The fat man began to softly clap his hands.

> "Oh, daughter of the hills,
> You have come to me naked,
> Your long tongue lolling,
> Flickering in and out.
> Your eyes are bright red coals;
> Your hair is loose in the wind.
> I hear your necklace of skulls
> Rattling between your breasts
> As you begin to dance. . . ."

". . . Very nice," Evan said. "And interesting, Detective Prasad. Really, very interesting, but if I may be
blunt, I'm not sure what this has to do with me. I saw
the girl fall—but I didn't see anyone cause it. And despite what you've said—and I suppose the Raos, like a
number of people in construction in this state and New
Jersey, are not angels—despite that, I think the girl
probably simply slipped and fell."

"First, Mr. Scott," the broad face patient, willing to
tutor, "—first, let me say that you are mistaken. That
song is not 'nice.' It is not nice at all. In times past,
more than two million—two *million* of my people
died, strangled traveling the roads of India. After
which, their murderers might sing that same song of
love, eat the lady's sacred sugar, and give thanks to
her. . . . We are talking, do you see, about a very ancient evil. Oh my, yes. Being very wise, and very
cruel." Prasad leaned to the right, dug in his jacket
pocket for more gum, chose a slice and unwrapped it.
"Now, to be sure, they are not what they once were. In
the last century, the British have damaged them se-

verely. But a few of the faithful remain." He put the
slice of Juicy Fruit in his mouth, chewed for a moment, apparently blending it into the mass of veteran
gum ... then reached up, took the increased lump out
of his mouth, examined it and put it back in. "And as
to your involvement—and seeing nothing, nothing un-
toward and so forth—what is important is simply that
you saw anything. You *saw*—that is what is important.
And you went to her funeral, where another of my
slender young colleagues observed you, even took your
picture. . . . And then you talked in your Fairport Club,
and you were telling the so-charming Sonny—what,
exactly?"

"That I'd seen her fall. That ... it certainly didn't
seem to be a suicide."

"Oh, dear."

". . . And I believe I mentioned seeing a bearded
man, very tall, and wearing a long coat—a raincoat, I
think. I mentioned seeing him looking down from the
structure."

"Oh, gracious me. . . ."

"Meaning?" Evan was beginning to be a little bored
with Oriental vaudeville. Feared another song if it kept
up much longer.

"Meaning, Mr. Scott, that your life, and my life,
would be a great deal simpler if you had said nothing
at all. Nothing ... at all. You see, the Raos will now
believe you were lying. That surely you saw a *little*
more. . . ."

"I didn't."

"Well, I suppose it's possible—you people are so
very strange. I suppose it's possible they'll believe
you."

"And you're saying Josephine Fonsecca was definitely murdered, thrown off that building?"

"Oh, if we were knowing that, if we had *proof* of

that, the Raos would now be under arrest. —Or at least their Pathan would be under arrest; we think they use a Pathan—a Dond savage—for some . . . tasks. You know the Donds?" A weary glance now, at having to explain so much to this skeptical white face. "—You are not knowing the Donds. Well, a small, primitive, and extremely ferocious tribe of Afghanistan. You might ask the Russians about the Donds—very unpleasant experiences with them in their war. A mountain people; they are not minding heights at all, if you catch my drift."

"I catch your drift. . . ." Evan considered the parking garage's exit. Would have to be single-lane, all the way through to the back of the building.

"So if we *knew*, if we were having proof—but unfortunately we don't. Still, I think it. Because Rao Electric is supplying all the controls and motors and wiring for that immense building you and your clever people here have designed. And because Mr. J. Fonsecca, the girl's father, commands the ironworkers constructing that building. . . . The precise *why* of the business, I'm not knowing—but the naughtiness I'm certain of."

"She was his eldest child?" Single-lane into parking area . . . all right. But only the single lane out?

"His eldest. He has two small boys left. Twins. —How many children do you have, Mr. Scott?"

"One."

"Ah. . . . One."

"And your advice in this situation, officer, would be?"

"It's a sad thing for a policeman to have to say—and my captain, my commander, would take violent exception—but my advice to you, Mr. Scott, would be to never speak of this matter again. Not another word. Not another word to anyone."

"And not to you either, of course." Evan thought of

mentioning the note, the phrase from Yeats ... and Willie's little silent golden bell. Then decided not; it would encourage the policeman to say more, chatter on about the possibility of trouble.

"Oh, most particularly not another word to me." The fat man rocked easily forward, and used that impetus to stand.

Evan stood with him. "Well, officer, thank you for coming by. . . ." And reached out to shake a warm cushioned hand that as it gripped grew suddenly much stronger, as if there were another and harder hand inside it. An odd sensation. "And I'm sure you're right, and there's some possibility of this becoming unpleasant. But frankly, it does sound a little improbable."

"*Improbable?* . . . You really are an extraordinary culture. It occurs to me—if you'll forgive a flight of fancy—that a certain Western blindness must have given your people, *gora log,* the great advantage of simplicity over those races, such as mine, which saw all sides of everything."

"I simply meant it all seems a little bizarre, a little—to use your phrase—Third World."

"Does it really, Mr. Scott? Then you must not have noticed how 'bizarre,' how 'Third World,' your city has already become. Believe me when I tell you that these people, the Raos and others like them—many not Hindu, not Indian—are finding your city more and more like home."

Evan waited a little while to go out to lunch, waited until he was certain Prasad had gone on his way, so he wouldn't encounter the policeman on the street, have to listen to more elaborations about a possible but unlikely murder.

After a few minutes, he set the Rapidograph pen down at the drawn close of a properly sloped entrance to the parking garage, then got up, put his jacket on, and walked out through the empty office—Sanchia and the others not back yet.

The fat man himself, of course, had been proof of his point—such an exotic type for a New York City cop. And perhaps with an Easterner's tendency to dramatize and complicate. Create the most interesting explanation, then believe it.

Evan passed the newsstand on the corner, noticing that the old man—usually glowering behind piles of papers, ranks of news and soft-porn magazines—had been replaced by a plump young Indian woman in a light-blue sari. She had a red caste mark between her eyes. . . .

He ate a slender, watery hot dog at a steel cart two blocks north, had a can of Dr Pepper with it, then—after four tries—flagged a worn Yellow Cab heading uptown in the midday rush.

The cabby was a small middle-aged woman with curly graying blond hair and a jockey's starved foxy face. She was a very good driver—the first Evan had seen in years who used a turning knob on her steering wheel, gripped that one-handed, and spun her way in swift left and right circles through the shifting traffic the long blocks up to the corner across from 366.

. . . There was no mark left in the middle of the cross street beside the building. No spot right there that might be anything but drops of a run of oil some elderly delivery van had left behind. The wreckage of her head, the collapsed body, had left nothing behind on blacktop pavement, as if Josephine had died in mid-air, and struck the ground a ghost. . . . The hurrying traffic ran over where she'd been.

Evan walked to the building site, through the wire gate, and across low drifts of graveled dirt to the office trailer parked far to the right amid neat heaps of reinforcing rods, cable coils, light steel members and a quarter acre of stacks of gray ten-gallon cans of red-lead paint.

Four office trailers were ranked down the site: Harris, diNunzio's, the excavating company's, then Receiving, and at the end, Rao Electric's (secondhand, its paint a chipped white). . . . Harris, diNunzio's office trailer had erected many big buildings, and its original dark green was creased and rumpled where brute machines had brushed by and thumped it accidentally—and showed slighter dents, here and there, where other contractors or subs had lost their tempers, and kicked it. Bill Budnitz was at his desk inside, sitting staring at columns of numbers scrolling slowly up a small computer's sky-blue screen. Budnitz was a leathery man—looked like an ironworker, but wasn't and never had been. The site comptroller, he almost never left the office.

"Yo—you're a Ward & Breedon guy, right? Responsible for the genesis of this pile?" He'd only glanced up from the CRT for a moment.

"Evan Scott—is Fonsecca around?"

"Not around; he's up top. . . ."

The work elevator was a big cage tracked up the building's side, painted bright orange and open to the air. Except for a section of tall vertical bars fencing off its motor and cable wheel, there was only waist-high wire mesh along its edges to prevent a fall. —The starter, an old man in a blue hard hat, had asked to see Evan's site pass, then shrugged when Evan had none to show and said he was with the architects.

"Well, go the hell on up," the old man had said. "I don't know who the fuck's supposed to be goin' up—supposed to have fuckin' passes. . . ."

When Evan pressed the top of the big steel button, the wire cage surged slightly as it began to rise . . .

then climbed steadily up alongside the building's steel
latticework, electric motor whining, sparking occasionally behind its barrier of bars, laboring a little. The elevator trembled in contact with the building, rattling
against the rails it ran on. . . . Evan was glad no workman was sharing the space as it rose, so he could watch
alone as other buildings' roofs presented higher, then
slowly sank . . . sank away below, until only the tallest
structures—and most of those several blocks north or
south—could still match his height, their serried rows
of windows, reflecting the summer sun, flashing in series like fireworks.

Here the river wind blew fresh through the great
steel framework, and gusts shook the cage as it
climbed.

Unsteady, Evan reached out to hold the elevator's
steel handrail, its chipped yellow paint rough against
his hand. It felt like the infantry handhold along the
flank of an M-3 tank . . . same veteran sturdiness.
"Hold on to me," it said to a man's hand, "and you
may be all right. Or maybe not. I've seen it go both
ways. . . ."

At the top of the cage's run, the seventieth floor, the
building's skeleton seemed slowly swayed by a buffeting wind—leaning very slightly to one side, and
stopped there as if by opposing pressure of the harsh
afternoon sunshine—which then, soundless, shoved it
slightly back.

It hadn't occurred to Evan before that Jerry Fonsecca's daughter must have been deafened by the wind
as she fell through it. Perhaps the reason she'd only
shouted above him, and never screamed as she fell—
overwhelmed by the wind's roaring past her ears. . . .

Fonsecca was working in a little plywood knock-
down cabin set up on the west side of the floor, across
two acres of temporary decking . . . odd planks and

plywood sheeting stretched across great gaps where a bank of elevators was planned, or where fire stairs were intended. The wind, whining up out of these spaces as Evan walked past, made one unstable plank thump softly, rocking back and forth where it straddled space.

Paul diNunzio, a large handsome man, his hair iron-gray and carefully styled, was talking with Fonsecca in the closet-sized cabin. Three ironworkers (one a Mohawk, Phil Dowson, whom Evan recognized from a downtown job the year before) were standing by, apparently waiting for some decision.

DiNunzio, dressed in a tan sports jacket, lighter slacks, looked up and saw Evan at the door. "Hey, Scott—Ward & Breedon got a problem?"

"No, Paul. Just wanted to speak with Jerry, when he has a minute."

"OK. We're finishing up. —Jerry, I don't care what Lawrence says. The hell with the city. We want all this laid in just according to the blues, all right? You have my authority to tell those heating people stay out of your guys' way until the steel is up. Then they follow, lay this ducting out exactly. I don't want people jumping ahead—which is how we got in trouble on the forty-seventh. Right?"

Fonsecca—shorter, heavy-shouldered in worn blue work shirt and jeans—only nodded, his dark face expressionless as he stood, staring down at plans lit by a battered gooseneck lamp.

It was a ducting diagram—even from the doorway, Evan recognized a section of Sanchia's dense, neat draftsmanship. All connections specific, all runs straight as possible and tucked away. No octopuses left untidy.

"OK." DiNunzio stepped out of the cabin, turning

his shoulders as he did to avoid getting his jacket dirty. "—How things going, Evan?"

Evan said, "Going fine," to diNunzio's back as the contractor walked away. Then he stepped into the cabin. "No problem with the layout, Jerry?"

Fonsecca said nothing, stood staring down at the plans.

"The runs are all right?"

"Listen," Fonsecca said, so quietly Evan could barely hear him. "Listen . . . you got no business up here. We got a problem with prints, Talbot is the guy takes care of it for you people. So—"

"That's really not what I want to talk about, Jerry."

"So . . . why don't you just turn around and get down off of here, where you don't have any business at this time? OK?"

"I told you, there's something else I think we need to discuss. I can meet you after work—"

"You are not goin' to meet me for shit!" Fonsecca was speaking louder, still only conversationally, still staring down at the diagram. "An' speakin' of mindin' your own business—*Evan*—what the hell . . . what were you doin' hangin' around out there at the funeral? An' I saw you out there. Are you a member of our family or somethin' we don't know about?"

"I'm sorry if I intruded, Jerry—"

"Mr. Ward was invited, an' he came out, because we got a long workin' relationship with Henry Ward. You weren't invited out there. I don't know you except to say hello. Period."

"I saw her fall, Jerry."

Fonsecca folded the plans lengthwise, then across— doing it carefully, then smoothing the paper to lie flat. "I know what you saw."

"The reason I came up is that a detective just came to see me. Very odd person . . . an Indian officer,

Hindu. He had a fairly far-out notion about what happened, and it seemed I should at least let you know—"

"Hey! Are you deaf or somethin'? Are you *deaf*?" Fonsecca turned on Evan, dark face paling in rage so his brown eyes looked black by contrast. "I don't want to hear shit from you! I want you to stay the hell away from my family—stay the hell away from me!"

Evan was so surprised, he knew he must look like a fool. His heart was hammering. "Wait a minute, now . . . just a minute—"

"You," Fonsecca said, his face savage, "you stay the *fuck*," and put up his hands and shoved Evan so suddenly he staggered back out of the cabin onto unsteady decking, "—fuck *away* from me!" Then Fonsecca followed up and shoved him again—looking as if he'd like to hit him, was barely restraining himself—and Evan saw the three ironworkers' startled faces as he tripped going back and fell against one of them.

"Hey, come on you guys. . . ." Phil Dowson.

"You understand me?" Fonsecca shouting, furious. "You stay the fuck away! You don't talk to me! You mind your own fuckin' business or I'm goin' to bust your ass!" He raised his hands to shove again.

"Don't do that," Evan said, feeling odd. He said it very calmly, so that Fonsecca wouldn't push him again. And to make certain, since he felt he might be pushed too far—saw himself pushed back and back and off the building to fall as the girl had fallen—he reached down with his right hand to Dowson's tool belt, lifted a chipping hammer out, and made sure of his balance.

"Jesus, Jesus, come on, come *on*!" Dowson caught Evan's arm, and another man was behind him, bearhugging, also saying, "Come on, come *on*," while Fonsecca stood staring.

"What the hell is this? What the hell is this?"

DiNunzio came running back over rumbling decking. "What the hell . . . ?!" He was calling as he came, exercising control at a distance—then arrived, bulled past Dowson, put a large hand on Fonsecca's shirtfront, and said, "Out of line, Jerry!" Then turned to Evan, said, "*Really* out of line," and reached out to take the hammer. "Are you guys crazy? Are you guys crazy havin' a fight up here? You guys are out of your fuckin' *minds*, havin' a fight up here!"

Evan noticed that excitement had coarsened diNunzio's accent. "Sorry, Paul," he said. "I'm feeling better now."

DiNunzio appeared to think that was a strange thing for Evan to have said, and stared at him for a moment. "Listen, you guys . . . I don't know what your problem is, but this shit does not happen again. This shit does not . . . go . . . up here! You understand this? Jerry, you understand this?"

Fonsecca said nothing, turned and went back inside the small cabin.

"Evan?"

"It was a misunderstanding, Paul."

"No more 'misunderstandings' up here. I mean it." DiNunzio reached out and took Evan's arm, drew him aside. "You ought to know better." He'd lowered his voice. "I don't care what the problem is. Jerry just lost his girl, for Christ's sake. . . ."

"I know, I saw her fall."

"Oh, shit, that's right. —Well, then you ought to know better than come up here, remind him of the whole fucking tragedy. You know . . . come *on*, Evan. You got to use your head, here. You're just a reminder to him, you understand that?" DiNunzio stood patiently, waiting for Evan's reply. The contractor was heavy-featured beneath his handsome hair, his face weather-roughened by years of construction work at cruel heights.

"I understand," Evan said, to satisfy him.

"Good man." DiNunzio patted Evan heavily on the shoulder, and called to the three ironworkers still standing by, interested, "*Hey,* you guys got nothin' to do up here? You got no work up here?"

chapter 6

....

The Dond drank black coffee, very sweet, every morning—and with this, often ate two or three cinnamon rolls.

That was his food till evening—then, always at either George's Acropolis or the Golden Horn, he ate lamb and rice and lentils. At the Acropolis, the Dond ate at the counter—habitual spaces being left by regular customers at either side of him. At the Golden Horn, he ate in the kitchen. Its proprietor, Mr. Arslan Sarnischuk—after weeks of urging by his wife—had asked him to eat there, at the small counter beyond the stoves, and the Dond had agreed, seemed to consider it a reasonable request.

At either restaurant, the Dond ate only lamb, rice, and lentils. He'd tried the bread at each, the first few times—then didn't eat it anymore. And when the bread continued to be offered, began to drop it on the floor, thinking they were being rude, joking, making fun of him by serving him bread his mother and sisters would never have recognized.

Both restaurants stopped serving him bread.

Mr. Sarnischuk's wife had wanted to call the police the first evening the Dond had come in, sat at a corner table amid surprised families, and waited to be served.

But Arslan Sarnischuk, an immigrant as a child, still retained some instincts of the East—instincts of this city as well—and had his waiters serve the Dond ... went to the table himself, caught a word for lamb not dissimilar to the Turkish, and saw that that was brought.

At the Acropolis, or in the kitchen of the Golden Horn, the Dond, eating always only lamb, rice, and lentils, scooped this food from a basin into the palm of his right hand ... rolling that into a wet brown ball, popped it so neatly into his mouth he hardly stained his beard. It was a large amount of food, and he ate it slowly ... chewed slowly, contemplating. ...

At either restaurant, when he had finished, he stood, took a twenty-dollar bill out of his coat pocket— always that amount—and put it down to pay. The staff always offered him change, but he never accepted it— and once, when an elderly waiter, a friendly man, tried to stuff the change into this odd customer's coat pocket, the Dond, upon being touched, slowly turned with a look of such ferocity that the old man had snatched his hand back—dollars fluttering to the floor—and used it to cross himself.

After that, the Dond was not troubled, even with kindness.

"He hit you?" Sanchia vibrating, furious in Bien Sûr.

"He just pushed me. He was ... very upset."

"Fuck him! I don' care that he lost his girl—that don' give him the right to hit nobody!"

"He just pushed me."

"I don' care. I don' care. That son of a bitch. ..." She turned away (a neat coarse little Spanish pony caparisoned in tomato-red jacket and dark-green slacks) and began rolling navel oranges around their small, mounded display, looking for perfect fruit. "They always got these, an' they don' taste like anything. Japanese ones are good; taste like tangerines."

"He pushed me, and I suppose I lost my temper. Picked up Phil Dowson's hammer. . . ." Evan stood in the aisle holding a basket of vegetables, waiting to see what Sanchia thought of that—if she thought that was strange, an inappropriate thing to have done.

"Should have hit that asshole in the head," Sanchia said. "Shouldn't have put his hands on you. . . ." Examining a particular navel orange. "These things always look so good, then you're disappointed with 'em."

"Well, something's certainly going on. Going on with Jerry Fonsecca, for one thing. There was no reason for him to behave like that. He seemed . . . my impression was he was simply terrified."

Sanchia put down the orange so decisively that two others were dislodged and fell to the floor . . . rolled away as if attempting an escape out to Prince Street. Sanchia went after them past two couples looking at goat cheeses, caught them near the entrance, and brought them back. "Listen, you think some people killed his kid, an' now they got him scared, too. Scared they're goin' to kill him he don' go along with whatever. . . . That's nothing new."

"That level of threat is something new, I think. Not just your usual construction kickback situation."

"Come on, Evan—you know how these buildings get built. Not by no sweeties, tell you that, an' I don' know that much about it."

"I don't think he was afraid for himself."

"I don' know him. I don' care about him. He don' have any right to be putting his hands on you."

Sanchia, drifting, stopped a moment at a pyramid of quinces, picked one up, sniffed at it, then put it down again.

"From what that detective said—"

"Cop that came an' talked to you? —Evan, you can't believe everything a cop says. An' he was a foreigner, too. Fuck him. Cops just care about getting promoted on the force. They don' give a shit about anybody more than getting that promotion. An' believe me, Evan, I grew up with people knew a lot about cops."

Sanchia always said "Evan" in a slightly stilted way, as if referring to an exotic acquisition. "My shy Anglo," she'd called him once, after he'd taken her to McSorley's one afternoon, where she'd had cheddar cheese and mustard, crackers, and two pints of ale. "I'm goin' to be peein' for a week. . . ."

More than a month before that, at the Central Park Zoo, she'd called him "a gentleman," after he'd bought a small boy a new helium-filled blue balloon to replace one floated up and away into sunshine. She'd called Evan a gentleman, then glanced up at him again as they walked alongside the sea lions' pool, apparently to assure herself that diagnosis had been correct, that such a *rara avis* strolled along beside her (much older, much taller) in a gray cord summer suit.

"Here we go—here we go!" The Japanese oranges discovered across the narrow produce counter. Sanchia led him through other shoppers, worried the small heap of wrinkled golden citrus might be bought completely up before she got there. ". . . OK. This is them. These are the good ones."

". . . I think Fonsecca was afraid for his boys. He has two little boys."

"I don' believe it." Picking swiftly through the fruit. "Those kind of guys don' go around killing little kids."

"Supposedly, with these people that isn't so."

"I got a dozen—you want some?"

"No."

"Where's the bags?"

Evan reached up to tear a plastic bag off the roll, held it open while she dropped the oranges down into it.

"Hey—you want to find out if something's goin' on, or what? You really want to know?"

"I think I can do without knowing. . . ." Closing the bag with a twist-tie.

"You know, sometimes I don' understand you." Sanchia reluctant to leave the Japanese oranges. "You think they're goin' to get more of these in? . . . Listen, Evan, you saw that girl falling, an' you're telling me you don' care how that happened?"

"I care. . . ."

"But not much, right? —They'll get more of these Japanese ones in. They're too good. . . ." She turned away and trotted along the fruit display to the checkout line, Evan in her wake.

"It's a little late to save Josephine, whatever happened."

"You ever meet that girl?"

"No." There was only one couple ahead of them, West Africans of some sort . . . dashikis, *kente* cloth. The woman, very young, had been scarred with four small chevrons down each cheek.

"Reason I ask did you meet her, you talk like you knew her . . . you know, like you met her, anyway."

"I never met her." Evan looked at his watch—forty minutes now to catch the train. Wouldn't be time to walk her home.

"I bug you too much, right?" Looking up at him from a background of patterned ocher and black, the wide back of the African's robe behind her. "You're goin' to be looking to get out—get away from this little bitch. 'I get enough of this shit at home'—right?"

"Wrong," Evan said, but couldn't help smiling.

"See—I knew it." The dashiki moved away from behind her. "I sound just like I'm your wife an' I'm bugging you."

"Not at all." At the cash register, Evan took out his wallet, paid for two avocados, two yams, an eggplant, four zucchinis, and the oranges—all then packed in a small shopping bag decorated with scenes of Paris in the rain. $27.39.

On the street, Sanchia paused amid hurrying people going home, opened her large purse, and looked into it as if something surprising might be there. "How much was all that?"

"Not much."

"Come on—we got an agreement. How much?"

"Twenty-five." Their agreement was that Sanchia pay two thirds for all groceries bought together. "Hey, I'm goin' to eat most of it. . . ."

"Jesus—is that ridiculous or what? But I love that store." She found her wallet after a search, took out a ten and four singles. Then another two singles . . . a quarter, a dime, and three nickels. "Is that OK?"

"Perfect," he said—and satisfied, Sanchia closed her purse and took his free arm as they walked. "Listen, I'm taking a sick day. Taking Friday off, the whole weekend—three days. Goin' out to the island tomorrow morning. . . . I tell you that?"

"Yes, with your girlfriends."

"Lucera and Nita. We're just goin' out for the three-day weekend; goin' to Nattituck. Lucera just took off; she doesn' ask her boss nothing. She's crazy; she wants to go—she goes. . . . An' I'll be back Sunday, in the evening, OK?"

Sanchia had begun, a few months before, to check with Evan before she did this or that . . . her schedule, her plans. As if in that way she wove strands to hold him closer to her.

He heard her skip a step to stay in step beside him,

walking fast to keep up with longer strides. "So, you
don' want to know what's goin' on that girl got killed?"

"There's no way to know if anything's going on."

"Oh, yes there is. Evan, we can find out. Ward &
Breedon gets a copy of every spec sheet, work order,
every piece of paper—whatever; you name it, we get a
copy right up to completion. . . . We don' use 'em. We
don' need 'em, usually, but Carol Passman gets a copy
of everything on that building—everything on everything we design. Period. An' I mean everything. Keep
all that paperwork to completion, an' right after sign-off
we ship it over to Newark, to the warehouse."

"I know we keep a lot of the paperwork—" He
guided her, arm in arm, to a segue left, out of the path
of a bicycle messenger riding down the sidewalk.

"Not 'a lot.' *Everything.* Keep it in the basement—
then ship it over to Jersey, put it all in the warehouse.
So, if you want to know what's goin' on at 366—an' I
mean everything that's goin' on at 366—then we got
paper on it."

"Yes, I suppose we do. . . . Sanchia, I won't have
time to walk you home."

"That's all right. Evan, you want to find out about
this shit, or not?"

"I think I can do without finding out about it. And
it's really the sort of thing the police prefer to handle."

"*Cops.* . . . They won't do shit—an' pardon my language. An' the cops don' have the paper we got on this
building."

Evan saw he was walking too fast for her, and slowed
down.

"So, you want to find out, you stay in town tonight
an' we can check the invoices, memos, every little piece
of paper. We'll see if these Rao guys are screwing with
the specs, purchase orders, see if they're messing with
anything."

Evan stopped on the corner of Spring, looking down-town for an oncoming cab. ". . . Let's think about it."

"You just don' want to get in trouble."

"I certainly don't, not if I can help it." He looked down and saw her surprised, disappointed in him. "It's just there's probably nothing to it, sweetheart." The "sweetheart" something new—at least out of bed—and offered for peace.

Offer rejected. "We could find out for *sure!*" Sanchia so eager, Evan saw her as she must have been when a child. "Don' you want to know?"

"No, not very much." Regretting he'd mentioned the fat policeman, the notion of gangsters, extortion or whatever to her—hadn't left the probable accident only an accident.

"Oh, come on. Come on!" Gripping his free hand, tugging like a small muscular dog on a short leash, tow-ing him down a sunset street now striped with shadows. "We can have an *adventure*! We don' have to tell no-body. . . ."

"No."

"OK. You don' have to! —You don' have to do it; I'll do it by myself."

"Are you goin' to lock up when you go, Mr. Scott? 'Cause if you don't, I could get in trouble."

"We'll lock up, Larry."

"You sure?" Larry, elderly and fat, was a constant evening pilgrim, supported by the staff of a mop or broom along the building's three narrow floors. Occa-sionally he carried a plumbing tool, or small box of light bulbs.

"We'll lock up."

" 'Cause if you don't, it's my butt goin' to be in trouble."

"We're goin' to lock up," Sanchia said. "You go on, Larry—we're goin' to take care of everything."

"Research," Evan said.

"OK. . . ."

Ward & Breedon's cellar file room was large as the office and drafting floors above—had been storage for tobacco bales shipped into New York Harbor from the Carolinas, from Georgia, from Brazil in the early eighteen hundreds.

The basement air still carried the faintest powdery bite of those ancient bales, captured in wide oak shelving worn black with age.

. . . They were working at a long plywood-topped table under yellow-white fluorescent light. The steady faint buzz of these long lamps seemed to underline the silence of the rest of the building, the night only shaken now and then when a heavy truck rumbled past on the street outside.

There seemed to Evan to be a comfortable domestic air about the two of them, sitting across from each other in folding metal chairs. The long table between them was loaded with stacks of paper in infinite varieties of color and size—forms, folders, files—all labeled *366 Mad,* and all, in the past two hours, searched for and pulled from file-cabinet drawers.

Bills, invoices, invoice orders, work orders, reports, plans, alterations, changes, requests for changes. Plans— architectural; plans—engineering; plans—electrical; plans—structural; structural steel. Contracts: design contracts, architectural contracts, construction contracts, union contracts. Bids: bids, counterbids, counterbids and agreements. Orders and shipping orders, bills of lading, progress reports. Delivery agreements: deliveries received and signed for; deliveries, late or unforthcoming (complaints and resolutions). Specs: specs on steel; specs on steel wire and cable; specs on electrical wiring (specs on electrical wiring of all capacities), junction boxes, transformers, boards, breaker boxes, motors (half-horse, two-horse, four-horse, six-horse, and all major motors), fans and fuses, routing and rewiring.

Architect's inspections and sign-offs (Henry Ward's scribble). Contractor's inspections and sign-offs. OSHA Plan and Confirmation (queries, reconfirmations, queries, reconfirmations, queries, reconfirmations). City inspectors' inspection notes, queries, reports, sign-offs. State inspectors' inspection notes, queries, reports, sign-offs. New York City Fire Department inspections and sign-offs.

Violations, reinspections. Violations, reinspections. Reinspections to date. Violations corrected. Violations uncorrected to date. Reinspections. Reinspections pending. . . .

Evan had called Catherine from his office phone—heard faintly Mrs. Hooper and Beth talking in the background—and told her he'd be staying in town tonight.

"I'll be in the office till late, and I'll sleep on the couch, here. It's the Hartford bank thing . . . the damned underground garage."

"All right."

"Be out tomorrow afternoon. . . ."

"All right, Evan."

"Let me say hello to Beth."

"She's upstairs, having her bath."

So smooth and strange a little lie that Evan, still hearing Beth's voice at a distance from the phone—certainly with Mrs. Hooper in the kitchen—was made too uneasy to question it, afraid to hear Catherine's reason. . . .

He was going through inspection sign-offs now, stacks of them, most yellow or pale blue, with an occasional full-sheet white, the city's seal stamped on it.

"Evan, you noticing anything strange?"

"Yes." And wished he hadn't. Wished he'd somehow avoided everything . . . been delayed in the cab, hadn't seen the girl fall. Had heard about it in the office the next day.

Now night's stillness seemed less restful, less warm with silence, yellow-white light, and only Sanchia's presence. This harsh light, vibrating beyond the competence of human vision and unflattering to most women, seemed to make Sanchia prettier . . . had softened the fierce colors of her clothes, brought out light honey browns, lighter toast browns in the shades of her skin.

"You still seein' something strange?"

". . . The fruit of the tree of knowledge."

"What?"

"Yes, I am. Everything Rao Electric has done on 366 so far, is perfect."

"Evan, you ever know any contractor do perfect work?"

"No."

"I got no complaint memos on them, no late memos, no late delivery, no short deliveries, no equipment problems, no supply problems, no replacements. . . ."

"No, I haven't seen anything like it—not on Japanese jobs, not on Swiss or German jobs. Truth is, it's simply not possible to do this sort of large-scale contracting without some problems coming up."

Sanchia said nothing more for a while. Sat across the table and slowly leafed through slips and receipts, bills and time sheets. Evan considered that they might have enjoyed making love down here . . . awkward in pleasure, lying on the harsh commercial carpeting. Perhaps leaving the humming fluorescents on—perhaps not. . . . He and Sanchia might have made love, but not now, not with Rao Electric having done so improbably well in its contracting.

Sanchia sighed, a breath of satisfaction Evan usually heard after she'd eaten—when, as he undressed her afterward, her narrow little belly would be swollen as a just-fed puppy's. "Evan—You know Marcello Hauling?"

"Yes. They worked the Seaport project for us."

"They're bad guys, aren't they?"

"Supposedly. I don't know that they're any worse than some other New Jersey haulers."

"I heard they were bad guys. You know. . . ."

"Maybe." The fluorescent light was becoming tiring; it left no shadows, only muddier illumination where a shadow might have been.

"Well—there's a lading bill here; they hauled off eleven tons extra for Rao Electric at 366: cut wire, cable debris, spools, pallets, broken box frames an' fasteners, crates an' insulation an' packing."

"And?" Evan shaded his eyes with his right hand, wished he had a gambler's visor, green plastic. Could see why people wore those things, sitting at a table under harsh light for several hours.

"An' . . . *an',* they hauled after regular hours, an' they billed overtime an' Rao didn' pay it."

"So?"

"There isn' any record in this file that Marcello Hauling complained they didn' get paid for that extra hauling."

"Probably requested payment verbally."

"No way. 'Cause no payment was ever made—none showing here, and none on the ledger copy. Marcello just ate that hauling charge, instead of pushing it. An' what I hear, Marcello doesn' eat no charges."

"Probably an explanation for it." Evan slid a new

piece of paper out of his stack, yellow billing receipt—
and nothing to do with electrical work, thank God. . . .

"Hey, Evan—explanation is, these Rao people are
scarier than those New Jersey people. That's the explanation. . . . You finding any mistake at all these people
made? Anything?"

"No. Nothing but very creative record-keeping
where they're concerned."

"Marcello don' do creative record-keeping—not like
this. The structural steel company doesn' do it. Paint
contractor doesn' do it. Welders don' do it. Ironworkers an' riggers' union doesn' do it. City doesn' do
it. . . . I got more than a hundred cross-complaints,
screwed-up inspections, shortages, late deliveries,
faults, redos, unscheduled overtimes, memos about this
an' that an' everything goin' wrong . . . but not one
single little piece of paper says Rao Electric's contracting is not absolutely perfect. —Never late, never
wrong, never miswired, no do-overs. Never fucked up
in any way on 366. —You believe that?"

"No, I don't believe it."

"Means they're crooks, is what this bullshit means."

"It means they *may* be crooks—and even so, it's not
really our business. Let the city deal with the Raos."

"You're goin' to see—we're goin' through this
whole tableful of shit, an' we will not find one little
thing out of line about those people. Not one complaint. Nothing."

"Could be. . . ."

Evan, back aching from hours in the folding chair,
felt, instead of any triumph, a slow apprehension grow
in him—and impatience with Sanchia, so mindlessly
pleased, so unconscious of consequences. The difference in their ages (usually, he'd hoped, not too apparent) now seemed to him to expand with the certainty
that much of this mass of Rao Electric's paperwork

was fake, a sort of Potemkin village, too perfect to be believed. And if Sanchia hadn't insisted, he wouldn't have had to know it. . . .

And if it was true that the Raos were hoodlums of some sort, criminals—what sort must they be to intimidate Marcello Hauling? Evan had met Michael Marcello—or seen the old man, anyway, on site at the Seaport. Marcello and his two sons had looked like wild boars, shaved, dressed, and walking upright.

. . . More than an hour later, while Evan was reading through a transfer memo once more (he'd already read it once, forgotten the contents immediately), Sanchia said, "I got one!"

"One what?" He shoved the folding chair back, stood up and stretched, yawning. No use pretending to be tireless.

"I got a complaint. Six . . . five weeks ago, ironworkers' union complained to the electricians' union about the electrical contractor. Look. . . ." She passed a pale purple tear copy across the table. "Read that."

It was a late-generation copy, barely legible . . . an informational circulated to all contractors on 366. "Under State Labor Relations Act . . ." Boilerplate for two paragraphs, then "Rao Electric Co. for improper scheduling of overtime. . . ."

"See what happened?"

"I see what happened. They pushed their people to work beyond overtime—"

"No. Not just that—an' by the way, the *electricians'* union didn' complain. It's the ironworkers complained about it, because they had to follow up that work past *their* scheduled overtime. Threatening not to complete improper overtime work, is what they're doin' there. —An' that is the first fuckup paperwork we found for Rao Electric."

"And it doesn't seem like much."

"But it was a complaint—a threat, from the iron-workers' union. An' Jerry Fonsecca is the union rep. An' last week his girl fell off 366." Sanchia's small face bright with discovery. "What do you think of that, Evan? What do you think? You want to bet this is the only record of any complaint against those people? You want to bet there will never be complaint number two?"

"Honey, I'll tell you what I think." Evan, too tired to stand, sat down again. "I think a single filed union grievance is not sufficient motive for murder. That's what I think."

"No? We didn' find any complaint before that one—an' we damn sure ain' goin' to find one after that. Those Rao people just made real certain nobody calls them on anything."

"And why? Sanchia, why would they do that? Just to avoid the usual problems typical of any large-scale construction? It doesn't make any sense."

" 'Cause, Evan, they don' *like* problems. An' maybe they got big stuff in mind on 366. Maybe already done big stuff, an' they're making sure nobody gives them a hard time on anything whatsoever."

"And what would 'big stuff' be . . . ?"

"Evan, I don' know. Something these guys would kill people for. —Money. We got to be talking about money. They got to be doin' something worth a lot of money."

"And we have no idea what. . . ."

"Evan, come *on*. You're sittin' there like you wish we never found out! I know you don' like trouble. I know you don' like that, but we wanted to find out, and now we found out."

"We found something suspicious. Not proof." The chair was just too damned uncomfortable. Evan pushed

it back, stood up, folded the thing, and stood it against
the wall.

"Hey—I didn' go to Yale, all right? But I know
when something stinks. An' this stuff stinks. These
guys are not hiding something—these guys are hiding
everything."

"I'll talk to Clive about it."

"That won' do any good."

"I think it might."

"Evan, that won' do no good at all. . . ."

A weary breakfast in a weary café—the Soho Special. Evan sat in a narrow little blue booth for two,
watching Sanchia eat three pancakes (extra syrup) with
one egg (over hard) and a double order of slender
tasteless sausages.

Evan had ordered scrambled eggs and sausage—
found the sausages inedible. The Soho Special prided
itself on traditional hamburgers, fat and rosy, their
juices running onto Thomas's English muffins, toasted.
It had once received a pleased review in *New York*
magazine for its hamburgers—but breakfast, served to
tired night-workers and delivery people from six in the
morning till eleven, had received less attention.

"You don' want the sausages?"

"No. You have them."

"You don' like 'em?"

"Not this morning," Evan said, and watched Sanchia
lick her fork clean of syrup, then lean over toward him
and neatly spear both sausages in turn, transfer them
to her plate. Reminded him of Catherine taking his
breakfast sausage patty a week or so before. Another
sausage transfer. . . .

This was the first time Sanchia and he'd had breakfast together. Lovers . . . friends, for more than a year,
and this was their first breakfast. Evan had the odd no-

tion, watching Sanchia eat, that he'd been betraying her with Catherine rather than the other way round.

"So today, you go an' see Clive, see if he's goin' to do something or what. . . . I wish I wasn' goin' out of town this morning."

Evan thought of the pleasures of presenting the best of various things to this girl. The south of France *en fleur* . . . or simply driving up to New Hampshire with her, to the Stonefence Inn, perhaps, so she could eat a proper breakfast—everything freshly, perfectly prepared. Their sausage, whole-pig and homemade, sagely rich in her mouth. . . .

It occurred to him it might do her no favor—to introduce her to fine food, lovely landscapes . . . all the satisfactions of comfortable money. No joy then for Sanchia Fuentes when he dropped her off in the East Village, afterward. After using the small dark body for this and that on perfectly mended old Irish linen over charming antique bedsteads. In Colonial or Federal New England bedrooms. . . . Sanchia, so fond, so eager to please him. As happy, Evan had come to realize, with hugging as with sex. Perhaps happier.

"Some guys like to spank girls," she'd once said to him.

"So I understand."

"I don' want nobody hitting me," she'd said. They were lying in her narrow bed at lunchtime, watching a few minutes of a soap opera before getting up, getting dressed and back to the office.

"—I don' want nobody hitting me, but if you like to . . . you know. If you like to spank me or something, you know, with your hand. I heard some guys like doing that."

"I don't."

"Well. . . ." She'd turned on the pillow to look into his eyes as if to check that answer, searching for some concealment. "I mean—not just that. I mean if you want to do anything, that's all right. You can do what you want."

It seemed to Evan that love was bound to be mentioned next—that she loved him, and what he wanted she would give. Would allow ... even welcome, for his pleasure, his relief, his peace afterward. Evan had been certain that love was going to be mentioned next, and he'd smiled and told her not to be silly—then got up to get dressed.

Their next time together, wary, Evan had stuck to fucking—kept at her and at her, and allowed no time afterward for talking, for resting together. That time, and the next two or three times, he'd treated her with a sort of distant heat, as if she were—and after all, she was—only a fairly ordinary young woman, Puerto Rican, small, dark, barely educated. Not wonderfully complex, except as any woman was.

He'd had her kneel (both still dressed) on the floor beside her bed, and unzip, extract, and service him. She had done that very gently, slowly, licking him, sucking, but with her eyes closed all the while, as if to be doing that—and only that, and still dressed—made it a sin. The gentleness had angered Evan in some obscure way, so he had thrust into her mouth roughly, and excited by his own unfairness, his perfect selfishness, had come and seen her swallow.

The next time with her—or the time after that—he'd turned her onto her stomach and put his finger up her narrow rear ... played with her there while she lay trembling, her face in her pillow, so he almost became used to just those harsh liberties she'd frightened him by offering.... When he realized, when he recalled doing those sorts of things with a bar girl—two different girls—in Vietnam, he stopped, and resumed treating Sanchia as he was most comfortable doing, with a remote tenderness. Happy to accept her richer response in return, pleased by hugs and foot rubs as much as making love. Pleased by her ever interest, her caring for him, so much more direct, so much warmer than Catherine's oblique regard.

Catherine, of course, pleasing him in other ways. By strenuous fucking . . . by her cool concealments, otherwise. An odd reversal, Evan supposed, to rely on his mistress for affection—his wife for sex. And he of course a common liar, a user of them both, with no honor due.

". . . What do you think?"

"About what?"

"The electric guys! What do you think?"

"I think they're crooks, sweetheart." Second "sweetheart" this time together. Sweethearts would begin to add up, if he wasn't careful.

"Well, I'm sayin' do we go to the cops, or what?" She finished her coffee, the cup tilted up so that only brown eyes peered over, waiting for an answer. . . . An undistinguished young woman, physically. Eyes only plain brown—almost muddy brown. And still waiting for an answer.

"No, I certainly don't think we go to the police. We have nothing to be bothering the police with."

"Hell, yes—" Coffee cup back to saucer.

"No, we *don't*." This was plainly unsatisfactory; her last forkful of sausage was put down with a click and clatter. "I can see Clive. It's the partners' business."

"They aren't goin' to do shit." The fork was picked up again—bite of sausage eaten, chewed hard. "Man, you are really white, you know? I mean, Evan, you are Anglo to the max."

"More Celt, actually."

"I mean . . . shit."

"I'll see Clive on Monday."

"Come on, go see him today."

"All right. If he's in, I'll go up and see him this afternoon."

"You promise? —An' tell me what he said when I get back." Reassurance Catherine had never required; Evan couldn't recall her ever asking if he promised anything.

"No, I don't promise. I said I'd do it, and I will."

"Don' get mad."

"I'm not; I'm just tired."

"I didn' mean to insult you. . . ."

"You didn't insult me, sweetheart." Third "sweetheart." . . .

Evan, dreamily weary after a morning finishing penciled elevations for a townhouse remodel on East 72nd Street—elevations Talbot was supposed to have completed—pushed through Ward & Breedon's double doors and out into noon's heavy heat and hard sunshine . . . grinding, thumping traffic shuttling past on Spring Street.

The nearest café was the Gallery, trendy and painted a dead white, glaring under industrial fixtures. Lunch salads . . . odd greens.

Evan walked left to the corner and stood waiting for a break in the traffic. The sunlight sparkled up along the pavement, painfully bright, and he stood with his eyes half closed, recalling too-perfect paperwork . . . feeling imperfect himself, as if he'd already made a mistake. . . .

Someone—a woman, he thought—called his name. *"Mr. Scott."* Evan looked around behind him along the crowded sidewalk . . . saw only people he didn't know.

"Mr. Scott!"

It was a young man's voice, after all—and coming from across the street. Evan looked over and saw a man in a white suit waving to him. Black man ... no, not black. Vijay Bhose—Sonny Varma?—stood at the curb in his too-white suit, waving. He was smiling.

The young man stepped off the curb, still smiling at Evan across the street as if they were the best of friends, as if they had an appointment for lunch. This hoodlum apparently about to present the sort of social situation that could only be dealt with rudely.

Young Bhose—Varma—stepped into the street, glanced both ways, and started over—and an engine rumbled suddenly to Evan's right and when he looked that way he saw a delivery van with red gladiolas painted on its side. He read PARKHURST FLORAL DELIVERY as it surged roaring past and suddenly swung over into the oncoming lane and hit the young man as he stopped and tried to turn back.

The hit was musical—it rang with harsh clanging through the traffic racket—and as if lofted by the sound alone, the Indian (his white suit glowing in sunshine) sailed very gracefully up and through the air for several yards, his arms outspread as if, impatient, he'd decided to fly.

He hit the pavement in seeming silence amid a squealing animal confusion of brakes, trumpeting horns, and a shower of bright headlight glass, fine as diamonds sprinkled along the blacktop.

Evan saw him, a paintbrush streak of broad bright red down his trouser leg, rise almost quickly to his hands and knees ... stand and begin a broken hopping toward the curb. Then the van—that had slowed almost to a stop, idling as if in shock at what it had done—suddenly snarled, lurched forward and rolling gathered speed and ran him over so that his legs—one white-trousered, one wet red—spun and twirled like tassels. Then the van blared and thundered and swung away into uptown traffic, blundered in and out of lanes ...

and with the changing of a light a block away, drove
off through tangled confusion.

Evan—seeming to be traveling in some sort of soft
slow air—ran across the street and reached the boy and
saw at once he was dying. Had to be dying, since his
pelvis and stomach had been crushed so blood was si-
phoning up, spouting out of his mouth in a little pumping fountain.

He would drown before he died of anything else.

Evan had seen something just like this, when Private
Neil—Teddy Neil—had been hit by a rare good-shot
sniper in Charlie Woods. So familiar was this dying
boy's gargling and spouting blood that Evan yelled,
"*Corpsman . . . !*" turned to look, and for only an instant saw Lance Corporal Frejus come galloping across
the street to him with his morphine and pressure packs.
Frejus, bent as if he ran against strong wind, looked
very frightened and tired. And then he was gone and
there was nothing in the street but sunshine.

Evan sat on hot pavement beside this dark young
man—no longer so dark, now bright with blood, his
white suit ruined—and cradled the spoiled head in his
arms, surprised just as he used to be by such a volume
of blood pouring out . . . as if it had waited all these
young men's lives for the chance to escape them.

"Oh, *Ram* . . ." someone said beside him. "*Ram* . . ."
and then something more, a phrase in some lilting language. Evan saw it was the Indian from the newsstand,
the angular old man kneeling beside him in faded
slacks and a worn white dress shirt, kneeling and holding the boy's hand.

Horns were blowing around them—a symphony of
horns, as if to herald the dying man's departure.

The young man—Vijay . . . Sonny—stared up at
Evan with one unbloodied eye, rich brown, that glared
as if to tell him everything with a look alone. Every se-

cret. Then the boy was overtaken by a convulsion so severe his body twisted and knotted upon itself, and that seemed to cause such agony his mouth stretched wide as Private Neil's had stretched, as if shrieking in a soundless world.

He smelled of shit. And something like a loop of blue-white hose showed at his belt.

People were watching from the curb—Evan saw each man and woman more clearly than he'd seen anyone in years, excepting only Beth. He felt he knew them all.

"Sir . . . *sir!*" The elderly Indian was up on his feet, tugging at Evan's jacket sleeve, pulling at him. "Come, *come,* come away from here now, sir!"

Evan slowly rose, feeling stiff as if he'd sat there on the hot pavement for many days, so that his knees hurt him as he straightened them, standing. . . . Vijay— whatever his name had been—lay dead and distorted in the street, his blood now sliding from him more slowly, lazily, little of it left.

"*Sahib* . . . sir, do come on now." Pulling at him. Evan got tired of being handled, and reached up to take the old man's hand away, then walked beside him back across the street, feeling blood running down his wrist, dripping off his fingers onto the pavement.

"A bloody murder," the old man said, "and who should know, if not I? A damned bloody murder. . . ."

The old man ushered Evan into the closet closeness of his newsstand, shut the narrow door behind them, then reached up and out to slip the catch on the heavy front display panel, swung it down and shut.

"Now they will be stealing from me what I've left outside," the old man said in the dark, then switched on a dull yellow light.

Evan looked down at his soaked jacket, deep red down the front and dripping here and there.

"Sir, take that off—and put this on." The old man reached under a shelf, took out and unfolded a large worn gray cardigan sweater. "For the winter," he said. "There is a small hole by the left elbow. . . ."

Evan, contorting in close confines, wrestled the jacket off—felt the material slippery with blood—and dropped it on the narrow strip of sidewalk the newsstand rested on. . . . He saw his slacks were splotched with blood.

"I have no trousers for you," the old man said. "The sweater is what I have—and I would expect one to clean it before returning."

"I'll have it cleaned." Evan felt slightly nauseated, anxious to get out into more air and light, where the dying boy might not take up so much room. "Thank you. . . ."

"I am Ram Dass Lal," the old man said, standing so close in the close space that Evan could smell some sharp spice on his breath.

"Evan Scott. . . . Can I get out through here?" He fumbled with the catch to the narrow steel door, very anxious to get out into the light. "I'll bring your . . . sweater back, tomorrow."

"Cleaned?"

"Cleaned."

"Dry-cleaned, please, since it is fine woolen."

"Dry-cleaned," Evan said, wondering if he were dreaming—opened the little door, and stepped out into bright sunshine he welcomed, and terrific noise.

Here was no quiet death as Josephine Fonsecca had seemed to die, viewed from sixty stories up. This patch of pavement was surrounded now by bedlam. The traffic had come to a clotted halt in battering horns and curses, and the lunch-hour crowd, clustering to watch, peeped over each other's shoulders. The men, Evan noticed, had forced their way to the front—young men, usually—then older men just behind them. Then women (also young) had come to steal small glances, confer with their friends ... then look again at what could be seen between the legs of two policemen, and past a third man kneeling beside what lay crushed in the street.

"You knew that young man." The old Hindu was following Evan along the sidewalk. "I saw you being his friend very much when he died."

"Excuse me," Evan said, imagined this elderly ghost following him forever, and walked faster, looking for a phone booth. "I'll return your sweater tomorrow, all right?"

"And do you understand what has happened to that young man?"

"I do, yes. Look—I'm trying to get to a phone to call the police; I will return the goddamn sweater!"

"Don't call the police on to me, sir. I am having nothing to do with police! I tried that long ago."

"Oh, for God's sake." Evan walked faster, threading through people who seemed to be doing a slow group dance of observation, stepping up ... stepping to one side, then to the other to see better.... "Listen, thank you for your help, but you'd better get back to your stand, because you're right; someone will steal your papers."

"Oh, my goodness," the old man said, reminded, and turned back through the crowd. Then called back, *"Dry-cleaned...."*

There were two women in line at the left-side phone of a two-phone stand. The other apparently vandalized and broken.

Evan stood waiting while the first woman put in her quarter, then told a friend of the accident. He stood hearing the uproar just behind him, then keening sirens coming from uptown.... No passerby seemed to notice his stained trousers. He might have murdered young Vijay—or Sonny, or whoever the hell he was—with a knife, then strolled away spotted and blotched with blood, and no one would be noticing. He found it not unpleasant to be standing in hot sunlight, separated—by precious minutes, by precious yards—from what had happened.

When the second woman was finished (she had spoken with her mother), Evan put his quarter in, and dialed 911.

"I need to speak to a Sergeant Prasad—he's a detective at headquarters, downtown. P-r-a-s-a-d."

"I have to have your name and address, sir."

"I only need to talk to the sergeant."

"I have to have your name and address, sir."

"Evan Scott—I'm calling from the corner of Spring and Wooster."

"I have to have your home address, sir."

"Christ—!"

"I have to have your home address, sir."

"Three Cove Lane. Fairport, Connecticut."

"I'll transfer you, sir."

". . . Police Plaza." This voice a young black woman's, still richly Southern after probable generations in the city.

"I want to speak with a detective, a Sergeant Prasad."

"And your name, sir?"

"Evan Scott."

"And would you spell that officer's name, sir."

"I don't know his first name. Last name is Prasad. P-r-a-s-a-d."

". . . I show no detective with that name."

"Well—he's on the Indian Squad. Would you try again?"

". . . I show no officer of that name active with the New York Police Department, sir."

"Well . . . then the office the Indian Squad works out of."

"Is that I-n-d-i-a-n?"

"Yes—Oriental, not Native American."

". . . I show no such unit, sir."

"Oh, for God's sake. Get me . . . get me Captain Gernsbach."

"G-e-r-n-s-b-a-c-h?"

"I presume so."

". . . I show no officer of that name active with the New York Police Department, sir."

"A captain?"

"No sir; I have no one with that name. See no alternate spellings. —I have no one with either of the names you've given me, sir. . . . Sir?"

"All right. . . . All right. Thank you." He hung up the phone, the fat man smiling at him as clearly as if he stood there, and had watched and listened as Evan made his phone call, much too late. The fat man smiling as he had before, sitting talking in the office, listening as Evan—busy, superior—had answered his questions.

"And will you call downtown, call Captain Gernsbach and check on this plump police officer's bona fides? No, you will not trouble. . . ."

chapter 7

······································

Clive, upset, had come down from his drafting stool to pace and repace the space beside his desk.

"Absolutely not. Oh, *absolutely* not."

In baggy khaki trousers and khaki T-shirt just bought at Military Sales on Lafayette Street (his bloody shirt and slacks left as trash with a clerk beyond surprise), Evan sat in one of the cream-leather armchairs, watching the little man shuttle back and forth. ". . . Clive, it seems to me the police are going to have to know about this. I don't see how it can be avoided."

" 'Know about this.' Evan, there is nothing concrete to know!"

"Clive—"

"No. You listen to me. We . . . this firm has certainly dealt with what might be called questionable entities, particularly in the last few years. There is simply no way to get major buildings designed and built in this city without some contact with people you wouldn't care to have come for dinner."

"I understand that."

"I don't think you do." Clive stood on his toes to slide back up onto his drafting stool and settle there. "You and Talbot and Swann down there on the second floor only have to worry about design; you don't have to do the *business*. You're not responsible for the contracts, the unions—the goddamned unions—and the city, which sends some really unspeakable people over to our sites."

"I believe we're talking about murder here, Clive—not annoyances or minor kickbacks."

"Evan, you don't know anything about it. You're a babe in the woods. You don't know—and you never have *wanted* to know about the business end, the responsible end, of Ward & Breedon. For years, you've been perfectly content to sit down there and draw, and you do that very well. It is really . . . really a little late to suddenly do a bull-in-the-china-shop routine and want to call in the police and so forth on your unsupported—"

"The man came to *see* me, Clive. He said he was a police officer, and he wasn't. He was very real—not my imagination at all."

"I don't think that was your imagination, Evan." Clive shook his small head to show how little he thought that. "—And I suppose the Rao people are not above chicanery—particularly since they are apparently preparing to sue our pants off, along with Harris, diNunzio, for damages to their company's reputation by creating 'unsafe working conditions.' No, I don't put it past them to play some games here—and perhaps try to trick us into false accusations, for which, of course, they could sue additionally."

"*Murder*, Clive. I saw one about forty-five minutes ago—and probably another last week."

"Evan, please. . . . You come to me with this tale, and it's an improbable tale. And your only evidence is the apparent—and I do say *apparent*—perfection of Rao's contractual fulfillments." Clive was bending forward from his stool, looked as if he might fall off it. "And I must tell you that I might tend to excuse a mur-

der or two on a two-hundred-million-dollar job if all
the contractors could perform half as well—even on
paper." Clive smiled, revealing dull-yellow slightly
bucked upper teeth, to show he was joking. "Now, you
have seen two terrible accidents—and within a week of
each other. But no matter how odd that seems, how co-
incidental, you have no hard evidence of a *crime*. And
I can tell you that Ward & Breedon has no interest in
being involved in a situation of this sort on mere sup-
position. —Do we understand each other?"

"Yes."

A satisfied nod across the desk. "Evan . . . I really
don't think you want to pursue this. Do you?"

"Of course I'd prefer not. . . ." True enough, and no
retreat to admit it.

Clive nodded, apparently relieved to see reason enter
in. "Very wise. It's just the sort of nasty mess where,
win or lose, you always lose."

"But I *saw* it. Saw a deliberate killing. —And I do
think the girl's death last week was another."

"Evan, if we all pursued every possible felony we
noticed year by year in this city, we would find no end
to it, and no satisfaction in it. You agree?"

"In most cases, probably. . . ."

"Tell you what—and I have to be getting uptown to
talk with some damn insurance people. Why don't we
leave it at this: we will certainly keep an eye on our little brown brothers in Rao Electric for the duration of
the project . . . and if any *evidence* of serious misdeeds
surfaces, take that immediately to the police. —Well?
Honor satisfied?"

". . . I suppose that it is."

"Good. Sensible. Done. . . ." He slid down from his
draftsman's stool, appeared to slightly shake himself
like a small fat bird settling its feathers. "And Evan,
please let's not noise this about downstairs. Ms.

Fuentes helped you search the files? Very well—that's done, and doesn't need to be rehashed for all our people. . . . I would frankly be very angry if the Rao people got wind of this little investigation of yours, and the implied accusations, and proceeded to use them against us and the general contractors in court. In fact, your little visit by the Hindu policeman or whatever—which I'm sure did occur—may have been intended to persuade you to do that very thing, make that mistake."

"I understand."

"And there's something else. Henry Ward is not—and I mean it—is not to be troubled with this. You understand me, Evan? He's not to be apprised or appealed to. We are working on the Aegis Insurance thing, and Henry needs to be left strictly alone."

"I won't mention it."

"Good, I'll rely on that. —And by the way, Evan—and I know this is not a major subject—I notice you're dressed perhaps a little more casually than is appropriate, even for an architect. Clients do come to your floor. . . ."

"Blood on my other things."

"Oh, *oh*. Of course. I'm sorry; stupid of me. . . ."

Trotting down the flight of stairs to the second floor, Evan was slightly ashamed of his relief at the postponement of any necessary action. Enjoying the stretching leisure of nothing having to be done—certainly worth a little shame.

"I won't use algebra. I will never use it."

"Suppose you have to build a bridge?"

"Daddy, in that case I'll hire somebody else to do the algebra."

"And if you can't afford to hire someone else?"

"Then I won't build the bridge."

"OK. Let's forget the bridge—let's just work on the idea of x equals . . ."

Catherine, in her gray silk bathrobe (dully shining, patterned intricately as a snake's skin), stopped at Beth's room door, her short hair haloed brighter blond under the hall light. "Evan, it's getting late."

"We're just finishing. . . ."

"Beth, it's your homework—not your father's."

"Mom, we're having quality time together."

Evan, sitting beside Beth at her small cherry-wood desk, watched as she wrote a wrong answer, left-handed, with an oversized yellow Ticonderoga pencil. The desk lamp's light glinted on tiny gold hairs along her small forearm, already, this early in the summer, tanned to beige.

"That's a wrong answer, pea pod."

"Beth, have 'quality time' in the morning before breakfast, if you need help." Catherine still standing framed in the doorway, as if crossing the threshold to them were taboo.

"OK. . . . Daddy, what's wrong with it?"

"You figure it out—but remember, what you do to one side of any equation has to affect the other side. That's the whole point."

"Oh. . . ." Beth bent in warm lamplight, as if looking more closely would help.

"Beth, it's *bedtime*."

"OK. . . . OK. . . ."

Beth got up as Evan did, stood momentarily beside him in T-shirt and shorts, a little taller than she'd been at Christmas. Her hair, rich brown as pouring maple syrup, was pinned up like an older girl's, revealing tender ears, a mouse's ears . . . delicate, nacreous, translucent. And a narrow nape, fragile and pale.

* * *

"She's been behind in math all year." Catherine lay beside Evan, but not touching him.

"No talent for it. History and English—fine." Conversation in dimly moonlit dark. The moonlight shone down through the bedroom windows portioned by their panes, and lay in long rectangles across the blanket.

"It's because she might not have a knack for it that she needs to learn to work harder. Everything doesn't have to be easy for her. I think it's important that everything *not* be easy for Beth. —And I don't think it helps that she depends on you."

"A point. I'll back off the homework a little. . . ."

After that, no talk. No discussion of the day. No turning to kiss, though Evan supposed he might have been the one to do that. . . . It was odd how his admiration for her seemed to grow as if there was deep affection just under it, waiting to be spoken. He admired her—that was it exactly. Admired her beauty—had once or twice imagined it was she he was with, while making love to Sanchia. Had imagined that once or twice. . . . but never the reverse.

Years had taught him what he knew of Catherine. —That now, for instance, she lay awake, too still to be ready for sleep. She almost always introduced herself to sleep by turning once or twice, settling, unsettling, then settled at last. . . . He knew much less of Sanchia.

Evan reached over in almost darkness, found Catherine's face, found her mouth, and gently began to trace her lips with his finger as if her mouth was new, and he'd never done this before. She seemed remarkable, as if he'd found himself in bed with a strange woman, available to be caressed. Someone so similar, but not quite Catherine.

He lightly, lightly stroked and followed . . . outlined her mouth. Gently, thoroughly, as if he were blind and had to know. Catherine lay still and let him. Let him do what he wanted as if she had no say, as if she'd given that up when the moon cast shadows.

After a while, Evan left a fingertip resting there, and touched her lips with nothing else but that. Left it there for the waiting that seemed to make her comfortable, and when that was over, felt her mouth move ... and open to lick his finger, then commence to suck it. In such mottled darkness she might have been anyone, any woman but Sanchia.

Evan raised up on his elbow, bent closer to her ... tugged the finger gently out ... slid it in again for her to suckle, then pulled it from her mouth.

He stroked her throat, and down, found the buttons of her pajama top, but left them alone. Found a moon-paneled fold of sheet and blanket lower, pushed them away and off her, then could see under the same moon pattern her sleeved forearm, and down to her slender wrist where it lay just under the elastic waistband of her pajamas, and moved in slight slow motion. Evan reached farther down and rested his hand over hers, felt the fine bones of the back of her hand through soft cotton, felt the slow cupping ... the small sliding motion its fingers made.

"Get your pants off," he said, and Catherine sighed as if she'd been asleep, and he heard and felt and could see something of her fumbling with her pajama bottoms and then lifting her hips to shove them down into darkness ... raise her knees to pull them off.

When she'd done that, her pajama top left on, Catherine moved and he felt her knee against him. Evan put his hand down on it, faintly rough and rounded, then slowly slid his palm from there along her thigh, a more polished roundness that took the moon's light smooth as glass as she lay spraddled.

Now he smelled her. And barely heard the faintest small *kiss-kiss,* the slightest brushing of her arm and wrist along her bare belly as she worked. Evan ran his hand along her thigh to where she was stretched widest, and found her hand paler out of dark, her fingers busy beneath damp fur.

"Oh, Christ . . ." Catherine said, and he watched in a moonshone landscape while both her hands, fingers damp white spiderlegs in silver light (one leg banded in gold, one in diamonds), played and trembled, tugged color gently open to deeper color, folded that back to show him . . . then let him bend to it as her hands grew still to rest along her thighs, and she lay whitely naked from the waist, her knees spread wide. Evan leaned down to kiss her cunt, unfolded, wet as a mouth that seemed to him to kiss him back, and tenderly, as if her heart lay just behind it.

After a while she grew restless, thrashed and tried to push his head away. But Evan, as if he were a different man from Evan in daylight, gripped her hips and held her down a little longer.

Then urgency required him to stop what he was doing and ride up onto her, brace himself above her and use his knees to hold hers wide. He reached down and notched his cock to her . . . then shoved so it hesitated, then slowly slid oily in. Catherine grunted, took it into her, and lay under him open as an open book to be read by moonlight. First lying almost still, receiving his cock, allowing it, and wet enough for liquid sounds. Evan, during this, felt himself permitted to kiss her hair, breathe in the scent of it . . . to lie over and along her, cradled in her, against her sweat-slick belly, hot as if her life were burning there . . . hold her against him with the excuse of what they did, so that these kisses, this clasping and closeness seemed one thing, and the activity below, where he fucked into her and felt that slippery clench and heard her grunt with taking, was something separate.

Then, after a while, when her soaked sex and its necessity prompted her, Catherine gripped him, held him hard, groaned and then groaned louder . . . said, "Oh, do that . . . oh, *do* that," and heaved up to him very powerfully so they smacked hard together, worked together at what each wanted, and after a while of striving Catherine said, "Momma . . . *Momma*," and apparently accompanied by her mother's observant ghost (drifting out of some warm sunny indoor memory of stroking, diapering, holding or hugging), she thrashed and came, bucking beneath Evan, struggling hard, kicking as if he were strangling her. . . .

Then Catherine lay relaxed beside him, but not touching, her knees still spread in moon-decorated darkness light enough for faint gleaming along her sweated belly and thighs. Her sex scented the bedroom with sea. . . . Then she slowly closed her long legs, sat up and got out of bed—her right hand, Evan knew, held cupped to her groin to keep his semen from the carpet—walked into the bathroom and closed the door.

Both finished again with lovemaking—fucking—so free and almost unhampered by affection that it seemed to Evan rich in the discovery of spaces as a strange house, large and several-storied, that had been empty for years.

She was still in the bathroom when the phone rang, and Evan rolled to his right to pick up the receiver.

"Yes?"

"Mr. Scott?" A man's voice, a lilting tenor.

"Yes. . . ."

"You fail to take my so good advice . . . and then, you become a nosy parker! So, this morning? This morning was your wake-up call . . . !" The last almost sung.

Evan recognized that merry voice, heard street traf-

fic behind it. Pay phone. "You have just made a serious mistake," he said, "—you fat piece of shit."

"Oh, chut! Bad language." And the man hung up.

"Who was that?" Catherine, out of the bathroom,
sliding into bed.

"A drunk," Evan said. "Wrong number." And feeling oddly relieved—as if something he'd waited for
had come at last—he turned in cool sheets, felt his
muscles ease, and went to sleep.

No doubt the genuine article, Detective Sergeant
Cameron was young, black, and bored behind a desk—
the fourth or fifth in a row of gray metal desks beside
other rows of desks, all under ranks of fluorescents.
This was a full-floor office in a grim new building.
Narrow, grudging wire-glass windows admitted only a
little of morning's light.

"Man identified himself as a police officer?"

"Yes, he did. He showed a badge, no other ID."

"Any witness to this, Mr. . . . Scott?"

"No. It was lunchtime, and I was alone in the office."

The big room's low composition ceiling muffled an
uneasy surf of ringing telephones, conversations, clicking computer keys. "Um-hmm, well, no witness
doesn't help. . . . And his purpose in doing that, impersonating an officer, was to accuse this electrical
company of maybe throwing the girl off the building—
some sort of extortion thing?"

"Yes, that's about it."

"Tell you what's got me puzzled, Mr. . . . Scott.
What's got me puzzled here, is why the hell this fat
guy would come to you with that accusation. —If he
was one of the guys killed that girl last week—maybe
killed the insurance guy yesterday—then why the hell

come to you? Why tell you his own people were bad guys? Doesn't make any sense."

"From his point of view, a lot of sense. He wanted me to trust him, to tell him what I'd seen when the girl was killed—and what I'd told Vijay Bhose. And it worked, I told him. And also, of course—"

"Also what?"

"Also, of course, it makes for more confusion."

"Yeah, well, you got a lot of that. . . ." Detective Cameron, stocky in a short-sleeved white summer shirt, tapped several phrases into his computer keyboard—the computer's screen turned so only he could see it—then waited for a response. "Got a lot of that. . . ." He looked across the desk at Evan, a pleasant, observing, almost medical examination. "Doing architecture keep you busy?"

"Yes, fairly busy—here in town, and work in Connecticut, too."

A woman in a powder-blue summer suit came down the aisle—a tall blonde, thin except for a small bulge of pregnancy. Her hair, straight and falling almost shoulder length, a little too long for her long face. She stopped at the desk, looked at Evan for a moment with pale blue eyes blank and acquiring, then leaned down to Cameron. She wore a small steel nameplate pinned to the lapel of her jacket. CAPT. E. SHEA.

"Freddy, I don't have Chris's report."

"He's supposed to be getting it up."

"Freddy—you tell Chris to have that on my desk shift-change tomorrow morning, or I will tie his dick in a knot."

"OK. Yes, ma'am."

The woman straightened up, looked at Evan again, and walked back up the aisle.

". . . What's your first name again, Mr. Scott?" Detective Cameron had been drinking an extra-large

Coke; its tall red container stood at the near corner of his desk. What seemed the remains of a prune danish rested on a paper napkin beside the backs of two small silver picture frames.

"Evan."

"Evan. Right." And having apparently noticed Evan's casual glance at the picture frames, "You have a family, Evan?"

"Yes. Wife, and a daughter. . . . Believe me, I'm not—this is not the sort of thing I usually do. I'd much rather not be here."

"Hey, welcome to the club." Detective Cameron sat staring at the computer screen, still waiting for his readout. He made soft clicking sounds with his tongue . . . saw what interested him, and keyed another entry. "Your wife know about this, Evan? You know, your coming in?"

"No. I haven't discussed it with her yet."

Detective Cameron glanced at him, said, "Um-hmm," and went back to his computer screen.

The machine chirped, and Cameron looked at the screen, made another short entry, and waited for the machine's reply to that. He read it, seemed suddenly annoyed, said, "God damn it," and gave Evan an unpleasant look. "Tell you what I'm doing here. What I'm doing is checking this Rao outfit through the database—and guess what? Guess what? . . . There's information here from the county clerk's office shows a five-million-dollar lawsuit for damages to reputation filed by that same Rao Electric against your company and the contractor . . . Harris, diNunzio. —Hey, aren't computers great?" He keyed an entry into the machine, then turned to Evan. "Mr. Scott, did you know about that before you came down here, tried to get these Indian guys in trouble?"

"No, I didn't. I knew there might be some legal involvement. . . ."

"A fucking five-million-dollar lawsuit, and filed just a couple days ago. Could call that 'some legal involvement.' —You wouldn't be trying something cute here, would you? Use the department to pressure these people?"

"No, I wouldn't."

"Oh boy, I sure hope not. I really hope you're not trying something like that. The department would take something like that very personally—very personally, if you get my drift."

"I . . . there's no such intention. In fact, a partner, one of the owners of my firm, refused to have anything to do with this. He advised me to drop it. —But nonetheless, Sergeant, I *saw* a man murdered yesterday! Then I received the phone call. . . . And now I believe the girl, Ms. Fonsecca, was also murdered."

"Yeah . . . well, I'll tell you something, pal. What you think is fine, but I can tell you what my commander's going to say. —You see that lady was just here?" Detective Cameron took a silver pencil out of his shirt's breast pocket, arranged a yellow legal pad before him on his desktop. "She's going to say most likely you saw two accidents . . . and just so happens your company and these Indian guys are going to court for a major amount of money concerning one of these accidents— which, *which* maybe your company wouldn't have to pay if they can raise the possibility it *wasn't* an accident."

Cameron was making notes on the yellow pad as he spoke, as if recording his own statements as evidence. He was left-handed, like Beth. "And the only proof you got, you're bringing to us here, is your records showed these guys did too good on the job! . . . And I have to tell you, Mr. Scott"—looking up from his note-taking—"have to tell you that far as my commander is concerned, all that would add up to jack shit, pardon my French."

"That was no traffic accident yesterday. It was deliberate murder—and if you'd been there, you'd have known it."

"But I wasn't there, Mr. Scott—and you're upset and it was a terrible thing to see and so forth, guy got killed you knew." He reached over for the last of the prune danish, and ate it in one bite . . . sat chewing for a moment, looking at Evan. "I notice you didn't call us in on that immediately—make those charges yesterday, right at the scene. To the officers arriving right at the scene. Didn't say anything to those people about that van, about any murder."

"No, I didn't. I was . . . reluctant to become involved in that way."

" 'Reluctant to become involved.' " Detective Cameron smiled. "Tell you something—best thing you said, right there. *That,* I believe. . . . So, you back off, figure you'll wait and see about this supposed homicide you witnessed. And you waited until this phone call last night. That's what set you off, right?"

"It's true that decided me. It made the matter . . . inescapable."

"And you had a witness right there at the scene—the old Hindu guy, right? But I notice this witness didn't come down here with you this morning."

"He doesn't want to be involved with the police."

"Right. And I notice this girl's father—that other homicide you're suggesting—I notice her father, works the same job, foreman or something on the job, I notice her own father has entered no complaint. None. Guess he figures it was a tragedy, an accident. Guess *he* doesn't figure it was a homicide. . . . So that just leaves you, Evan, and what you have adds up to noth-

KARMA 159

ing, as far as Sufficient Cause is concerned—OK?"
Cameron looked over at the crumbs of his prune danish, appeared to wish there was more left. "We have
zero, zip, nothing at all derog on this Rao Electric
outfit—paid all fees, licenses, everything. Just regular
business guys got a big beef with *your* guys. And—
and, if they did send some dude around to pull your
chain, maybe to get you to do just what you're doing—
making a mess here, making unsupported allega-
tions—we got no way to prove it."

"This seems . . ." Evan intended to say, ". . . seems a
pretty stupid response on the part of the police." Then
thought better of it.

"But . . . and I suggest you listen up, Evan. Have I
got your attention, here?"

"Yes."

"All right. What I'm trying to tell you is, we have no
record of previous complaints, no laws broken in this
country, far as we know. —And we're talking about
American citizens here, Evan. You understand that?"

"Yes."

"The Hindu community here—all the people from
India are very solid citizens as far as we're concerned.
Honest people, law-abiding. We have no trouble with
them. See what I'm saying?"

"I understand, Sergeant. But what *I'm* saying is that
these particular people, these few people, apparently
are the exception to the rule. —Apparently were dangerous criminals in their own country, and now have
shown up here."

"So you say. Listen, these guys may be giving you
business problems; they may be naturalized and talk
funny and have dark skins—but they are American citizens."

"I don't care what color their skins are."

"Sure. . . . Now, we will check this out—you made

an accusation, we're going to check it out, send some people over to talk to people, look around. And if you get anything we can *use* —if your boss wants to come in, or the girl's father, and back up some charges, show this doesn't have anything *whatsoever* to do with this five-million-dollar lawsuit thing—then fine, we'll take a real hard look. But from what you say to me, your boss and the girl's dad, they aren't interested in doing anything like that. Am I right or wrong? Well ... am I right, or wrong?"

Evan, the Hartford Bank's first elevations complete and handed over to Swann, left work early, even for a Friday. There'd been only a short, unpleasant call from upstairs in the afternoon. Clive. ". . . Evan, two detectives have just left my office. And I am very disappointed, frankly, since I'd assumed we'd come to a reasonable agreement on this thing."

Evan had mentioned the phone call to his home, but Clive had only said, "I am also disappointed that, having changed your mind, you didn't choose to inform me before you made this fairly absurd and possibly damaging complaint to the police. . . ."

". . . I'm thanking you for returning my sweater, Mr. . . . ?" The elderly Indian had seen Evan coming through Ward & Breedon's double doors, and hustled out of his newsstand to intercept.

"Scott. Evan Scott."

"Oh, I've seen you going in and out, Mr. Scott, in and out of this building here." Said in singsong so rhythmic he seemed to sway with it. The old man, slender, gray-mustached, and almost tall as Evan, looked very much like a retired British officer—an old cavalry officer perhaps, burned permanently brown by India's sun.

"Yes—I'm an architect with this firm; they own the building."

"Yes, yes. . . ." The old man did a little dance to stay in front of Evan, hold him there at the corner to be talked to. "And may I ask you one question, Mr. Scott? No, I must be asking you three questions."

Evan saw himself plagued by this elderly man for as long—which perhaps would not be so long, after all—as he worked at Ward & Breedon. The Indian stood waiting for a nod, and got it.

"Oh, thank you. First—have you seen the police, and do they have an interest in me?"

"Yes, I went to the police, Mr. . . ."

"Ram Dass Lal."

"Ram Dass Lal—and no, I don't think they have any interest in you."

"Ah, now I am pleased at that—you see, I had, many many years ago, nothing but disappointment with the police in my country. When I was a young man, severe disappointment with the police. Severe disappointment thereafter with myself, too, of course. . . . And my next question, my second question is, the young man was a friend?"

"No. A business acquaintance."

"Ah. . . . And my last question, my very last . . . are you an important man, Mr. Scott? Do you have powerful friends? Friends with influence?"

"No."

"Are you a rich man?"

"That's four questions, Mr. Ram Dass." Evan stepped to the left to walk past the old man, but Ram Dass, likely a soccer player in his youth, stepped right to match him.

"Mr. Lal—Ram Dass Lal is my name; it is a Rajput name. I am of *chandravanshis,* the moon's children. You know Rajputs?"

"I believe I have heard of Rajputs, Mr. Lal—and that's the fifth question, and I have to be getting along. . . ."

"Oh, I am so rude—two questions too many. But I only asked to see if you were a prepared man, is it?"

"Of course. . . . Well, good-bye." Evan reached out to shake the hand of this odd specimen—who, like Bhose and "Detective" Prasad, appeared to have read too much Kipling, too much Forster. —Shook Lal's hand and stepped left again, was allowed to pass, and walked away uptown looking for a cab. He missed Sanchia's after-work farewell, a discreet small fluttering wave, her hand held down at her waist.

Evan imagined her still at the beach this late afternoon—a beach occasionally crossed by cool early-summer winds. At the beach with her friends, Nita, a retail clerk (a plump girl, unlucky in love from what Sanchia said about her), and Lucera, a court stenographer and tougher article. Sanchia would be lying, oiled and sun-blocked, on a striped sandy beach towel alongside those two. —And probably discussing her difficult attachment to an Anglo—not young, not single, and remote and reclusive by nature. Certainly not the sort of man to fall in love with a *portorriqueña* (unless, of course, she was very beautiful). Not likely to fall in love with her, leave his wife and daughter for her. Leave his other life, his Connecticut life, for her.

"No way. . . ." her tawny friends would be saying, chanting in unison, lying lotioned side by side on the sand. *"No wayyy. . . ."* And Lucera adding, "You got a rare-lamb-chop guy—he's not goin' to go for a rice-an'-beans girl. *No wayyy. . . ."*

chapter 8

••

It would have been better practice to have worked the
Crealock's sails dockside, using only the boat's limited
space to maneuver, and if Evan had had a crewman to
help, he would have done that. As it was, with Beth and
Catherine, it made more sense to take the sails—
together a half acre of Dacron—up one by one, folded
over the wheelbarrow. Take them up to the lawn, unfold
and shake them out across the grass in hot sunshine . . .
refold and set them for packing into *Anywhere*'s lockers.

In the egg-yolk light of afternoon, Evan worked and
watched Beth and Catherine, both barefoot in shorts
and T-shirts, tugging, hauling together . . . marching
over snowy fields of Dacron canvas so they seemed
separated by brightness from ordinary earth . . . until
they reached the cloth's border and stepped back on
grass to gather a heavy-stitched hem weighted with
steel eyelets—gather it, heave it up and over for the
first long fold.

While he watched, Evan rehearsed a way to mention
the city trouble to Catherine without disturbing, frightening her. "There's been some difficulty on the Madison Avenue job; one of the contractors appears to be a

fairly criminal outfit. And apparently, since I'd seen the Fonsecca girl fall, I've become involved."

Could say that much, and really shouldn't have to say more. Unpleasantness, with unpleasant people. "Some violence there, involving an insurance man on the job, so I had to check in with the police, strictly pro forma. Ward & Breedon intend to step aside, and so do I, of course . . . and that's about it. Not all that unusual on these big New York projects."

Something like that—an annoyance more than anything. Nothing could have been done to avoid it. Certainly not a case of looking for trouble. . . .

"Mom! You didn't get the corner; it's going to be crooked!" Beth, springing and slender, high-stepping in sunlight through heaps and folds of white.

Sunday, Catherine made pancakes for breakfast, with low-nitrate bacon, and—once Beth had finished and taken her bike out, gone riding with Cindy Wooten— Evan mentioned the firm and general contractor having some problem with one of the subcontractors of 366. Apparently thugs of some sort. . . . Situation had been reported to the police.

"*You're* not involved with that."

"No . . . well, peripherally I have been, as a member of the firm."

"That city . . ." Catherine said. "You do most of your work in Connecticut. I don't see why it's even necessary for you to be going in every day."

"It's where the firm's decisions are made," Evan said, and thought he'd told enough without upsetting her, frightening her, without having her feel he'd been a fool.

"You want the last pancake?"

"Split it with you."

The morning sunlight, reaching across the breakfast

table, had turned the raspberry jam to jewelry . . . filled
the little white pot with rubies.

Sanchia had never cared for baths—her mother said
that was because she'd gotten soap in her eyes as a
child. But Sanchia had never cared for baths, really,
because of being in dirty water—not dirty to start with,
but dirty soon enough. Look at the stuff left in the tub
afterward. No way was that clean. . . .

She stood cramped in her small shower stall in a
seething fog of warm vapor, and already soaped with
yellow Camay and rinsed, now began to shampoo her
hair, wash out the last of the ocean's salt. Her soaked
hair lay heavy, slippery wet when her fingers combed
through it in the shower's rushing water.

The spray stung her nipples, made her small breasts
(sore, slightly swollen) ache a little. . . . Sanchia stood
swaying with pleasure under the shower's flood, gently
wringing shampoo foam from her hair, wishing (as
she'd wished many times) her hair was blond. Or if not
blond, then at least a soft light brown. Long straight
hair. . . .

She supposed Evan would like that better—wouldn't
find her so strange, so unlike Catherine Scott, who
came into the office every now and then, down from
Connecticut. Come down shopping—Bloomingdale's,
Bendel's. . . . More friendly than she'd looked, staring
so cold out of the picture with their little girl on Evan's
desk. The little girl smiling, Catherine Scott not smiling.

Sanchia thought Evan would like most of all a
woman who looked like Catherine, but smiled . . . was
a warmer person. Was crazy about him, loved him very
much. —This thinking about Catherine always troubled Sanchia with the notion that Evan's wife would
come to visit the office again, would come in and

somehow be standing right beside her, so when Evan came out of his office he saw them side by side. Saw how small and dark and ugly Sanchia looked beside his wife, could see she had *negro* blood, and then he'd say to himself, "I must be crazy—crazy to waste time with something like that"—Sanchia—"when I have Catherine. . . ."

And that would be the end of Sanchia Fuentes and Evan. —Which was coming now anyway, for sure—and would have come even without this, if she didn't learn to keep her mouth shut and stop talking to him like a wife, telling him what to do. He already had a wife, didn't need her talking like another one.

Last thing Lucera had said, dropping her off. "Don' pretend you're the dude's wife, honey—'cause you are not." Easy for her to say, when she didn't know as much as she thought she did.

Nita had put in her two cents from the backseat. "Believe it, girl. . . ." Lucera couldn't say anything without Nita agreeing with her, kissing her butt. Friends—but even friends could be a pain. Always giving advice whether you want it or not. All you had to do was mention something—a relationship, whatever—and they had this advice, as if they weren't all fucked up themselves.

Sanchia looked at her nails under the falling water. Good shape. She had nails as nice as anybody—any lady. No glue-on shit; all natural. And Warm Pink—that was her color.

But there was always a chance, because life was crazy. Supposing Catherine died—nobody wished that—but supposing it happened in an accident up in Connecticut, with her car. And Catherine was gone, was dead for a year or two—then, even if Evan had broken up with her over this, then he found out he couldn't forget her, understood how much she loved him . . . then one day he would come to her desk, and say, "It seems I can't get along without you," in that cute Anglo way, and he was always shy except when he was fucking her. Then he looked different. He looked like a tough guy then—sticking it in her and he didn't care what she wanted. He just wanted her pussy and he got it and used her up. She'd be coming and he didn't care. —Poor Francisco was always thinking about what she wanted, and that was part of the trouble. That would never have worked out, even without his family always bugging him, saying too-close blood and all that shit. . . .

Sanchia rinsed out the last of the shampoo, took the conditioner down from the shower basket, squirted some into her right palm and stroked that into her hair, combed it in with her fingers. She leaned back as if Evan were standing behind her in the shower, so much taller, strong and warm against her, so she wasn't alone.

. . . When she was out of the shower, and feeling tired, feeling sad, the entrance-door buzzer sounded from downstairs while she was drying her legs with a butter-yellow towel (the set $18.99 at Macy's).

Wrapped in the towel, Sanchia went down the hall, crossed the small living room (leaving damp prints on splintery old wood), and pressed the speaker button by her door.

"Who is it?" Hoping for Evan, could have come in town today, said he had work at the office.

"Police, miss."

"Who?"

"Police!"

Sanchia wanted to ask what it was about—perhaps to do with the girl who died—but the cop already sounded impatient at having to identify himself twice.

She pushed the unlock button, held it long enough,

then trotted back to the bathroom to hang up the towel and wrestle into her blue bathrobe. Then she came back to the door, waiting until heavy footsteps sounded on the stairs . . . creaked down the corridor.

Sanchia looked through the peep just as the doorbell rang, to see a fat man in a light-gray summer jacket smiling at her—saw him lean in, knowing she was looking, until his brown eye was opposite hers. Then he leaned back and brought a small gold badge in a black wallet swimming into view.

Sanchia unlocked the deadbolt, then the Fox lock, and opened the door inches on the chain.

"Police, miss," the fat man said, smiling at her over the chain. He brought the badge up again. "Really. No kidding!" He looked Hispanic, but his accent was different, not Spanish. "I understand some of my countrymen have been *very* naughty. Your Mr. Scott may have told you we spoke about it the other day. . . ."

Sanchia closed the door, took the chain off, and swung it open. "He's not my Mr. Scott—"

"Oh, dear," the fat man said, and strolled in. "I've made a gaffe—a social solecism. Only a working relationship, is it?"

"That's right," and Sanchia might have said something else, was thinking of repeating that about their only working together, but couldn't. Her mouth opened—stayed open in surprise—but no sound came out, since the fat man, as he'd walked in, had reached down to touch his waist where his shirt was tucked, whipped swiftly out a shimmering length of white silk—weighted at a corner by a coin—and snapped the cloth around her neck. Sanchia had seen the beginning of his doing that, but the rest had been too fast to follow.

Silenced, she jumped in shock and then began to struggle, but much too late—and the fat man, still smiling (smiling even more broadly, so Sanchia imagined for a moment this was some rough joke), neatly skipped behind her, very light on his feet—then spun once, spun completely around as if he were her dance partner, so she ended hanging down his back, feet off the floor, her blue bathrobe swinging open so she was naked, strangling.

Then the Dond came in.

Sunday All-Star Country was on, and the fat man, whose name was Vasud Rao—it was a cousin of his, very unpleasant, who'd been called Prasad—Vasud Rao had no intention of missing the program. A music lover, he had found after several years in this nation that the only music of theirs he cared for was this "country." It had at least a little of the steady, twanging, ringing beat of music from his home. Very crude, of course, a music for uncultured children, but still pleasantly reminiscent.

Now a pretty young woman (playing a guitar very badly) was singing in a high pleasant whining style about mistreatment by her lover. The young woman, like most in this nation, dressed like a prostitute, so that (in this case) she exposed her knees and calves beneath a short skirt. It was incredible to think some respectable man might be married to such a thing, no better than a sow.

The fat man sat at ease on Sanchia's sprung living-room couch, comfortable on its worn green corduroy, and toyed with the remote control occasionally to raise or lower the volume in concert with noises from the bedroom.

Most sounds were not the girl's; slip-knotted silk still kept her nearly silent, barely breathing, allowing only smothered squeals, thin, piping, tremulous. Difficult to hear through the music.

Her companion, however, was noisy as a feeding beast.

This the second Monday morning in three weeks that Evan had been invited up to the partners' floor. On this occasion, sensing a change in the firm's weather concerning this particular architect, Mrs. Koskovic had offered no coffee, certainly no tea.

". . . It just seems to me we had come to an agreement, an understanding—and now, for some reason, Evan has come up with something different."

"Harley, it's simply that I felt it might be more . . . elegant, for the two bathrooms to be combined, while still allowing for separate entrances, separate toilet areas and so forth."

"Not what we *agreed* to."

"Let's forget about agreements, for the time being, Harley." Henry Ward looking more alert as he grew annoyed. "You and Sybil asked for the best work we could do for you—and I've checked the plans and it seems to me that the two-bathrooms-side-by-side notion was one of the more asinine I've seen. *I* wouldn't have agreed to it from the start, and I assume Clive was busy and passed over that detail. —Probably didn't believe his eyes; thought he was seeing things. . . ."

"It's what we want." Sybil Martin, brunette and very slender, had been a model but now was commencing to wither.

"Well, dear, sometimes what we want in life we just can't have. And Evan is quite right, and I'm telling you that you will have no ridiculous twin bathrooms squatting side by side with Ward & Breedon's name on them. Period. You want something *outré* as that, you can go to another firm to have it designed."

"It's what we wanted. . . ."

"You can't have it—not out of this shop." Ward sat

back in his leather desk chair, fat in a coffee-colored summer suit, his face an irritated pug's with a person's eyes.

Sybil Martin, sitting erect, recrossed her legs. "Harley is very messy in the bathroom. We've had a lot of arguments about it, and I just said, 'Well, we're each having our own.' "

"Not with our name on it, you're not," Ward said. " 'Mess' is your cleaning woman's business, not mine."

"But Mr. Scott *agreed*. . . ." Harley was a large man, flush-faced, crew-cut as a colonel.

"In a moment of weakness," Evan said. "But you know, Harley, everyone who's seen that set of plans thinks the double bathrooms look ridiculous. . . . And now we have a workable, handsome fix—which I think we need to go with."

"Oh, shit." Sybil Martin lifted a hand to keep Harley quiet. "I mean, we are paying for it, and surely it's our decision what gets done. . . . I don't believe this."

"Ordinarily," Ward said, his fingers restless on his chair's padded arms, "ordinarily you'd be right. You want it; we do it. But *not* when possible generations of guests at your home—people of taste, naturally, and some influence—will look at that absurd arrangement and say, 'Ward & Breedon? Really? Henry Ward must have lost his mind!' "

"We can have someone else do it."

"Go right ahead." An angry pug now.

"Sybil, please don't do that." Evan smiled at the woman as if he liked her. "It really isn't necessary. You have a beautiful living space designed there, something to be proud of. You don't need—you really do not need a nonsensical arrangement for people to make fun of. It's an injustice to the space—and, in my opinion, an injustice to the two of you. It misrepresents your very special taste."

Harley sighed, not colonel enough for his haircut. "Oh, well . . . for God's sake. Doesn't money buy anything anymore?"

"It'll buy you that Alabama marble, if you still want to go twenty-seven thousand for it. We found some varied-brown stored upstate. Or rather Chuck Bartels found it."

"True brown?"

"Sybil, it's true brown—Chuck called down, said it looked like a maple-fudge sundae just beginning to run."

"Twenty-seven thousand. . . ."

"That's right. Eight-inch block. —And that's installed."

"Well. . . ."

"Very sensible," Ward said, and stood up behind his desk, not very much taller than when he'd been sitting. "I've learned to depend on the ultimate good judgment of our clients. Very rarely disappointed. . . ."

"Evan, they went for it?" Swann was eating lunch at his desk—two cartons of Chinese take-out and an apple.

"Kicking and screaming, but they went for it."

"Damn fools. . . ."

"Swann, has Sanchia come in this morning? I have a possible addition for the Conners' saltbox, and codes out there is definitely going to insist on a total redo for wiring."

"Hasn't come in today. That smart little cookie's taking a four-day weekend. She's still at the ocean—and we're stuck here. . . ."

Evan walked back to his office, called Sanchia's apartment, and heard only her recorded message—the answering machine a recent, prized acquisition. *"You [the Y carefully not J] have reached the Fuentes residence. You may leave a message after the tone. . . ."*

A half hour later, Evan left the Ferguson preliminaries (for a Vermont cabin, and slightly overdue) on Swann's desk . . . then went downstairs and out past the old man's stand—Ram Dass, busy cutting newspaper bundles, offering a brisk nod.

Evan strolled through Soho's lunchtime crowd, noticing the women out in full flower as if hot summer sunshine, a long-awaited lover, was now worth undressing for. . . . He walked east for six blocks, then walked downtown. The sun, straight overhead, flashed reflection off every piece of glass—windshields, store windows, broken bottles here and there along the gutter—and made the mica scattered through the pavement's cement sparkle before him step by step.

There were two squad cars double-parked down the block in front of Sanchia's building, and Evan felt an odd electricity of foreboding he denied and then accepted and walked faster for only a few steps, then began to trot . . . and embarrassed, ran down the block (still not running as fast as he could), jacket flying open, his loafers awkward, slipping at the heels while he galloped along, noticing interested faces, brown and black, as he passed them.

A uniformed patrolman (white, stocky) stood on the sidewalk, watching Evan run toward him. Their eyes met before Evan was close enough to speak with him, so they seemed already acquainted when Evan, slowing, reached him and stopped, out of breath as if he'd been running for several miles. "Is there a problem, officer? I know someone in this building."

The patrolman pursed his lips, and still looking into Evan's eyes, maintaining that contact, said, "Couple junkies broke an' entered. TVs an' shit. Nobody was home 'cept an old guy. He got hurt. —Old black guy." The last apparently added to reassure Evan it could be no friend of his.

"Thanks. Thank you. . . ." Evan went up the brownstone's steps, saw the heavy entrance door swung open, hooked in place, and went through the narrow, white-tiled entry and up the stairs.

Another white patrolman, a taller, younger man, stood on the second-floor landing, and as he passed him, Evan saw two large men talking at the end of the hall, a splintered door, yanked off its hinges, leaning against the wall beside them. A little boy, black, came down the stairs from the third floor as Evan went up.

There were no police on the third floor, Sanchia's floor. Evan walked to the end of the corridor, pressed her doorbell, and listened. Waited, then pressed it again. ". . . Sanchia?"

He supposed she and her friends had decided to stay out on the island another day. *"Sanchia. . . ."* She'd never offered him a key to her apartment. Apparently knew he preferred not to have it. . . .

He pushed the button again, heard the two musical notes sound inside. . . . Then, in case she was in but didn't care to answer—had at last gotten tired of him, the whole unsatisfactory business (her girlfriends must have talked to her over the weekend)—he knocked, called, "Sanchia?" Then knocked again . . . and the door, painted a thick black, withdrew a little. Moved . . . swung open only a few inches, so he saw sunlight through window blinds stripe the wall across the room.

"Sanchia? . . . Sweetheart?"

Evan stepped into a mingled odor of patchouli and acrid perspiration, as if Sanchia—trying new perfume, and her system fiery with a weekend of Latin spices— had just furiously exercised there with some leotarded

TV instructor. Harsh sweat . . . not what he usually smelled lying braced above her, looking down into that small, sweetly simian face, damp, childish with satisfaction. . . .

"Sanchia . . . ?"

There was an empty place in the far corner of the small living room; a green lamp had been set on the floor there where the big TV had been.

The low bookcase by the kitchen door had been tipped over, and books lay around it on the floor. The CD player had been on the bookcase, stacked with the tape deck. . . .

"Sanchia!" Evan stepped in, turned to look back at the inside of the treacherous door, and saw a long splinter had been ripped off its frame, the chain lock's grooved plate torn free—and he ran, felt he was running much too slowly down the hall when she probably hadn't even come home yet. Stayed out on the island another day. . . .

The bathroom light was on as he went past, and he was in the shadowed bedroom, caught his breath, smelled shit—and saw Sanchia sitting up in bed, smiling at him.

Not smiling. Doing something else. Sticking out her tongue.

She was naked, sitting up with her thin brown legs spraddled wide. Her arms were stretched out, tied at the wrists with electric cord to the bedposts at either side. She glared at him, her eyes bulging, huge, and black with blood, her hair a dark tornado around her face. Her tongue, mottled pink, lolled out long as a dog's and she sat naked in her shit, the center of a silent storm of death.

Evan said no, no, no, and as he went to her saw she wore a tight white scarf, then saw a broken green chair

leg protruding fatly from her presented vulva, breaking
her apart in clotted red.

The patrolman on the floor below had seen expressions like Evan's once or twice before. A detective,
just then walking up that corridor, had seen such expressions many times—a look not of shock or horror,
but rather of illumination, as if the person had, just a
moment before, been told an extraordinary secret.

The patrolman stood staring, he and the detective
watching a gesture Evan made to them as he came
down from the landing, a sort of offering motion with
his hand—a generous motion, as if indicating treasure
for them just up the stairs.

Then Evan and the patrolman stayed in each other's
company, listening to the heavy hammer of the detective's footsteps up the flight, his footsteps down the
hall above . . . to the end of the corridor, the only open
door.

When, after a few moments, they heard no returning
footsteps, the patrolman sighed—pointed to the floor at
Evan's feet to show he should stay where he was—and
climbed the stairs, in no hurry.

chapter 9

....

This was a different precinct, different detective—his
L-shaped desk the only one in a small office space, partitioned off in a row of similar spaces. Marquez—LT.
ABRAHAM MARQUEZ on a steel desk nameplate—was almost elderly in summer slacks and shirtsleeves. Bald,
his skin brown as tobacco leaf, his eyes a faded paler
brown behind black plastic bifocals.

"Mr. Scott," he said, "—Evan Scott. Sorry to keep
you hanging around here all day long. And after a
shock like that . . . somebody you cared about. You get
something to eat?" Marquez had no accent but New
York's.

"Yes. From McDonald's."

"Used to better than that, right?"

"It was fine, Lieutenant."

The short side angle of Marquez's desk was weighted
with paperwork, not a computer terminal, and he was
sitting facing it, slowly shuffling files, readouts, and
legal pad notes like decks of cards. "OK. You volunteered, made some accusations previously over
at another precinct, uptown. And for your information"—he looked up at Evan as if making sure he was
speaking to the right man—"for your information, that
was checked out in a preliminary way, and those electri-

cal people, those Raos, said it was—excuse me for saying so—just bullshit, and they're suing your company, and you people and the contractor as good as killed that woman speeding up the work." He paused, apparently to see if Evan had anything to say. "That was their story, but the uptown guys ran a check on them anyway. And guess what? No record of any trouble whatsoever. Far as law enforcement's concerned, righteous law-abiding citizens. . . . Oh, in big construction, so they probably cut some corners—OK. But nothing serious we know about." Marquez stopped talking again, waiting for any possible comment. Evan supposed the detective had found those pauses useful—chances for a suspect to make one remark too many.

Marquez sighed and said, "But you're a respectable citizen made these accusations, so we had some of our own people following up on that all afternoon and up to right now. Just in case—possible multiple homicides and so forth."

He turned three papers over, one after the other, and read their backs. "So, first—nobody saw any guy with a beard, and wearing a raincoat, long coat, or any kind of coat come up the work elevator in that building on shift or after shift. *Nobody* saw any guy like that come up, and at least a few people were working around there all day, all evening. So, my people say if your guy got up there, he had to wait until end of shift in the evening, when most of the people were gone off the site. Then he had to pick the one corner of the building that's in deep enough shadow that early . . . so he wouldn't be seen from the street, the next block over. And then, he had to climb ten, twelve stories up the outside of that ironwork before he could get to where guys had been working that day, left ladders up floor to floor." Marquez smoothed the papers on his desk as if he were stroking a pet. "Would you do that? *I* wouldn't do that. —Could you do that? *I* couldn't."

"There must be someone who can," Evan said, "because I saw him."

Marquez stared at Evan as if he were more interesting to see than listen to. Then he looked back down at his paperwork. ". . . And we also called that insurance outfit in Canada. Did they have any reason to believe their man . . ."—shuffled his papers quickly and found his reference—"*Bhose,* was victim of a homicide? Answer—no, they don't. He hadn't sent in a report on that situation yet, and they weren't expecting much when he did." Marquez put the paper down.

"OK. So now we come to that accident. Bhose guy got run over—and do you know we didn't find one witness said that was deliberate? And my people interviewed two persons were right there on the street when it happened. Neither one—and being interviewed by detectives that believe me had a shitload of *real* work to do—and neither one of those people said they saw anything but a guy getting hit and then run over when the other guy couldn't stop in time. . . . Now, we have a hit-and-run. And that's all we have."

"There was another witness."

"Right, so you say. But Evan—OK if I call you Evan?—your witness, whoever the guy is, he won't come in here and talk to us. Am I right? You know we put three men on this, today? Three detectives. And that doesn't count the guys uptown. And these are busy officers with cases backed up and so forth. Believe me, they don't like to be wasting their time. . . ." Marquez searched his desk top for some particular paper, couldn't find it . . . then did.

"OK, last thing. Mr. Fonsecca, the girl's father up there at Madison Avenue—her *father*—also said the charges you made were bullshit. Man said his daughter slipped. An accident, period." He shuffled that paper back into the pile. "—And Evan, I have to say we think it's all bullshit, too. Only thing we couldn't cover was the Indian guy you said came in impersonating an officer. But you told us the guy waited until the rest of your office people were out to lunch. And that's convenient, and it's inconvenient, because again . . . no witnesses. See what I'm saying?"

"And Sanchia?" Evan said. "And Sanchia Fuentes?" It seemed odd to him to be saying her name in such a removed way after spending several hours waiting here, being shifted from one office to another—and occasionally seeing Sanchia sitting naked, spread-eagled on any chair opposite, her small lightly furred vulva exposed to him, impaled. . . . And above this wreckage, her bloated face furious, ferocious as an attacking animal's, its spoiled tongue out and swelling.

"That Fuentes thing. . . ." Marquez paused, considering.

Evan sat waiting, willing to wait. This new interview—his story, his accusation sounding with repetition less and less likely, odd as a fairy tale—this interview at least had relieved him of Sanchia sitting opposite . . . seeming not dead, but dreadfully alive.

". . . What that Fuentes thing was—and I'm really sorry that happened; terrible, terrible thing to happen to a young woman like that. Disgusting." (A grim Catholic weight to "disgusting.") "But what that appears to be is a pair of junkies, probably were two of them, coming through that apartment building burglarizing, breaking and entering. Found the old man home, and choked him to death with a cord from a venetian blind. —And by the way, Evan, we'd appreciate it if you kept details on this stuff to yourself. OK? I'm talking to you about it because you were involved, cared for the young lady and so forth, and you have other matters you tried to bring in. —But that's what we have. Went through the building, robbed four apartments there, killed the old man. And then, unfortunately, found your lady friend at home, ripped her place off, and dealt with her in a brutal fashion."

"I'm sorry, but that's nonsense."

"Hey. . . . Pry marks, doors kicked in, kind of food they took out of the refrigerators—all sweet stuff. And we found two popped crack tubes. Everything exactly according to MO—that kind of crime."

"I'm sure everything was exactly according to the usual *modus operandi*. Tell me, Lieutenant—how many crimes have you found where everything is exactly as it should be?"

". . . Maybe a little unusual here, but not unheard-of. No way unheard-of."

"And you believe that?"

"I'll tell you what I believe, Evan." A little edge to the "Evan." "I believe in witnesses—plural—and I believe in evidence. And let me tell you a little secret about homicides: usually there's more than one possible motive—reason, cause, whatever you want to call it—but the biggest cause of all is just shitty *luck,* being in the wrong place at the wrong time. But nobody that loves these people, these victims, ever wants to believe that. —Now, we will get those perpetrators; that I guarantee. In time, we will get them. Meatballs . . . morons like that, they can never keep their mouths shut."

"No," Evan said, "you won't get them. Because the people, the junkies you're looking for, don't exist."

"They better. . . ."

"What?"

Marquez set some of his paperwork aside, leaned forward to face Evan directly, and pushed his glasses up onto his forehead. His brown eyes had an aging man's oily sheen. "You mind if I talk to you about something, Evan? You don't have to discuss it if you don't want to—I know you had a bad time today. And not the first bad time."

"I saw the Fonsecca girl fall—"

"I'm not talking about that." The lieutenant looked down at his desk again to search for a slip of paper in a stack of papers, and found it. "Tell you what I'm talking about. I'm referring to this." He shook the piece of paper so it made a soft leafy sound. "And this is confidential information which is not leaving this office, period. So don't worry about that. . . . Let me ask you, Evan, what's this 'episodes of violence'? This 'poor impulse control' stuff . . . ?"

"What the hell are you talking about?"

"I'm looking at privileged medical information here—which is no longer so privileged, since the subject volunteered accusations in a possible multiple homicide. The Veterans Administration records show you were hospitalized—is that right? And I'm not saying it's anything to be ashamed of. I got in Korea with the army last year of the war. —You see those *M*A*S*H* TV programs? Well, that's what I did. I drove for a MASH unit before I went in the MPs. So Evan, listen, it doesn't mean a damn thing to me a guy had to go in for treatment, had the war you had. OK?"

". . . You must be joking. That was twenty years ago—more than twenty years ago!"

"Hey—don't get defensive. What I'm saying is, you had some problems and you worked them out. Period. Is that right?—And I'm only asking because of this 'violent episodes' thing."

"This is fucking ridiculous!"

"Hey—I know that. But we need to look into everything. That's all this is, Evan, looking into everything."

"Listen, Lieutenant, I was having trouble sleeping, and a friend woke me in the dark in the BOQ and I

was confused and smacked him. That's all there was to
it."

"Wasn't dark."

"What?"

"It wasn't dark. . . . Says right here you assaulted a
First Lieutenant David Ornati, oh-nine-thirty hours—
that's in the morning, Evan—January eleven, 1972.
Says you broke the poor guy's jaw."

"That's not really accurate. The bone wasn't broken. . . ."

"Hey, Evan—relax. I don't mean to upset you, talking about this. It's very very ancient history. It doesn't
interest us at all. Only reason I brought it up was just
to check the thing out with you. You know, see where
we were—and also maybe remind you that you do
something, or say something or get involved in something . . . and it's there forever. It's always on paper
somewhere, always on those computers somewhere.
Do I make my point? You see my point?"

"I see your point. And I had some reactions at that
time—twenty years ago—some trouble sleeping. And
that once I took a swing at Dave Ornati—who, by the
way, didn't hold it against me. He woke me in the
dark—well, it was dimly lit . . . dark in the room."

"So, you were really hospitalized for a rest, more
than anything. . . ."

"That's right. For a few weeks."

"Three months."

"If you say so."

"You know, I get that all the time." Marquez shook
his head. " 'If you say so.' You wouldn't believe the
type of asshole I get across this desk saying, 'If you
say so.' Difference is, of course, they did something
bad, and you didn't. You just got worn out, am I
right? . . . Am I right?"

Evan felt an odd sort of insistence rise in him—as if

it were his body demanding it, not his mind—that he get up and leave Marquez, leave this desk and chair. As if there were going to be a disaster—an earthquake or fire—and he needed to get up and get out of the building. . . .

"—And I see a Navy Cross here, Evan. Which doesn't always mean anything, because a few years ago I had a Medal-of-Honor winner sitting across my desk. Not this desk; way uptown. Sitting there, and the son of a bitch had killed his own brother to get a shitty little trucking business. Made it look like a mugging, but he didn't even take the poor guy's watch. Medal of Honor. . . . But I see the Navy Cross here, and so I'm going to just forget about this 'violent episodes' stuff." Marquez put the piece of paper down, covered it with others. (Gone, practically forgotten.) ". . . Did you have another incident? I ask because of the plural, there—'episodes.' And this 'poor impulse control' stuff."

"Lieutenant," Evan said, "why don't you just kiss my ass."

Marquez smiled. "That's the young marine officer talking, right? You must have been a pistol, Evan. But listen, know what gets a guy in trouble? Temper. Nine times out of ten, it's because he loses his temper."

"I withdraw the remark."

"Well. . . ." Marquez looked down at his paperwork. "This stuff isn't important, this late date. You had your war; I had my war; and that's the way it goes." He stood up and came around the desk, a smaller man than he'd looked, sitting. "Let's head downstairs, OK? Getting to be time to go home, anyway."

Evan stood, much taller, and the lieutenant led around the partition and down a long aisle of small offices where men and women, most younger than

Marquez, were busy with computers and paperwork, looking more like tired clerks than law officers.

"Take the stairs; four flights is good exercise up and down. Good for the heart." The lieutenant, a small revolver comfortable on his right hip, pushed open a heavy red metal firedoor with a large 4 painted on it in white, and went through onto a creaky wooden landing. "Your Ms. Fuentes had a door like that, probably still be alive...."

The wooden stairs were worn, sagging under the dim red light of the stairway's painted bulbs. The precinct's building (nineteenth-century iron and brickwork) would be cheaper to wreck and rebuild than repair.

"You seem to me to be a competent officer, Lieutenant—good interrogator." Evan heard his voice echoing around them as he followed Marquez downstairs, the risers moaning softly at their weight. "Unfortunately, you're being taken for a ride by some even cleverer people. Too clever for you—and, it would seem, too clever for me.... I simply think it's unfortunate, tragic that they're going to get away with murdering a wonderful young woman. Murdering three people, as a matter of fact."

"Whoa, whoa—matter of *opinion*." Marquez speaking up over his right shoulder, stepping lightly downstairs like Alice's rabbit leading below to Wonderland, but armed. "—Not fact. I know ... I know the young lady, Ms. Fuentes, was special to you. I appreciate that—more, I bet, than your wife does." He glanced back up with a painfully roguish expression, a priest's at a cocktail party, then continued on down the stairs. "Mrs. Scott's been waiting for you outside Processing quite a while. We called her up in Connecticut a couple hours ago, and she drove in—can be useful to get a wife's point of view and so forth, got serious charges flyin' around.... And I would guess, ladies being ladies, that she's put two and two together about Ms. Fuentes." Marquez waited for Evan on the landing. "And what that tells me is, you got about all the trouble you can handle without making more. —Mind if I sneak a smoke?"

"No." Evan, who of course had known that—had known that now there couldn't be that secret—still felt an edge of nausea, as if he was in peculiar motion and it was beginning to make him ill.

"Real reason I like to use the stairs, is not have some asshole come up, tell me I can't smoke in the office." Marquez plucked a bent cigarette out of a pack in his shirt pocket, took an orange plastic lighter from his trouser pocket, and lit up. "What we were just discussing, you know, about trouble, I wonder if you'd like to hear the kind of way police officers think, you know— like the lawyers say, 'hypothetically.' Would you like that?"

"Go ahead, Lieutenant. . . ."

"Now, for example, say there's a traffic accident, witnessed *as* a traffic accident by people. And say a guy, a respectable citizen, comes to us making charges about that—and also concerning a previous accident, a girl who fell. . . . Our hypothetical guy makes these charges against some business people, very serious charges. And those charges are checked out—and nothing to them. No evidence, no witnesses, no motive. And he claims somebody impersonated an officer. —No witness to that, either." Marquez paused, drew on his cigarette the way Evan remembered his grandfather smoking cigars, relishing them. . . . "So, this hypothetical guy has now made *two* separate serious charges against these business people, some Indian guys his firm is having a legal hassle with—a civil problem, by the way, not a criminal problem."

Marquez indicated the next flight of stairs with his

head, then led on down them, almost skipping now, very coordinated for a man his age. Rattling down like a boy, almost tap-dancing down the stairs, his bald scalp tinted rose by the stairwell's lights.

"Now," he said over his shoulder as he went, "we have Ms. Fuentes, who *is* a homicide victim. And our hypothetical guy makes serious charge number *three*: those same Indian guys did it." Marquez held up at the landing, and stood watching Evan come down after him. "So, everything is checked out again, this time by this precinct. —Result? Zip. Zero. *Nada*." Marquez flicked ash off his cigarette. ". . . Tell you something about that kind of behavior, Evan: it makes cops curious. That's the way they think. 'What is this person up to? What's he *after* . . . ?' Guy comes around the police like that, keeps making charges that don't check out, it causes them to be curious." Another savoring drag, the cigarette's tip burning bright.

"And when"—gusty exhalation, cloudy gray—"and when it just so happens the last victim was this same guy's on-the-side girlfriend, then I have to tell you it occurs to cops that maybe this hypothetical guy we're talking about, this respectable citizen, was setting something up all the time. . . . Sees a bad accident. Then, a week later, sees another one for God's sake! Disturbing, horrible, people killed. But it gives our hypothetical guy an idea—a golden opportunity to charge these Indian people with responsibility for those accidents, and set up a pattern to cover a crime he himself *intends* to commit." Marquez turned and stepped off down the next staircase, so his voice floated up behind him in a trailing cloud of cigarette smoke.

". . . And his firm's having trouble with these Indian people on the job—so, it's those foreign electrical guys did everything. They throw a young woman off the building—her dad had annoyed them with a complaint about overtime. Then they kill this insurance guy because he knows too much about that . . . or something, right? And then—*then,* guess what? They kill our guy's girlfriend." He glanced back up as Evan came down the steps behind him.

"—And why do they do that? Well, because she found out they did too good a *job.* That's why." He started down the stairs again, very lively, cantering down the risers. ". . . And I have to tell you, just talking hypothetically, your average investigator is probably not going to be convinced by that. You see where I'm heading, Evan?"

"I'm sorry to say that I do, yes." Evan felt he was talking in a dream—his voice unlike his voice, with an odd humming undertone to it. The unreality of this scene on a staircase, its tragicomic unfairness, made the situation so funny he felt himself smiling, was afraid he'd begin to laugh.

On the next landing, Marquez looked up at him, seemed annoyed by the smile.

"I know this isn't funny," Evan said. He thought of saying, "Outrageous, but not funny," but didn't.

"No, it isn't funny," Marquez said. Another drag on his cigarette, held in his lungs, savored. "As I was saying, Evan, that's the way law enforcement people think. Very suspicious individuals—especially homicide people. Least thing they'd do in that hypothetical I was giving you—least thing they'd do is go back and take a look at that guy's motivation, take a look at where he's coming from. If he had a motive. . . . If he had opportunity—like maybe contacts with a lot of connected-up contractors come over from Jersey to work on projects he's doing." Marquez tapped the cigarette's ash away. "If one of those people owes our hypothetical guy a big favor—maybe recommended them for a heavy-money hauling contract, just for example—wouldn't be hard for them to find somebody who knows somebody who knows somebody else could send a couple of creeps to rip off apartments . . . and just incidentally kill two people, one of them being our guy's on-the-side girlfriend." Marquez glanced at Evan in a friendly way, crossed the landing, and started down the next flight of stairs—this time at a quick collected trot. Apparently enjoying variations in descending steps.

". . . Maybe"—calling back into his own soft echo, his voice reverberating from the staircase angles above them—"maybe some reason, she was starting to look like trouble to him. Trying to put him in a corner. Could be she pushed our hypothetical guy a little too hard over this or that. Maybe something came up, and she just got to be trouble." At the foot of this flight, Marquez turned again to wait. He seemed to enjoy racing down the stairs, forcing Evan to catch up. "Hey, it happens. It happens, and very respectable guys—"

" 'Hypothetical guys.' "

"That's right. They lose their tempers, feel they have to get out of situations any way they can. And, Evan, don't think things like your old VA stuff, that 'episodes of violence,' that 'poor impulse control,' don't think that kind of thing wouldn't come up with our hypothetical guy. I don't give a damn how old that information is, how far back."

"*Jesus Christ.* Listen," Evan said, "speaking as your 'guy,' Lieutenant, I assure you . . . I *assure* you you can forget all that 'hypothetical' crap. You are wasting your time. You're wasting my time." It seemed to Evan he was being very reasonable; he certainly wasn't smiling, certainly didn't feel like laughing anymore. All that had turned to anger that seemed to make the air vibrate around him. It gave him trouble catching his breath.

Marquez drew on his cigarette a last time, dropped it on the landing's worn wood and stepped it out. "Hey, I sure hope that's so, Evan. —And I know the other thing's unlikely. Really, it's unlikely. It would be such a dumb thing for you to do, that frankly I would be embarrassed for you if you did it. . . . My opinion? My opinion it was probably junkie meatballs after all. But that's just my opinion—not shared by all."

"Not shared by who?"

"Well, for example, you know your Connecticut cops up there? Sergeant Milano talked to those Fairport people—see if they had anything, you know, any record of problems you may have had and so forth. . . . Just familiarizing ourselves, find out what we're dealing with and so forth. Strictly routine. But now—remember what I said about how cops think?— now *those* guys are interested."

Marquez shook his head. "Small-town cops, always dreaming about a big case, catching some leading citizen stepping on his dick." He shook his head again, smiling at the dreams of small-town policemen. "So, I wouldn't plan any trips flying to Brazil right away"—he started down the last flight of stairs—"get the locals excited."

Evan followed Marquez down, and found himself anxious to keep up, catch him at the bottom of the stairs—as if it were important not to let the detective get away from him. "Lieutenant, I don't give a damn how it looks to you or the Fairport police or anyone. —Listen to me! . . . I had nothing to do with Sanchia's death. I had no reason to do anything like that. The only, the *only* thing I feel responsible for, is getting her involved at all. I do feel responsible for that."

Marquez, his hand on the first-floor fire door's heavy handle, waited while Evan came down to him. "You know, Evan, I'd like to ask you something—and you don't have to say a word. You can tell me to take a hike and not say a word, you understand?"

"Lieutenant, you can ask me any goddamn thing you want. Just get to it."

"OK. Here's what I'd like to know—just for my own personal satisfaction. What I'd like to know is, when did Ms. Fuentes tell you? That, I would like to know."

"When did she tell me what?"

"When did Ms. Fuentes tell you she was going to have a baby?" Marquez watched Evan with a bird's bright attention. "Medical examiner's office called in to us a couple hours ago, people actually got their work done fast, for a change, and they say that poor girl was almost two months gone."

". . . You're lying."

"I wouldn't lie about a thing like that, Evan. That, I wouldn't do. Just wondered when she told you."

"She . . . didn't tell me."

"No?"

"She didn't tell me."

". . . If you say so," Marquez said, pushed down on the handle, and swung the heavy door open.

Evan walked through shifting groups of police and civilians (some in handcuffs), their noise and traffic. As he passed, these sounds seemed to grow less and less, until he felt he walked in silence down a corridor of glass, transparent but unbreakable.

At the corridor's end, Evan saw Catherine, holding her largest purse, rise from a crowded bench to watch him come to her.

All through late-evening rush-hour traffic to the Bruckner Expressway—having assumed the right to drive them home (he a moral invalid, diseased with stupidity and treachery)—Catherine perched in silence behind the Range Rover's big wheel. She always used the bulky dark-blue vehicle driving into the city, as if its heft and capability might protect her from New York surprises.

On the expressway, settled into its swift river of traffic, she suddenly said, "What in God's name ... what in God's *name* have you been doing?" Gently pounding the steering wheel with a small white right fist.

"I've become ... since I saw the Fonsecca girl fall, I've become involved. I didn't intend to be. Tried not to be. Those people—the Rao people—have simply kept pushing matters. And now this...."

" 'Peripheral involvement, as a member of the firm.' Didn't you tell me that? Isn't that what you told me?" Small fist striking the steering wheel again.

"I didn't want to frighten you."

"And you've also been 'involved' with that dwarf Hispanic thing—that spic out of your office that was killed. So I have to go down and get you out of a police station! What ... what the hell am I going to tell *Beth*? 'Beth, your father has been screwing ... screwing a little spic whore from the office'—and for God's sake I *knew* her; she looked like a damn monkey for Christ's sake! 'And she got herself murdered in some sort of drug thing, and I've just had to go and get your father at the police station.' "

Catherine stared along the highway as if searching for something to run into. "How would you like to explain this to your daughter, if you appear in some disgusting New York paper, or on television? Would you like to do that? Mention it to people at the club? Or will I have to do that, lie about it so she'll still respect ... respect her wonderful handsome father who plays such a hot game of polo and is such an ass that he is only comfortable screwing a thing like that." Catherine seemed to rest then, leaned forward braced on the wheel, and had nothing more to say.

When they reached the New England Thruway, the evening was darkening to night, and Evan felt more comfortable sitting in shadow, watching other cars traveling beside them ... then slowly pulling ahead, or more often dropping behind; Catherine was a steady fast driver. Evan imagined himself in one of those cars—in any of them. He thought he would do better in any car than this one.

He glanced over at Catherine, and she noticed it. He saw her face grow grimmer in the dash's dim light, and wished he hadn't looked at her, had kept looking out the window.

"Evan," Catherine said, watching the road, "you have been asleep for years. For years I have been waiting for my handsome ... *talented* husband to wake the fuck up, so I might have something more interesting to do with my life than shoot goddamned clay pigeons. ... And now, it seems sleeping beauty *has* been awake—he's been a goddamned *fireball* in New York. Casanova, Sherlock Holmes—"

"It hasn't been like that—"

"How dreary," Catherine said. "How boring. ..."

"I lied to you. And I betrayed you with a very nice young woman, who was very fond of me. I betrayed both of you, in different ways ... and I have no excuse for it."

"Boring. ..."

"Catherine, her murder is ... beside all that, and none of it has been my fault—it's simply happened to me! A sort of grotesque accident, a New York *thing* ... seeing that girl fall, becoming involved with those people. Just the wrong place at the wrong time—and it has certainly killed Sanchia, no matter what the police think."

Catherine swung the Range Rover right, surged past a station wagon, then swung left again, into the speed lane. "Oh, for God's sake—stop trying to turn your nasty little lunch-hour screw into part of some big drama. It is truly painful to listen to. I heard all that this afternoon, from the police—your *second* visit to them, apparently. I mean, I am sorry, but your little love object was bumped off by a bunch of druggies— probably her own countrymen—who also killed an old man in the same building and robbed several apartments! I know it; the police know it—they checked your nonsense *out,* Evan! And they are definitely not interested in any more fairy tales. They think you're a nut case, by the way, if that's of any interest to you . . . thanks to those months you spent rotting in that VA hospital. —Months I spent in agony for you. I was the crazy one; I would have done anything for you. You broke my heart every goddamn day in that hospital. You were dead, Evan. It was just your corpse walking around." Catherine took a deep breath . . . drove a little slower.

"—And that nurse, Joyce Bonner? She was the one who first called you my 'Sleeping Beauty.' At the time, I thought that was charming. . . . I didn't realize you would never wake to any kiss of mine, Evan. And I'm not talking about fucking. We fuck like strangers—you do realize that? Like strangers having a good screw. Very hot *fucking.* . . ."

Evan saw by passing headlights that Catherine was crying, or had been crying a little while ago. There were tears on her face reflective as drops of gold, but she looked furious. "And speaking of fairy tales, your firm's lawyer, Springman, told me on the phone he was definitely not interested in hearing any of them, either. 'Complication,' is what he said. 'We don't need more complication.' I called him when I thought they might be going to arrest you—which would probably have served you right. I think one of the detectives believes you had her killed."

She speeded up, tapped the horn. "Oh, come on, you idiot. This is the fast lane.... Counselor Springman, by the way, declined to come down to the station house; which makes me think Ward & Breedon might very well do without your services if you make much more of an ass of yourself—after which, you can devote yourself entirely to sailing and polo and go right back to sleep, Evan."

"... Catherine, that officer thinks I may have done it ... because Sanchia was pregnant. And I knew nothing about that, Catherine, I give you my word of honor. She hadn't told me."

Catherine said nothing, seemed to concentrate on her driving, staring ahead through a red swarm of taillights.

"—And I am so ... I am so terribly sorry to have hurt you this way."

Holding the wheel with her left hand, Catherine suddenly leaned over toward him and hit him in the face backhanded, with her right fist.

Evan saw a flash of light in his left eye as she hit him, and slowly put his hand up in case she hit him again. Then he put his hand down. It seemed improper to guard himself against her.

Neither of them said anything the rest of the way home.

chapter 10

....

After the first silent half hour in the house—Catherine's only conversation an apology to Mrs. Hooper for being back so late for dinner—Beth came up to the bedroom, and trying to drawl as older Fairport girls did, said, "I suppose you two are fighting about something. . . ." Then stood by their bedroom door, frightened, waiting for an answer.

"Something bad happened in the city, Beth," Evan said. "A woman in my office was killed in her apartment—and it's upset both of us."

"Who was it?"

"Miss Fuentes."

"The little one," Catherine said. "The little ugly one."

"Oh, I remember her. . . . What happened?"

"Burglars," Evan said.

"Now, that's enough—let's go down and help Mrs. Hooper get dinner on the table. It's late, and you have homework to do."

"Mother, I've already *done* my homework. . . ." And Beth trailed Catherine out—relieved that the trouble was only a distant murder of a distant person, and not her parents in argument. . . .

Evan went into the bathroom, closed the door, and

profoundly relieved to be alone, sat on the toilet with
his eyes closed, trying to think of anything but Sanchia, how she'd stared at him, her savage dead face exactly the one the false policeman had made, portraying
his murderous goddess.

Evan managed, after a while, to think of his ponies
instead of Sanchia, closed his eyes, and imagined
stroking Dodo, leaning against the warm animal side to
rest. . . .

He began to feel uneasy, then gradually sick . . . then
sicker, and had to turn and kneel to vomit into the
bowl. He'd eaten nothing since morning except a bite
of the McDonald's hamburger the police had brought
him, and the seizures twisted his stomach so severely
that straining, he watched for blood, but saw nothing
but watery bile.

After a while, he got to his feet and flushed the toilet, then went to the sink and rinsed his mouth, his
hands trembling as he cupped water in them.

When he came out of the bathroom, he found Catherine sitting on the bed, composed, attentive as a child,
her hands tucked under her thighs as if it were a chilly
evening.

"Are you all right?"

"Yes."

"Was that a mourning vomit, Evan? . . . Or shame?"

"Regret," Evan said, walked past her out of the bedroom, and down the stairs into the distant sounds of
Beth's voice, then Mrs. Hooper's—and at the foot of
the staircase, faint odors of dinner warming in the
kitchen. Broiled chicken, sweet potato . . . and probably with succotash, a Monday standby.

After dinner, a quiet dinner, with squash rather than
succotash—during which he pretended to eat, and
maintained conversation with Beth about school and

about an improbable boyfriend, Jake Tobey (a boy so shy he could hardly speak)—Evan went to the den. Went in, shut the door, then sat at his desk and tried to think of nothing but the Conners' saltbox ... its small addition. He worked for almost two hours, planning it fairly thoroughly, including trim.

Finished, he turned off the desk light, undressed, and lay on the sofa's cool leather in T-shirt and shorts, chilly under an afghan. The night wind blew gently through a half-open window, scented by woods, and the salt of the Sound. . . . Then Evan thought of Sanchia, of their child, and found such a tide of shame rising in him that he couldn't weep for them, hadn't earned by love and attention the right to weep. Not even for the agony she'd suffered.

He'd cried the night Beth was born; by commitment earned the tears of joy. But not yet the tears of sorrow. Evan lay in darkness, his eyes ... his throat aching. Then he turned over, settled into the sofa's soft cushions in refuge, and went to sleep as if nothing new and worse could come to him. . . .

Deep, deep into the night, he dreamed he woke to distant music, barely audible, drifting through the den . . . and thought the kitchen radio had been left on.

Then, after a little while of dream-listening to what sounded like some very faint classical piece for the flute ... with perhaps soft drums under . . . he seemed to wake, tossed the afghan aside and sat up in darkness complete, the moon apparently down.

There was some soft music playing. A flute. . . . A tapping drum measuring out the melody.

Evan got up and walked out of the den into the hall—bumped the doorway with his left shoulder; not yet morning; no light at all.

He drifted down the hall—brushing his fingertips

along the right-side wall to stay oriented—came to the kitchen doorway, stood, and still heard the flute, but from outside.

He found he was at the back door then, opened it, opened the screen . . . and stepped out on the stoop into dreamed starlight and cool air. The stars were scattered like sugar against a night sky darker blue than black, and Evan could see by their delicate light a fair distance across the back lawn . . . down into his grandmother's Chinese garden.

The music was there—or farther, in the boathouse, and he couldn't recall if he'd turned the radio completely off after he and Willie had sat out, days ago, listening to jazz. . . .

There were no insects shrilling in the dark, no sigh of wind from the Sound, though he could smell salt in the night air. Some breeze was blowing, though—Evan could see branches moving in darkness down in his grandmother's garden. One branch moving as if in time to the music . . . a distant branch in shadow that became a long misshapen arm with an awkward elbow as he watched, moving in time to the flute and drum.

Evan stood in starlight, the softest light, and was able to see several branches moving down there in the oddest angular way, certainly in time with the music. And, as if he'd watched just long enough, all the branches came together in uncertain light and he saw a spider—but large as a woman—a huge spider standing upright on two long back legs, and doing a deeply rhythmic dance that turned it and turned it with its furry arms or legs so it slowly cartwheeled over and folded into itself then pulsed and rose again and positioned and repositioned, stretched and crawled along, then rose upright again and danced to such strong rhythms in so strange a way that Evan's heart began to hurt him, and he saw a white face above where its legs came together—a face small at this distance, but not small, not distant enough for its eyes to be unseen— black eyes in a white face among its legs, that gazed at him while the monster danced.

Evan said something to himself, dreaming, but didn't hear it and backed away. Away and back through the screen door and door, back across the kitchen in the dark. Then he was afraid if he kept retreating, the thing would come dancing up the lawn and into the house, the kitchen. Dancing so powerfully, so perfectly, shaggy angled legs rippling in motion as it came down the hall in slow scuttling to that plangent music. Its white face watching as he went back and back, so it danced after him to the stairs . . . then climbing up after him . . . dancing, dancing up the stairs in a really wonderful way, almost beautifully as the music sounded so much faster, beautifully to the drumbeats swift as horses' hooves. And then, in the upstairs hall, would follow him no longer—would leave him, leave him alone and not follow, not watch him anymore— would turn and stop instead to dance before Beth's door.

Evan had stood on the Fairport platform—had nodded to Mick Pierce, said good morning to Ted Humphreys—then hadn't boarded the seven-thirty-five train. He'd stood watching while the train was in the station, then as it slowly pulled out down the tracks. He stood there, occasionally folding and unfolding the *Wall Street Journal* to read about the national money supply.

When he finished that article, Evan walked back through the station to the parking lot, unlocked the Lexus, and sat behind the wheel for a while, listening to the car radio. They were playing some Bud Powell sides.

Evan thought of driving home . . . then decided not to, got out of the car, locked it, and walked back to the station platform.

He took the next train in, and sat in the aisle away from the window, reading a different article in the paper, reading about debentures as he rode. He was traveling, it seemed to him, from sunshine country certain to fade more completely with each departure into an irrecoverable past—leaving that country and approaching another, darker, whose time was come. There, as he drew nearer, the train's contrapuntal sounds might blend with others—the distant thump and tapping of small-arms fire; the harsh rattle of helicopters . . . their mini-guns' coarse zipping sounds as they swayed across a dark horizon.

Evan avoided looking at Sanchia's desk, avoided looking into people's faces as he walked by and into his office. It occurred to him it might become impossible to continue working at Ward & Breedon. To forget—then remember—expecting her to pause at his office door . . . to catch up with him outside, at lunchtime. How could he shop at Bien Sûr anymore? Have to walk all the way up to Dean & Deluca. . . .

Evan sat at his desk, thought of going over the Hartford building, or looking at the Greggs' house plans—they'd submitted a bastardized Lloyd Wright plan (apparently by some California "designer") of a twenty-room two-story for a waterfront lot at Southhampton, and Ward had left a note for him with the drawings. *Evan—Please transform these into something less embarrassing. I will finish. H.W.*

Evan thought of going over those plans, then decided not. . . . He wondered if the police might be right, after all, and tried to imagine two hoodlums, worn and nervous junkies. Black men. Tried to imagine them tangled with Sanchia, wrestling, contorting that small body as it pleased them ... somehow muffling shrieks as one came grinning in from her small kitchen, having broken her chair (her only kitchen chair), broken it and was bringing in the length of leg, its end splintered. ... Then the other man, as she struggled, hitting her in the face, hitting her hard several times, swift slugging punches as if he were fighting a man. And forcing her thin legs apart, reaching down to spread her wide for the other one to fumble with, fit the sharp wood at that small place, then grunt with the great effort it required to force that thickness in and up ... and deeper as she tried to scream, convulsing—while, murmuring comments, instructions to each other, they labored over her.

The effort to imagine this made Evan close his eyes and grip the edge of his desk as if his balance was gone. And imagining it as thoroughly as he could bear to, still felt he'd imagined wrong, that it hadn't been done by those men, and not that way. It made him, sitting with his eyes tight shut, more and more angry that the truths of her dying—how it had been accomplished, and by whom—he would never be certain of. ...

He opened his eyes and saw Pete Talbot standing in the office doorway.

"You OK?"

"Fine. ..."

"They want us upstairs," Pete said. "Moral support." He wore a black armband for Sanchia.

As Evan followed Talbot to the stairway, Swann and the draftspeople, who'd seemed to know nothing about Evan and Sanchia when she was alive—alive only yesterday—now appeared to know everything, and watched Evan from their desks as he walked by as if expecting him to commence to weep, stagger in the aisle, perhaps fall down. . . .

"We do want to save money on the building—but not in the public areas, and not where longevity is concerned." Two senior Hartford bankers had come to town—both handsome men (one balding), and very tall in summer-weight suits. The balding one was doing their talking. "We don't want to save money on the stuff that counts."

Pete Talbot, sitting with Evan on a cream leather loveseat—set right-angle to the long sofa bearing both bankers—sighed softly in boredom.

"So—a handsome structure of obvious quality, and well built." Henry Ward stood alongside Clive's high draftsman's stool; Clive perched there, an aging bird. Ward was present, apparently, out of respect for the capital position of the Hartford bank. "Well built, but no cash to be wasted on the clerical drones in the back offices."

The executive who wasn't losing his hair smiled pleasantly. He was sitting, long legs crossed, very much at ease. "That's a little harsh, Henry. Let's just say there are areas where some extra expenditure is called for—and others where restraint is common sense and good business."

"Right," the balding man said. "Exactly. For instance, the parking-garage entrance is right beside the front entrance, and that . . . that doesn't seem, from the preliminary plans, to make the sort of impression we'd like the building to make."

"Evan?" Henry Ward gestured slightly with his left hand, introducing a response.

"Gentlemen, banking isn't primarily a walk-in business anymore, as of course you know better than I." . . . Evan found he felt better now, talking to strangers. His voice, however, sounded odd, as if what he was saying had been recorded earlier, was now being played back. "We were raised when it *was* a walk-in business, and naturally we have that expectation—a formidable front entrance, usually classical or massively modern. But we're designing your bank—not for yesterday's customer, but for today's and more important, for tomorrow's. . . . Tomorrow's customer is going to drive, and he or she is going to want to drive as *close,* and as *convenient* to business as possible. Tomorrow's customer will be more and more reluctant to get out of his car at all—particularly downtown. Safety will be a concern. Convenience will be a concern. . . ." He felt much better, talking. "I don't mean that your customers won't want a bank to look solid, even formidable—but they'll want convenience and safety more."

"And," Talbot contributing, having some say, "I understand more and more banking business is being done by women. Which means that safety becomes of prime importance. —I think Evan's done a hell of a job with that plan."

"At the same time," the balding man apparently the nay-sayer of the two, "we don't want our downtown branch, our main offices, to look like a shopping-center drive-through. This building is supposed to *represent* the bank."

"Evan . . . ?" Henry Ward made his small permitting gesture again.

Evan was happy to be distracted from thinking of anything else—pleased to be called on again, like a bright student in elementary school. ". . . All right, let's see if we can't split the difference. I'll come up with a redesign on the entrance. Enhance it, see that it's a little more striking. And we'll leave the parking garage inlet very simple in comparison—so the building will make the sort of impression the bank wants, but not at the cost of customer convenience."

"Seems sensible to me." Clive's first words, while he shifted on his uncomfortable stool.

"Seems sensible to me, too," said Henry Ward. "Phil?"

"Well," the balding man said, "we'd have to see it. It really does have to have an important, very downtown look. . . ."

"For Christ's sake," Evan said, surprising himself by becoming impatient with the man so quickly, "you're bankers. Haven't you seen the projections for your 'downtown' in the next decade, the next two or three decades? I looked those up. The city's figures—reading back thirty years, projecting thirty years in the future. Your 'downtown' is going to be *black*. It's going to be dirty and dangerous. If you have any customers coming down there at all, they're going to be driving, and they're going to be very reluctant to get out of those cars!"

"Evan. . . ."

"—You people are dreaming of a nineteen-fifties downtown bank. But this is not the nineteen-fifties, and never will be again."

"*Evan*. . . ."

"What you should be building down there is a fucking fortress—if you were smart. Reinforced concrete, slit windows, emergency generator and all that crap. —You people need to wake the fuck up!"

Having said something that seemed so direct and sensible, Evan was disconcerted at the expressions he saw on all their faces. They looked like startled children, and he supposed he'd frightened them, insulted them—something. "I'm sick of this shit," he said, stood up, and walked out of the office.

He heard Ward's voice behind him. ". . . apologize

for that. We've all been upset. There's been a death—one of our employees was murdered in her apartment on Sunday. . . ."

Evan went down the first flight of stairs, then stopped at the landing and leaned back against the wall. In this simple space, painted white—the steps rising up, the other flight coming down. Ceiling angled. . . . This space was simple enough to be comforting. No window. He wished he could stay here for a week, more than a week. Months. Stay here until everything outside was solved.

But he rested there only a few minutes, then walked down to the second floor and past the draftspeople's desks toward his office.

"Mr. Scott!" Lilly Basco, one of the structural people—a plump middle-aged woman, fairly new to the firm—was sitting at her desk, holding her phone up to him. ". . . Someone's calling you on my line. They called a little while before. . . ."

"Thank you, Lilly. —Hello?"

"*Wake-up call number twoooo . . . !* And I do hope we're in a better humor today." Traffic sounds, another pay phone. ". . . No comment, Mr. Scott? No bad language?"

Evan said nothing, oddly relieved to hear the fat man's chuckling voice, to be reassured of its reality.

"—Ah, no ready reply, and no bad language." The fat man was calling from a busy corner. "You've been a slow learner, is it? But you've learned at last, by example of the so charming little Spanish lady? . . . Oh, I do hope so." A bus, some heavy vehicle was passing the fat man's phone booth. "Now, this is what we would like you to do. We would like very much for you to get in touch with the police—for the *last* time—and we would like you to tell them what a silly man you've been, how foolish, how mistaken in everything you've said. And, of course, that would be in the form of a sworn affidavit. . . . If you do that—precisely that, and today—and if you keep your mouth absolutely shut hereafter, it may . . . it *may* not be necessary to wake you a third time." And hung up.

Evan's office phone rang as he walked in, and he thought the fat man might have something else to say, but it was Clive, calling from upstairs.

"Evan . . . Evan, I'm sure, after that outburst up here, that you would have to agree some action needs to be taken. I'm very, very sorry you're having such a difficult time. Henry and I are both very concerned about you. . . . Evan?"

"Yes, I'm here."

"Concerned about you. But we do feel something has to be done. We cannot, we really cannot have this sort of behavior in a business environment. It is simply not *on*. And I'm certain you agree with that."

"No, I don't, Clive. I don't agree with that. I'm tired of telling fools what they need. I'm tired of doing that and not being listened to."

"Well . . . I think we *can* agree that 'tired' is the operative word here—and Henry and I would like you to take a rest, Evan. A serious rest, and, if you and Catherine think it would be helpful, perhaps some counseling to control what seems to me to be very self-destructive behavior. Really, terribly self-destructive."

"Bullshit."

". . . I'll ignore that—and I do understand now, that there are some . . . specially tragic elements to Miss Fuentes's death where you're concerned. Anyway, Henry and I would like you to take six weeks, or more, if necessary. Take that time from right now as a leave of absence. A time to get yourself together, get some rest. To simply relax."

"Why don't you just fire me, Clive?"

"We're not going to do that, Evan. You're on a leave of absence—at . . . oh, half-salary. A leave of absence. Go over to France and look at cathedrals, or whatever you care to do. Get some rest."

"I don't need rest. I've been resting for years."

"Yes, well . . . then some diversion. Whatever. And when you're better, feeling absolutely yourself again, in a month or two, we'll expect you to call in and come back to your desk. You'll find it exactly as you left it. . . ."

Outside the building, Evan carried his briefcase in one hand and, in the other, a shopping bag borrowed from Lilly Basco filled with pens, pads, graph paper, his notebook computer and the photograph of Catherine and Beth. Down the steps, he turned to the right to avoid the old man at the newsstand—but heard the small access door slam, footsteps hurrying after him.

"Oh, sir! It is Mr. Scott—"

"Yes," Evan said, and turned as the old man came up to him. The Indian was almost as tall as Evan, must have been a big man, thick through the shoulders when he was younger.

"And the police, sir—will they be helping or will they not?"

"They might have helped if you'd come with me. Now, just leave me alone and go on about your business, Mr. . . . Lal." Evan walked away, and after a pause, heard the old man come trotting after him.

"Ram Dass Lal, Mr. Scott. Ram Dass. . . ."

"Very well. Ram Dass Lal. . . ." Evan kept walking.

"Call me Ram Dass."

"Listen—"

"Ram Dass."

Evan, tired of being run after, stopped and stepped into a failed gallery's dark entranceway. "Listen, you . . . 'Ram Dass,' if you had just come with me, it would have helped—it might have. Then the police might have done something. Because you didn't, you helped those people get away with that. And now they've murdered someone else. A friend of mine."

"Oh, yes, that is certainly so—the little lady who worked in this building. Her picture was in two of my newspapers this morning. It was certainly the Raos who have killed that little lady." Ram Dass sighed. "But Mr. Scott, it would have made no difference if I had come to the police; please believe me. Was there evidence? There was not. Were they believing you—a sahib, a white man and respectable American citizen? No, I wager they did not." He shrugged, raised both hands and held them out, empty. "And would they have believed me, a stranger, an old man and a Hindu? No, I wager they would not have done. They would have called the immigration police instead, and then I would have been in so great difficulty. I am here as a visitor, now, for four years—and so I would be in great difficulty, and could never become a citizen."

"I believe we're talking about murder, here, Mr. . . . Ram Dass—"

"Yes, 'Ram Dass,' or you may call me 'Dass.' "

"We're talking about a . . . about killing a young woman. And frankly, compared to that, I don't give a goddamn about your visa problems."

"You think I am a coward, Mr. Scott."

"I don't know what you are, and I don't care. Now, I'm going to get a cab, and I'd prefer you stop following me down the street."

"But I'm not a coward! A man and another man came to me last evening, right there on my corner. Hindus—I could smell no meat on their breath at all. And these men threatened to kill my daughter-in-law! And what do you think of that?"

"This really happened?"

"I am not a coward, Mr. Scott. And not being a liar, either."

Evan, tired of holding the briefcase and shopping bag, put them down against the entranceway wall. "All right. I didn't mean that you were a coward, Mr. ... Ram Dass."

"Just 'Dass.' "

"—Or a liar. What were these men like?"

"Well, one was small, very dark—Dravidian, I believe, very dark. An ugly little man. The other person did all their talking for them, and he was, oh, very jolly. He was a very jolly person—fat as a man who is lending money."

"What did he say?"

"He wanted to know what that young man was saying to us, when we went to him in the street as he was dying. And I told him he said nothing to us, but this fat man just smiled and said, 'Nothing? Not even a few last words? Not a phrase? Not even a single little word? Not a peep?' And I said, 'Nothing,' and this fat man smiled as if I were lying.

"—He said, 'We know you, Mr. Ram Dass Lal, and we know of your son in Arabia, doing computer work for those savages. And we know of Vashti, your daughter-in-law, the woman of your house.' " An uncomfortably good imitation of the fat man's chortling speech.

"—And I said, 'Then you ought to know better than to be saying a respectable woman's name in the street.' And he said, 'We can do worse than that, worse than rudeness if you speak to our American architect again, if you speak to anyone else about what should not be spoken of. We can kill her.' And I said—and then I did lie, I lied deliberately—'Please, do me that favor and I will be in your debt—because I chose her for Mandu,

and she has been the most complete failure, which re-
flects on me in the worst way. She has revealed herself
to be a nasty woman, overbearing and cruel and a bad
cook, who is not letting me smoke my pipe in my own
room.'

"And when he heard me say that, this jolly man
laughed. And I said, 'You can laugh if you like, but if
you go to the Bronx to kill my daughter-in-law, you
had better take help, and not approach her in the
kitchen, where the knives are.' Then the man laughed
again, and said, 'Now you are telling fibs. We know
better; we know the little lady is very amiable. But in
any case, if we do not deal with her, we shall deal with
you directly.' And I said, 'I'm not young, but you may
still find me difficult to deal with.' And he laughed and
went away with his friend—a very jolly man."

"Did he have a car?"

"You want the license plate, isn't it?—No, no car,
Mr. Scott. He walked; he walked like a sailor. . . ." And
the old man rocked back and forth, took two sauntering
steps. "Just as I, I walk like a soldier, and I should,
since I was thirty years in the Army of India. Sergeant
major in the last year." The old man paused, seemed to
consider something. "Honorary, really, because I was
mustering out; I don't wish to be misrepresenting myself. . . . And I must make clear I lied about the woman
in my house, but the fat man was knowing it. It is true
that she doesn't allow me to be smoking my pipe, and
it is also true that she is not a good cook—but those
things beside, I have no complaint about her. She's
very nice."

"I see. . . ."

"You are wanting to laugh—oh, yes. Is my way of
speaking English so funny as that, Mr. Scott?"

"No. No, you speak very good English."

"But with an odd accent, isn't it? . . . Amusing?"

"Perhaps a little—but still, very good English."

"Well, let me ask you something, Mr. Scott. Are you speaking the Hindi?"

"No."

"Oh—then Pushtu?"

"No."

"Hindustani? Urdu . . . ?"

"You've made your point."

"Well . . . my point, the point I am making to you is, if you did speak any of those languages, and did not have an amusing accent in any of them—then perhaps you might be justified in finding my English amusing. . . . Do I offend you?"

"Not yet."

"Ah, now there is an honest smile—a smile between men. And of honest amusement, not slyness. What I wished to ask you, Mr. Scott—if the police believed nothing, will do nothing—is what are you intending to do?"

"I don't know."

"You find it hard to believe that this could be happening—it seems so very strange?"

"Yes. Very strange."

"What a difference there is between us, between our peoples. You see, I find it very easy to believe—and for good reason. My father, who owned a small factory where shoes were made, he was killed by men precisely like these—*goondas,* in Calcutta. He refused to contribute, do you see? And he had an accident. He fell into an open sewer—rather, was thrown there—and was held under the filth with sticks until he drowned. My mother and I were told this by the police, who did nothing. And that is what happened to my father."

"I'm sorry."

"So am I, Mr. Scott. I was sorry then, and I am sorry now. —But now I am thinking of doing something about it. I am thinking of resisting them. Though I am not a fighting man; I was at the depot, a sergeant in stores, in supply do you see? The Vindhaya Horse, my very fine regiment, an old regiment. Of course, very few horses now. Lorries. Light tanks. . . ."

"Fighting, you'd be playing their game."

"But sir, Mr. Scott—we are both already playing their game, and losing. And these shits are by no means being finished with either of us. They certainly intend to kill me, and I mean no insult to Bengalis—there are many fine Bengali people—when I say that these particular Bengalis are men who keep their word."

Evan was home by midafternoon, and found the house empty—Beth still at school, Catherine out shooting or playing golf with Kelly Sims.

He left the briefcase and shopping bag on the entrance-hall bench, walked through the parlor and into the den. He opened the cabinet, poured three fingers of Scotch into a tumbler, and stood looking out at the side lawn as he drank it.

There was room to extend the garage for four cars . . . add a graveled turnaround. The stables that had stood there once had occupied even more ground, if the riding ring was included. There was a photograph on the den desk showing his grandfather, as a young child, riding a Morgan mare in that ring. His grandfather—in miniature jacket, breeches, and boots—looking very determined, a little boy with a man's decided face. . . .

Evan finished the Scotch, put the tumbler on the silver drinks tray, and walked out through the parlor into the hall and up the stairs to the second floor . . . then down that hall to the narrow service corridor and up narrower stairs to the old servants' quarters and attic steps. It was pleasant to be in the house alone, walking through streaks of sunshine lying across the old wide-board floors, grooved, pegged and fitted fine, then polished for ... two hundred and twenty-three years, on this top floor. Hot clarified tallow, linseed, and lemon oil, all hand-rubbed in. ...

Here, just beneath the roof—modern trimmed slate, not the original long slabs—the house's ancestry showed itself in massive barn joinery (first-growth chestnut and oak), notched and fitted mortise and tenon, key-cut to keep from slipping. All work by local builders—farmer-fishermen, their sailing crews and farm laborers—boatbuilders and barn builders to a man. They'd built as if time were an ocean to be sailed through every weather. ...

Evan went up the attic steps, pushed open an old pintle-hung door, and stood on rattling planks in a long chamber beneath the roof peak. The loose-laid floor was struck with sunlight in slender shafts through sawn soffit vents ... and spattered, in two places down the left, with small shit where swallows had maneuvered in from time to time.

Evan switched on the attic's row of four bare bulbs.

Trunks, wardrobes, chairs, and two old brass bed-steads, stacks of crates and labeled boxes ranged along the right ... ancient suitcases, cracked harness and tack, a box or two of old china ... several ranks of sheet-draped pictures Catherine had found no place for downstairs—including seven pictures of women who'd lived in this house. One of these painted by Eakins, the others by local men, less distinguished.

"I don't want those women looking over my shoulder," Catherine had said, though her great-aunts' house in Maine was a gallery of grim seafaring faces, the faces of their grimmer wives—many of whom had sailed with their husbands for years at a stretch on the

China trade, or killing whales off the Marianas ... biting leather straps so as not to scream when giving birth, the crew stomping barefoot at its work just above their heads. ...

Evan found his footlocker between two huge ancient wood-and-leather steamer trunks, and hauled it out.

The old combination lock was still snapped through its hasp. His birthdate had been the combination. Evan dialed right to three ... left to fourteen ... once around right and stopped at fifty.

He lifted the open lock away, flipped up the hasp, and raised the locker's lid to rear-echelon odors of Vietnam—mildewed jungle-green shirts and field pants, crumbling paper (notes, old letters, separation papers), and damp-spoiled leather. Boot polish, Brasso, spilled toothpowder, spilled aftershave, spilled Japanese brandy.

His Class A uniform, blue, red-striped, carefully folded and bulky in a big, stained paper bag. No cap. ... Beside the uniform, several photographs floated loose among folded green T-shirts, skivvies, tropical shorts. One group picture—of First Platoon, B Company—Evan set aside, avoided looking at. Then a photograph of company officers only. Glancing at that, Evan was startled at how young those men were— looking much more like high school seniors than college men and veteran Marine Corps officers.

—Young, and tired. He was there, standing beside Bobby French, and looking very young ... very tired. Hickman, Drexel, and Bruce Cummins. Hickman and Cummins had died in-country of Lieutenant's Disease—the Fatal Follow-Me's. So called by Bobby French, after Hickman had led out from an LZ at the head of his first squad, the chopper blades still swinging behind him, and received "numerous wounds, penetrating and ablating," that knocked him over, screaming like a rabbit. —Still screaming through the morphine (his intestines coiled out onto his lap) all the way back to base, while the corpsman in the copter soaked the guts with halazoned water to keep them moist.

Photographs of those young men, and two pictures of the same Vietnamese bar girl, looking twelve years old and grinning into the camera in front of the Bing-Bong bar in Danang. Evan couldn't remember her name . . . nickname had been Pokey.

Boot socks, and one pair of battered jungle boots, nylon mesh and rubberized leather, cleated soles still carrying crusts of red mud hardened to stone. . . . Beneath those, at the bottom of the locker, folded camouflage pants, two Class A shirts, some equipment webbing, and a plastic canteen wedged beside a fat rolled green issue towel, stained with oil.

. . . And in that towel when unrolled, like an odd heavy insect revealed in its cocoon, a Colt .45 semiautomatic pistol—its dull Parkerized finish so oily it looked wet. There were four empty magazines lying alongside it like nursing young, and two small, heavy, paraffin-sealed boxes of forty rounds, U.S. Government ball ammunition.

Beneath that, lay Sergeant Beckwith's knife.

A long wide leather scabbard, dark with old neat's-foot oil, was wrapped in a flaking yellow copy of the *Ia Drang Times*. And beside it, nested in more crumbling newspaper, Beckwith's knife, rescued from the corpse counters at Regiment—a Randall Classic Bowie, brass-hilted, its grip staghorn, its blade fourteen inches long, deeply curved and double-edged for six inches from the point. Thereafter, nearly wide and thick through as a cleaver.

Evan picked the heavy knife up, balanced it in his hand, then touched the bright blade's edge with the ball of his thumb. The bowie, its steel fine-honed and stropped as a straight razor, cut him there immediately, as if possessed by Beckwith's ghost, instantly aggressive and quick to teach hard lessons. —As he had in so many afternoons at base, behind the dump, dancing a knife fight with his lieutenant (their shadows in savage motion beneath them) as if he and Evan had not achieved, not received, quite enough damage in weeks of long-range patrolling. Fencing and feinting to three-cuts-and-out, their occasional blood cheered by a small audience of battle-weary potheads, dreamy on Buddha Grass.

Evan—depending on four years of saber fencing at Yale to offset Beckwith's speed and ferocity—had wielded a short issue machete in those practices, and recalled that mild steel's mild clang when it met the balanced weight of the bowie's bitter metal, its surgical sharpness. . . .

Now a small drop of blood trembled on its edge.

chapter 11

∙∙

The Dond, who slept at no set hour, lay in a white room, clean, bare, and bright. Its three lamps on, the room was washed with light. There were only cushions scattered through it—gaudy reds and blues and acid greens. But four carpets of more complicated colors were laid across the floor. These were tribal carpets, hand-loomed (three by women—the fourth, the finest, by blind boys).

The rugs told stories no one remembered, stories so ancient even the oldest pattern weavers had no notion what odd shapes meant, what angled patterns represented. In the smallest carpet, lying along the window wall (the window always shut, its blinds closed tight), there had been woven a silver lattice of irregular squares over a field of what seemed flowers, intricate knots in green and gold.

This carpet's story, of a chief's daughter who fell in love with a ram, and who lived with that handsome beast in winter in her sorrowing father's garden, in summer among the stone fences of high pasture, was now known to no one.

The Dond lay asleep, undisturbed by lamplight or the thrum of traffic through his shut window. He lay, mouth open, eyes closed, wrapped in his long brown coat as if about to be buried in it, shot in some high frontier skirmish. His snoring was deeply regular, harsh as if an animal were trying to learn to sing. And in his sleep, his age presented itself most clearly—beard growing grayer, the lines in his long face scored deep by savage weather.

He was not dreaming. And since he was not, the Dond awoke at once and completely when someone knocked at his door.

"Have I disturbed you, brother?" said Chandra Rao, standing in the hall, and his long face and dark eyes were sorrowful as a mourning god's.

The Dond knelt to him and kissed his feet.

"Come up and say good night to Beth." Catherine standing at the den door, already in her robe—this robe dark blue, nearly a gown, reaching almost to the floor. "And stay upstairs tonight. I'd rather we didn't upset her with this."

Evan had been drawing at the desk by the stained-glass azures and maroons of his great-grandmother's Tiffany lamp—working in a big sketch pad, outlining a new plan for the first floor of the unfortunate California-designed house, giving it a kitchen opening directly into its dining room at last. He put the pen down. "Catherine, I think we're in serious trouble."

"You're certainly in serious trouble, Evan." And turned to the door.

"I mean we may be in some danger—Beth, too."

"Oh, spare me."

"These people have no compunction about killing the children of anyone they think poses some sort of threat to them."

"Not only nonsense, but contemptible nonsense." And started out of the room.

"They've already murdered a child of mine ... when they killed Sanchia."

There was no expression on Catherine's face—it was still, contemplative for an instant in the soft lamp-light from the hall, before she stepped out and swung the den door closed behind her, as if on an empty room.

Evan put the sketch pad in the desk's center drawer, turned off the lamp, and followed Catherine out through the parlor, and up the stairs.... Beth stood watching them by her bedroom door in pajamas with teddy bears on them, old pajamas now too short in the leg, too short in the sleeve. She stood uneasy in her pajamas of two years before ... worn perhaps as magical garments to ward off a disquieting present, perhaps made too evident this evening.

Evan caught up with Catherine, put his arm around her waist—felt her pause an instant, then relax against him. "I thought the hyperactive Emily Wandsey was due to be a gossip guest overnight this week...."

"Daddy, Emily's still up at the Cape. She's coming Friday."

"Well," Catherine said, "when she stays over, if you two have to run through the house half the night—"

"We didn't—"

"If you have to stay up late, and you want to get something to eat, then please remember to wash your dishes when you finish. Mrs. Hooper doesn't need to be greeted by dirty dishes in the morning."

"We will...."

"Good night, sweetheart." Evan kept his left arm around Catherine, bent to gather Beth in his right, and hugged them both, drawing them to him—not caring for Catherine's anger or disappointment, caring only to be fenced by them on either side, bodies so different and so similar, the scent of their skins rich to his left, delicate to his right—holding them at either side as if their beauty might become an armor and a residence.

". . . That didn't fool her for a minute." Catherine from the bathroom.

"Listen—I think we're in serious trouble. Trouble in which the police are not likely to be any help at all. You and Beth should go up to Maine, to Aunt Nan's cabin. It's not property many people know about, and it's not in our name."

Catherine came out of the bathroom, took off her robe, draped it over the rocker's arms, and got into her side of the bed. She was wearing yellow pajamas. "Why don't you go up to the island—if the police don't object to your leaving the state. I think we can get along without you. . . . And Evan, let me tell you something. I think—I know—that already the local police have told their wives, their wives have told their friends, and their friends, beauty-shop people, whatever, are telling our friends all about New York. Your girlfriend getting herself killed, your involvement . . . the fact that you've been happily screwing that woman probably for years. And all my friends will know it, and they will all get a certain satisfaction from it. 'Poor Catherine—how humiliating for her. Evan busy screwing this little spic in New York. . . .' Let me tell you, I do not enjoy being the object of other people's sly nasty amusement. That has never happened to me before, and I don't like it. Now, whenever I meet anyone, the first thing . . . the first thing I think of is, Does she know yet? That is the first goddamn thing I have to think about when I meet my friends. . . . And it is your fucking fault."

Then reached up and turned off her bedside lamp.

. . . It was odd to be lying beside such a separate Catherine, knowing her untouchable. Of course, it

made him wish to touch her. He thought of her
ashamed before her friends—thought of placing an eccentric ad in the *Courier*. . . .

For a time, I had a relationship with a young
woman in New York. I was very fond of her, and
I haven't really recovered from her death.

Though I found things in Sanchia I had not
been wise enough to find in my wife, Catherine,
my love for my wife has been a constant and remains a constant. Our sexual relationship is and
always has been wonderful. She breaks my heart
with her beauty half a dozen times a day. She is
what the loveliness of woman has always meant
to me, and she has given us a spectacular child.

I am bitterly sorry that in seeking something
else, some difference, some more direct and ac-
cessible affection, I have wounded and betrayed
my wife. If any friend of Catherine's takes advantage of my betrayal to hurt and embarrass her,
they will only be revealing their own long-held
jealousy of a woman wiser, braver, more beautiful, and always better dressed. . . . Her husband,
Evan Scott.

. . . Evan decided to sleep for just four hours—it was
an old accomplishment that had worked very well in
the war. And having decided so, he breathed in Catherine's scent as a way of touching her. Breathed her scent
in with the odors of the night . . . and its sounds, insects and small frogs singing from the woods and
cove. . . . Then slept.

—And woke on time, he was certain, without checking the Vacheron's glowing dial. Woke to a cooler, quieter night, sounding only with Catherine's easy
breathing. —Listening to her, Evan wondered what

dreams she enjoyed, what dreams frightened her. She never discussed them. . . . Sanchia had related her dreams to him wide-eyed with excitement, as if they'd been adventures and actual. . . .

He lay for a while enjoying being awake in a world of sleep, then rolled out from under his light covers (folding them carefully back), sat up, took the flashlight from his bedside table, then reached down to slide its second drawer slowly, silently open. He picked the heavy pistol up, checked the safety with his thumb, stood, and strolled past the bed and around its foot to the bedroom door, finding the late moon's minor light satisfactory.

The Colt's weight rested in comfortably familiar conformation to his hand—its rectangular grip eased and rounded at its edges—though he'd killed only four people with it. All in two days snaking through a tunnel complex honeycombing the earth beneath Ka Moc, that nasty village. Work that Beckwith—dead then for nearly a year—would have enjoyed, though tunnel ratting was not their unit's specialty.

Walking down the stairs barefoot, at ease in boxer shorts and T-shirt, Evan recalled the first—a terrified VC, an older man who'd frozen crouched in a dirt niche twenty feet down, staring in horror as if Evan were a demon with a flashlight rising through the narrow trapdoor from an Oriental hell.

This older man had squealed, very much as a rodent or rabbit might, and commenced to handle an AK desperately—poor armament in such cramped quarters dripping loose dirt down on them.

Evan had shot him center mass—and as the man (looking even older) squatted staring into the flashlight's beam, mortally hurt, had shot him again neatly through the head, and the man had huddled and shit.

Deafened by his first shot, Evan had fired and seen the results of the second in mime.

Next had been a medic (from the brown cloth kit he'd left behind) writhing away into the dark down a steep tunnel two feet high, two feet wide, that was collapsing behind him. Evan had shot this man in the anus, or near it, and tired from hours of crawling through darkness the flashlight only momentarily relieved, had backed out on bleeding elbows and knees as the tunnel crumbled down and slowly, by degrees, silenced the shrieking.

Third had been a woman, a little nurse with a knife in a larger chamber lower down.

The fourth (happening the second day) he couldn't quite recall. Some man who'd shot at him twice out of the dark, and missed. A man who'd seemed to sigh with relief after Evan killed him.

The fifth (end of the second day) he hadn't shot. The Colt's first round, a miss, had jammed stove-piped, and the man—a boy—had come out of the dark with a bayonet, stabbed into Evan's ribs, but caught his point on bone (worth two weeks, after, in Japan). That one, Evan had killed with Beckwith's bowie. One of only two men he was to kill with the knife—hand-to-hand contact (even in long-range patrolling, even in night work) so unusual in a war of mortars and sniping, booby traps, ambushes. . . .

"I used to carry one of them good Ek stickers," Beckwith had told him one steaming afternoon in monsoon rain, while leeches swam like stretching drops of ink through the flooded ditch they lay in. "All the knife a guy needs, usual way things go. Most people carry a big knife, they got a little dick. But then we started patrollin' in the hills, an' some of those VC up there carry bush choppers long as your fuckin' arm. Good luck you tangle assholes with one of those mothers, an' all you got is a sticker. So, I went major metal." A pause then while the sergeant had said, "Ouch!" and raised his left arm from the water to expose a very large leech fastened to his wrist.

"What are you, a fuckin' piranha?" And drawing the subject of his conversation from its submerged scabbard, had surfaced it like Excalibur and sliced the leech away in a swift bright flash of steel, a blurt of blood. A movement that brought a quick little burst of fire popping, thumping along the path. "—Just said fuck that, man. Gave the Ek to Norrie Thomas—shit lot of good it did him—and sent to Orlando for the biggest bowie they make, Swedish fuckin' tool steel." Beckwith had then settled back into the ditch's water (rich with sewage run off from the flooded field behind them) like a stocky alligator in rotting field green sinking into its element. It was one of the sergeant's essential infantry talents, making himself almost always comfortable and at home. . . .

It seemed to Evan the most natural of all walks to take, to amble down through his quiet house through a quiet night, with the flashlight (carried switched off) in his left hand, the Colt in his right. He thumbed the pistol's hammer back, left the safety on . . . and walked silently along the hall . . . paused to listen, standing against the wall, listening between the measured ticking of the grandfather clock. Then went into the den . . . and after a while, out of it and into the hall again. Paused to listen, then barefooted down the ancient thick Turkish carpet runner to pegged old wide-board oak in the kitchen—from roughly soft to smoothly hard.

It took Evan some time more, a restful time, to patrol his house. Then he patrolled the grounds. There was moonlight, but not too much. . . .

After an hour or so, he came up to bed, sat and put

the flashlight and pistol away, wiped his damp bare feet on the coverlet, then slid beneath the covers next to his wife—and slid, as if in continuation of that movement, into a pleasant dream.

The second squad was marching in extended order— none of them dead. He was walking tail-end Charlie with the slight radioman, Billy Torrance, and was saying something to him—he couldn't remember what— and then, when he looked up along the scattered line of route-stepping infantry, saw one in an odd helmet. One was swinging along in a blaze-orange hard hat, and he saw it was Josephine Fonsecca, pacing in work boots with her tool belt sagging at her hips, keeping good interval from Kershner, in front of her. . . . She turned to say something to the grunt marching behind, and it was the first time Evan had heard her speaking voice—at this distance rather high and fluting, a slender voice for so sturdy a young woman.

He felt such enormous relief at seeing her he said, "Thank God," and Torrance, handsome black face running sweat, turned and said, "What?"

"Thank God," Evan said, but couldn't recall why . . . and the second squad (one slighter marine bright-helmeted) ambled on, the men burdened with packs, ammunition belts, MG belts, canteens, 20-mil grenades and rifles, relaxed as much as mines and snipers would allow, marching in rotting sweat-silvered uniforms in extended interval along a paddy, through paddy country green as cut limes and shimmering with heat, with apprehension of gunfire. . . .

Breakfast was a pleasant meal, Beth apparently relieved as they stayed in routine, in the house and speaking, whatever their disagreement had been. . . . Catherine, in her blue robe, cooked bacon for them. And Evan made toast and talked tennis with Beth to watch her think, watch her eyes and mouth as she answered him.

Mrs. Hooper came in while Evan was dueling Beth with spoons over entrance to the marmalade pot—said good morning, and set a big brown paper sack on the counter beside the sink—various produce, red potatoes, Swiss chard, carrots and early tomatoes from her sister Evelyn's ever enlarging garden. Then unpacked these and stowed them while the Scotts finished breakfast.

"Do you want a cup of coffee, Mrs. Hooper?"

"No, Mrs. Scott, I don't. I had tea this morning, when I got up."

"Tea?" Beth, making an amused face at Evan, the family tea drinker. "I thought you didn't drink tea, Mrs. Hooper."

"I tried tea this morning, and I still don't like it. I tried Tetley's. Gerald likes that and I just don't see why." She tugged open the tin-lined potato bin under the knife drawer, and handed a dozen small redskins in one by one, each to a minor metallic note.

Midmorning—Beth gone to school; Catherine, after an hour of cool unspeaking, gone shopping in town— Mrs. Hooper came into the den and wandered, dusting bookshelves repeatedly, until Evan put down his pen and asked her if she wanted something.

"Mr. Scott, a man called me at my house this morning—called me at quarter to seven."

"Yes . . . ?"

"Person said he had a message I should give to you." Mrs. Hooper seemed to seek for something new to dust . . . chose the lamp table by the window. "And I told him if he had a message for Mr. Scott, he could just deliver it himself. That I wasn't a messenger boy."

"What did he say?"

"Oh, he just laughed. Thought he was funny. Some sort of foreigner."

Evan closed his notebook, shutting the California house away from assistance, at least for a while. "What was the message, Mrs. Hooper?"

"He just said you didn't do what they told you to do, and he was very surprised and disappointed. And I told him you didn't have to do a damn thing you didn't care to—and he could run up a tree and branch off. And he laughed and hung up. A jerk."

"Well . . . if that man calls again, Mrs. Hooper, don't talk to him."

"Oh, I wouldn't listen to that jerk again. He wasn't funny." Finished with the lamp table, Mrs. Hooper stood at a near attention in a flowered summer dress, spindly pale freckled legs descending to white Keds sneakers, her short-handled feather duster held at a sort of port arms. "—Calling people in the morning don't even know who the hell the man is. I should have let Gerald answer the phone. Gerald would have told him where to get off."

"Mrs. Hooper—"

"Edith." The first time in eleven years Mrs. Hooper had offered her first name to him.

"—Edith, I've had . . . a friend was killed in the city. And that man was probably involved—was certainly involved. I'm very sorry he troubled you."

"Foreigners don't trouble me, Mr. Scott. My people shot the britches off some English soldiers right down there in Salthaven. Cavalry troopers under that Major Clay. Anybody troubles us Hoopers or Wilsons, we trouble them right back." Narrow face expressing determination, brown eyes indignant, slightly bulging.

"Still, Mrs. Hooper—"

"Edith."

"—Edith, you need to stay absolutely out of this."

"I know about that city stuff"—Mrs. Hooper made a quick dismissive gesture with the feather duster that released a small soft cloud of sunstruck dust—"and nobody in the township except some fools on the police force, who were the dumbest boys in high school and haven't got any smarter, nobody believes for a minute you had a thing to do with that. . . . I guess a man can make a jackass of himself and hurt his wife to her heart and worry his little daughter half to death. I guess a man can make that kind of a jackass of himself and still not go around murdering a girl in her bed— and that's all I have to say about it."

Then, her bright dust cloud slowly swirling by the window, Mrs. Hooper left the room.

Evan sat at the desk a while longer, thinking only in passing of the fat Hindu hoodlum . . . threats. Of Sanchia, only for a few moments. He sat relaxed, almost daydreaming but never quite, and watched the sunlight falling radiant through the tall den windows . . . pouring in like molten gold and running, pooling . . . puddling in the room's Oriental carpet—a Persian carpet, faded scarlet, faded emerald, and very old.

Wearing loafers, jeans, shirt and windbreaker, Evan drove the silver Lexus to the station, waited, and took the eleven-forty train into New York. On the trip in, he saw no one he knew.

Rao Electric & Contracting was listed in the Fifties on the East Side. The Lederer Building. Perhaps out of habit, Evan left Penn Station, hailed—after several attempts—a cab that pulled over for him, and went downtown to Ward & Breedon. Not intending to go upstairs, or even into the building, but only to arrive there as a familiar point of departure. . . . Then walk those blocks where he and Sanchia had walked. Perhaps to discover he'd dreamed everything bad, and would now wake to good ... see Sanchia come out to lunch, looking for him.

And if he was given only a little control of the flow of hours, days—only some small influence over time— what he wished would be true; what he didn't, would not. Then he could correct all deaths—step between death and Jo Fonsecca. Between death and Sanchia. Could then (those young women being safe) row back through time as he'd rowed crew at Yale, stroking an oar of years to stand in furnace afternoons and monsoon mornings between his men and death, however it had come to them—in blast, or humming. Or twanging, hissing just above the grass.... He could shove Beckwith onto the path, away from the wide puddle of mines—and say, "Don't get your boots wet, Sergeant," so Beckwith, startled and annoyed (not liking to be touched, even by his officer), would shrug off Evan's hand and say, "Will you get fuckin' serious?" but walk on, his life saved for a doctor, perhaps, to signal an end to it fifty-three years later.

But even as a lord of time, Evan could only save them once, from a particular death. Jo Fonsecca, Sanchia, and all his men. Save them from that single death only—or else go mad, and roam time in desperation trying to prevent any dying by all those he knew. Above all, for Catherine and Beth. —Beth never to die, if he had to spend forever standing constant guard.... But then, who would be patrolling to keep death from him?

It was a five-dollar-and-thirty-five-cent cab ride; Evan left a dollar tip and got out at an intersection changed. Old Ram Dass's newsstand had been burned down. RAG HEADS GO HOME printed on the building wall beside it, in black spray paint. The words had been scrubbed, but not scrubbed away. There was no scorched smell from the remnant low rectangle of blackened plywood, black shrunken crumbled interior; the fire had been a day or two before.

Beyond it, halfway down the block and past the entrance to Ward & Breedon, a man in slacks and polo shirt was sitting on the level head of a red double-cap fire hydrant, smoking a pipe. Evan recognized Ram Dass as the old Indian recognized him, raised the pipe in salute, and beckoned him over.

"Do you see how clever they are, Mr. Scott? Hindu thugs"—he pronounced it "tugs"—"leaving *anti*-Hindu slogans when they destroy a man's business?" Ram Dass stood to shake Evan's hand.

"Yes, I saw it."

"I have returned to the scene of the crime, you see, even when it is not my crime. We are being such creatures of habit."

"I'm here by habit as well."

"Oh, I supposed you would be. . . . When my father died—when he was murdered—I went to that street, I went down that alley there, in Calcutta—oh, a hundred times. I mean it, absolutely one hundred times, as if one of those times he would surely come to me. And I knew, of course, he was already burned and with Darling Ganga, going down to the sea. I knew it, but I couldn't believe it, so I was coming back and back again to that alley. To the sewer there, I came back and back again. . . ."

"And in dreams."

"There you are! Now, you see, I knew you. I have definitely known you in a life before this, Mr. Scott— although of course I know Westerners don't believe a word of it. 'The statistics are all being wrong for everyone to have had a past life' is what they say. Even as a beetle or a moth or a frog. Statistics are all wrong for that.—But I am not giving a damn. It feels right to me."

"Dreams," Evan said, standing by the fire hydrant, watching people walk past in ignorance.

"Yes, dreams." Ram Dass bent to knock the dottle out of his pipe on the curb. "I ruin all my pipes this way; I am too rough with them. . . . My father was such a dignified man. Such a complete man. He was a *formidable* man. I never saw another person—not even my mother—shout at him, or treat him rudely. When the British buyers came to his factory—and it was not a large factory, and they were not important British businessmen; they were not gentlemen or officers. They were small businessmen, salespersons, coarse people. But even these men treated my father with respect." Ram Dass sat back down on the fire hydrant. "I'm going to have another pipe. Are you minding?"

"Of course not."

". . . Even those lower-class British, Liverpool people, Irishmen and so forth, even they treated my father courteously as they knew how to do." Dass paused, filled his pipe from a small plastic sandwich bag, then lit it with a translucent blue-plastic lighter. "And that, you see, is precisely why the *goondas*—once he refused them, refused to share his business with them— waited in an evening when there was no moon, and seized him and took him down into that alley and threw him into the sewer and took sticks, poles from a *dhobi,* a laundry there, and held him under the filth until it entered his mouth and his ears and his eyes, and he died of it. —They did that *because* my father had great dignity and courage. And doing so, they spoiled my dreams of him. For after that, when I am calling 'Daddy' as I dreamed, and he turned smiling to me, I saw that filth fell from his mouth as he smiled . . . and from his ear as he turned his head to listen to my calling . . . and from his eyes when he looked down at me. And so, the *goondas* had spoiled even my dreams of my father." The old man paused, puffed on his pipe, then took it out of his mouth, looked at it. "A Clarkson pipe. They are not bad."

"My grandfather had briars," Evan said, "and a Washburn calabash. He had a pipe for every day of the week except Sunday. My father smoked cigarettes. Luckies and Old Golds."

"Ah, Old Golds. My father smoked only Senior Service—never *bidis,* except when he was a boy and had no money. I'll tell you something, Mr. Scott—"

"Evan."

"Evan. And you must call me Dass.—I'll tell you something, that old damn newsstand was meaning nothing to me. It was a business I didn't care for, and if those fools think it's a warning to me, to Ram Dass to keep his mouth shut about that young man they ran over with their lorry, then they have wasted their efforts. I was tired of selling printed foolishness to fools. Dirty pictures . . . nonsense. —You see, it is not the bullying I am minding. It is the contempt behind it, do you see? —That I am an oh-so-suitable subject for bullying. That, I am minding very much."

"Well, I was going up to their offices—the Rao offices, uptown. How would you like to go up there with me, see the ones who are giving the orders? See if they're as fierce, face to face."

Dass sat a moment more, looking at his pipe. Then sighed and knocked the tobacco out of it into the palm of his hand. Brushed hot ash to the pavement. "Wasting tobacco. . . . Goodness, that is an idea, isn't it? An American idea—to look into their faces. . . ." He stood up, slender, dark as old horse-tack leather scored by years and parching weather. Stiff to bend, but perhaps still strong enough. "I have my parade saber at home, and now how I wish that I'd brought it. . . . Just funning, of course. At least I suppose that I am funning. . . ."

A long cab ride crosstown, then uptown, Dass sitting silent and very erect beside Evan, like an attentive dark-eyed child inexplicably aged, grown taller, wrinkled and mustached. He smelled of his tobacco (some inexpensive scented blend) . . . and a spice. Not curry, but a component of curry. Perhaps cardamom. Dass's hair, thick as a young man's though almost white, was oiled, combed very neatly.

At 43rd Street and Third, while they waited in impatient traffic (edging through an intersection light that stayed red too long), Dass said, "Actually, I am of a warrior caste—Kshatriya—even though my father and his father were business people. So, it was a natural thing, perfectly natural for me to go into the army when I was grown, even though my mother wasn't liking it. Oh, she was bitterly opposed. . . ." And having said that, sat silent another few blocks while the cab driver, a young black man named L. McNickel on his hack license, exchanged a glance with Evan in his rearview mirror.

"You served in the U.S. Army, Mr. Scott?"

"—Evan. The Corps, Marines."

"Ah, well . . . the United States Marines. The British NCOs—and I met many that were coming over in advisory cadre and so forth—had nothing but good to say of the United States Marine Corps. No, nothing but good. . . . I was mustered out a sergeant major; I believe I told you that."

"Yes."

"And you were an officer—of course an officer."

"I was a lieutenant, Dass. Discharged a captain. And we lost the war. . . ." Another mirrored glance exchanged with L. McNickel.

Surging start-and-stop uptown, Evan looked through the cab's dirty side window as if he were a stranger to the city, had never been this way before. And slowly, slowly as he passed, realized the sidewalk crowds as people he could never know as he knew his own. Afro-Americans, Hispanics, Orientals, the crowd threaded through by only a bare majority of white men and women.

A new country was being formed out of the old, and it seemed to Evan difficult to determine any longer what was his ... what he could be certain to leave for Beth, her children and grandchildren.

At the uptown corner where the Lederer Building loomed over a half-block square, Evan took out his wallet to pay the cabby, and Dass protested.

"Oh, I must pay half, Captain." The old man hauled a large zippered brown change purse out of his trouser pocket.

"*Evan*. And you don't have to pay half. You've just lost your business, Dass. Let me pay the damn cab fare."

"No, no. I must pay half." And tugged out and un-folded four worn dollars ... a handful of change.

Out on the sidewalk, they stood deep under the building's shadow, the structure's sheets of stamped bronze-colored aluminum stacked and stacked like immense brickwork sixty-five stories above them. The Lederer a thick building, monumentally ugly—and rumored among the city's architects to have been an act of revenge by Charles Gaddis, who'd designed it, against Dolph Lederer, who'd intended the building to be his monument, but perhaps not so accurately.

Student architects came from abroad to see this building, as a cautionary example.

The entrance and lobby were low-ceilinged as a basement, where people passing seemed to duck their heads beneath massive dark detail set into the ceiling in foot-thick sections of stepped metal. Ram Dass hurried a little to stay at Evan's side as if they might be separated . . . he become lost. The directory, framed in bronze on the wall between two banks of elevators, listed "Rao Corporation" on the forty-seventh floor.

. . . The elevator echoed the building's exterior, and as if weighted by ugliness, rose very slowly to the thirty-ninth floor, after many stops . . . entrances, exits.

At the thirty-ninth floor, the last other passengers—two squat young men in shirt-sleeves who'd murmured together—got off.

"I did tell you I was in stores, actually—a 'depot wallah.' " Dass stood against the elevator's side wall, watching the small swift parade of orange double digits. "Not to mislead. Though of course I passed the infantry course; everyone had to pass the infantry course, even though we were a cavalry regiment, Vindhaya—well, Seventy-first Mechanized Regiment now. I did small arms for four weeks. And saber exercise. And small-unit tactics. I passed Leadership. . . . And Storage, Numbering, Record-keeping, Residuals and Excess." Still staring up at the floor numbers flickering in addition. ". . . I don't wish to mislead, sir."

Watching this nervous old man, listening to him, Evan felt himself more and more at ease. A familiar weight seemed to settle around him like warm cloth, the recollected weight and uneasy pleasure of responsibility for his men. One man, in this case. Surprisingly like what he felt for Beth, for Catherine. . . . What he should have felt and acted on for Sanchia, and had failed to do.

"In our company," Evan said, "Chris Dunfey was senior supply sergeant, and he was one of the few real grown-ups we had. Went up to the line during Tet."

Dass seemed to consider that ... stopped looking at the elevator telltale. "It's true; we were grown-ups in the depot—and the men so like children, isn't it? Always coming to us wanting this or that, angry if they had to sign a chit. —Officers, too. Officers, too. As if webbing equipment grew on trees. . . ."

The elevator slowed and clicked, stopped, clicked again and opened its sliding door onto a corridor as grimly dark bronze as the lobby had been. Evan led to the right, down twenty feet to a frosted glass double door labeled KILLGORE INVESTMENT TRUSTS in thick black script.

He turned and walked back the other way, Dass skipping into step on the right beside him.

Several office doors along the left as they went. Design ... a design firm—its logos on three doors. Then double doors, laminated walnut. RAO ELECTRICAL CONTRACTING inscribed on a long brass plaque across the left-hand door.

"Face to face," Dass said, and they went through the doors into a contractor's work space—the floor torn up, its old tiles (black and buff) piled to the right, the new flooring, floating flooring (inch-thick strip red oak), stacked in long bundles to the left, against the lobby wall.

Two workmen, the older with a striking handlebar mustache, were sitting on heaps of tile against the right side wall, eating lunch. Hero sandwiches ... tall cans of beer. They watched Evan and Dass cross the floor area on long planks laid down over a pour, apparently releveling the floor.

"Stay on the planks, guys." The young man, around a mouthful of sandwich. "Wet mud under there."

"Should have locked them doors," the older workman said.

Across a space still tiled in one-foot checkers, a woman was watching them from a reception desk against the lobby's back wall. As they crossed over, she stood and came around the desk to meet them—tall, lean as a model in a beige business suit, a handsome woman in her thirties. She wore glasses.

"Yes . . . ? May I be of help?" Her upper-middle-class English accent still so popular in receptionists, as if British good breeding and a decent girls' school might at least gloss dubious American businesses.

"We don't have an appointment." Evan smiling, feeling more and more relaxed, as if Clive had been right, he'd only been working too hard . . . and this visit was vacation. "No appointment, but we'd like to see a senior executive, a member of the family. I'm an architect on one of your company's projects."

The receptionist smiled and glanced at Dass.

"A colleague. We have a few questions. . . ."

"Oh, dear. Mr. . . ."

"Scott."

"Mr. Scott, I'm afraid the office is being redone through the summer, and unfortunately no one is here." The woman was older than she'd seemed coming toward them, in her late thirties, early forties. The fine-boned face was lightly lined, the eyes behind her silver-rimmed glasses a softer blue than they must have been before. "The staff and our executives are all on vacation now. Canada . . . India. There's really no one available, so, if you do have questions, then perhaps the general contractor might be able—what project are you working on?"

"366."

". . . Well, the general contractor on that is Harris, diNunzio, and they would probably be the ones—"

"We'd like to see one of the Raos."

"I am sorry. But I don't believe any of our people are in town. In a few weeks—"

Evan looked down the corridor past the reception desk, saw open office doors. "Mind if we take a look?" And started down the hall.

"Oh, no—oh, no!" And the woman hurried to step in front of him, light on her feet in high heels. "You can't do that. Really, there's no one, and I can't let you go into the offices."

"If no one's there," Evan said, "it should be no problem; we won't steal the paper clips." He started to pass her by, but the woman moved in front of him again, a quick little dancing step. "Please. . . . You can't go in there!" Her voice had risen; Evan heard one of the workmen say something behind them.

"Lady, please to be getting out of our way!" Dass stepping up beside Evan. "We would like to see one of these lords of creation—face to face."

"Please, oh *please* don't do this. I can't, I can't let you . . . !" Frantic now, the angular face gone paler, blue eyes desperate behind her glasses, her mouth open so her teeth and tongue showed wet.

"Hey! You heard the lady!" The young workman, behind them.

"Petey. . . ." The older man.

"I don't give a shit; guys are out of line!"

Evan glanced back, saw the young workman standing.

"You," Dass said, "you mind your business, please."

"Fuck you, dad."

"I'll have to call the police! Please—just . . . just leave!" Tears in her eyes now.

"By all means, call them," Evan said, turned and walked back to meet the young workman. "Everything's OK. There's no problem here."

"Yeah? Then why don't you leave her alone. She's just doin' her job." The young man was stocky, and looked strong. He was dark, heavy-featured except for his nose. His nose was delicate and slightly snub, too small for his face.

"Where are you from?" Evan said. "Are you from the city?"

"I'm from fuckin' Queens, and what's it to you?"

"Even in Queens, people have to know when to mind their own business. Now, you can either go back there and sit down and eat your lunch, or we can have trouble. Your choice." Having said it, Evan was surprised to find he meant it, and genuinely didn't care which the man chose. He supposed, if it came to trouble, he'd duck under the workman's fists . . . get a grip on his testicles through the trouser material.

"Petey," the older man, "will you get the fuck back here?"

"Nobody's going to hurt this lady in any way," Evan said. "We just need to check those back offices."

"*Petey,* for Christ's sake. . . ."

The young workman hesitated and thought about it, and Evan saw there wouldn't be any trouble.

". . . I'm going to call the police. I'm going to call the police," the woman said as Evan and Dass walked past her, and Evan heard the older workman behind him, talking to his friend. "Are you outta your fuckin' mind? Get back down here an' eat your fuckin' lunch. What are you, the Lone Ranger . . . ?"

There were four offices, all almost exactly alike, and a fairly large meeting room. All empty of anything but expensive office furniture (good walnut veneers, dark-brown leather upholstery) and large file cabinets. Nothing was locked. And a few scattered documents, plans, computer printouts, faxes, had been left on desks, on top of the file cabinets.

Working offices, but not today—perhaps not for a week or two. Offices, but nothing more—no indication, no comfortable disarray of a daytime life led in them. No mess.

Evan stood in the second office on deep coffee-brown carpeting, and smelled the room's air, listened to its silence as if odors of the men who'd worked here might remain, and echoes of their voices. There was an odor of cigarette smoke, and another, very faint, like crushed sugarcane. But the room recalled no sounds for him. This office, like the others, might have been movie sets done by very good designers. Sets so well done that they could be worked in . . . used as actual offices.

In the third office, Dass found a silver-mounted photograph on a miniature refrigerator in the corner. And two small bottles of Schweppes Bitter Lemon in the refrigerator.

"Now, here they are! Here they are, you see—in St. Clarges's colors. It is their school."

Three boys in cricket whites (certainly brothers) smiled from the silver frame with a field of lawn behind them. They were dark, with eyes beautiful as Arab horses'. The boy on the left, plump and grinning, had certainly become the man who'd visited Evan, pretended to be a policeman. The boy on the right, very slender, very handsome, was also smiling. But the boy in the middle, the tallest and it seemed the eldest, had a sadder smile than his brothers. He, only a little older, seemed to know a secret they did not.

"Do you see how dark they are? They may be Bengali, but their blood is not Bengali. They are not *arya*, not in the smallest part."

"St. Clarges's. . . ."

"It's their school. Those are St. Clarges's colors on their caps. Light blue and white. The Anglicans run it—monks—for rich Indian children to try to be British ... European."

"You know that school?"

"Everyone knows that school in Pondicherry. It's for children of people who are ashamed to be Indian. There they are permitted to speak only English."

"Dass—you speak English, and with a British accent."

"Oh, no. No, no, no. That is a different matter, do you see? It is a traditional matter of the army. Quite a different thing. It is a regimental matter, and besides, I already knew it. My sisters and I learned English at home, a valuable second language."

"I see. . . . Can you remember these faces? —Much older now, of course. I'm asking because I don't want to take anything out of here. I want to leave this place just the way we found it—except they'll know we've been here."

"Oh, yes. If I see these brothers again, I would know them if they were a hundred years old. Look how dark they are ... see how they smile. When my people conquered—oh, thousands of years ago—they met just such darkness, such smiles. These people keep dirty secrets, and when I was small I was taught that those dirty secrets make their skin so black."

"Handsome, though." The boys smiled up at Evan out of their sporting afternoon ... out of a well of years.

"Oh, yes. The women extraordinary—white eyes. There is a saying. 'A Dravidian woman carries lanterns in her head.' ... That's what they say. Of course, you don't know what may happen if you go with one. You could lose your purity; anything could happen."

"If these are the sons—let's check for a picture of

the father. It would be nice to know what the whole
family looks like."

"Captain—there won't be a picture of their *bapu,*
their daddi-ji."

"Why not?"

Dass shrugged. "Just . . . not."

" 'Just not'?"

"Yes. Just not."

There were no other photographs in any of the offices, and none beside the large brass tea urn in the
meeting room, at the window end of a polished refec-
tory table. . . . In the farthest office, the largest, the
beige walls were hung with seascapes, all featuring
warships from the earliest days of steam. Against the
back wall of that office, to the left of the desk, stood
a massive glowing commercial soft-drink machine. Dr
Pepper.

"No, no one here. No goddamn face-to-face." Ram
Dass began striding from office to office as if to find
a Rao by surprise, perhaps just come out of the bathroom. —Though they'd looked in there, seen only
dark-green wallpaper with foxhounds and pink-
jacketed riders trotting across it.

The tall receptionist had come to an office door to
watch Evan sorting through folders, checking desk
drawers. . . . She'd fluttered, then gone away.

"The police." Dass paused in patrolling, uneasy.

"I think she knows better than to call the police into
these people's offices. She may not know much, but
she probably knows that." Evan was opening desk
drawers in the last, largest office . . . finding nothing
but would ordinarily be there. No locked drawers.
"Well, they're running a contracting business here; no
doubt about it."

"Oh, yes, and other businesses elsewhere. Shall we
leave them a note?"

"I don't think so. I think with people like this, silence is the way to go."

"Oh, yes. I like that. 'Silence is the way to go.' "

The workmen were laying the first section of flooring along the lobby wall when Evan and Dass came down the hall. The men didn't look up as they went past, walked across the bridging planks, and out the door.

It was a wait for the elevator, and when it arrived, and they were in it and the door hissed closed, Dass said, "I am being honest. I was a little relieved they were not there. I am not a coward, but I was a little relieved."

The elevator stopped at the next floor down, but no one stepped in when the door slid open.

Then a white, long-fingered hand gripped the door's edge, and the woman receptionist stepped into the doorway, smiling, and looked at them. It was a gleeful smile, full of some sort of promise, and Evan saw himself and Ram Dass reflected in the bright lenses of her glasses.

"I know you two," the woman said. "I knew you when you swanned into the office. I know exactly who you are. And I must say you were very rude to a poor frightened woman just trying to do her job." The angular face was rich with pleasure, with suppressed amusement. Her eyes the brightest blue, as if she were becoming younger as she watched them. "—And if my husband, Chandra, and his brothers *had* been here when you came, they would have taken you into the WC, into the shower stall, pulled down your knickers, tied strings round your sacks, sliced off your balls and made you eat them. . . . If you've never seen men eating their own genitals; they make the most extraordinary *faces*."

And still smiling, radiant, she stepped back, released the door, and it closed on them.

They rode down several floors in silence, then Evan said, "Face to face."

Ram Dass said nothing.

chapter 12

· ·

The Dond had paused at the Reitmann Project playground one afternoon last autumn. A scarecrow figure,
he had stood outside the wrought-iron fencing for three
hours, watching the little children play.

The mothers at Reitmann, black and Puerto Rican,
had studied him from their benches as he watched the
children—that day and the same day every week for
two months.

Then, on one of his Wednesdays, an early-winter afternoon, noisy older boys had come into the small
playground, pushed the little children aside, and
lounged on the swings and seesaws, one saying, "Ladies, kiss my ass," when the women protested.

Then the Dond had come from behind the fence into
the playground, and gone up to this older boy and
stood looking at him until the boy got off the swing he
was sitting on, and left the playground. Then his
friends left, too. . . . And when, in spring, a man in a
Buick LeSabre made a habit of driving by and double-
parking to watch the children—and then had spoken to
Buster Bateman, five years old, and asked him if he
wanted to go for a ride—the Dond had gone out into the street and said something to the man in Pushtu,

hen smashed the car's windshield with his fist. And
he man drove away and didn't come back.

So, by summer the mothers were content to have the
Dond sitting on a bench of his own among them, an
odd figure that occasionally—if a child came over and
tugged at his long coat—would rise to his great height
and participate in a game of chase. He always the pursuer, trotting in immense slow strides after a cloud of
little children scattering before him, shrieking in delighted terror while their mothers smiled.

In these slow-motion chases—the Dond's huge rap-
tor's head cracked in a wide yellow-toothed grin of
pleasure—he never quite caught a child, never touched
one, but only clawed at, reached for, tried to seize but
never quite. And when in these chases it sometimes
happened that his coat would billow back in his long
stride so the great knife could be seen sheathed at his
belt, the mothers chose not to notice it, but accepted
that as sadly as the occasional pistols some of them
found when their sons came home to have their laundry done.

And one morning, early, the Dond came by with pre-
sents for them all. Four big cartons of ice cream bars
still smoking from the dry ice they were packed in. He
carried them across the street from an ice cream truck,
where a friend waited. —It was much too much ice
cream for the children to eat, so when the Dond left,
the truck's bell ringing merrily, the mothers called their
friends down to share it.

It had been at least three or four years since Evan
had been on the subways. The system hadn't improved.

He hung from a metal handhold above a seated Ram
Dass—the old man preoccupied, frowning. The visit to
the Rao offices, the appearance of the woman afterward at the elevator door, had upset the old man—

perhaps had revealed too grim a reality. So, once out of
the building, he'd asked Evan to go up to the Bronx
with him, apparently as an ally in dealing with his
daughter-in-law.

"Oh, she is furious I was calling Mandu. And he
said, 'She is coming with the baby to me,' and that was
that. But she is furious; she doesn't want to be going to
Arabia. She thinks all sorts of nonsense about Arabia,
and she's saying the baby would have been American—and now what will it be?"

The old man had asked for company—really moral
support—and Evan, with a twinge of commander's satisfaction, had said yes. And now, in a jolting, poorly
ventilated train lit weak lemon-yellow, thundering up
to the Bronx, he bent his head to hear what the old man
was saying.

"... Do you know what that whore has done? And
it is only an accurate term I am using, not to be vulgar.
—I'll tell you. That brother, Chandra, has married a
European, that Englishwoman—and do you know what
she has done?"

Evan recalled the woman's malignant relaxation, her
bright blue eyes. "I'd say she's done quite a bit."

"Oh, yes. She has fucked with them all, and please
be forgiving my language. —With all the brothers.
That is what a few still do in the South. Not many,
now, but some still do it. . . . She goes to bed after the
wedding, and then all the brothers are coming in in
their wedding clothes, and when she is undressed, they
fuck her like dogs on a bitch. All of them together in
disgusting bedding. And she is doing anything they
ask. And that is what they do in the South. . . . Well,
most of them don't. Most of them don't, but a few of
them still do it."

Evan, standing swaying with the subway's motion,
imagined for a moment that long body years before,

naked, lean and white, its glasses off, sweating in furnace heat and jolted, penetrated, doubled this way and
that by three dark men in a darker room, plangent music still played for the guests downstairs while here, by
lantern light, is great striving, effort as she accommo-
dates. So that just below, in a small room decorated
with ribbons, candles, trays of sweetmeats, the women
of the family—wives, aunts, sisters, mothers, all singing to handclaps—hear her, after a while, begin to sing
above them the oldest song of all. . . .

"And now, Captain, certainly they will not forgive
us for going to their offices. But I am very damn glad
we did it."

"Yes. . . . They're used to doing the hunting—being
the wolves preying on sheep. I don't think they ex-
pected two of the sheep to look them up. It may upset
them . . . make them careless, do something the police
will have to notice. I think it's much better that we
hunt them, rather than wait for them to hunt us at their
leisure. It's a question of the 'best defense.' "

"Yes, yes, Captain, I understand. But what will the
sheep do when they are finding the wolves? And the
wolves now will be even angrier."

"*Evan*, not 'Captain.' Oh, then the sheep either become tigers—or lamb chops."

Ram Dass said something in another language, then
sat silent, rocking slightly with the train's motion.

In that same language—Hindi or Hindustani, but
higher-pitched—Ram Dass's daughter-in-law, plump,
brown, pregnant, and very angry in a raspberry-colored
silk sari with a gold stripe at the hem, addressed the
old man for almost an hour, while she packed. Evan,
after an awkward introduction (certainly regarded as
part of the problem—Anglo and odd), sat on the sofa

in the apartment's small living room, reading *TV Guide,* keeping quiet and out of the way.

The apartment smelled of curry and wood incense. Otherwise, there was nothing exotic about it; it was furnished like a motel suite. Ram Dass's son—in a color computer-painting from a photograph—smiled from the wall over the television. A handsome young man with a bad haircut and skin the shade of chocolate milk shake, he was wearing a white dress shirt with open collar and no tie, and looked very much as his father must have looked at his age.

The angry daughter-in-law had pointed the portrait out to Evan when he'd come in. "Fool of a daddy"— nodding at Ram Dass—"fool of a son." She'd brought Evan a cup of tea, a saucer of white almond-paste candy, then had gone into her bedroom to finish packing and to punish her father-in-law. Ram Dass had answered back only for a while . . . and when he came out to the living room, looked more than an hour older.

"I am begging your pardon for her behavior, Captain. She is absolutely a well-brought-up young woman—of so good family—but she is very upset because I telephoned Mandu in Saudi Arabia. She is loving it here"— Dass sat beside Evan with a sigh— "and she doesn't want to go and fly to Saudi Arabia. And this is the reason for her behavior. Really, she's usually being very nice."

"I'm sure she is. It's enough to upset anyone. And Dass, don't call me 'Captain.' "

"I'm sorry; I won't. . . . Mandu was the one who was upset. I was very calm, but he was upset and insisted she fly to Saudi Arabia right away. Actually, she is going to have to go to Bombay—and then get a visa and go to Saudi Arabia."

"Bombay. . . ."

"Yes, yes, I know, but for two days, perhaps three

days—and she'll be staying with her uncle there. It would take them more time than three days to know she has gone, then find out where she has gone, then discover her uncle's house. Even if they trouble to do that, they will not be in time, so the boy is safe."

"What boy?"

"My grandson. She carries my grandson. —A boy, not a girl."

"I see."

"Not that we would want anything to happen to a girl-child either. . . ."

The ride out to Kennedy was more pleasant, the three of them in the wide backseat of an ancient Checker, Vashti's three suitcases, tied and covered basket, and a major purse crowding the jump-seat space in front of them.

". . . Daddy, go to the police."

"Oh, yes, and then they can send me away to the immigration and say this man has overstayed by two years and now is causing trouble with the police so he will never be a citizen! The Captain—Mr. Scott has already tried the police twice, isn't it?"

Small, plump, tucked between them, Vashti Lal pouted. "I think you want an adventure—and you are too old to have an adventure; isn't he, Mr. Scott?"

"I think we're both too old to have an adventure, Mrs. Lal. Unfortunately, we haven't been left any choice."

"I don't believe these men would hurt my child."

"Yes," Evan said, "they would. My family's going to have to leave our home."

"But they won't have to go to Saudi Arabia. In Saudi Arabia, I cannot go out in the town without people pointing at me and saying, 'Cover up your arms,' as if I were a bad woman."

"And who is telling you that?"

"Oh, Daddy, I know it; I read it in *National Geographic*. Now, what do you have to say? . . . See," she said to Evan. "Now he has nothing to say, because he sells magazines but he reads only *Country Life,* as if he was English and had a place in Kent."

"What nonsense. You're just talking nonsense. . . ."

When they pulled in to unload at the terminal, Evan paid, despite protests, then stood with Vashti while Ram Dass checked the baggage in, curbside. And Vashti stretched up like a child to murmur into Evan's ear. "Take care of him, Captain Scott. Those *goondas* would not have burned his newsstand if they knew what a very nice old man he is. —And he can't eat hard-cooked eggs. They upset him."

"I'll try," Evan said. "And I'll watch out for the eggs."

"Soft-boiled, soft scrambled . . ." Vashti said at the gate, later.

"What?"

"Daddy, I wasn't talking to you; I was talking to Captain Scott." And she kissed Dass on the cheek and was gone, a small brown pouter pigeon in silk and sandals.

"Thank the Lord Krishna," Dass said, watching her go. "Though they will certainly stop her basket; it is full of food and they will certainly stop it at Customs when the plane lands. Indian Customs is terrible. . . . I am so glad she is gone; she is very dear to me. Mandu has a jewel of a wife, and it is my doing . . . I found her. An old friend was a friend of a regimental surgeon—an infantry regiment but well thought of. He is a very distinguished person, and she was his second daughter. . . ."

Evan phoned Fairport from the terminal. After four rings, Mrs. Hooper answered.

"Mrs. Hooper, everything all right?"

"Right as rain."

"I'm still in town, but I'll be out in a couple of hours. Please let Catherine know."

"All right, but you're going to miss dinner. I won't do roast beef well done."

"I know. Just leave me some, sliced for sandwiches, and I'll have that when I get home."

"All right."

"And it might be a good idea to lock up, now it's evening."

"Already done. Mrs. Scott went around and unlocked all the doors I just locked—so I went around and locked 'em all up again, and she's lettin' 'em be."

"Good for you. I'll be coming right out."

... It was a long wait in the hack line for a cab back to the city, and Ram Dass, so talkative through the afternoon and evening, now settled into a long silence as they sped thumping over ruined roadways into New York's constellation of lights.

"Dass ... we've had our meeting, at least with one of the Rao women, which—I'm sure you're right—won't have pleased the family. And since I suggested we do that, I'm responsible for your being involved."

"No, you are not responsible."

"Let's say I feel responsible—and I also feel it would be very sensible of you to say enough's enough, before matters get more serious."

"I am responsible for myself."

"Still, I don't think it's too late for you to step aside here, Dass. And if you'd rather leave the city, get out of this, I'll provide any money you need to do that."

"I don't need any money. I have my own money. I'm not going to go anywhere. I don't know if you think I'm being too old or a coward or whatever. But I'm not too old, and I'm not a coward. —In the war with Pakistan, I was assigned to stay in the regimental depot. It was not my fault, and it was not what I wished to do. Now, no one can order me to the depot to count boots and underdrawers." The cab, crossed under the East River, now slowed, thumped and rattled up out of the Queens Midtown Tunnel into the city's streets, passing streetlamps, traffic signals—individual lights now, no longer sidereal. Passing pedestrians on nighttime sidewalks. ". . . You are making me angry and I have to tell you I am not a funny old brown man who cannot be depended on in trouble. Yes, my ancestors were brown men, not white men—but I am assuring you, Captain, there was nothing funny about them."

"I don't mean to insult you, Dass. I mean to warn you. There's a very good chance these people will kill us. An excellent chance—I want you to understand that."

"I have understood that long ago, and it is not the most important thing to me."

". . . All right. All right, you're in. But you can't stay in that apartment; they know about it. So, we're going to need a different place. Somewhere to hide in the city for a few days while we try to learn where they live, and what the hell they're up to on 366. Perhaps find enough to interest the damn police. . . . We can't use a public accommodation, a hotel, nothing like that. So if you can, find us rooms somewhere—but a place that involves no one else, where no one else is put in danger from these assholes."

" 'Assholes.' That's right." Dass smiling in passing rose light from a restaurant's neon. "I'll find a place to stay. Already I am thinking of a place. . . ."

"I need to get my family away, Dass—it's going to take two or three days, probably, before I get back to town. Let's meet . . . in front of the Museum of Natural History. Do you know it?"

"Of course I know that. I have been to it twice, for

the whale. Well, once for the whale and once for the dinosaur."

"If you'll be there ... say ... from nine o'clock to ten every night from the day after tomorrow—"

"Twenty-one to twenty-two hundred hours."

"... That's right, Dass. I'll see you there as soon as I come in. It will depend on how long it takes to get my family away."

"You have an American wife, and she won't do what you say, isn't it?"

"That's very likely. ..."

"Sorry, Evan, I stopped being afraid of the bogey-man years ago." Catherine sitting at her dressing table, brushing her hair.

Evan, just returned from a late bedtime visit with Beth, was standing at the dresser in pajamas and robe, eating the remaining half of his roast beef sandwich. Beth, very sleepy, had not been too sleepy to eat the other half. "Mrs. Hooper had a call from one of the bogeymen, yesterday."

"So I was made to understand during a ridiculous lock-up-the-house duel this evening—Mrs. Hooper running around with pepper spray in her apron pocket, if you can believe that. And only the first in a series of nasty crank calls, I suppose, thanks to your New York activities." Angry, she brushed her bright hair harder, so it picked up static electricity and rose slightly to follow the brush at every stroke. "Edith Hooper believes in witches, for God's sake. There are two women in this town she'd have burned if she could get away with it. I'm not surprised she's picking up on your unpleasant fantasy life."

"And if there is a bogeyman, after all?" The sandwich had been very good; he missed the other half.

"Then I'll apologize, Evan. Though I suppose he

would have done me a favor by eliminating your little office prostitute. No great loss."

"Matter of fact, I met one of the bogeymen this afternoon—a female variant. The newsdealer and I—"

" 'The newsdealer'.... Oh, yes, your elderly Hindu no-show. I remember the police were *very* impressed with him."

"We went up to the Rao offices—"

"Oh my God. I can't believe you're acting all this *out*—and you are going to get us sued! You went up to their offices?"

"No one there, except one of their wives. You'd have been very interested to meet her."

"Listen—I'm not interested in any of this ... this sick elaboration of some really unpleasant fantasies. Really, I'm not. And I'll tell you what I would like. I would like you to go downstairs and sleep in the den, and spare me any more of your bullshit." For an instant, Evan saw in Catherine's face a cold decided weight that seemed the perfect counterbalance to the Rao woman's savage heat that afternoon. "—Evan, I am getting very very tired of it. And I'm getting tired of you."

He waited for more than an hour, then came up from the den, stood listening to Catherine breathing as she slept ... and went in to take the flashlight and the Colt from his bedside table drawer.

Resting while he walked, feeling rested, he patrolled the house barefoot, in shorts and T-shirt though the night was cool. He stood by Beth's door for a while, until through its thick wood he was certain he heard her easy dreaming breaths, light as sketching.

He patrolled, and imagined Pete Diller scouting for him down dark halls. Lance Corporal Diller easy on his feet, shifting from shadow into shadow as if alive

again, and with both his arms. . . . Evan stopped in the
kitchen, sensed Diller halted at the cellar door, then
waved him down . . . was sure he saw him by moonlight as the tall man (the cigarette pack in his helmet-
cover strap a spot of pale) stalked like a folding rule,
crossed the pantry entrance, eased the cellar door open,
and went downstairs making no noise. Then Evan
crossed to follow.

In the cellar, he stood taking deep breaths . . .
smelled only Diller's ancient sweat, and damp earth
and stone. Smelled no foreign spices, no one freshly
showered but himself, no hair oil. Heard no one else
breathing, a useful part of Diller's being dead. . . . The
cellar, absolutely dark except beneath rare grimy small
half-windows that allowed faint moonlight, lay a half-
acre pit walled by granite hand-laid foundation stones,
partitioned here and there into root cellars, coal bins,
apple keeps, furnace surround, woodpiles, water heat-
er, work sinks, old zinc laundry tubs, and, in the south
corner beneath the kitchen, well housing and hand
pump he still occasionally came down, primed, and
worked for a few gushes.

Cobwebs stroked Evan as he moved along. He'd lost
Diller somewhere ahead . . . forgotten him for a moment and let him slip away.

It took a long time to cover the cellar so thoroughly
he knew he'd left nothing behind—and he climbed up
through the slanted double doors out to the east side of
the house. Swung them quietly down and shut behind
him, decided to padlock them in the morning, and
walked down along the plantings to the front lawn . . .
and across the lawn once a cloud had obscured the
moon. He glanced down when the moon came out, and
saw the moonlight lick his pistol's steel, frosting it as
it had all weapons in the hills, years ago. . . .

Evan stood near the road in moonlight, stood still beside a beech tree for some time. No traffic came by.

In the morning, Catherine, in her white robe, made pancakes . . . came between servings and rested her hand on his shoulder in almost a natural way as she talked to Beth about being nicer to Susan Tedesco.

"Mom, she's a slut."

"Don't talk like that."

"Mom, will you relax? I don't mean a grown-up slut. I *mean,* she will be friends with anybody. Boys . . . anybody."

"Disgusting," Evan said, enjoying Catherine's hand on him, even in demonstration.

"Well, it is. . . ." And Evan saw behind her childishness a different attention being paid to her mother's resting hand, her father's shoulder.

"Didn't fool her for a minute," he said when Beth went upstairs for her book bag.

Catherine ran water at the sink, rinsing dishes.

"Catherine, use your head. If there's even a chance in a hundred that I'm right, that I'm telling the truth about all this—my personal betrayal of you to one side—then you need to get *out* of here. You need to get Beth out of here. And as fast as possible."

"Jesus H. Christ," Catherine said, opened the dishwasher, and put three dishes into its rack.

"—I think they might consider her life some sort of debt I owe them for seeing too much, for going to the police—twice. For just having been an annoyance. More of an annoyance all the time."

"Well, here's what I think, Evan." She closed the dishwasher door, pushed the on button. "I think it's disgusting for you to involve Beth in this, your excuse-making, whatever it is. . . . All that happened is that some junkies robbed your girlfriend's apartment and killed her—and you showed up and were caught with your pants down. And as far as these so-called criminals are concerned, I'm sure Ward & Breedon have dealt with worse, working in that city." Catherine dried her hands on the dish towel. "I don't want to hear any more about it. And I mean that." She hung the dish towel on its rack under the sink, and walked out.

Evan drove the white Lexus, the .45 under the driver's seat, and followed the school bus to the Academy—waited a half block away until he saw Beth walk up the entrance steps, then turned and drove the long way to town.

Connecticut Shore Bank was on the corner of Chandler and Shore Road—in an old two-story building, clinker-sided and painted white, that had been a sail loft and warehouse since 1809. Some of the *Constitution*'s storm sails, and the *Chesapeake*'s, had come from this loft.

Evan drove alongside the building, parked, and went in the side door. He wrote a check at the counter, saw only one person at Susan Nash's cage, and went to wait behind him.

"Hi, Mr. Scott." Susan, cheerful, pale and plump, was Carrie Nash's daughter—and now in a wheelchair from a beach buggy accident. She'd been Beth's babysitter.

"Susan . . . how goes it?"

"No complaints. How's Bethy?"

"Growing up, but I think she misses you."

"Well, I miss her. . . . Oh, this check is for two thousand?"

"That's right."

"Well . . . I just need to look something up. Be a minute." And wheeled back, turned, and rolled away toward the offices.

"Evan. . . ." A wiry Spencer Dunn in espadrilles, sun-bleached jeans, and white T-shirt, his skin cracked and brown as worn leather, still the yacht club's commodore at seventy-one.

"Mr. Dunn."

"I hear you have a Crealock. The big one."

"Yes, just got her."

"Well, perhaps you'd want to consider running the Bermuda race with us, Evan. If you get lucky, sail into some weather, you might do pretty well with a heavy boat."

"I'd like nothing better—but this year I doubt if I can do it."

"You might want to try to make it. We have some people coming out from the West Coast—could show them a little Atlantic autumn sailing. Show them a little real ocean sailing. . . ."

"I'd like to."

"Well, think about it, but don't think too long. I would like us to have one heavier boat in the race, something that can take a little weather."

"I will think about it, Commodore. And I'll let you know."

"All right. Yes or no, I'll expect to hear from you." And sauntered away, stepping easily as a boy. A boy somehow preserved through decades by sun and salt air, salt water and Scotch-and-sodas.

"Mr. Scott, I'm sorry." Susan Nash had rolled back behind her cage. "—But would you mind going back and seeing Mr. Burton? It's . . . he just wants to see you for a minute."

"Am I out of money?"

"No, you're not. He just wants to see you for a minute."

. . . Carl Burton was up and around his desk as Evan

went into the small office, a pleasantly sunny room with seascapes on every wall.

"Evan, thanks for coming back. . . ." Burton, a very good tennis player, had a strong handshake.

"What's the problem, Carl? I thought we had a constant ten thousand balance kept in checking."

"Oh, you do. Your account stands at just that amount. Down a couple of days ago, and brought back up to ten thousand by end of business, yesterday."

"OK, Carl, then why am I here?"

"Want to sit down, Evan?"

"Less and less. What's this all about?"

"Well . . . really bizarre. An unpleasant kind of situation. . . . Truth is, we've known each other a long time. And also, of course, you keep a good deal of money in the bank one way and another—very considerable sums."

"And so?"

"Truth of the matter is, two detectives came to the bank beginning of the week, Tim Nearing and Bud dePau, and they requested that we inform them if you came in to withdraw a significant amount of money. 'Sufficient,' as dePau put it, to 'flee the country.' "

"For Christ's sake . . . !"

"Now, Evan, we are under no legal obligation to do any such thing. . . . On the other hand, the police are the police. So, with this withdrawal"—Burton held the check up between thumb and forefinger, as if it were already somehow dubious—"with this amount, Susan had to come back and run it by me."

"And now that she's run it by you?"

"Well. . . . Now I apologize to you, cash your check, and keep my mouth shut as far as the police are concerned. I don't feel that two thousand dollars is germane."

"In that case, let's make it three thousand. I have some expenses coming up."

"You've got it. And of course, you can have any money you want, anytime you want. Don't misunderstand, Evan. —Only there would be some pressure to keep the police informed of a really major withdrawal. Unfortunately, with the largely specious excuse of keeping track of criminal activity, the government now has its nose deep into the banking business and everyone's private financial affairs. It would be very easy for the law enforcement people to suggest that federal agencies target us for continuous audits, investigations . . . and of course let this be public knowledge. I'm sorry."

"I understand. . . . Would you like us to take our money out of here?"

"I would not."

"All right, Carl. I appreciate your candor."

"May I say something else?"

"Your bank—your office."

"Concerning that New York stuff—and forgive me for mentioning it—no one in town thinks the police are doing anything but wasting their time."

"Thanks, Carl."

"Give my regards to your beautiful wife—and tell her Marie expects the usual heavy volunteer duty at the Sea Cubs things."

"I will. . . ."

Leaving the lot, driving on through to Dock Street, Evan turned left—watched the rearview mirror as he went, as if a police cruiser might suddenly swing in behind him—and drove down Dock to the corner of Hillside, parked, and put a quarter in the meter. Then he walked up the block to Lufton's, and went into the store under the spring-bell's jingle.

Rows of fishing poles to the left—limber fly to stiff

strong deep-sea trollers—and to the right, glass-topped counters over gleaming rows of reels. . . . In the store's addition, through a wide entranceway (his job, one of his first remodels for Ward & Breedon twelve years ago), were ranked tennis and squash racquets, golf clubs, soccer balls and shin guards, polo helmets and mallets.

As he walked through, Evan smiled at the girl behind the fishing-gear counter. Gail Quillow, tall, sturdy, and suntanned—and a working mate on her brother's boat in season. He smiled and went past to the back of the store. Camping equipment along the white-painted plank walls, some rock-climbing gear, then racks of guns.

Terry Lufton, very tall, thin, prematurely gray, and stooped as a heron, was standing behind the counter, working the slide of a semiautomatic pistol. He looked up at Evan, said, "Hey, ol' buddy," and put the weapon under the counter. "Glock makes a great handgun— then he sticks soft sights on it, come off if you look at 'em, and fixes the extractor so it throws those hot cases right back in your face. At least on this piece, couple others I've seen. Right back in your face. Those two items and a gimmicky trigger. . . ."

"But reliable, I've heard."

"Oh, yes. Accepts major punishment. You're walking the banks of the Amazon, this is the handgun you want. I'd skip the forty, though; take the nine-millimeter in Cor-Bon's best."

". . . Speaking of ammunition, Terry, I think I need some fresh."

"What I've got, you can have." Still smiling, stooped and kind. Terry Lufton and Evan had made a pair each summer from ten or eleven on. Bicycle days . . . crabbing off Collins's dock, or the town pier across the harbor. Fishing. Later, quail shooting upstate for several autumns when Evan was home from Groton for Thanksgiving holiday. Upstate, first with Evan's dad, then Terry's father after Frank Scott died. . . . And masturbating together once, after watching George Halleck screw Anne Osbourne out behind the club course shed. Evan and Terry had been ball-chasing after driving practice.

Sweet summers roaming, wandering . . . discoveries of the town and township slowly becoming rarer as they grew older, until school and friends made at school began to take up Evan's holidays . . . summers, so that finally he and Terry Lufton only nodded, smiled, perhaps talked a minute or two when they met in town.

"I got my old forty-five out—"

"Regular issue?"

"M1911-A1."

"Nothing the matter with that pistol, if it's been taken care of. Could use better sights."

"It's in good shape. Our armorer had throated the bore for me, polished the ramp. And I disassembled and greased it, then put it back together before I came back to the world. It seems fine."

"Seems fine may not be fine. I'd put a few rounds through it. . . . What ammunition you using?"

"Only rounds I have are the same vintage."

"Right. Well, you do not want to use stuff that old. It'll probably cook off, but no way reliably. Planning on target shooting, plinking? . . . What?"

"What."

Lufton stood hunched, leaning on the counter, and Evan saw into and through his adult face—long, almost sad, a face weighted by some care Evan had not stayed a good enough friend to know. Saw, through this grown-up face, a younger man's face . . . then, a boy's, intelligent, considering, more thoughtful than Evan's had been at that age.

Terry sighed and walked away down the counter, stooped to a drawer underneath it, and came back with six small heavy boxes stacked in one long-fingered hand.

He put them down before Evan in a short row, one two three four five six, each with a soft thump.

"That GI ball was not a major stopper, even fresh. This is the most effective forty-five cartridge going. Federal Hydra-Shoks—high-speed hollow-points. Two hundred and thirty grains, traveling very fast. Deep penetration for forty-fives . . . go through a car door. A solid torso hit with one of these is guaranteed to spoil that person's whole day." The rollicking gun talk of a man who had never been shot, never even shot at. Terry'd wanted to go to Vietnam, but an army doctor had heard odd comments from his heart, some muttering as it worked.

"All right in an old pistol?"

"All right in that model of old pistol, as long as it's in good condition. —You'll notice she'll come back in your hand sharper than you're used to. Make a louder noise, too. But if . . . but if it's a matter of saving somebody's life, you'd be well armed . . . in that sort of situation." Terry looked at Evan, then back down at the glass counter.

"I'd better have a couple of new magazines, too."

"OK." Terry went down the counter to the left, through a door . . . and after a minute or two came out again, fumbling through a small gray cardboard box. He took two flat black magazines out and put them on the countertop beside the ammunition. "Now, I'm supposed to register this sale. But I think I have just mislaid that sales slip, or miscounted my stock, some damn thing, and if I get caught on that, I'll just pay the fine."

"Thank you, Terry."

Terry stood, looking down into his display case as if there was something worth watching there. "Evan . . . I could be way out of line, so you just tell me to mind my own business, and I will. . . . You know, we still have a small town here, even with all the money coming in last few years. And what I'm getting at is, that trouble in New York City with the Spanish girl? Well, people know about it, but there's not one person I know of who thinks you could ever hurt a girl like that. Not one." He looked up. "And if you wished I hadn't mentioned it, I'm sorry."

"That's all right, Terry. Just got another vote of confidence at the bank. And thank you."

"Still have problems, though? Whatever that situation was?"

"Yes."

"Um-hmm. . . . Catherine's staying with those big Remington twelves, isn't she? Heard she went up to the state shoot last year."

"Yes, she's doing very well."

"Right. . . . I'll tell you something, Evan; I hear those clay pigeons are getting tougher and tougher. Tell you what. . . ." And bent behind his counter, shuffled a few crouched steps to the right, slid the back of a display case open, then stood with four square red-and-white boxes, and slid them down the counter. ". . . Double-ought buckshot, magnums. Just in case a few of those clay birds don't want to break."

"Might be a good idea."

"Hey, you never know."

"No . . . you don't. What do I owe you, Terry?"

"Hell, you don't owe me a thing."

"Terry, this stuff costs money—let me pay you for it."

"No. Not a penny. Old times' sake, Evan."

"Times before I became a prep-school snotnose?"

"Oh, that was just the natural course of events. Kids have to grow up."

"No, it wasn't 'the natural course of events.' It was my fault; no time for old friends. I apologize for that, Terry."

"You went to the war."

"Yes—and I'm glad you couldn't. Buddy, I wouldn't have wanted to see you over there."

Evan called home from the corner.

"Scott residence."

"Mrs. Hooper—"

"Mr. Scott."

"Mrs. Hooper, is my wife still at home?"

"No, she isn't. She went over to the Peddys' to go shopping with Mrs. Peddy—they're giving a barbecue."

"All right, thank you. No calls?"

"That jerk thinks he's funny didn't call here, if that's the one you mean. Better not, either."

"All right. You might lock—"

"I got the doors locked, and I have my pepper spray, too."

"All right. Thank you, Mrs. Hooper."

Evan hung up and walked back to his car, put the small sack of ammunition and two spare magazines on the floor of the passenger seat, then backed out into traffic grown busier year by year, and drove down Dock Street to Mill, turned left, and stayed on that road to the strip ... McDonald's (a subdued Fairport-styled McDonald's), then to Ripley's. He cruised the supermarket's big lot ... and, the second time around, saw Janice Peddy's maroon Jaguar parked at the end of the fourth row of cars.

Evan circled the lot once more—and parked in a space in the third row where he could see both the market's front entrance and the Jaguar. Then he reached down under the front seat, slid the .45 out, removed its magazine, racked back the slide, picked up the ejected round and put that and the magazine in the Lufton's sack. —He glanced around the parking lot, saw no one near, no one interested . . . reached into the sack, took out one of the new magazines and a small heavy box of Federal ammunition, tore the box open, and loaded the magazine with those stocky gleaming rounds, pressing each down against the magazine's stiff spring until, with some effort, he thumbed in the seventh and slid the magazine up into the Colt's grip. . . . He held the pistol down between his legs and pressed the release so the slide snapped forward to chamber a round—then ejected the magazine, loaded one round more for a full seven again, and reinserted the magazine. Then he tucked the Colt under his right leg and sat back, watching.

He sat for some time, enjoying the car's heat, enjoying being so alone . . . such an oddity, sitting in Ripley's parking lot with a gun resting under his leg. For a long time he watched handsome people (their children trailing like ducklings) wheeling their groceries, the basket carts piled overflowing with food—rich, various, and always more and more to come. More, it seemed, than they could ever eat. . . .

He saw Janice first, just out through the automatic doors, Catherine appearing from the store's cool shadows to follow her. Janice was wheeling her cart, heavy-burdened. They both walked, side by side now, in shorts and bright summer shirts. Both wearing sandals. . . . Janice Peddy was a tall woman, tanned, very slender (rumored to have had an affair with her husband's father). She had a long stretching stride, tanned toes almost prehensile in the sandals; her black hair was pinned up in a casual bun. . . . Beside her, Catherine was sunlight to moonlight, strolling collected, white skin only burnished by early summer, her short hair the same shade as sunshine and reflecting it. Dark and gold, their long strong bare legs pedestals for privileged beauty. It was for them, it seemed to Evan, for women like them, that the sweetest of civilized country had been groomed to fence them from an ignorant, hungry, and savage world. It was for them and their children that he worked, and most men he knew worked, or spent money their fathers and grandfathers had worked for. For them, for Catherine in any case, he sat in this parking lot with a pistol.

They crossed to the second row of parked cars and walked past it, Janice pushing her laden cart one-handed. They were talking, bright head and dark head together, Janice smiling, the muscles in her lean thighs delicately defining step by step as they walked . . . and at the near end of the lot, a big delivery truck—white with brown-gold lettering along its side—grumbled and came rolling, then roared and came rolling faster.

Evan was out of the Lexus with the .45 down at his side—afraid to yell across the lot to Catherine, afraid she'd only stand still, staring at him as the truck came to her. He ducked behind his row of cars and ran down the line to cut the white truck off, and saw as he went past a little boy in a blue T-shirt stare at him from a station wagon, seeing the gun.

Evan came around the row, running hard (heard his own fast footsteps on the blacktop)—saw the truck, accelerating, just pass—and ran faster to catch it, get alongside and up onto the running board for his shot. And was almost there, running faster, felt he could run

faster than any machine for that moment—when the
truck suddenly lurched and took a sweeping right turn
... turned and turned away, left Evan behind ... and
swung down an access drive along the side of the
building, toward the loading docks.

Evan, still running, stumbled as he slowed—finally
trotted to a walk, hurriedly tucking the Colt into his
waistband, under his shirt ... sure everyone had seen
him, the police already called. He looked across the lot
and saw, over rows of cars, Catherine and Janice
Peddy at the Jaguar, unloading groceries. Another
woman was coming down this row carrying two white
plastic sacks, a little girl just keeping up with her.

Evan was breathing hard—not from running; he'd
run fast, but not far. It was close-call breathing at such
near disaster. He turned, reached down to check the
pistol beneath his shirt, make sure it couldn't be seen,
and went back along the row of cars the way he'd
come, keeping his head down so if Catherine glanced
across the lot, she wouldn't notice him.... Still close-
call breathing. If the vehicle hadn't taken that right
turn away, he would have been up on the running
board. Might have fired and blown the truck driver's
brains out.... And then been left to the police, a murderous and mistaken fool.

He walked past a parked station wagon—saw the
little boy again, still staring at him from the backseat—
walked a few yards more, and reached the Lexus.

Listening for sirens, Evan pulled out of the lot,
turned right on Mill, then drove four careful blocks and
took another right into McDonald's, parked ... and sat
watching the highway and listening to his heart slowly
easing its beat.

... No sirens.... No police.

After a few minutes he saw the Jaguar go by, and
pulled out to follow it. The Peddys lived on Chestnut.

Easy to park down the road there, watch their place until Catherine left, and he could follow her home. . . . But the dangerous nonsense in Ripley's parking lot had been warning enough; there could be no bodyguarding Catherine and Beth through their days, perhaps for weeks, while the Raos decided when and where to teach their lesson of silence. He would always be too eager . . . or once, too late.

Naomi Grinspun looked younger than her age despite a uniform and blaze-orange Sam Browne belt too big for her, despite skin webbed with fine wrinkles from chain-smoking. Despite white hair cut short as Hamlet's in a movie she saw after she came to America, eleven years old—a subject of Jewish War Relief.

Moved younger than her age as well—had always been small, quick-moving, lively. Little Leafbug, her mother had called her, because she so often skipped along when her mother went out to their garden.

She'd made a German officer smile at Ravensbrück, by playing hopscotch along the loading platform while her mother called to her, afraid. The German officer had smiled at her, but not smiled at her mother when she stepped out of line to come get Naomi. Then he'd frowned, and kicked her mother hard, even though she was such a pretty lady, so well dressed. He'd held his gloved hands away, so as not to touch her mother with them, but only kicked and kicked her until she fell off onto the tracks. *"Du Vieh!"* he'd said, and unbuttoned a leather thing at his side and took out a gun and pointed it down at her mother as she was getting up. And it went off with a noise that made Naomi wince and cover her ears while she watched her mother seem to sneeze, and red stuff flew out of her head and hung down over the side of her face, so she wasn't pretty anymore.

Naomi's mother fell down and lay beside the railroad tracks and made a grunting sound. She was kicking with one leg the way Putzi did when you scratched his stomach—and Naomi saw that her mother's stockings were spoiled.

Another German, in not so nice a uniform, walked over, and they both stood and watched what her mother was doing. They were looking where she was showing her underwear, kicking like that, and they laughed and the other German said something dirty that boys say, but the officer glanced at Naomi and said, *"Halt den Mund! Da ist doch ein Kind."*

In America, later, Naomi had many dreams of her mother. In those dreams her mother always looked pretty—had always been happy, and sometimes was eating candy.

Of the many jobs Naomi'd had—until now, all in the city, in the garment industry—she enjoyed this part-time job the most. First, because it was outdoors in the country, and second, because it gave her time to think, often about her son, Louis. He paid her tiny apartment's rent—was happy to have her here, near him and Kris and Georgie, while her old friends stayed in the city, terrified of the blacks every time they went out for groceries. She thought of Louis a great deal of the time while no kids were crossing. Thinking about him was like patting his cheek, hugging him, giving him kisses like a baby, for his goodness to her.

The worst part of this job was the kids. So many of them spoiled so they only knew how to make noise and show off their clothes—too expensive, and badly sewn—show off and talk about their trips. They were always taking trips.... And they walked across the street talking about spending money and didn't look where they were going, look out for traffic. The boys were the noisiest.... It would have been a nicer job if it was at a public school, where the children at least knew what it was to work, at least had parents that went to a job, instead of just taking trips all over the place, spending money. Louis could have afforded here, but instead Georgie was going to public, to Hillside.... Even this young, in grade school, so many of these children were spoiled as if the world was made just for them....

Standing on the corner curb, Naomi saw the seventh grade starting to come out of the gym—the boys looking so ridiculous. Pants down over their knees so their legs stuck out ... terrible, long, stupid-looking shirts. Not even cotton; just junk. The girls a little better, but not much. And the fat ones—terrible in those clothes. These were the worst fashions for girls that were fat; it was hard to imagine what their mothers were thinking of to send them to school looking that way....

Some car's tires squealed far down the block, and then an ice cream truck's bell was ringing.... That was all she needed for gym class letting out. The kids would buy ice cream in the middle of the day over there—anything but get back across the street to the school building. Just so spoiled....

Here came at least some of them—boys, very noisy. Naomi went across to lead them over.... Never would just stand and watch them cross the way that fat woman did at Alder. She didn't do anything; took no responsibility; just watched. —Naomi went and brought the boys over, looking right and left, and said, "Morgan, come on, come on." A handsome boy, looked like a young prince, but those awful clothes....

And they were over and there was the ice cream truck, parked down the block ringing its bell. Shouldn't even be allowed near schools in the middle of the day....

"Come on, come on, children!" Girls now. Silly

things. If she'd behaved like that when she was a little girl—and such language they used—she would have gotten slapped. Never liked girls as much as boys, anyway. Louis ... Georgie.

"Come on, come on with me. Michelle, are you crossing the street, or what?" And they made fun of her accent; she heard them do that all the time. "Come on ... get across. Never mind ice cream."

Now more girls—and that truck had started up. Oh, *now* it had to come, with children in the street. ...

The ice cream truck, that had started so slowly, now made noise and came faster down the street, its bell jangling—then suddenly swerved to the right, clear across the street, missed a moving car going past it and kept going and ran into a car parked in front of Peabody's Stationery. Hit the side of it with a bang so loud that all the children turned to watch.

"That fool is drunk!" Naomi said. And the truck kept going after hitting the car—came even faster and swerved back to the left side of the street, and Naomi knew.

"An accident! There's going to be more accident!" Forgetting English pronunciation, forgetting everything as the truck came faster, its bell so loud.

Nancy—something—and the Scott girl, that was who was in the middle of the street, and Naomi ran to them, jumped to them in the street as if she was a girl herself again and grabbed that Nancy's stupid shirt and threw her—threw her to the side. Off to the right side. And the truck steered to the left as if it had gone crazy, as if the driver was crazy, and Naomi saw a laughing man, a little dark man's face behind the windshield and the truck's bell rang as it came to them while the Scott girl stood like a frightened deer in the street.

Naomi shouted, *"You!"* and didn't know who she shouted at—the girl, the stupid truck so fast with its stupid bell right here. She reached the girl as the truck reached both of them, took her by the arm and swung her—swung her away and the truck hit Naomi and knocked her down so she heard her head break, and then drove over her.

One boy, braver than the others—some children yelling, or crying, or running for help—came out into the street as the truck drove on, drove away, and a teacher was running down the building steps. The boy, Jesse Demuth, who was eleven, helped Beth Scott stand up; she'd scraped her knee. Then he knelt by the old lady in all the blood and said something to her to see if she would answer. Then he took off his long shirt and put it over her. The old lady lay with her right arm stretched out from under the shirt, and her arm had little blue numbers on it.

chapter 13

....

Catherine swam pale into Evan's sight, the only person in a long white corridor off St. Jude's emergency room. "Evan, she's fine, she's fine. She only . . . her knee was scraped, that's all. A policeman was just here. A drunk apparently stole a truck somewhere and drove over half the goddamn township, running into things."

Catherine looked frightened. She looked frightened of him.

She said, "Now, I suppose you're going to say—" and had no time for more. Evan took her by the back of the neck and shoved her toward a rest room door so she stumbled and one of her sandals came off, and he pushed her into that smaller, tiled white space and held her by the back of her neck so her head was bent down and said, "You just keep quiet, and listen."

His voice sounded to him like some other man's. He saw her eyes and mouth wide as a frightened child's—realized he was hurting her and let go of her neck. And when Catherine straightened up—but slowly, as if to stand erect might offend—he stepped back by the bathroom's sink so she wouldn't be so afraid of him.

"Now, listen. We'll check her out of here and take her home. Then you start packing. You and Beth will drive out this evening. You're driving up to Maine, to the island. Do you understand me?"

Catherine nodded.

... Beth, still dressed and seeming slight as a younger child, lay on a gurney with her right knee lightly bandaged. She was looking up at the ceiling as Evan paused in the examining room's white-curtained doorway. Beth, her face still, colorless, was staring up at the ceiling as if reading there a message sent to her long ago, written in a language she only now had learned to read.

It seemed very bad news had been written on the ceiling, and Evan saw some permanent damage had been done after all, more serious than a sore knee.

"Hello, honeydew," he said. He hadn't called her that in years. And when she turned to him, he saw his mother's eyes in tears.

"How is she?" Mrs. Hooper gone home at last, Evan was in the kitchen disobeying her orders, making ham sandwiches rather than reheating the ragout.

"She's packing, Evan. I told her ... I told her it was possible that some New York people, some gangsters, might be trying to hurt us."

"Sit down and eat. Milk or coffee?"

"Oh, Evan. ... I'll have coffee."

"Sit down. I've got a sandwich for her, and a piece of the apple pie; she can eat in the car. I put milk in the thermos."

"Christ. Christ, I can't *believe* this! What about the police? Really—what about the police?"

"As it happens, I was told today at the bank that the police are still very interested in me—and I don't think one apparently drunken hit-and-run will change their minds. Particularly since, after all, our daughter wasn't hit, wasn't killed." Evan wrapped Beth's sandwich, started on one for Catherine, with Durkee's salad dressing. "Oh, sooner or later, the Raos will interest the New York police. But too late for Josephine Fonsecca. Too late for Vijay Bhose and for Sanchia. Too late for that woman today."

"Grinspun. Naomi Grinspun."

"Too late for her. And, if it hadn't been for her, too late for Beth."

Catherine sat at the long kitchen table, looking down at her piece of pie. "There must be someone who can help. . . ."

"There is. We can help." Evan put her sandwich on a plate, brought it over. "—Here. Start eating. . . . I got some buckshot shells from Terry, in town. Take both your shotguns, and keep one—loaded—within reach in the car. You'll take the Range Rover, and drive backcountry roads all the way up into Maine." He went back to the counter for her glass of milk. "Here. . . . Stay *only* on county roads, unimproved roads. No state highways, no interstates; I'll trace a route for you. . . . If any car tries to follow you back-country, you'll notice it right away. And tonight, tomorrow night out in the boonies, there'll be no place to stop, so just drive well off the road and sleep in the car. Take blankets and pillows."

"All right. . . . All right." Catherine was eating slowly, reluctant bite by bite.

"Don't use your credit cards for food or gas. Don't use them at all—I have enough cash for you. You should get to Shaddock in two days' driving. When you get there, stock up, buy all the groceries you'll need for two or three weeks at least—it'll be all right to give them a check. Don't try to phone me; don't phone Aunt Nan. Don't call anyone from Shaddock. Don't write to anyone, don't contact anyone."

Catherine had stopped eating. Sat with her head bowed.

"Sweetheart, eat the sandwich.... Park the car at Ableson's, inside his shed. Inside, not out in the lot. Then see Clyde Pope or his boy, and have them take you out to the island. Fred Pell should be there; Aunt Nan said he'd come back to town and was staying in the shanty, going for lobster in the cove.... Don't lie to him. Tell him there's trouble, that people are looking for you. And after that, sleep light, keep Beth close, and never, *never* leave the cabin without taking one of the shotguns with you."

"All right. All *right*."

"These are clever people, Catherine. If you don't do what I've told you—if you do something careless, something stupid—they'll find you, and they'll kill Beth. She's the one they really want."

"If it's all true—if this is true, why don't you come with us?"

"Eat your pie. —It's a matter of offense being the best defense, sweetheart." ... Another "sweetheart." If he wasn't careful, "sweethearts" would begin to add up.

After dark, Evan followed them ... the Range Rover's red taillights glowing down the road before him. They ran along Cove Lane ... turned right onto Spring, and stayed on it to Mill. On Mill Road for only a mile, then a left turn up into the hills, first on Red Maple ... then Chestnut to the old township road. Berry Road ... then Branch going east.

He rode after them up winding ways in full dark before the moon, so their lights ahead were the only lights. There were none behind him.

Seven miles on Branch ... and Catherine paused at

the crossroad, likely looking at the map, then turned left on the old Cross Pike road—graveled dirt—blew her horn, and drove up that hill and out of sight.

Evan turned the Lexus's lights and engine off, and sat in the dark for a long time, listening. He sat until the moon came up, then started the car, lights still out, and drove slowly back by moonlight—drove a different way, first to the north of town, then down Post Lane to the Sound. Then south, to Club Road.

The stable was dark when he drove up to it ... let himself in through the narrow entry framed inside the wide left-side stable door. The rows of stalls, lit by single bulbs far down each walkway, were rich with the smell of hay, grain, and horses. He heard them shifting in their boxes, smelling him, hearing him come in. . . . Evan walked down the first row to number six—found Dodo alert, waiting, black eyes reflecting what there was of light. Evan reached over the half-door and stroked that blocky hammerhead, the rough-smooth coat over a neck thick with muscle and bone. It seemed to him some of the small horse's warmth, his courage and stubborn strength, might be transferred by touch, by stroking.

"Have you been good?" Evan rubbed behind Dodo's ears, and the black pony gazed at him in animal innocence. Simply very strong, and very brave, with goodness having nothing to do with it. . . .

Then Evan petted Tulip, next stall down, said, "Good girl," and left ... unbolted the narrow sally door, climbed through, and bolted it behind him.

. . . At home, he found a folded note half under the front door—stooped to pick it up, unlocked the door, went inside and turned on the entrance-hall light. The note had been written on the small, lined white page of a pocket diary.

*Returning your visit of yesterday. Terribly sorry
to have missed you and your lovely wife. And
even sorrier to have missed your charming
little daughter. Better luck next time.*
                              A Concerned Friend

Evan stood reading and rereading as if the note, if he
could only read deep enough, might tell him much
more. He knew the merry fat man had written it. Could
see him leaning chuckling on the door for a flat writing
surface, squinting a little in the coach lamp's glow.

There would have been another man with him. And
they must have come out, stopped by on the chance of
finding him, or finding Catherine and Beth unready
and at home. They hadn't come into the house. There
was no faint new odor, no recent memory of sound, no
other presence in the place.

Evan folded the note, put it in his pocket, and went
to the hall phone to call Mrs. Hooper.

"Hello. . . ." Gerald, Edith's slow and amiable
brother. An aging bachelor and plumber's assistant.

"Gerald—Evan Scott. Is Edith there?"

"Yep. . . . *It's Mr. Scott.*"

"Hello?"

"Edith, Catherine and Beth have left, they're driving
out to Texas to visit some friends of ours. And I'll be
leaving, too—probably be gone a week or two."

"You don't want me to come in?"

"If you could come in tomorrow, just clean out the
refrigerator and lock up the house. —Oh, and capture
Willie if you can and take him home with you."

"That cat chewed up my rag rug last time. My
kitchen rag rug."

"Well, if you prefer not to, or you can't catch him,
then please come by every two or three days and leave
him his dry food and fresh water. Your check will be

on the kitchen counter—and we'll call as soon as we're
back."

"Oh, dear. Oh, dear. . . . Are you going to be all
right, Mr. Scott?"

"I'm going to be fine, Edith. And remember to be
careful, yourself. When you do come by, it might be a
good idea to have your nephew come with you. Have
Tom come with you after work; and it wouldn't hurt if
he had his deer rifle with him in the pickup."

"Holy cow. . . ."

"You said it, Edith." And after he'd hung up, was
sad to have lied, mentioned Texas to her just in case
she was forced to talk to interested people—tell them
everything while they listened, smiling.

He walked down the hall, past the den, and on back
to the kitchen. Turned on the light, went to the refrigerator and took out a wedge of cheddar, an apple, and
a bottle of Boston Lager. He took a small plate and
paring knife from the dishwasher and sat at the long
plank table, eating, drinking the beer—wonderfully relieved to have Catherine and Beth away, turning
through the night down odd and narrow roads. Beth,
Manning's sedative still with her, would be asleep
curled in the passenger seat, head nestled on a pillow—with Catherine, a guardian goddess, driving her
heavy vehicle through the dark. And between them, its
long, gleaming muzzle up and alert, one of her twin
Remingtons, packed with buckshot shells, would be
resting potential, as all guns rested.

The cheese was off a wheel of Vermont rat cheese,
hard, crumbling, and sharp. The apple, a spotted small
tart pippin from Prendergass's, just sweet enough to
balance the beer. Evan ate and sat at ease, the house
resting around him. He had never felt solitary in the
house, had always considered the house a companion. . . .

He chewed a bite of apple, reached down and pulled the .45 out of his waistband, cocked it, half turned toward the old kitchen fireplace, and triggered one round into the blackened bricks at the back.

The noise smacked him across the face, made the table jump to its resonant crack, the row of copper and steel pans ring on their rack above him. The largest black chip of blasted brick had hummed away. . . . Evan's ears seemed to creak awake, listening for more such sound. Gunpowder's bittersweet odor drifted. . . . No doubt the pistol recoiled harder, a sharp whack back into his hand, with the new ammunition. His hand still remembered the GI ball's slower, more measured thump. And the sound of this shot harsher, higher-pitched, not the old simple slamming noise.

He'd aimed at a lighter mottle in the brickwork, and missed it by four inches. Poor shooting, even offhand, even after twenty-odd years—and a stupid thing to do; might have caught a ricochet. . . . He stood, and took his beer with him to go upstairs for two of the boxes of ammunition lying on the bed to be packed . . . came down with those and spare magazines. Then downstairs again, into the basement. . . . He turned on the single bulb that lit the longest rough whitewashed corridor from foundation to foundation, propped a stack of several thick old planks of two-by-twelve scrap against the stonework at the end, then walked back forty feet to the opposite wall, turned and began shooting.

Evan fired a little faster than he had time to aim—never, in firing forty shots and reloading magazines as he did, taking quite enough time for aiming. Only he kept the front sight in mind, and watched over it as the distant lumber, smashed, punctured and split, sneezed away long ragged white splinters.

When he finished the first box, he was no more accurate than he had been. But he was more comfortable.

When he finished the second, he was shooting better, and stood satisfied and deaf in a haze of gunsmoke, the big pistol hanging hot in his hand.

"Could be worse. An' shit sure could be better. . . ." Exactly what Sergeant Beckwith would have said, standing beside him.

Evan collected the empty cartridge cases, filled his pockets with them, turned off the light, and went upstairs to clean the weapon and finish packing a big blue duffel bag.

He slept wonderfully well, didn't dream, and woke at twenty minutes after six.

He showered, dressed in chinos, sneakers, and shirt, and carried his duffel and an old oversized safari jacket downstairs. Then went to the kitchen and made scrambled eggs and ate them with whole-wheat toast and orange marmalade, tea—Irish Breakfast—and the last of the ham, heated in the pan. He washed the pan and his dishes, put them away, walked to the entrance hall and checked an address in the phone book. Then he picked up his duffel bag and jacket and left the house by the garage entrance, locking the door behind him.

He took the white Lexus, went down the drive, turned into the road, and slowed to look back through the trees as the house woke into morning sunlight just come over the hill.

At Harbor Drive, Evan turned right . . . then right again onto Hillside, passed two houses on small half-acre lots, and parked at the side of the road near the driveway of a large cream-painted saltbox with improbable dormers on its second floor. There were several cars parked along the drive.

He walked up to the front door—a Federal door, wrong for the house—rang the bell and stood waiting, enjoying summer morning's warm and lavish air.

The door opened to a pretty woman—small, freckled, middle-aged, and still in her bathrobe. A redhead, the red fading into gray and worn long, to her shoulders.

"Yes?"

"I'm sorry to have come by so early. I wanted to see Louis Grinspun. . . . I'm Evan Scott, Beth Scott's father."

"Oh, God, oh my God. It's all right . . . Louis! *Louis!*"

"What?" As if expecting trouble, a bulky man in shirt and slacks came to the door behind her. Dark hair, and darker eyes. "What do you want?"

"Louis, this is Mr. Scott, the little girl's father."

" . . . I see," Louis Grinspun said, and he and Evan both saw, stood looking into each other's eyes.

"I'm sorry to come by so early—"

"No, no. . . ."

"I wanted you to know that my wife and I understand very well that we only have our daughter because Mrs. Grinspun—because your mother gave her life to save her. As soon as it's possible, my wife and daughter would like to come and see you, thank you for your mother's courage."

"Well, that's . . . that's not necessary."

"I think it is necessary. My wife and Beth have had to leave, have to be somewhere else for a while, or they'd be here with me this morning."

"Well. . . ."

"Until they can come and speak to you personally, I want you to know that you have my deepest gratitude—and my congratulations on having had such a woman for your mother."

"Thank you," the big man said. "A very nice thing to say. And you bet . . ." There were tears in his eyes. "You bet we're proud of her, proud of her memory."

"Come in, Mr. Scott," his wife said. "—Come in."

"I can't, not this morning. I'll be traveling, myself, for a while.—Something that couldn't be avoided. But I would like you to know that my wife and I will be very hurt if we ever learn that you or your family were in need of any kind of help or assistance—anything— and haven't come to us for it."

"Well . . . that's very nice. And we're glad your girl's all right. At the hospital, they said she was fine."

"Scraped her knee," Evan said, standing at the door in dappled sunlight, and the Grinspuns nodded, smiled.

He reached the city at searing noon, the sun's light yellowed, its heat doubled by reflection from concrete and occasional brickwork as he drove down to Soho and past Ward & Breedon's building, past the street's blacktop where young Bhose had died, past the patch of scorched sidewalk that had held Dass's newsstand. Evan found a parking place on a side street two blocks east, locked his duffel in the Lexus's trunk, and walked back, feeling a stranger to the neighborhood.

He went to the Soho Special, took the two-person table at the window where they'd eaten breakfast the last time he saw her, and pretended to wait for Sanchia . . . then imagined he saw her crossing the street to come to him for lunch. Small, hurrying, compact as a fine pony. Evan recalled her face, its expression whenever they'd met to be alone together—a look of satisfaction, of accomplishment and kindness, as if he, superior, selfish, and removed, was a prize of prizes and worthy of her.

Remembering this, he felt such sudden shame, such sorrow, that tears came into his eyes and he held up his paper napkin . . . pretending he was blowing his nose. When the waiter (young, plump, and gay) arrived at his table, Evan glanced up, saw a concerned look on the young man's face, and said, "Sorry. I lost someone

... very dear to me." Startled at having said it and, to this stranger.

"Oh, honey, join the club," the waiter said. "I'll get you another napkin."

... When he'd wiped his eyes (then had really to blow his nose), no one else in the café had seemed to notice, or perhaps had not cared to notice. The waiter brought him a large bowl of onion soup, a hot seeded roll, butter, and a glass of milk. "Soup," the waiter said. "Mother knows best. . . ."

Feeling much better after he finished the food (he'd imagined Sanchia sitting across from him, reaching over with her spoon to try the soup), Evan left a five-dollar tip in gratitude. But the waiter came out of the restaurant and after him down Spring Street. "I never take advantage of sorrow," the young man said. "That's the creepiest thing a person can do," and handed him four dollars.

Evan walked back to the Lexus, and found that someone had broken off the aerial.

... He spent the rest of the day in the Museum of Natural History, wandering through dark hallways into darker exhibits. Most, except for the new models of dinosaurs, he remembered from those two years of his childhood when, ten and eleven years old, he lived in New York with his mother during the separation. And was left here as she went shopping with friends—or perhaps, met lovers. He'd roamed the huge building, so stifling in summer, as if it were his palace, its wonders created for him. Then, he'd almost always had an egg-salad sandwich on whole-wheat bread for lunch, usually with a tangerine. He'd carried them in a small paper bag.

Old friends from his childhood stared out through slightly dusty glass . . . and the family group of African elephants lumbered through the dark past bright dioramas of the East African veldt ... distant herds in almost motion, and just behind the glass, a greater kudu, alert, displaying its thick high shoulders, long thoroughbred legs, its tall spiraling horns.

Evan went through the old dinosaur room, the one he remembered, with only bones—great towering racks of bones to represent what beasts had once surrounded them with muscle and blood, had moved with those bones as scaffolding. Hissing ... muttering. Each of their moments in sunshine as actual as any moment now. —He felt as he watched them almost the slight swinging weight of his lunch in his right hand. Felt he might go downstairs where bronze tribesmen threw their spears at bronze lions across the marble entrance hall. ... Wait there for only a little while, and see his mother coming through the revolving doors. And on her long, white, handsome face, that constant mild preoccupation as if there were something else to be thought about, somewhere else to have been, someone else to be there with. Still, she held his hand as they walked away, went down the wide steps. And still held his hand while they waited at the curb for the taxi— usually a Checker—that always seemed to arrive for her without delay. ...

When the museum closed, Evan crossed the street to sit on a bench along the park's stone wall. He sat there through a long bright twilight, and thought about his mother for a while. His father and his mother, who had seemed more like acquaintances than married people. Very much, he supposed, as he and Catherine must seem except when they were fucking. And he supposed his father and mother had done much the same. Met as acquaintances in a familiar bed, and fucked.

Which was why, possibly, Elaine Scott had taken to going up to men's apartments. City men—brothers or cousins (or husbands) of friends of hers. Seeking perhaps what he'd sought in Sanchia. . . . Then, tired, abstracted, come to the Museum of Natural History to get her son . . . walk down the wide steps and wait for the taxi sure to arrive, and soon.

Ned Lacey at Groton had let Evan know. "Jere Brown's brother has screwed your mother on several occasions in his place on Gramercy Park in New York. —Elaine Scott? Tall, very pale? Good dresser. *Definitely* a lady. And he reports she enjoys it from behind, with her face in the pillow, and is a moaner. Keeps her bra on, apparently beginning to sag." An occasion for the only serious fight of his boyhood . . . blood and near expulsion. But only confirmation, no surprise.

Evan sat into the evening, thought about his mother and father—doing his best to recall their voices, as if those sounds, any of their words spoken, might be the beginning of explanation. But he couldn't hear them clearly enough. He thought perhaps a musician might be able to remember his dead parents' voices. One of the great jazzmen might have been able to remember his parents' voices. Might have been able to play them. . . .

It was growing cooler with the night, and Evan wondered where Catherine and Beth were in their second evening riding, driving north up narrow roads, some barely paved with failing county blacktop—and soon, in another two or three hours, would be looking for a place to pull over, to drive deep among trees, lock the Range Rover, arrange the pillows and blankets in the back, and go to sleep, Catherine holding Beth closer for longer than she'd usually found comfortable. . . . The treasures of his life now sheltered in a machine under leaf shadows shifting in moonlight.

"Hey—you a faggot?" Tough white boys walking past through the streetlamps' harsh yellow light.

Evan sat and watched them, not very interested, and

the same boy said, "He's a faggot," and they walked on.

. . . Then, having considered his family long enough, Evan set them aside, set his parents aside, and sat in the shadows committed to his mission as if briefed and ordered to it. Odd that his men, his recalled and imagined men, seemed more distant now, with this small battle pending—as if, creatures of remembered war, they required peace to come to him.

At nine o'clock, Ram Dass, across the street, walked from lamplight to lamplight to the museum's steps . . . stood and waited. He was carrying a long narrow roll of cloth or carpet under his left arm, slung from his shoulder by string.

"Captain, I'm having a flat—well, a basement flat, that no one could know of. It is the basement of the first place I lived in this country. The superintendent, Louis Salcedo, is a so friendly man; he was friendly to me before I moved into the better place in the Bronx that was my son's. . . . Louis says it is quite OK to stay in the basement flat for two hundred dollars a week. But if it becomes rented, then we have to go."

"We can pay for a week, Dass, but I doubt if we'll be there that long."

"Not that long?" Dass, walking alongside, skipped to get into step.

"Not that long. I think this'll be settled in three or four days, one way or another. Settled quickly."

". . . I see."

"Where is this place?"

"On Twelfth Street, the East Side. It is not a fine neighborhood, but it is not a terrible neighborhood."

"It sounds perfect, Dass. Good job."

"But there is no telephone, however."

"Not important. . . ."

"And your family has gone away?"

"They've gone away." Evan saw the Lexus down the block. A young white man in streetlight shadow was standing by the car, bending to look inside it.

"It is difficult to get a woman to go places she does not want to go. The woman of my house—my wife—was very difficult when she was alive. She did nothing she did not want to do. She wasn't obeying my mother; she wasn't obeying anyone. It is said—I know it is said that Indian women are put upon. But no one was putting upon my wife."

"They tried to kill my little girl. With a truck." The man looked up, saw them coming.

"Oh, my God."

". . . A woman died saving her."

"Oh, my God. Oh, *Ram.* —Those bastards, and that is all they are."

Dass's bundle, his roll of cloth, was bumping against Evan's arm as they walked. ". . . Is that a prayer rug, Dass? I thought you were Hindu."

"Ah, ha. Ah, ha! This is a surprise. What you ask about is a surprise." The old man stopped on the sidewalk under a streetlight, fumbled in the carpet roll's narrow opening . . . and drew a length of steel shining, then a sword swung free in his hand—a light, slightly curved saber with a simple bright-brass hilt.

The blade shimmered in running reflections as the old man swung it.

"A *tulwar,* Captain. A parade saber. Regimental property at first, but given to me on retirement, since I retired a sergeant major. Not troop command, mind; I don't claim that."

Stepping back a little as Ram Dass practiced a cut, Evan looked around for interested observers. ". . . Really a handsome blade, Dass—but you'd better put it away."

"Oh, yes, I'll put it right back away." He fingered out the scabbard opening, and slid the saber home into its narrow roll of carpet. "But isn't it clever? Everyone is seeing an old Hindu man with a little rug of some sort all rolled up. What could be more Oriental, more natural?" Dass settled the wrapped saber under his arm, the carpet roll's string over his shoulder. "But so I have a weapon! And one I know how to use, oh, yes. I drilled so many many hours of saber when I was recruited. Then we still had our horses.... Lorries as well, of course."

"Here's the car."

"This is your car? Oh, it is splendid. It is not a Jaguar, but it is very very nice."

"... And you'd be able to use that sword on a man, Dass? Use it to kill someone?"

"Oh, yes. Oh, yes indeed." Dass stood at the passenger side of the Lexus. "If my father had had such a weapon, if he had had a fine sword by his side, do you think the *badmashes* would have killed him in such a filthy way?"

"No, I imagine not." Evan got into the car, pushed the unlock button.

Dass got in, passed his carpet roll over into the backseat. "You are damn right, not.... Of course, I am not the man my father was." He glanced at Evan. "Shall I tell you a secret?"

"If necessary." Evan started the engine ... pulled the car out into an empty street.

"Oh, you are smiling; you are humorous, but I'll tell you. It seems to me the sword is braver than I am. I am thinking of it as a dear friend of mine. If I am afraid, it will not be afraid.... Is that nonsense?"

"No."

"It seems reasonable to you?"

"Yes." Evan took a left on Columbus Avenue, head-

ing downtown. "In Vietnam, I heard of a man who was
in love with a tank."

"A tank. . . ."

"An M-4. Big machine, obsolete now. Man was a
regimental clerk, had been on the line and maybe was
afraid he was going back up—apparently obsessed
with this particular tank. Always going to the emplace-
ments, sleeping by the machine at night. Always
around during the day, bothering the crew. . . . But they
couldn't keep him away. Orders—wouldn't obey orders. The man had to be near that tank. Maybe just
needed something very big, very strong, very hard to
hurt . . . something like that to be his friend."

"What happened to this man?"

"He slept behind her one night, too close. They
started her up in the morning and backed over him."

"Oh, dear. . . . I suppose my saber might cut me."

"It certainly will if you're careless. You might imagine it's teaching you a lesson in that case, Dass. That
it cares enough to do that."

"You're making fun, Captain. You're thinking it is
all nonsense."

"Evan, not 'Captain.' " The traffic was getting heavier as they went down the avenue. One driver, then another, ignoring a red light. ". . . I'm thinking it's beside
the point. I've known men try to imagine their way out
of the sort of trouble we're in, during the war. It didn't
work; it couldn't work because that sort of trouble, this
sort of trouble, is so . . . absolutely real."

"Yes, I see what you mean. It is, it is very real."

"Remember that woman at the elevator door? How
she looked at us?"

"Oh, yes. That, I am never forgetting."

"There's nothing more real than that look, Dass. Everything else is dreaming."

* * *

The apartment was grim—after a grimmer entrance through a labyrinth of basement corridor. The entrance hall was painted pea green ... the small living room, the tiny kitchen, were painted pea green, the paint flaking away here and there to reveal a darker green beneath. The ceiling was a low tangle of ducts and piping—steam pipes, water pipes that rang and gurgled as if welcoming them in. There were no windows.

It was spectacularly ugly, and it seemed to Evan that this space and the hundreds of thousands of others in the city just like it (though most of those were required to have windows) did their part in disturbing and making furious the people who lived in them. —And most could be improved just with fresh paint. In this place, a false ceiling painted cream white, walls a very pale beige. ...

"That bedroom is the biggest bedroom and it is yours, Captain. And that's settled because the smaller is mine and I am already absolutely moved into it. We are prepared; I have gotten everything. We have sheets and pillows and towels; I have a very good first-aid kit from the army-navy in case of wounds. And hydrogen peroxide as well. And a flashlight."

Evan put his zipper bag down by the bed in the larger bedroom—a cot really, and neatly made up, military-fashion. The bedrooms and the bathroom were also pea green. "I think it's perfect, Dass—I'll give you my half of the rent."

"All in good time." Dass back out in the living room, apparently moving furniture. "After we're having a late dinner. ... Have you eaten?"

"No." Evan began unpacking ... put a spare loaded magazine—one of the new ones—into his jacket pocket.

"Perfect, perfect. I have already been in the kitchen this afternoon and I have made a curry and it is hot on the stove. And *paratha* in the oven keeping good and hot. A spicy curry, but not too spicy. And I have used small bits of lamb in one portion, for you."

"Sounds wonderful."

"And I bought beer." Calling from the kitchen. "Taj Mahal beer."

"Sounds good." Camping out with the boys ... one elderly boy in this case. And there was a release to it, this odd change, this kink in the cord of his life. It had about it that odd element of shared masculine fantasy that the years in the Corps had had. Fantasy that turned to reality so edged it cut no matter which way a man turned.... Evan walked back to the living room. A card table had been set up outside the narrow kitchen's doorway, set with paper plates, white plastic knives and spoons. No forks. "... But we'll share the cooking, Dass."

"What do you cook, Captain?"

"*Evan.* I cook chicken, steak.... Well, we'll forget the steak—excuse me, Dass, of course you're vegetarian. And I can bake potatoes and so forth."

"... Maybe better that I cook, I think."

"No, we'll share the chores. Now ... can I help?"

"No, no. All done. Everything almost all done."

Evan spent the next few minutes sitting in the living room's only armchair—upholstered in worn tufted yellow, its seat sagging—listening to rattling pans and reading a year-old copy of *Cosmopolitan* ("He Loves you—But Does He Listen to You?").... Then Dass appeared from the kitchen carrying a battered black tray with several bowls on it, and two bottles of beer.

"And here it is; here we are with it!" He set the tray on the card table, reached into his back pocket, and took out two plastic forks. "I know, I know—you thought I was forgetting forks...."

* * *

". . . My God."

"It's too spicy."

"No, no, Dass. It's really delicious."

"Too hot—but I made it less hot than usual."

"No, it's really wonderful; I was just surprised. In restaurants, it's usually not so . . . spicy."

"Oh, of course, they're cooking for Westerners. But I made it too hot for you?"

"No, no. I mean it, it's really good." Proving it with another mouthful.

"Do you usually eat lamb, Captain?" Dass was chewing away, his mouth open. He had good teeth for a man his age.

"Oh, yes, very often."

"And how do you have it cooked?"

"Well . . . usually cooked fairly rare."

"Rare?"

"Fairly rare. Chops, rack of lamb. Needs to be fairly rare."

"I see. . . ."

Evan smiled. "Don't worry, Dass; I won't cook. You can cook, and I'll do the dishes. . . ."

Comfortable enough on the narrow cot—not minding the faint smell of ancient urine from the mattress beneath worn sheets—Evan lay with the .45 on the small nightstand beside him, and turned himself over to sleep as he had done in the Annamese Hills . . . set all concerns aside, and slept.

He woke toward morning, listened a few minutes to be certain nothing, no odd sound, had wakened him . . . and heard only the intermittent murmur of water through the basement pipes . . . the old man's minor rattling snore down the short hallway.

Then he slept again, and dreamed a dream of such heat and light that he squinted in his sleep to keep out glare. Nhu Lat, or the narrow road to it, lying in slow narrow rising loops of red dust winding away into jungled hills. Indian country.

He dreamed he drifted ... perhaps flew slowly, steadily rising along the road. Saw two burned vehicles—burned long ago. Someone was waiting, his men were waiting for him, and he sailed slowly through baking air ... then settled down to walk the last quarter click, so as not to startle them.

Second squad was standing in a ville—barely a village for half a dozen families of mountain farmers. His men were clustered around the largest hut—all smiling, weary, successful at something difficult. The rest of the platoon was out of sight—perhaps farther up the road ... perhaps dug into the hillside among the trees.

The Vietnamese, only a few (so much smaller, slighter), stood back, expressionless. There were no young men; four old men stood smoking little twisted cheroots.

Sergeant Beckwith called, "Lieutenant," and came to meet him. "You are not going to believe this shit," he said, and fell into step alongside Evan. "This shit, you are not going to believe."

"I'll believe anything."

"Not this shit you won't." Beckwith as happy as Evan had ever seen him, though looking so tired, sandy, freckled, sturdy as a stump. His uniform was rotting off.

The men were relaxed, pleased to see him. "Come look, Lieutenant!" Kershner, looking not quite old enough to shave.

"All right, here I am. What have you guys been up to?"

"Look what the fuck we got." Jack Miller, no longer bloody, no longer so badly hurt, was grinning and pointing at the hut.

"Take a look," Beckwith said. "Look in that window."

Evan walked, or almost walked—really drifted over—and looked in through the hut's small paneless window (the framed window so unusual in a country hooch), looked into darkness and saw, after his eyes became accustomed, something large and darker. It almost filled the hut, dark and round as a huge chocolate cake. But small things moved in it.

"Death," Beckwith said. "Believe that shit? Took us the whole fucking morning. Found the motherfucker downslope—down on the road! Took us all morning to drive it up here. You know how much death this is? Lieutenant, couldn't be any more of this shit in the area. This is it ... in one big pile. All the death there is around here."

"What are we goin' to do, Lieutenant?" Miller looked as if he'd never been hurt at all. Looked fine. Only tired. . . .

Evan looked into the hut again. The death was trembling like muddy water when artillery came over. Perhaps their voices disturbed it.

"How does it move?"

"Lieutenant, it rolls," Beckwith said. "The fucker rolls like a big ball of tar."

"But it's smooth, man." Billy Torrance, his radio a permanent hump on his back. "You can see your reflection in the motherfucker. . . ."

"We got this piece of shit, now," Beckwith said. "An' not one fucking thing dies for maybe seven, eight clicks any direction. Even a fucking lizard doesn't die. Not a goddamn weed withers. Believe that?"

"Yes. . . ."

"No, watch this." And Beckwith turned a little to his left and fired a short burst (silent in the dream, though his rifle trembled), and one of the old men's black pajamas were struck with three quick holes across his belly. The old man looked startled, then annoyed, threw down his cheroot and lifted his long pajama shirt up to examine it, angry at the damage . . . put his fingers through the torn cloth.

"See? How about that shit?" Beckwith said.

"What do we do with it, Lieutenant?" This was a man who hadn't been with them long before he was wasted. Tedford. Harold Tedford.

". . . OK. First, numbah-one job, guys. Congratulations, and nice work, Sergeant. Second . . . we will burn the motherfucker."

"All riiight!"

"Burn the hooch, Sergeant." And Evan drifted back, watching, heard the tiny clangs and clicks as the Zippos came out, and saw the hooch's thatch singe and then turn bright as sunshine to run up in ribbons of fire. Beckwith and the men stepped back from this new heat that began to seethe and rumble into slow rings and then at last completed to a blazing shell that caught the whole small structure up so it shook as if in the jaws of fire, imploded in a haze of sparks and thundered up in flames thirty feet high.

What was inside, just visible through trembling heat, could be seen stretching and folding . . . but then slowly commenced to cook so the small things within it crawled like flies to its surface.

At last it began to burn, and although black, it burned into smoke a wonderful silky white that twisted smoothly and rose and rose up to the jungle's treetops and above them, silver-white against the sky's hot and vacant blue. It burned, and death made no noise dying.

"But if that can die," Evan said, and wished he hadn't realized it, "—then there has to be another kind of death still around."

"Oh, shit," said Beckwith, "that's right." And Evan woke.

He lay on the narrow cot smelling an odd breakfast. It smelled like bread and hot salad oil. . . . And seemed to him, when he was out of bed and seated at the battered card table eating it, to be some of the same rich layered bread they'd had for dinner, and a dish of hot vegetable oil with mashed peas or lentils in it.

"Only *dal* and pickles and *paratha* is what we are having for breakfast. And oranges." Ram Dass sitting wide awake and very neat opposite. The old man, scrubbed and shaved, was wearing plaid polyester trousers and a short-sleeved white shirt. "I made this breakfast yesterday, and kept it in the refrigerator until this morning."

"Coffee?"

". . . Tea."

"Good news. I'll get it—"

"No, no!" Dass waved Evan back down. "You are the officer; I am the sergeant." And got up and went into the kitchen.

Evan pushed back his chair and followed him, took the kettle out of his hands, and poured tea (already brewed and with milk in it) into two yellow plastic cups. "Listen, I'm not the officer, and you aren't the sergeant. We're two men, comrades in arms, attempting something dangerous—besides, you're old enough to be my father."

. . . The lentil soup or stew seemed to Evan fairly grim. The pickles were good, and familiar as a New England breakfast relish. The bread—thick-leaved, hot and oily—delicious as it had been at dinner. Evan had had the bread before, in Indian restaurants.

"Wonderful bread. . . ."

"Ah. So, you see, you like my cooking. And let me tell you, it is no joke to make that bread in this oven, and with these pans. . . . I have forgotten all about purity. I have had to forget all about that. Soon I will go to the *pundit* and be purified no matter how much trouble. —And we have fruit for our dessert."

. . . Dass's lentil soup soon gone, his bowl mopped with bread, he got up, went into the kitchen and came out with a green plastic plate of oranges and mangoes. "I will prepare you eggs for tomorrow morning's breakfast. Tomorrow you will have eggs. The British NCOs had soft-boiled eggs and bacon—and all the Muslims had to run out of the mess kitchen when the bacon was cooked. They did not even want the smell of it."

"And when the British had beef?"

"Oh, absolutely same. Then the Hindu cooks all walked out of the kitchen. The rest of us stayed there as hosts for the mess, regimental hosts for these British NCOs, but we didn't eat. We had little cakes, and tea, and some little vegetable pies. That's what we had."

Evan finished his lentils, washed down with the tea. Then he had the last bite of *paratha,* skipped the mango, and peeled an orange. ". . . It must have been odd, Dass, British and Indian troops sitting down together, with all that history behind you."

"No, Captain, really it wasn't. It was very comfortable." Dass tilted his head back, poured a little tea neatly down his throat. "They had killed our people and conquered us. Then we mutinied and killed their people. And then they reconquered us—but they grew too weak to keep us and we became free. More than two hundred years . . . more than two centuries of living together. They not so much the conquerors as they imagined; we not so much conquered as we imagined." Dass sipped more tea, a noisy sipper. "We are understanding the British; and they are understanding us. We were so many years lying in the same bed—very much like a long quarrelsome marriage, isn't it? And I will tell you something: Sometimes we miss them, and I believe that they are missing us. So we NCOs did very well together."

"And of course, a sergeant is a sergeant."

Ram Dass smiled, and began peeling a mango. "Oh, that is so true. Officers come and go. But sergeants are forever—even sergeants of supply."

"Particularly sergeants of supply. . . ." It seemed to Evan, as he ate his orange slices, that the old man—talkative, leaning on his past, his old regiment—was vulnerable as a child. Easy to recruit, to take advantage of.

"You know, Dass—what we're after, what I'm after, is exactly like trying to find a spider crawling in your clothes, before it bites you. . . . In Vietnam, we had kraits—little brown snakes, very poisonous."

"We also—we also have those in India! They will kill a man in five minutes. Five minutes!"

"Well, we'll be snake hunting. Spider hunting. Nothing . . . nothing romantically military about it."

"Oh, you don't want me to call you 'Captain.' I know, I understand that."

"No—well, that's true. But what I'm saying is that this is a very nasty business. Ugly and dangerous."

"It is like a real war, is what you're saying."

"Yes, that's exactly what I'm saying."

"And you remain concerned about me. I see, I see that, and it is so nice. . . . But let me tell you something, if I am old enough to be your father. Let me tell you that I know more about these creatures that disgrace decent Indian people than you do. And let me be telling you something else, young man: This will not just be a 'nasty business.' It is more likely to be a fatal business. It is most likely that these *goondas*—who have a thousand years of wickedness behind them—

will be finding us before we find them, and will kill us. *That* is what is likely. . . . So, you see, this particular old man is not needing your concern. He is needing—we are needing—what you have learned in your war, Captain. And no nonsense."

"All right, Dass. Then no more horseshit." Evan ate his last slice of orange. "And, by the way, you just hit the nail on the head."

" 'Nail on the head'. . . ."

"The first rule of jungle warfare. The one who finds—wins. The one who is found, doesn't."

"I understand that. That makes good sense." Dass was cutting his mango's flesh into small squares, slow going with a small plastic knife.

"—A rule I'm sure our unpleasant friends know very well. So, they'll be looking for us, and certainly looking for my family. And if we give them time enough, they'll find us, find my family. No doubt about it."

"No, there is no doubt about that whatsoever."

"So, Dass—how do we find them first?"

"Their goddess." Dass ate one of his small pieces of mango. Chewed with his mouth open.

"What?"

"Their goddess, Captain. They will live near her. Be near her. We are not talking about atheists here, who are believing in nothing. These are devout persons. It is their strength. Their tradition is to be that way."

"You may be right. The one who came to see me did a lot of talking about that. Sang a song to her and so forth. . . . But I'd say locating a goddess is a hard way to go."

"No, no; a goddess cannot be located. —Though she may locate us. But a temple, a place of worship, can be located, isn't it? And there they would be. Kali's servants must be there." Dass ate several pieces of mango, eating swiftly as if Evan might reach over to take some of the fruit from him.

"Dass, it all sounds extremely bizarre, but I suppose it's a notion. —Actually, I was thinking about 366. The building."

"Oh, yes. . . . For why they have done everything!"

"Because of something to do with that damn building, these people have killed a girl and young Bhose, and have killed someone I loved. And now an elderly woman who died saving my daughter's life. . . . That's quite a list. I don't give a damn how bloodthirsty these people are supposed to be; that's quite a list. And it means they have a very good reason—and that means money."

"Oh, yes. They are loving money. They are not so devout they are not loving money. Money is how they know she cares for them."

"Right. . . . Well, where *is* the fucking money? Excuse my language."

"I don't care. We are saying that sort of thing ourselves."

"When we find that, we'll find them coming around to check on it. And it has to be at 366. That's where their company contracted; that's where they started killing."

"So—first the goddess, or your tall building?"

"The building first, I think—starting with the man who built it."

"Very well. To me, it sounds like a sensible plan." Dass tilted his head far back, poured the last of his tea into his mouth.

"Dass, mind if I ask you something?"

"Am not at all minding."

"Why don't you—why do you drink like that? Holding the cup away from your lips?"

"Oh . . . to keep a dirty cup away, is it. Some person

of a poor caste might have used it. Or, here in this country, a very unfortunate person of some kind. I am not prejudiced; don't imagine I am prejudiced. It is now only custom, not that I am afraid of being polluted."

"... I see."

chapter 14

∙∙

The cabinet held no metal of any kind, no fasteners, no nails, no screws—only dowels, perfectly fitted. It was framed in kiln-dried maple, with ash runners for its small drawers. The drawers were birch, and had been very difficult to work. And the drawers were dove-tailed all three sides, each dovetail hand-cut with a tiny Japanese pull saw, with barely visible teeth. What the saw had not been able to accomplish—narrow work deep into the corners, shaping the olive-wood dowels and plugs—had been done with wood-carving knives for the left hand, special orders from Lomax & Doyle in London.

The glue was calf's-foot and fish-bone, mixed and heated over a spirit lamp.

The cabinet, though incomplete and only two and a half feet high on its low bench, already had about it an air of importance, of careful work beautifully accomplished. Its several woods seemed to sing together as a string quartet might sing, and their cabinet, even unfinished, balanced between craft and art.

Evan and Dass had sat in the Lexus through two hours of darkness, parked deep in tree shadow well down the block.

"He's got a shop back there. The garage is a shop,"

Evan had said. "Woodworking. DiNunzio mentioned last year he was quite a woodworker.... It's worth waiting to see if he goes back there after dinner."

And he had, twenty minutes ago.

Evan reached up, switched the Lexus's dome light to off so it wouldn't light as the doors opened. "Let's go." And they stepped out into a summer night as cool, as tree-shadowed, as insect-noisy, as darkness in the country. There were lights on in the small houses up and down the street, occasional faint conversation from televisions.

They crossed the street side by side, Dass with the slender roll of carpet under his arm—and a small dog traveled its mesh fence along that sidewalk with them for a yard or two, yapping—then, as they moved away, out of a streetlamp's light, was quiet.

Evan led across a narrow front lawn ... then down the driveway side of the house. A woman was talking with a child in the kitchen as they passed. The child's voice a boy's.

There was a door at the side of the garage, and Evan paused there, listening. Dass stood too close behind him, almost touching, and Evan reached back, put his hand on the old man's chest, and gently pushed him away for more room to kick the door open if it was locked.

Evan listened a moment more, heard nothing but the gentle snoring of a small saw ... reached out to the knob, turned it, and tried the door. It swung open silently, hinges well cared for, well oiled—and Evan went in running, hit Jerry Fonsecca from behind and knocked him sprawling half across the workbench, throwing bucking shadows from the low hanging light set swinging.

"Close the door," he said to Dass over his shoulder, and the door closed as Fonsecca thrashed to get to his feet, a small silvery saw still in his left hand—and a beautiful cabinet tipped over and fell to the floor, cracking a corner.

"Hey!" Fonsecca, half up, still startled, stared at Evan and recognized him. "You ... you fuckin' asshole! What the fuck you think you're doin'?"

"They've tried to kill *my* daughter, Jerry. And now I want to know anything you can tell me."

"What the fuck?" Fonsecca stood up. "You cocksucker comin' in here—" He glanced over at Dass, and Evan reached out, shoved Fonsecca hard with his left hand, and as Fonsecca knocked that hand aside, brought the Colt across in his right as if he were slapping the man with it. The .45 struck Jerry Fonsecca across his left cheek, broke that bone, and knocked him down.

Fonsecca was a strong man, and had been hit before. He rested a moment on his hands and knees, then got his feet under him and was hit again. This impact made a stony sound, and it put him down on his face in aromatic sawdust.

"Captain, don't kill him!"

"Oh, I'm going to kill him," Evan said. "If I have to I'll kill him, all right." And feeling larger and oddly shaped, as if he had a longer reach than he'd had before, Evan leaned over Jerry Fonsecca and hauled him up. Fonsecca half lay against his bench as if he were filled with sand. His hand was empty; no more small saw. "Do you hear me?"

Fonsecca seemed to be listening, but hadn't heard, and Evan put the pistol back into his waistband and looked for something else to hit Fonsecca with. He was concerned for the pistol, that he might have damaged the slide hitting bone with it.

There were only little tools scattered on the floor, little knives twinkling in swinging light, so Evan stepped

back, and—as Fonsecca recovered himself, stood up
and shook his head to clear it—stepped in again and
kicked him in the groin. Fonsecca grunted and bent in
a half-bow, and Evan, as if this had been rehearsed,
reached out with both hands to grip the man's head,
held it down, and brought his right knee up into Fonsecca's face to break his nose.

Jerry Fonsecca made noise then, a shout, almost a
scream, and Evan was on him and had his hand over
his mouth and broken nose, and that hand's fingernails
pressed against Fonsecca's eyes. "Listen," he said.
"Are you listening?" And now Jerry Fonsecca was listening, and Evan could feel blood slippery against his
palm, could feel the man trying to breathe.

"I've killed a dozen better men than you. Two
dozen! —I don't even know how many poor fucking
people I've killed, and they were all better than
you. . . . Let your daughter be murdered by those people and didn't do *anything!*" Evan felt Beckwith's
knife, its scabbard leaning against the small of his back
like a friend's hand.

"Captain. . . ."

"Just watch the door," Evan said, and leaned back
from Fonsecca and took his hand away from the man's
mouth. "Now, listen to me," he said, and could see that
Fonsecca was certainly listening. "You let them murder
your daughter and get away with it. —I saw her fall. I
saw her fall. . . . And now they've tried to kill my
Beth, and a woman died to save her! Now, I'll tell you
something, Jerry," and he reached under the back of his
safari jacket and drew Beckwith's knife. "To save my
daughter, my wife, I would skin you alive. And I know
how, because I've seen it done."

". . . I . . . can't say nothin'." But Fonsecca's eyes
had changed, seeing the knife, as Evan remembered
seeing a VC officer's eyes change during an ARVN in-

terrogation outside Hue. Now Fonsecca's eyes admitted other possibilities, now understood that anything might happen. They were a new person's eyes, not Jerry Fonsecca's anymore.

"Waste him," Sergeant Beckwith said from the corner.

"Captain. . . ."

"Too bad . . ." Evan said, and thought that was absolutely true, it was too bad—and brought the big bowie back and poised. He thought he might turn the blade to strike with the flat. He thought he might do that, if he remembered—and Jerry Fonsecca said, "Oh, no, no, no!"—sounding odd with his broken nose, with blood running down to his chin—and held his hands up to his damaged face like a grieving woman, as if having them there would somehow prevent the blade.

He spoke very rapidly through guarding fingers, talking while he watched the knife's bright steel to see what it might do next. "They asked me to withdraw an overtime complaint. An' I said fuck you hell no. And Mr. Rao, Chandra, he was there with his brother—I didn' get his name. . . ." And then stopped talking, sitting half propped on his workbench, watching as Evan lowered the knife. Then, very slowly, as if he were terribly tired, Jerry Fonsecca tugged a white handkerchief out of his back pants pocket, and held it to his nose. He looked older, looked ill as the light still swung back and forth above them, but more slowly.

"And you said, 'Fuck you.' "

Fonsecca brought the handkerchief down, looked at his blood on it. "That's right. An' he just smiled at me and patted me on the shoulder like we was big buddies, and him an' his brother walked away an' I figured that was it an' fuck 'em. . . ."

For a while, no one said anything. Dass cleared his throat.

"Then Josie went. Then she fell—an' it killed me. Just bein' an accident it killed me. But the next mornin', the boys were gone right out of the yard. Four years old an' gone right out of the yard! My wife went crazy; she went *crazy*. . . . We looked through the whole neighborhood and no dice, and we were goin' to call the cops and they were back. —Back playin' right in the fuckin' front yard like they was never gone. An' their faces. . . . Guys who got 'em, those people made up their faces like they was girls, like they was whores. Lipstick, an' eyelashes an' all that shit. —But they didn' touch 'em. Didn' molest 'em. Just took 'em somewhere, Joey said, a fat guy an' a little guy—dark guys talked funny—an' got 'em some ice cream. Then they put that stuff on their faces, made 'em up like they was girls. . . ."

Jerry Fonsecca sighed and seemed to doze under his worklight, as if he'd paid his debt with enough words. He swayed.

"Hang on, Jerry." Evan reached back to slide the reluctant knife into its long scabbard, and Dass came to hold Fonsecca up.

"So," Dass said. "Then you knew."

"This is Ram Dass Lal, Jerry," Evan said. "The Raos don't like him, either."

"Oh, no. They are not liking me; they are intending to kill me. I am a loose end. Men like the Raos are not liking loose ends. They are very neat people in their business."

"I don't feel good," Fonsecca said. "I don't feel good." And as Dass held his arm, kept him from falling, he bent over and vomited, and stayed bent, gasping. He'd eaten a big dinner.

When Fonsecca recovered, though he was making a soft continuous humming sound—perhaps so as not to have to vomit anymore—Evan said, "Jerry, what's going on on 366? What's so important to them up there?"

"Nothin'!" Fonsecca seemed to wake with that question. "There's nothin' goin' on on that buildin'. Hey, some friggin' kickbacks and shit—but *nothin'*. That's good steel, an' it's goin' up right!" He looked for his handkerchief, but it had fallen on the floor.

"Well, we're going over to take a look at all that 'good steel' tonight, Jerry." Evan stooped, picked the handkerchief up and shook sawdust off it, where it had stuck to the blood. "Here. . ."

Fonsecca took the handkerchief and made dabbing motions at his nose, but didn't touch it. He had vomit on his shirt.

"Surely," Dass said, "something must be rotten on that building, Mr. Fonsecca."

"Jerry . . . ?" Evan was feeling weary, as if he'd done more than what he'd done to Jerry Fonsecca. As if he'd been doing that sort of thing for a long time, and was tired.

"I don' know. I don' know. . . ." Fonsecca was leaning against his bench, still occasionally humming very softly. Now he was with them, though his face was oddly mottled, very pale everywhere but where he'd been hit—and there beginning to swell and darken. But that was over; now he was only a man talking to two others. It would be an embarrassment now to hit him; that was all over. "I tried to figure somethin' out, an' there's nothin'. All their electrical shit is put in to code, far as I can tell—an' you gotta be talkin' more than ten million bucks wirin' and labor and switches and motors in that buildin'. An' that's just so far. DiNunzio isn' complainin' about anything; he thinks they're doin' OK—no skin off his ass. City isn' complainin'. . . . So, I don' know what the fuck they're up to."

"Jerry," Evan said. "These people killed your girl, and they took your little boys and had some fun with them—all just to keep you in line, for now, maybe for later. I'll tell you something that puzzles me. What puzzles me is why you're letting them get away with it."

" 'Puzzles you,' huh? Listen, Mr. What-the-fuck crazy—I don' know what the fuck you are. . . . When Joey an' Gregory showed up back in our yard out there? With that lipstick an' makeup shit on their faces? I go to see a guy. An' while I'm goin' to see him, I got two friends, buddies of mine, sittin' up in my house with shotguns." The worklight now hung almost still, and shone down on Fonsecca's face as if to illuminate cabinetry needing complex repair. Needing a reversal of time and absence of trouble in order to fit properly together. ". . . So, I go to see the man, who ordinarily I would stay a long way away from. I convey the situation to him. An' he says, 'Oh-oh. Weirdos.' An' I say, 'You got that right, an' they killed my girl.' 'So,' he says, 'you goin' to do me a favor if I do you a favor, Jerry?' An' I said, 'You're goddamn right I will, help me with these motherfuckers. . . .' "

"And what happened?"

"Nothin'. That's what happened. His guy, Charlie Franco, comes to my house—and believe me, I'm not happy havin' this guy in my house. He says, 'Hey, sorry. Nothin' can be done.' This fuckin' Franco guy has personally put people away. We're talkin' about a giant guy I understand has personally killed people with his hands. A goddamn animal. An' he's apologizin', sayin', 'Sorry, no way. Chief says forget it.' "

"An' I say, 'How can I forget my daughter?' And this Franco says, 'Hey—we all got kids. Big guy's got grandchildren, and these people are unreasonable; they're so fuckin' foreign there's no use tryin' to talk sense to 'em. Period.' . . . So, I'm lookin' at this monster ordinarily would scare me shitless, an' I just lost it and I say, 'Listen, you fuck! You people go around hittin' people in the head and stealin' money and scarin' the shit out of everybody bein' so fuckin' tough. An' here I got a real situation, killin' nice girls for Christ's sake! A wonderful girl! Takin' little boys and playin' games with 'em? Think I don' know what that was, what they were tellin' me puttin' that makeup on those babies? Think I don't know what those motherfuckers'll do to my little boys next time? They'll cut 'em, make girls out of 'em. That's what they're goin' to do the next time.' " Fonsecca closed his eyes for a moment, but apparently saw what he imagined too clearly, and opened them again. . . . "So, I mean, I was furious with the guy. I didn' give a shit what I said. An' you know what he does? He just sits there an' he says, 'Hey, you got a point, Jerry. I know you got a point. . . .' An' that's it. This monster sits in the kitchen an' eats two pieces of my wife's poppyseed cake. He drinks two glasses of milk, an' out he goes." Fonsecca took a slow deep breath, as if he'd been short of air for some time.

". . . So now, let me ask you somethin'—you crazy asshole come in here an' goddamn near kill me—let me ask you why I don' do shit to bother those Rao fucks not even a little. An' I'm not goin' to. I am not goin' to do it. I'm out of it . . . I'm out of it. My Josie's dead. My little sweetheart is dead an' gone. Now I got the boys to think of. I got my wife to think of. . . . You don' like it, fuck you. . . ." And Jerry Fonsecca ran down like an old clock, unwound.

They drove down Hillside Avenue into a summer storm's first gusts of wind, come thumping out of the

darkness between the streetlamps' light. There was little traffic so late.

Dass cleared his throat. He'd cleared his throat before. He cleared his throat again, and said, "We didn't
receive much useful information."

"I didn't expect to. I don't think Jerry knows much
about the Raos—except what they've done to him.
And he knows that whatever hoodlums he went to, prefer to leave the Raos alone."

Evan glanced over at Dass, and saw the old man
looking older in intermittent sulfur light as they rode
along. The wind came again, a south wind and strong
enough to buffet the Lexus. If the storm reached the
Sound, any yachtsmen would have to run for cover in
whatever cove or harbor, to stay off the Connecticut
shore. At home, by morning, stray flotsam would have
drifted into the cove. Occasional planks ... plastic
soft-drink bottles.

"It seemed a ... drastic sort of a beating, for us not
to be expecting information from it, Mr. Scott."

No "Captain."

"Fair enough. I lost my temper with him, Dass, and
I shouldn't have.... But I didn't beat him just for information. I intended to mark him, so whoever informs
to the Raos on 366 would see he'd been leaned on—"

" 'Leaned on.' ... Oh, yes." Now rain came hissing
down in curving curtains. The Lexus sounded with it
as it struck.

"—Been roughed up by someone, for some reason.
And the Raos will assume, correctly, that the someone
was us, and that Fonsecca might have been persuaded
to cooperate.... So, Jerry can't just show up at work
looking like that. But he can't stay home for a week or
two, either, or *that* would make the Raos suspicious.
Either way, a badly bruised Fonsecca or a missing
Fonsecca, and the Raos will assume we had something

to do with it—and that Jerry might have said something . . . might have agreed to go to the police, and is now a danger to them."

"So, they will kill him—or be doing something dreadful to his little boys."

"That's right, Dass; they would. And Jerry will realize that. And he'll do the only thing he can do."

". . . He will call them." The rain suddenly slackened to almost haze as they drove through it, tires sizzling on the pavement.

"I think he's calling them now—telling them what happened, and that we're going to the building tonight."

"So they will not distrust him. Then they will think, 'Oh, my—what a sensible fellow.' "

"And they'll send people after us; they'll send people to 366. And then, if we're lucky—very lucky—we may get our hands on one of the Raos, on one of their hoods at least. And that man can tell us where they live."

"Oh me oh my. . . ."

"Dass, you know the phrase 'a piece of cake'?"

"I certainly do; it is a British phrase—and it is not applying here at all, Captain."

"That's right. I was going to say this will not be a piece of cake."

Rain came again with the next gust of wind, drumming in, flooding the windshield between the wipers' strokes.

"And if he does not call, Captain? If they do not come?"

"Then we'll have all night to find out just what it is about 366 that was worth all those lives."

They drove onto the Long Island Expressway into slowed and heavy traffic, and rolled over sheets of

draining rain that thrashed under the Lexus's wheels.
The windshield shimmered with water as they went.

They rode in silence for a while, and Evan lowered
the driver's side window for a moment for fresher air,
to feel the rain spatter in ... then closed the window.

"I did lose my temper with him," he said, and they
swung down the exit and into the entrance of the
Queens Midtown Tunnel ... and white reflecting tile
beneath the East River, beneath the weather.

Three six-six was wreathed in rain, misted with it
into an immense skeleton tower rising into night, and
barely lit every other floor by dim occasional bulbs.

Evan had brought a flashlight from the Lexus, but
hadn't switched it on when they came over the high
fence—its chain link rattling softly through the sounds
of rain.... There was no watchman on site when they
came over the fence. No one patrolling through more
than an acre of stacked equipment and material as they
moved carefully through it. There was no watchman in
the site-office trailer.

"Is this unusual, Captain?" Dass looked sad with
weather, lit by a pole lamp across a heap of steel rebar.
His khaki zipper jacket drenched, his handsome white
hair soaked to his scalp, he looked smaller, wet, and elderly, tired from having climbed the fence.

"No watchman? It's very unusual."

"Oh, dear. . . ."

"We'll go up, use the work elevator to the top, then
search as we come down. They've started to lay wire
this week, so they should have ladders on every floor
now."

"And you think those people are here?"

"I don't know—but ordinarily there's always at least
one watchman, all night."

"I do not know which God to pray to," Dass said,

"—and I am most certainly going to be catching cold." He hitched his carpeted saber under his arm, and stepped out beside Evan as they crossed the yard, keeping to shadows along the building's east side.

They saw no one at the elevator stage—dark under the structure's loom. They climbed wooden steps to it, their human scale shrunk by the night, by the size of the steel framework rising alongside.

Evan wiped rain from his face. "No elevator. They must have left it high." He noticed he was speaking very quietly. Murmuring. He stepped back, looked up into fleeting rain, and could barely see the elevator's minimal cage high alongside the building's flank, six stories up.

"Then we climb. —And the ladders are where, Captain?"

They found the long wooden ladder (barely lit by a distant bulb) propped in the middle of an acre of first floor, resting on just-cured concrete at the poured lip of what would be a freight elevator's single shaft. A yard in front of the ladder's foot, the great black square of space opened in the floor, a gulf down to basement and subbasement. The ladder rose from the edge of that shaft, fifteen feet to the second floor and darkness complete. . . . Here, almost eighty stories down, the rain had found its way, and dripped musically into puddles among a forest of steel beams and uprights, supports and braces, plank and concrete flooring, cables and wiring—all now black with wet, and dark or dimly lit. This wilderness smelled of curing concrete, of sprayed paint and fire retardant, and of wet steel's faintly bitter scent. The odors were intensified by the rain.

Evan stood with Dass in the deepest shadow of a massive, boarded crate, well away from the ladder. Behind the crate's wide-spaced two-by-fours, a huge black electric motor, light just touching its paint's fine reflective gloss, bulked like a beast in its cage.

"Well," Dass whispering, "here we are."

Evan put his hand on the old man's shoulder to keep him quiet, and listened. Sniffed the air too, for cigarette smoke (hard to keep a light in all this wetness) ... or hair oil, or wet wool. Any odor but the building's, or theirs. He raised his head like a dog's to smell the air ... and also listened. He tried to recapture, to recover what he'd been so long ago. Then he'd hunted—too weary, too used to death to be afraid of it anymore—and nothing had been on his mind but going, doing what had to be done, then coming back.

... And after a while, when he was no longer trying, Evan became only a listener, a taster of the air, and nothing else.

Only a few minutes later, he heard a plank reverberate very high above them, the slight sound echoing down and down with falling rain. A plank had shifted slightly as many other long and heavy planks—loose-laid—had shifted slightly with the occasional buffeting wind.

But that plank, so very high above them, had moved between gusts, when it should have lain still.

Five stories up. Five or six. Five or six swift stories up steep ladders to be located in the dark. ... Dass's shoulder trembled with wet and chill under Evan's hand.

"Dass," speaking very quietly into the old man's ear, "I'm going up the ladders for the elevator. Can you stand guard here, see to it that no one follows me up?"

"I'm going with you." Whispering.

"No. It doesn't take two of us to bring that work elevator down—and we have to have it to survey seventy-plus floors before dawn. But I don't want to have to worry about my back when I climb. So, you stand guard—here, take the flashlight, but try not to use it."

"No, I will go with you." No longer whispering.

"Dass—"

"I can climb. I am not so old I cannot climb."

"Sergeant, you will please do as you are damn well told."

". . . Very well. I will do it, but it is unjust."

"Keep in shadow, keep quiet, and if anybody tries for the ladder, stop them."

"*Unjust. . . .*"

Evan climbed, annoyed by the weighty length of Beckwith's knife sheathed at the small of his back, the more compact weight of the .45 in his waistband. He felt encumbered, almost clanking with steel.

But not slowed. It surprised him how quickly, how eagerly he climbed—up two floors already, and almost at the third—as if something wonderful waited higher, up cluttered cavernous floor after floor of darkness and dripping water. Partly it was feeling the building to be a familiar place, and nothing strange. Though he hadn't designed it, Evan felt he knew it, and felt known by it.

. . . He'd gone up these first three ladders—each set one above the other—he'd swarmed up them almost as if he were slowly flying up into the building, only touching the ladder rungs as he went.

There was no ladder to the fourth floor, its absence announced by lightning, then thunder that made the steel columns around him hum in sympathy. A rain forest, but steel, and rising through darkness into a storm.

Evan—only impatient, late for an appointment—went searching the endless floor by lightning flashes, looking for the ladder, for anything to climb on. . . .

. . . Dass felt he was freezing, was certainly very

cold. It had been one of the trials of this country, the terrible cold. That, and rudeness. And now again a rudeness—left like an old fool to stand shivering in the dark. Left with nothing to do but be afraid. Even being afraid was more bearable in warm weather. . . . However, he was more uncomfortable than he was afraid. That was how wet he was, how cold. And this was summer!

He had heard the sound, and thought nothing of it—a ticking noise. When he listened now, it seemed probably the rain dripping . . . dripping. Striking metal perhaps, like footsteps. Like a man with those metal taps on his shoe heels.

The rain striking metal, Dass thought, and a man came walking just past him in near darkness, walking to the ladder.

"No no!" . . . Dass was astounded he'd called without thinking—so surprised he seemed more surprised than the man he'd called to. A small man, and he turned smiling in shadow as if he'd been called to by a friend. He was wearing a short blue raincoat with a belt, its shoulders wet with rain—and as he turned smiling and stared to see Dass more clearly, Dass saw him more clearly.

The man was certainly small, and very dark, with neatly cut black hair and long sideburns. He had a mustache, which looked odd on his face. It seemed to Dass almost a dog's face, as if the man had half changed into a *pi* dog, and stopped before that was finished. The man's teeth, his jaw, protruded almost into a muzzle. But it was his eyes that most made him resemble a dog. His eyes were small, golden brown as a dog's that understood people as all dogs do. But this was a savage dog, and had eaten corpses in the streets.

"Nao, wiw you tike a look at wot we got 'ere!" He spoke a hard cockney dialect, very like a British corporal Dass had known at Dum-Dum Depot. "Wot we got 'ere is a right fuckin' ol' *thakur.*" And the small man tugged a large tucked bandanna of white silk from his raincoat pocket, snapped and twirled it so it ended gripped in both hands, its fine material twisted into rope. Then he came strolling.

Dass wished he were younger; he wished it as he turned and ran away—ran to the right around the huge square black emptiness of the basement excavation for the elevator shaft. The small man broke into a trot behind him, splashing through a puddle, muttering something to himself in Hindi, and Dass wished he were younger so everything wouldn't seem to be happening so fast. He called, "Captain!" as he ran, and heard his voice swallowed in thunder that still allowed the rapid tick tick tick of the small man's shoes behind him.

Running, running, almost stumbling at the next corner—running like a child around that dark vacancy—Dass remembered some advantage . . . remembered his saber, and as he ran half-turned to fumble at the end of the narrow carpet roll slung under his left arm.

"Goin' to pry?" The small man was giggling just behind him. "Is it a Muslim, then, this brave *thakur*? Carryin' a fuckin' pry'r rug?"

And Dass felt the *tulwar*'s brass grip—seized it, tore the saber free—and turned in a rage of terror, yelling, the bright curved blade flashing down.

The small man stepped aside to the left, startled, but not afraid—stepped far enough aside for the blade to thrum down past him. And he seemed to hang there in emptiness above the elevator shaft—seemed to stand poised for that instant on a dead black floor. Then he fell, and left his silk kerchief floating in the air.

Dass, staggering at the edge, heard the small man

say, *"Kali,"* very quietly. Then heard him hit bottom two stories down in darkness—a complicated thud.

Evan found the fourth-floor ladder lying on the planking almost at the building's west-side edge—only found it by the last of several lightning flashes. Then he dragged it back across the floor in darkness, through an irregular shower of rain filtering down, splashing musically onto steel, drumming on the timber flooring.

He hauled the ladder to the edge of the freight-elevator shaft, lifted it, set it up, and climbed. There was a dim worklight a distance away on the fifth, and he found the ladder to the sixth floor in place.

At the top of the ladder, he eased off and crouched by an I-beam in the dark—no yellow worklight on this floor—sniffing the air again, listening. Now, the thunder rumbling away inland, Evan could hear the hiss of traffic down the avenue below. . . . Far across the floor, a small red bulb burned in the work elevator's cage. Except for that, only distant flares of lightning reflected every now and then on row after row of columns of wet steel. The night air was a haze of coolness, and as he waited where he was (waiting for a message sure to come), a gentle wind, trailing the storm, blew and eddied through the building as if to take advantage of its nakedness. And it seemed to Evan, resting against wet steel, that this bareness, this structure, was the building—and the rest, its skin and windows and furnishings, only a compromise for the comfort of lesser creatures.

Evan waited, and watched—felt he could wait until dawn. Wait until the first workmen came. And then wait through their day, and stay until the next night fell. He understood how a ghost might choose to haunt a place.

But a while later, considering Dass—elderly and nervous—waiting for him below, Evan stood and walked down an aisle of steel toward the elevator's small red light. None of his men had come from dreams to watch with him, to scout the forest of columns. Beckwith wasn't pacing at his side. . . .

The big elevator cage rested alongside the building, open above waist height everywhere but at the steel-barred side wall where the control buttons were backed by its electric motor and cable wheel. The cage wore a jewelry of raindrops shining ruby in its small bulb's light.

Evan stopped at the entrance chain, waited a while longer . . . then unsnapped the chain and stepped over six inches of space out onto the elevator's grillwork floor. The big cage trembled slightly at his weight. Trembled when he walked over to the control buttons set in a small stainless-steel box set bolted between two of the narrow vertical bars. The only light was red, after the dimness of the building's interior, and the last of the storm's rain fell through it, free down the structure's side.

Evan pushed the lower large steel button, and the cage jolted as the electric motor hummed, sputtered, then hummed higher into a whine and the cage began to sink fairly fast, shaking. Evan turned to look out over the city—saw it frosted with haze of the last of the rain, the lights of its buildings a galaxy slowly rising as he sank.

The cage trembled as if he'd moved, and something fell white before his eyes and took him by the throat.

Took him and in the same motion hauled him back so his head cracked against the slender steel bars of the cage's side. There was no breathing anymore. And soon, so terrific the pressure circling his neck, there would be no consciousness. The red light already pulsed in his sight, and swarms of motion stirred before his eyes.

Evan saw in a slow accurate vision—as if he stood in the air a few yards away—saw himself held strangling against the bars protecting the elevator's motor and moving cable. And behind him, crouched beside the motor's housing on the outside of the cage, a man made of shadow who gripped the throttling cloth with both fists (clinging, supported now only by that knotted cloth), his feet propped up on the bars before him to add to his leverage.

Evan tried for the .45. Got his hand on it, drew it from his waistband as he began to go blind—but still saw well enough to see a quick foot in a brown penny loafer kick between the bars, and catch his wrist hard enough to shake the gun loose ... send it skittering over the steel flooring.

An alert man, a good man killing him.

Now there was nothing to see but red, with darkness growing at its center. There was a pain somewhere that was becoming death, like a train rolling down dark tracks, and Evan asked himself to reach behind him, up under his jacket—to find and draw the bowie knife cramped against the bars in its scabbard behind his back. He asked that of himself ... and thought finally it was done, that the knife was in his hand and held away from kicking.

Now blind, he willed the knife to rise so the long blade was set at an angle beneath his chin. He felt the cool line of the edge.... Then Evan cut his throat.

—And slid down kneeling on the elevator's steel grating, the strangling cloth sliced away.

As he began to breathe—gasping, gulping air—he heard the man's shout echo faintly up as he fell, and an impact far below. Then Evan leaned forward, rested on his hands and knees to breathe better. Breathing mattered and nothing else mattered. . . . Then, as his vision cleared, saw bright drops of blood fallen from him.

"What a near-run thing. What a terrible thing!" Dass very pale, still at his post. Evan saw he had his sword out.

"I was careless—and then very lucky."

"Oh, Krishna—how badly are you hurt?"

"Not serious." Evan was embarrassed to see his hands were trembling.

". . . Let me look, let me look. Your skin is cut, and it is bleeding all over. You have blood all down your front. What a thing to do. . . ."

"It isn't serious."

"No, no. It is not squirting out. The blood is not squirting out. It is a cut . . . just a cut." The old man looked haggard by flashlight. "I must tell you I have killed a man here, Captain," he said. "I too. My ancestors came up in me and I killed him as they were killing men, with the sword."

Hearing that, a second man dead, Evan felt an odd swinging sensation, as if everything would soon begin to slowly turn . . . and turn . . . then faster and faster, becoming a tornado of killing. A war of only a few days. . . .

It took them almost an hour to retrieve the dead.

. . . They had to search for access steps down to the bottom of the freight-elevator shaft. Then, by flashlight, found the small man sitting up, penetrated by two long spikes of rebar waiting upright for a final pour. The first inch-thick corrugated steel had punctured him up through the buttocks into his bowels. The second, entering slightly to the side, had broken through his right hip and thrust up into his chest, his heart. Held upright by these two supports, sitting in a pool of blood and rainwater, the small man had watched them with dusty eyes ... had been heavy and uncooperative as he was hauled up and off impalement. Had farted as he was lifted free.

Then, after they'd heaved the small man—so heavy now—up the access steps from the shaft, Dass, resting bent over with his hands on his knees, had said, "I was telling a lie, Captain. I never struck him. You can see I did not strike him. He was chasing me around this hole in the floor as if I was a chicken, I was so afraid. Then I struck at him, still being so terribly afraid, and he dodged away and fell. And there, I've told you the truth."

"Dass, only a jackass wouldn't be afraid of these people. You did ... you were perfect." Evan had been crouched, searching the corpse. "—This man had a pistol." He'd stood and held it out to the old man. "Czech—a nine-millimeter. Take it."

"No, I don't want it. I know nothing of pistols, though I have fired a revolver, for familiarization."

"You sure?"

"I could not hit anything with a pistol. A man would stand laughing at me all day long while I tried to hit him with a pistol. . . . I am a good shot with a rifle. If we find a rifle, I would be a good shot with that."

Evan had tucked the weapon back into its shoulder holster, and searched the small man's body for his wallet, for identification. "This man has nothing on him at all. One hundred dollars in five-dollar bills, and not a goddamned thing else. No driver's license, nothing. Very professional. . . ."

"Your neck is still bleeding."

Evan had felt the torn strip of silk bandanna bandaging his throat, saw wet blood smeared on his fingers.

"Less. . . . There should be some wheelbarrows out there, Dass. I'll go bring one in for your friend. And then we'll take it and go looking for my friend."

"But to do what with them? Are we putting them in the car?" Dass had looked very tired, ready to cry.

"No. I think we'll leave them in the Rao office trailer. Let those people bury their own . . . give them something to think about."

"It is us they will be thinking about now."

"—And we can also take the opportunity to look through that trailer."

But after they'd spent some time searching—by faint streetlight through the site fencing, by cautious flashlight—they still hadn't found the other man, Evan's man . . . And all the while, the small man had waited patiently in shadow, lying in the wheelbarrow beside stacks of drums filled with fireproofing.

"Could he have gotten up, do you think, Captain, and walked away?"

"At least four stories down—and into all this? No, I don't think he walked away. . . ."

Still, they hadn't been able to find him, hadn't found him anywhere beneath the work elevator's track. . . . Then, after what seemed a very long time, Evan saw a hand and shirt cuff, and they found him lying with his back broken across a big wire spool, a surprising distance from the building. He was breathing when they found him, but as Dass crouched and spoke to him in Hindi, then Hindustani, his breathing slowed . . . and stopped. He'd been a tall man—younger than the other, though beginning to go bald, and not as well dressed.

Now, with both dead men piled into the wheelbarrow—Evan at the handles, Dass steadying—they slowly wended their way across the worklot, down corridors of supplies and material.

"I hope to God no watchman comes, Captain."

"I think the watchman was told to get lost."

"Get lost . . . ?"

"To stay away."

"Ah. I suppose no one has told the police to stay away?"

"No."

"The police would be so upset with us. . . ." Dass began to make an odd sound.

"Dass, are you all right?"

"I am giggling. I am giggling. It is so silly. . . ."

"No, no it isn't silly," and Evan began smiling, intended only to smile, but began to laugh and tried to stop—which made them both laugh louder. They tried to smother their laughter as they trundled their load along . . . tried to stop laughing to catch their breath.

"Oh, officer," Dass said, "we can explain everything. . . ." More laughter wheeling their dead from pool of light to pool of light. Until they sighed and stopped laughing at the Rao office trailer.

"Oh, God . . . Dass, what a character you are."

"I think we are both being characters."

Evan reached up to try the door—open; the two men must have waited there. The smell of cigarette smoke still coiled from inside. "Let's get them in. . . ." And as if in punishment for having killed them, for being humorous, he and Dass reassumed the burden of the dead, lugged and hauled them leaking up one by one— the tall man first—and shoved and slid them through the trailer's doorway into darkness. Then Evan climbed in over them, and pulled them all the way in onto commercial carpeting and clear of the door. ". . . That's it."

Dass came up the step into the dark. "Can we go soon and leave the trailer to these, Captain?"

"Yes. And thank God they only sent two."

"Three, actually." And the light went on.

A man in a gray silk suit was leaning, his legs crossed, against the edge of a desk at the far end of the trailer. An Indian, slender and very handsome in early middle age, his thick, beautifully combed hair an even dark iron-gray.

Evan saw, grown-up, one of the three schoolboys in the framed photograph. This had been the thin boy, on the left.

The handsome man had a stainless automatic in his hand, but he wasn't pointing it. The gun rested casually along his thigh.

"Old man, close the door. . . . That's right. Very good." He leaned at ease, and looked down the aisle at the two dead men. ". . . Goodness gracious, what a slaughter, what a hecatomb. Poor Piroo, and Vikran also." He shook his head. "It seems we should have sent in at least the second team. Sivastra will be heartbroken. She and Vikran are practically newlyweds. Really—only married six or seven months. . . ."

"Sir—"

"Shhh, quiet, old man. I am Dev Rao . . . and you, of course, are the stubborn Mr. Scott—and looking somewhat the worse for wear. But didn't I hear merriment? Didn't I hear laughter from outside?"

"We're easily amused."

"I see. . . . Well, and this old man is Ram Dass—Something?"

"Yes. Sir, I wish to—"

"You are not going to apologize, surely." Rao gestured with the pistol, only slightly. "This would seem to require a little more than that. Piroo perhaps lacked charm, but Vikran could be really good company, for an hour or so."

"This is going to require . . . what?"

"Oh, Mr. Scott, it is going to require that you and your old dog, here, stop breathing in and out. That's what. But, for the moment, if you care to prolong the moment—and who knows? The police, or the FBI, or an angel with golden feathers may come sweeping in to your rescue—but, for the moment, disarm yourself. And very slowly. Then you can live as long as I have questions, and you have answers."

Evan reached carefully to his waistband, pulled the .45 free, and stooped to slide it down worn linoleum to rest a few feet from the handsome man.

"Really sensible, Mr. Scott—but do you know something? Do you know—and I'm sure you must, from your experience of war—do you know there is a difference in posture, in attitude, between a man who is armed—and the same man, unarmed? Well, there is a difference. And I must tell you, I do not yet see that difference in you." Dev Rao, leaning against the metal desk, smiled. "So, you will slide another weapon to me, please. Slowly."

Evan reached to the small of his back, drew the bowie, bent, and sent it after the Colt.

"Good gracious, what an object! I see you share a taste for tradition with our redoubtable Sher Daula. . . . And you, old man, look too frightened to be armed— and are you Muslim, to be carrying a prayer carpet with you?"

"I *would* like to pray."

"You hear that, Mr. Scott? Your myrmidon would like to pray before answering questions. Not what one would call a 'strong right arm,' is it?"

"Please, *please,* sahib, allow me to pray. Then I will answer anything.'"

Dev Rao smiled. "A fine and traditional attitude. How could we not follow such sheep to these new fields, Mr. Scott?... Get on with your praying, old man. Consider it a dispensation of the Lady Durga, in the avatar even Muslims know."

Evan felt the time arriving, saw that Dev Rao did not, and didn't glance Dass's way as he heard the old man drop his narrow carpet roll to the floor, kneel to untie its string.

"What do you want to know?"

The handsome man examined him, smiling. "Very direct, very Western, Mr. Scott. First, what are you looking for, here in our beautiful building?"

"For what's profitably wrong."

Dev Rao nodded. "Very well put. And did you find it?"

"I will."

"No, I think not ... except perhaps in spirit. And now, the question of the police—"

Evan heard Dass grunt with effort to his left, and saw an instant after something bright rotating, flashing through the air down the trailer.

Dev Rao saw the thrown saber, watched it come to him, then ducked only slightly, glanced at it as the blade whirred past and above him to clang off the trailer's end wall. "Stupid," he said—and as Evan straightened from the small man's corpse with the Czech pistol in his hand, saw him and fired one fast shot that snapped past Evan's left ear so close it stung, then fired again as Evan fell behind a desk.

"You silly fucker," said Dev Rao, and he came down the aisle shooting twice more, striding behind gunshot blasts. He was no longer handsome.

Evan rolled from behind the desk and shot Rao once, in the narrow stretch of white shirt showing as he came, and Rao reached down with his free hand to hold that place and aimed and fired again so the carpeted floor jumped by Evan's head. Then—flat on the floor—Evan shot him in the groin and saw the man stagger, his hip broken so he came hobbling deeply, swaying, and raised his bright pistol.

Evan shot him high, and Dev Rao jumped in place and stumbled in a crippled half circle while his eyes stayed on Evan, considering him as coldly as if all choices still were his. Then he fell over, toppled sideways and hit his head hard on the edge of a steel wastebasket.

All in silence now for Evan, deafened by gunfire. All in a haze of gunsmoke, so rich in memory.

"There, there you filthiness!" said Ram Dass Lal, still kneeling on his small carpet.

Though he felt well, hadn't been hit, it was difficult for Evan to get up off the floor. He had to collect himself, grunt with effort, force himself to his feet as if the floor were where he belonged.

Dev Rao, lying stretched on his back, made a noise in his throat as if he were gathering phlegm. Evan saw the stainless pistol lying a few feet away under a desk, and walked over to the man.

Rao's eyes, dark and fine as a deer's, were dreamy with shock. "I hurt my head ..." he said, his voice bubbling up through blood inside. Evan, his ears still ringing, found it difficult to understand him.

"You hit a wastebasket on your way down."

"Embarrassing ..." Rao said, and the word sounded spoken by a fountain. He smiled, then stopped smiling and tried to draw a breath, couldn't, and grew first concerned ... then very troubled ... and finally desperate, making a huge gaping face for air, his eyes inhuman in their need. He began a crippled heaving, thrashing on the floor, his face a darkening tragic mask.

Evan bent over and shot him through the head.

Dass had come to stand beside them. "Return as a

spider," he said to the dead man, as the trailer's thin metal still rang with the shot.

. . . Then they were out of the trailer into cool night air. They'd hurried out, after Dass retrieved his sword, as if the dead men might have risen against them if they'd stayed.

The site was comfortably dark, the darkness concealing except where the few pole lamps shone sulfur-yellow amid rows of equipment, stacks of supplies.

"Are we leaving, now?" Dass slender in dim light.

"Dass, we're here. And despite all this . . . killing, we have a chance to find out what we need to know. Can you go back to the building? Do you feel up to that?"

"Oh, my goodness me."

"You'd rather just go home."

"Captain, of course I want to go home. I wish to be going home immediately. But, unfortunately, we can't because of our duty."

"Are you sure?"

"Yes, I'm sure," Dass said, and headlights came sweeping across the site, a car turning in at the distant gate.

Evan took Dass by the arm and half-lifted, half-ran him along the trailer's side, then around to the back as the headlights focused. The car came straight down the bulldozed access, bright rings of halation around each light.

"Is it them?"

"Quiet." Evan pulled Dass deeper into shadow . . . tugged him to the left behind a double stack of crates. "Just stay still. I don't think they saw us."

"Is it them?"

"I don't know. Just keep quiet."

The car, a brown Mercedes, passed under one of the pole lamps, the big sedan rocking a little on the rutted drive. It came on . . . and on to pull to a stop at the Rao trailer. Close enough for Evan to hear the soft squeal of its brakes.

"Oh, Ram, oh Shiva-ji."

"Quiet."

The driver got out first, an Indian, a very thin man in slacks and a white shirt. Then a man got out the passenger side, and two more men from the back—one of these was tall, older, dressed in a dark-blue summer suit. This man stood for a few moments in the faint glow of a distant light, looking over at the building's steel scaffolding. His face, bony, plain, and deeply lined, seemed pensive, almost sad.

"Oh, dear." Dass, whispering.

Certainly the eldest brother, Chandra Rao. This had been the boy standing in the middle of their old silver-framed picture. The mournful boy who'd already known what he and his brothers were to become.

The thin driver walked up to the trailer door, called something—then tried the door, found it open, and stepped up into darkness.

Evan felt his heart's hard rapid beat.

The light in the trailer went on and the man inside called out . . . cried out, and the others went in, the sad man last, as if he already knew what he would find.

"Oh, no." Dass started to scramble away down the wall of crates, and Evan reached to hold him as men came flowing out of the trailer into the night. A hunting pack with pistols in their hands. They scattered into the dark, circling, questing, and as they ran they called to each other, soft yodeling cries.

Then Chandra Rao stepped down from the trailer door, and only his eyes had changed.

"Please. . . ." Dass twisted in Evan's grip, almost got away. And Evan, wrestling to hold him still, made the slightest noise.

Chandra Rao slowly turned his head to look their way.

Then Evan was still, and Dass the same, as if a sudden terrible cold had come and frozen them motionless and silent.

Chandra Rao came walking toward them down the trailer's side. There was no weapon in his hand. He walked through darkness as if he saw them very clearly, as if he saw through them. His men hooted softly through the night on either side. . . . Then called closer.

Evan and Dass turned together and ran.

They ran down between the long rows of crates as animals run from predators for their lives. Evan found himself startled at his terror, felt himself carried along by his own body as if it had taken charge of him, as if it left him no choice but running. Running—then suddenly dodging to the right around the end of the row of crates, Dass still with him, keeping up. There were huge spools of cable here, and they ducked between and around them, wove themselves deep into a forest of stacked cable. They ran through this maze dodging, trying to avoid the light, and the Rao men called softly, hunting them.

Then Dass stumbled on the uneven dirt and fell— and for the first time, as if he'd been deaf before, Evan heard the old man's desperate breathing.

"Come on, *come on*," and he picked Dass up, hauled him up and ran with him, supporting him, half-carrying him along while the rug-wrapped saber swung and nearly tripped them. Someone called out nearby . . . then called again from farther off, beside heavy equipment. And the pack replied and seemed to swing that way.

Evan thought of letting the old man fall. He thought of two or three swift reasons why that was a good idea.

He thought of that while his body paid no attention to him, to how frightened he was, but only heaved and heaved the old man along, held him up for unsteady running.

The tall chain-link fence stretched across the back of a wide storage lot of diesel drums. There were pole lights over that field, and they went into it through alternating dark and light. Dass seemed better now, almost keeping up, and they threaded their way through and through the drums and were almost at the fence when two shots cracked and the rounds hummed past. Then they were at the fence and heard metallic thunder behind them.

Evan turned and saw Chandra Rao running toward them over the field of drums, leaping from one fuel drum to the next—from darkness to light, from light into darkness. There was still no weapon in his hand. But two of his men were loping behind him.

Evan went up the fence clawing, scrabbling, kicking his way up—and heard Dass call, "Captain," behind him. Then had to, *had to* turn back, hang from the fencing to reach down for the old man's hand, grip it and haul Dass up through the air until they both struggled in the wire at the top, rolled over it, tore themselves free and dropped to the pavement outside as Chandra Rao and his men struck the fence, one of the men shooting as Evan shoved Dass behind a parked car and dove after him.

The fence shook and shook; the men were climbing, and Evan and Dass got up together and Evan supported him as they ran again—ran past three cars to the side-street corner and around the corner as glass was blown out of a car window behind them, and pistol slugs sparked off pavement and whined away.

The Lexus was there, and Evan got his keys out as he ran ... unlocked his door, pushed the unlock button for Dass, got the key into the ignition, started the engine and pulled out into the street as a man came running firing at them, small quick bright blossoms of gunfire as he came. And other men behind him.

Evan drove out and down the empty street, swerved hard left then right to make a more difficult target, then stomped the accelerator to the floor and drove away. They were doing seventy past the second intersection when he began to slow for the turn to the avenue. He could hear Dass's labored breathing beside him.

"Are you all right? Dass, are you all right?"

"Yes." A long pause for a deep unsteady breath. "Yes, I am all right." Pause. "I am only a little too old ... for a great deal of running ... and then climbing the fence."

"Sit back, sit back and rest." Evan turned the Lexus into brighter streetlights and sparse traffic. "No more running. No more fence climbing for you, Dass."

"I apologize, Captain, for my panic, for being so frightened."

" 'Frightened'? You were only frightened, Dass? Well, I was fucking terrified."

The Dond was dancing.

Towering, bearded, he revolved slowly to that unpleasant Western music—paying attention only to the drums—then gradually began to whirl faster and faster, so the wide hem of his long coat floated out around him in moonlight.

The fat Rao, Vasud, had danced in the garden as well, prancing and shaking his behind, dancing with his strangling cloth like a woman with a gauze, making fun, as he always made fun.

He had made fun of the Dond for refusing to touch the stained panties, the bra. For refusing to drink any of the beer.

However, the Dond—who would not touch a filthy thing, who would drink no alcohol—did smoke a rolled cigarette of the West's weak *kif,* and had no objection at all to fire.

chapter 15

....

Evan and Dass came home to their basement as the night grayed toward dawn, came trooping down the narrow concrete entranceway, moving as if there were more than two of them. Unlocked, then locked the fire door behind them. The basement, so grimly ugly in flaking green paint, its ceiling woven of stained water pipes, worn conduit and ancient wiring, now seemed to Evan his home and refuge—while Connecticut, after a day and night, had become the World, insubstantial as wishing.

"Time for first aid." Dass very cheerful, bustling for his kit. "And I am MO. I say butterfly bandages for your neck, Captain," and sat Evan down in one of their two straightback chairs. He very gently cleaned the cut on Evan's throat. "Only skin and a little under is injured," Dass said, "no arteries, no vessels." He cleaned it, stinging ... then closed it neatly with small adhesives.

"There. . . . It will hurt, but it will heal. Would you like something to eat, Captain?"

"No, thank you, Dass. Just a shower. A shower and sleep. . . ." Evan had pulled over to a double phone booth on 54th Street, found the right-side phone still working, and reversed charges on a call to Clyde Pope, up in Shaddock.

After some hesitation, perhaps hearing Evan's *"God damn it!"* in the background, Pope had accepted the charges.

"Clyde, sorry to call so early. Did my family get in?"

"Yes sir, Mr. Scott. Got in this afternoon."

"And they're out on the island?"

"Sure are; my boy ran 'em out. That damn fool Pell is out there, too. Poachin' lobster."

"All right. Thanks, Clyde; sorry I woke you."

"I was up."

"And if someone goes out to the island with groceries or whatever, please have them tell Catherine I called, and I'm all right. —And have her reimburse you for the charges on this call."

"I'll see she gets the message, and I guess I will get my phone money, too. Can't afford to be givin' money away. . . ."

Evan had hung up, then stood exhausted in the phone booth for a moment, as if there he was closer to Catherine.

". . . For myself," Dass said, "I am going to heat some tea, and have Ritz crackers. And then I'm going to bed and will sleep forever."

"You did very well, buddy—and in that trailer, better than very well."

"Oh, yes, I am a fighting man now," and apparently cheerful, Dass went into the narrow kitchen and began to clatter pots and pans.

Evan stood for a long time in the grimy shower stall—soaped, then slowly turned under steaming water. He used a spare towel wrapped around his neck to try to keep the bandages dry. But when he turned off the water, stepped out in front of the sink's small mirror, he saw his throat was bleeding a little, the bandages wet through.

He dried himself, then collected a wad of toilet paper, and pressed it gently along the cut until the bleeding stopped. It didn't seem worth the trouble to have Dass redo the bandages.... Evan wrapped a towel around his waist and walked down the hall to his small bedroom, sat on the cot as it twanged softly with his weight, and put the .45 and bowie on the bedside table. Someone had painted the little table the same shade as the walls—perhaps missing grass and woodlands, but not quite recalling their green.

He sat on the cot, thinking about the three men killed. Two fairly accomplished brutes—though apparently only the "third team." And then Dev Rao. To the Raos, the first two would only be casualties. Wasted grunts. But their brother's death would be another matter.... Dev Rao had carried a wallet, unlike the others, but the only address in it had been the same address—Rao Electric's offices. And there'd been no paperwork of any kind in the trailer, all drawers empty, all desks cleaned out.

Evan looked down at his hands—steady, no trembling. They'd been very steady when he'd aimed the Czech pistol to kill Dev Rao, laying the front sight on that white shirt. He sat a while longer ... then stood up, dropped the towel on the floor, turned down his covers and lay down to sleep—worried he might dream of war, have no rest from killing.

... Dass (having eaten several Ritz crackers with peanut butter, and rinsed his dish and cup and put them away separate from the Captain's) came to Evan's bedroom door in stocking feet to find his officer asleep, exhausted, seeming much more tired than this elderly man—who was, after all, old enough to be his father. Dass stood in the doorway, quite satisfied, and thought of the Captain as his son—a son he might have had perhaps, if he had married one of the English nursing sisters, the missionary ladies he had noticed at the clinic in Gwalior Territory. If he had married the little plump one, white as a white pigeon. . . . Instead of Shakuntala.

Dass watched for a few minutes while the Captain slept, then went to turn off the hall light, and to undress and wash. . . . And when that was done, he took his saber from a chair in the small bedroom, leaned it against the wall beside his bed, and lay down to sleep.

He whispered to himself in Hindi, *"I have my ancestors' courage in me, after all. . . ."* And felt he had discovered himself as a new person, and not at all the man he had believed himself to be for all his years.

Catherine sat on the cabin's long deck in pale early-morning sunshine, and watched Fred Pell's old Sea Truck trundle out of the island's lee heading east, bucketing a little in the chop.

She could see Fred at the wheel, and Beth standing small beside him in her white sweater and red knit cap. They were going out to pick up lobster pots for Fred's brother.

Fred Pell had listened when Catherine told him of the possible trouble, had listened and not seemed surprised. Battered, bulky, almost toothless at forty, Fred was no longer surprised by any sort of trouble.

"That so?" he'd said.

"At least, it's . . . it seems possible, Fred. Evan believes—we believe they tried to hurt Beth."

"Well then, fuck 'em," Fred had said, and casually accepted when Catherine handed him one of her shotguns.

"Just in case. I know it seems ridiculous."

Fred had sighed, checked to see that the Remington

was loaded, then turned and lumbered away down the steep path to his shed.

"Poor Fred," Beth had said, and Catherine had turned to see her standing at the open cabin door with a half-eaten apple in her hand. "He's our bodyguard."

"Which we probably don't need at all, sweetheart."

"Daddy thinks we need him."

"Your father is not always right, Beth."

"You're just mad at him," Beth had said. "And I know why." And she'd gone back into the cabin.

Catherine had started to go in after her . . . then hadn't. She'd imagined herself and Beth in the kitchen—both angry and frightened, yelling at each other. Both of them saying too much. So she hadn't gone into the cabin, had just let it lie.

Now, watching Fred's boat well out in the offing—still able to make out Beth's red knit cap—Catherine felt relieved to be alone. It seemed to her that Beth had suddenly grown old enough to be difficult as another woman . . . be as much trouble to share a house with as another grown woman might be, with things unsaid humming under daily chores, errands. Two women alone now, no longer just mother and child.

And who to blame for this . . . this premature complication? Who to blame for his daughter's fear and his wife's humiliation? A selfish man and his entanglement with other selfish men was what it came down to. It was disgusting—and to have been with such an ugly young woman. A plain young woman, anyway, and very ordinary. To have been with her, and then come home to his wife and maybe not even have washed. To have said things to that woman about love. Perhaps to have loved her, and given love away that should have been his wife's. . . .

Catherine, who'd been sitting erect as if she might get up in a moment, now relaxed back into the deck chair and watched the sea. Fred's boat had gone out of sight around Little Rooster, the small island's steep granite and pine green.

... A plain young woman. Young. Perhaps it was that she'd been young. She hadn't had to look into her mirror yet as if it were an enemy. She hadn't seen herself as Catherine had, beginning to spoil; only the beginning, but it was there at the back of her arms. It was there behind her knees, the most delicate spiderweb of fine blue veins that had to be covered with makeup, foundation. But Evan might have seen them when she came out of the shower. Seen them and thought how ugly they were. . . . Perhaps that was what he had wanted with the Puerto Rican girl, a body that time hadn't marked. Perhaps he'd wanted that, or perhaps only a woman who didn't know him so well. Who only liked him, only loved him, and nothing more complicated than that.

A seagull, dark gray and immature, swung in from the sea . . . sailed up the island's slope, and up and over the deck. Beth had fed it the day before, and it had remembered. The young bird turned and turned above Catherine, wheeling in the air, observing her first with its left eye, then the right. Eyes lemon-yellow and merciless.

"Shit and you're dead," Catherine said.

The gull skated a few yards in the air, cambered its near wing, and swung back in over her. It was like a cat in its dignified begging, its cold demand that returned nothing.

Catherine sighed, got up from the deck chair, and walked into the cabin for bread. Two pieces, no more.

"Want to try for the goddess?" Evan felt quite well, and deeply rested. He had dreamed, but forgotten the dream.

"Oh, yes, that is certainly best. Where she is, they are."

Breakfast was fried banana, fried zucchini slices, fried eggplant. Lentils and pickles.

"Oh, I didn't get eggs yesterday—we were so busy rushing around, fighting. . . ."

"That's all right. We'll pick some up today. Bacon—is bacon all right for you, Dass, not offensive?" The cut across Evan's throat seemed to pull whenever he moved his head . . . a constant slight pain.

"The throat is bothering you?"

"No, it's fine."

"I will clean the cut, and be putting on fresh bandages right after breakfast. —And as for bacon, I don't give a damn about bacon. We Hindus can eat all the bacon we want to eat, if we are eating meat. But usually, we do not eat meat."

"Forget the bacon."

"No, we can have bacon."

"Forget the bacon, Dass. Now, how do we go about finding this goddess of theirs?"

"Oh, for that we must ask a *mahant,* a priest."

"Of Kali?"

"Oh, of them all—but mainly of Lord Shiva. We'll go to the temple, where I have been before several times, doing *pujas,* and asking blessings."

"Well, do us both a favor, Dass. Ask several blessings while we're there."

The zucchini was the best of the fried vegetables.

The Hindu temple was in the West Village, on a long loft floor above a drugstore. There was no sign or notice of it on the building.

"Here we are, Captain."

"Where?"

"Upstairs . . . and Captain, this priest, this *pundit,* is

a Brahman man, a holy man very clever about the best gods to help, the most interested gods. But you musn't touch him—no shaking hands or that sort of thing. No touching, and not be letting your shadow touch him, either, or he will be spoiled and have to go to a great deal of trouble."

"I understand."

"We will go upstairs, and I will go into the temple, and I will make *pujas,* and then I will ask the *pundit* to see us. . . ."

A fat man in a Hawaiian shirt and blue jeans sat at a desk at the top of the stairs, and Evan thought for a moment this might be the priest, but the fat man only stared at Evan, and grunted as they went past him.

Evan followed Dass into a small room with no windows—a room painted saffron-yellow, its floor painted the same color. There was no furniture in it, except several cushions apparently taken from different sofas and easy chairs, and scattered across the floor. The small room's walls were banked with flowers—some daisies, but mainly marigolds and yellow roses in thick ranks rising from the floor on wire racks, so the room seemed made of flowers. . . .

"You are waiting here, please," and Dass opened a door into sandalwood smoke, candlelight, and the sound of someone singing very softly. Evan saw for a moment a long room—and just past the doorway, a statue of a small gold woman smiling and riding a small gold tiger. The statue was above an altar wetly gleaming with what Evan supposed was clarified butter, and wreathed in flowers.

Then Dass was gone, the door closed, and Evan— enjoying the drifting odor of incense overlying the scent of blossoms—sat on the largest cushion and began to consider various choices of college for Beth. Early to worry about it, of course. . . . It would be wonderful to find one of the good schools that still taught with rigor, without the fakery that passed for serious subjects at most schools now. Special "studies" of this or that trendy and victimized group. Sociology and its attendant nonsense. . . .

The door opened and the priest—in white skirt, a scarlet string over his bare left shoulder—walked in smiling, chose a green cushion a few feet away, and sat cross-legged. Dass, following him in, picked up a cushion and settled beside Evan. The priest was a young man, his bare upper torso plump, smooth, and very light brown. His scalp was shaved to a topknot, and he had odd eyes, taffy-colored and set slanting.

"Good morning, Captain. . . ."

"Just Evan Scott, sir. Good morning."

"Good morning, Mr. Scott. Do you know what sort of face you have?"

"I imagine a fairly tired one."

"Of course. You're having adventures, as I understand from Mr. Ram Dass Lal, whom I already knew from coming to temple to do *pujas*—make his prayers. And adventures are always tiring, or they are not adventures, are they? No, what I meant was that you have a particular kind of face. A Kshatriya face. A man-of-duty's face—involving violence as a form of service."

"A form of desperation, in this case."

"And not . . . pleasure? Mixed, of course, with necessity?"

"Too frightened for pleasure, so far."

"Um-hmm. I understand that you have already been in a war—a war perhaps too dubious for you. And now, at last, a little war very much worth winning, isn't it? And a genuine peace to follow . . . ? Well, I will not prescribe for you, Mr. Scott. You have your own very understanding God for that—but, since you are both in difficulty with men descending on the wheel ... with men in unfortunate rebirth, I will be what little help I can."

"We need to know where they are, sir. Where they live. We need to find them before they find us."

Dass said something in another language.

"Yes," the priest said to him. "At what they call a temple, no doubt. ... You see, Mr. Scott, these *tugs*—an obsolete term by the way, and origin of your word, *thug*—these criminals, in damaging our good people here, are abusing the complications of a wonderful feminine power. To them, her energy is only to put money in their pockets, and they do not understand—cannot understand—that she is simply fashioning their *karma* through their own hands. They imagine she aids them in their criminal nonsense, which is so very foolish. Lady Durga, in all her attributes—of which Kali is only one—is concerned with much more important matters."

"But they have a temple?"

"Oh, yes, Mr. Scott. Somewhere in New Jersey, I believe. But it is only a temple of foolishness."

"Would you know exactly where?"

"No, I'm afraid not. I am very much a New Yorker, you see, even a Manhattanite. I never go to Jersey." And sitting at ease, watching Evan as if Evan were a landscape, seemed to have nothing more to say.

The flowers' scent had overcome incense, and the small room, yellow as its yellow roses and marigolds, now smelled richly of bitter-green and roses' perfume.

"Wonderful flowers. . . ."

"Yes, thank you. We have new flowers almost every day—at outrageous expense, I must say, even now in summer. In winter, you would not believe the bills. In winter, our flowers come all the way from the Jews, in Israel." The priest lifted his right hand, examined it for a moment as if it were something new. "Aren't they odd?" he said. "The gift of Hanuman. . . . So, the gods and we enjoy flowers together. I personally, and I wouldn't quote the *Gita* for it, but I personally believe that flowers are a sign to us. To persevere, do you see, in our attempts to understand the incomprehensible. I believe flowers are intended to comfort us while we seek. Does that seem odd to you?"

"No, it doesn't."

"No? Well then, perhaps there's something to it. Perhaps I am not mistaken—oh-oh, I hear them coming. . . ."

Evan heard footsteps on a distant flight of stairs.

"A bridegroom's blessing is due—and blessing is how we make our bread and butter, isn't it. And Mr. Scott, I regret to ask—"

"We have to go," Dass leaning to whisper in Evan's ear.

"Yes, I'm sorry." The priest made an exaggerated face of sorrow. "But if you would be so kind as to go away, or you will mar purities left and right and make for more work. Go away down the staircase you came up."

"Of course." Evan stood, stiff from sitting on the floor. The cushion hadn't helped much. "And thank you for giving us this time."

"I have not given you anything, Mr. Scott." The priest stood as easily as he'd sat down. "Time, least of all. For that you must ask the Dark Lady, when you find her. But now I give you my blessing, and for free. Ram Dass Lal, think of Lord Krishna for your Christian friend." The priest smiled at Evan. "Lord Krishna is the god for you, Captain. In him, all anger, all sorrows of the past, turn at last to laughter and sweet sleep."

"Then, sir, he is certainly the god for me."

"If you ever meet him," the priest said, "ask him to

open his mouth. And if he will, there you will see everything. In Krishna's mouth, the stars are burning."

In the corridor, Evan took out his wallet, then two fifty-dollar bills, and gave them to the fat man at the table. The fat man grunted and put them in a light-blue Florsheim shoe box drifted half full with money.

"Where do you order your flowers for the temple?"

"*Achchi-bat!* Oh, yes! So good a question," Dass said.

"Temple business," the fat man said.

"Answer the Captain," Dass said, "or we will take back our money."

The fat man shrugged. There was singing, and a drum began to tap in the temple. "Anan Prakash provides our flowers, and they are too dear. . . ."

. . . They found a phone booth with a phone book still in it on the corner of Carmine and Bleecker, and Evan looked through pages of Flowers (wholesale, retail) to the P's—to Prakash Blossoms, 141 37th Street.

It was a slow drive through dense traffic—Dass singing a song ("a very religious song") and accompanying himself with rapid little handclaps as the false detective had, singing his song to Kali. A slow drive, and impossible to park once they were there, all spaces taken by delivery trucks and vans. They had to circle the block, then circle two blocks . . . then park on 34th Street.

Prakash Blossoms was not at 141. It was several doors down, a first-floor store with two long windows. There were no flowers in its office, only a middle-aged black woman behind a high counter stacked with order books. She looked at Evan and Dass as if she'd seen them before, several times, on no interesting occasions.

"Miss, we're looking for an address—"

Dass standing beside him at the counter, elbowed

Evan fairly hard. "It is a purchase we are wishing to make. To send wreaths of flowers to New Jersey."

"We don't do retail."

"Oh, this is the first of several deliveries. It will be a wholesale amount—and it is going to New Jersey to a temple of Durga, as her avatar."

" 'Durga as her avatar,' " the black woman said, opened one of her order books and leafed through it. "I don' know anything about that. We got seven churches, four different temples in New Jersey take our flowers. One of them is a Jewish temple. A synagogue."

"Not that one, miss. It is a Hindu temple we are sending to. But I am so foolish, I have left their address at home."

"You don' know where you're sendin' these flowers to?"

"Yes, everything but the address." And lower, "—Excuse me for elbowing, Captain."

The black woman sighed and shook her head. "You can't send flowers if you don' have no address."

". . . Marigolds, miss. This temple would have been sent only marigolds."

"Well, that wouldn' even be in this book. . . ." The black woman sorted through several of her ledgers. "An' how much are you sendin', I'm wastin' my time lookin' all this up?"

"One hundred dollars worth."

"You got to be kiddin'." And she closed a book she'd just opened.

"One thousand dollars worth," Evan said. "Wreaths of marigolds to be delivered tomorrow morning."

"Not tomorrow. Goin' to be a two-day to deliver on that."

Evan took out his wallet. "And I'll need the address for taxes."

The black woman opened the book again . . . turned

the pages. "We send marigolds to all them Hindu places. . . ."

"But for one," Dass said, "that is their only flower. No other flowers but that."

More pages slowly turned. "They all get those marigolds. . . ." Then a page turned back. "Travelers' Rest Motel. Eastfield Exit. New Jersey Turnpike. . . . They don't get nothin' but those marigolds."

"That's it!" Dass slapped his forehead. "Stupid me to be forgetting it."

"That'll be one thousand dollars, please, cash or card."

"Cash," Evan said, and took out his wallet.

"Is there a discount, miss," Dass said, "if old flowers, flowers past their prime, are sent? We do not need to be sending all very fresh flowers."

"You don' want these flowers fresh?"

"They can be simply mature flowers. This temple is not needing wonderful flowers . . . is not needing the freshest of them."

"All right. . . . Eight hundred and fifty dollars," the black woman said, and reached to take the money.

"Do we go today?" The question apparently waiting to be asked as they'd walked two blocks.

"Let's think about it. Are you hungry, Dass?"

"Oh, yes—I am always a little hungry. It is a Hindu trait because we are usually vegetarian. A tiger eats only once a week, and is full of dirty meat. A deer must eat once in every hour, and is full of clean grasses. Full of flowers. . . . What do you think of that?"

"Poetic, Dass. Nicely put." Two rolling racks loaded with summer dresses were shoved out of a ground-floor warehouse, blocking the sidewalk in front of them, and Even led out into the gutter and around.

"Well, there you are, you see. My mother said that. She told me that, and she was right. You know Shakta?"

"Worshipers of the feminine principle?"

"How do you know that, Captain?" Dass skipped to get back into step.

"Another Hindu mentioned it to me."

"My mother perfectly expressed that spirit. In her, though she was a very small woman, and not pretty, a man could see how strong was Lady Durga, could hear the gentle voice of Saraswati. I loved my mother dearly, and she loved me."

"Then I'd say you were in luck, Dass."

"Yes, deep into luck. 'Never offend a woman,' my mother would say, 'or you will ruin your luck.' Where are we going now, Captain?"

"Going up to the park to have some lunch."

"Oh, what a good idea; it will be pleasant to be with trees. . . . Do you think I offended the Lady by sending wilted flowers? I'm a modern person, and I've seen a thing or two. I am not superstitious."

"I'm sure you're not."

"So, do you think I have offended her?"

"No. Women are very aware of budgets."

"Women, yes. But are *ranis* aware? Queens? Goddesses?"

"Dass, if Kali is dancing beside the New Jersey Turnpike, which is not a beautiful highway, I think she'll be glad to receive even slightly wilted flowers."

"I hope that's true. We are in so delicate a position."

"—Oh, for Christ's sake. I got a ticket. . . ."

They drove uptown, found a parking place on 62nd Street, off Third Avenue, then walked west to Central Park. . . . Now, in early afternoon, the summer sun seared the city, softening the streets' patched black paving and throwing hard-edged shadows under their

feet. Dass strolled beside Evan at ease, his carpet roll
swinging from its string across his shoulder.

"You don't find this weather hot, Dass?"

"No. Oh, no. This is not being hot weather. You
come to Calcutta, come to the Deccan, and I will show
you hot weather. Come to Kerala. There you will find
hot weather. This is pleasant, but it isn't hot weather."

Evan imagined Catherine and Beth walking with
him—walking with both of them. Beth particularly enjoying Ram Dass Lal . . . pausing to look into the little
stores, the elegant boutiques, she and the old man reflected together in the display windows, the sun-bright
slow traffic behind them, while they discussed fashion,
modesty, cost. . . . the old man making his pronounce-
ments as they moved on. Evan saw himself and Catherine walking ahead, talking about nothing important.
Nothing dangerous. Perhaps a sailing party for their
friends—a run up along the Sound and back, to work
the Crealock in.

Dass clicked his tongue in disapproval, and Evan
saw two girls in shorts, T-shirts, and sandals waiting
for the light on the far corner. "I would hate to be having a granddaughter in this country. I know she would
dress in that way no matter what I said, and it is a terrible way to dress."

"It's hot, Dass."

"It is not hot," Dass said, and glared at the girls as
they passed, crossing the street, so one of them noticed
and giggled.

Dass tongue-clicked again. "Not even bad women
dress like that in India. They would be ashamed. They
would be afraid they would meet their mothers in the
street, and then they would get a talking-to they
wouldn't forget."

"Different countries, different customs."

"And this is a bad custom. —Silly women. What are

young women having to offer, after all? They are ignorant of life; what can they provide? Nothing. Nothing except the beauty of their bodies, and perhaps, if a man is lucky, a certain sweetness of nature. And what do they do here in this country with these treasures of their bodies? —Why, I will tell you. They put it out onto the street like cheap goods in the bazaar, for any fool or ruffian to stare at. To oogle—"

"Ogle."

"What?"

"*Ogle.*"

"—To ogle at them to his heart's content. To see is halfway to possess. And what decent man would want to take for his wife a girl smeared with the looking of so many men? All of these have slept with her, made love with her in their imaginations. She has had their imaginary children, no better than a whore."

"Sergeant, I think you're hungry."

"I am very hungry. I'm most hungry."

"Hang on. We'll eat in the park; there's a restaurant at the zoo. . . ."

"I don't know how you can be doing it."

"Doing what, Dass?"

"Eating those things."

"Dass, hot dogs are very bad for you, and I love them."

"They are meat, and they are made of beef."

"If you're lucky. . . ."

"Well, Captain, please not to breathe on me while you eat. It is really a pollution. . . ."

Dass had ordered the seven-bean salad, and picked through a tray of rolls before selecting three. Then two cartons of milk and a piece of Boston cream pie.

Evan finished one of his hot dogs and most of his Coke, sat back in his chair, and watched the old man eat. Dass ate with the same steady attention that handsome young Vijay Bhose had directed at his food at the club, chicken sandwich and whatever. . . . Both men ate as if nothing else were important. An ancient lesson, Evan supposed, taught by a thousand years of famine.

"Oh, that was delicious," Dass said. "—What wonderful pie."

"You have some on your mustache."

Dass put out his tongue, searched for the fleck and found it. "What pie!"

And in this exchange about the Boston cream pie, Evan found he liked the old man very much. So much that it surprised him—as if in this odd storm of criminals and killing, a very small and lonely war, he rediscovered affection. He found he cared for Ram Dass more freely, more easily, than for Sanchia, though she'd loved him.

"Dass, do you want another piece?"

"Yes and no," Dass said, and took his pipe from his jacket's left pocket, a plastic tobacco pouch from the right.

"Come on, you have to smoke outside, anyway. Let's walk. . . ."

They walked by the sea lions' tank—no sea lions in it—then strolled past a tall wrought-iron cage of birds. Big tropical parrots, colors molten in afternoon sunlight, sidled restless along their perches, their voices harsh as cab drivers'.

Through an underpass, walking against a tide of children leaving the petting zoo, Evan smelled the faintest acrid remembrance of the big cats that had patrolled their cages down the path to the left. The trace of an odor of those innocent, captive beasts, mixed with Dass's sweetened tobacco—the old man leaving plumes of it behind as he walked, ambling along with the narrow roll of carpet swinging from its cord across his shoulder.

Tigers had paced the cells there. Bengals.... "Do you miss India, Dass?"

"I am not missing India, though I respect her. I respect my *rishi bhoomi*. But this is much better country for me. It is being very clean—like the army. Here, people do not do their functions in the street, and also there are not so many people anyway.... I am missing Indian films, very much. And the warm weather. And my friends, I am missing them a good deal. I have several very good friends that I miss, from the regiment and from my family." A pause, to puff on his pipe. "I am missing my family very much. I came here to be with my son, Mandu—and look, he has gone to the Arabs and is away from me. And now his wife is gone also."

They walked out across the meadow, Dass examining his pipe. "This one is a Carleton pipe; British. It draws very well, but it goes out. A fourteen-dollar pipe." He bent to knock the pipe dottle out into the grass, then stepped on it. "Am preventing fire...."

The meadow spread out before them broad in summer green and scattered with picnics, couples on small blankets and men alone stretched on the grass asleep, the sun in their faces.

In a few yards they passed a family—of Indians, it seemed to Evan, though the woman wore baggy trousers. The family—husband and wife, and three children—were sitting around several open plastic containers—of two kinds of rice, something chopped fine, bite-sized pieces of meat, and what looked like small pancakes. They were taking turns at each dish, eating with their fingers, licking their hands clean after.

"Pakistanis," Dass said. "Some of them are very

nice people. . . ." He put his pipe in his jacket pocket, reached out as they walked, and took Evan's hand.

For a moment, surprised, Evan almost pulled his hand away, then thought not and left his hand and the old man's together. Dass's fingers were slender, cool with age. Their arms swung together as they walked . . . Evan supposed people watching them thought they were homosexual, an unusual gay couple.

"Dass, we haven't talked about that fight, about those killings last night—and maybe we should. Are they troubling you?"

Dass looked startled by the question. "Good gracious, no. I am discovering I am a fighting man; it is in my blood. I don't mean that to my credit; it is to my people's credit that I am having that blood. And you, of course, were already a fighting man. —They would have killed us; we killed them instead."

"I thought you might be upset by it."

"Oh, no. Not the least little bit—though I was frightened. I was very frightened, but I said, 'Oh, Ram, the hell with it,' and threw the *tulwar.*"

"And damn well thrown, too."

"Oh, no. I wanted to split that man's head, and I missed him. I was too old when I threw it. —Did you see that his suit was silk?"

"Yes."

"And that is what they spend the money on that they have taken from my people. A suit made of silk, as if he were a prince instead of what he was. Did you see his wristwatch?"

"No."

"It was as thin as a quarter piece. . . ."

Evan glanced down at his Vacheron—perhaps a little thicker than that.

"And his shoes. British handmade shoes. My father

manufactured shoes, and I know British handmade when I see them. . . ."

Wending now through denser clusters of people. Blacks . . . Puerto Ricans, a few white couples. Evan saw another group, also apparently Pakistanis, a number of them—an extended family or two families together—lying amid their food containers like fed seals drawn up on a beach of grass.

"Pakistanis. . . ."

"Oh, no. Punjabis. Punjabis are very good people; even Muslim Punjabis are good people."

More and more the carpet of grass seemed to Evan an Oriental carpet as they walked it . . . with African woven through . . . and South American, as if, holding hands with his elderly guide, he were walking into whatever New York was becoming. And after the city, the nation.

"A lot of foreigners for you, isn't it, Captain? Pakistanis, Punjabis . . . and blacks, and those people and these people but not so many of your people."

"The city was made by foreigners, Dass."

"But not so many, Captain, is it?"

"Perhaps not quite so many. . . ."

"And not being *so* foreign." Dass took his hand away. "We are too many for you, and too odd."

"That's not true."

"Oh yes, yes it is true. You are afraid your beautiful country—where everything works and there is so much room, so much money, where everyone does WC inside and not on the street—is going to become nasty, and full of people who have spoiled their countries, and now are coming to spoil yours."

"Well . . . some of that may be true. But more important to me is the feeling I have . . . of strangers in my house. The feeling that however well these people turn out, whatever great contributions they make—even if they are all of the quality of Ram Dass Lal—they will change America into a country in which my people will no longer be quite at home. In that sense, our country will be taken from us, and changed so we can never get it back. —It's already happened to many of our cities. They're no longer ours, though we dreamed them, and built them."

"Oh, yes, that is sad. I do see how sad that is ... particularly to a man who builds buildings. Different people like different buildings, isn't it? And perhaps they will not want your buildings." Dass reached out and took Evan's hand again, apparently to comfort him. ". . . There is a Shakespeare theater in this park. A William Shakespeare theater. Mandu used to go, but I didn't. But I have read a Shakespeare play."

"And what did you think?"

"Oh, he is a wonderful writer; I'm certain he is a wonderful writer. But the play I read was about a Scotsman, and it would have been better with gods coming down. Otherwise, is nothing but men wanting a woman or money or a revenge or wanting to be a king. We all know this. There is not a bit surprising in those things. What a man does can never astonish grown-up people, after the first shock. But when a god comes down, you never know what to expect."

"—Or a goddess," Evan said, and was sorry he'd said it.

Dass let go his hand. "Oh my. Goddesses ... not even gods know what they will do."

Evan heard a man and woman laugh—looked back but didn't see them among the people lounging on the grass. —And he remembered, outside Hue, three marines in clean, pressed uniforms lying on navy blankets on the grass of a temple's grounds, though the temples were off-limits. The marines had been joking with two ar girls in silk trousers and *ao-dais*. The girls were

fourteen or fifteen years old, sitting amid the men mer
rily drunk.

These hadn't been Evan's people; he knew none o
them, though they'd had the pinched uneasy look o
men just off the line, despite their fresh haircuts
shaves, their ironed uniforms. The men had been smil
ing, but only the girls were happy—their giggling ha
seemed to float them all on their blankets a few inche
off the grass ... and as Evan recalled them, he imag
ined they were here in Central Park, and rising slowl
on the navy blankets, sailing slowly out and over th
lawn, then south and south to the small pond, driftin
over the water only a few feet in the air, supported b
the laughter of the girls.

"Dass, I'd like you to go to New Jersey this after
noon, and stay overnight. Stay until I get there tomor
row evening. Have you been to New Jersey?"

"I was at New Jersey once. Mandu drove me acros
the bridge, and then brought me home again."

They were driving south on Fifth Avenue, comfort
able in the Lexus's air conditioning. While it wa
parked, someone had scratched the car along its righ
side—a long, wavering line of damage through whit
paint.

"You'll need to go over by bus, from the Port Au
thority Terminal. We'll get you a ticket to Eastfiel
and if you can, get off at the turnpike exit. Ther
should be several motels, and you'll need to check i
to the one nearest the Travelers' Rest. And if possible
overlooking it."

"I can do all of that. But why aren't you comin
too?"

"Because I have some things to do here—and be
cause we need to find out as much as we can about th

Raos' motel or temple or whatever the hell it is, before we go in."

"But why can't we go over together?"

"Because I have things to do *here,* Dass. I need a wiring diagram of 366, and I'll be getting that. And, since I don't think our friends will be expecting another visit so soon, I'm going to go up on the building onight."

"Oh, my. I should be with you."

"And you will be, tomorrow night. We'll be going nto that place in New Jersey—and we have to know everything we can about it. Since it's a turnpike motel and apparently their headquarters, it'll probably be a big building, and we'll have to know the entrances, exts, emergency exits—any men going in and out of the motel offices, working around the place at night, and so forth."

"I would rather come with you tonight."

"And I'd like to have you with me, Dass. But this other thing needs to be done. For instance, where do their families stay? Their wives and children? Right on the premises, probably—but where? I'd rather not have us go charging into rooms full of little children, start some shooting in that situation."

"No, no, I understand. But you should not be on that 366 building all alone."

"Dass, we have no choice, and we have no time. I have to find out what these people have been up to on that building. Without that, there'll be no help from the police, from anyone."

"Oh, I see that. I see it. We have to find out the why.' I do see that."

"—And you have to learn what you can about their home . . . their headquarters in New Jersey. We've found them; at least I hope we have. We've found them—they haven't found us. And that's the only reason we're still alive."

"That's true. Oh, absolutely."

"Then get over to New Jersey, watch that place today, tonight, and tomorrow, and learn what we have to know. Do you have money?"

"I have a great deal of money."

"Stay in your room after dinner tomorrow, and I'll see you then. There should be at least two or three motels there besides theirs. I'll ask at each, until I find you."

"I'll register as R. Prakash, the name of the man who had the flower shop, is it."

" 'R. Prakash' it is. —And Dass, no mistakes. Don't go into the Travelers' Rest. Don't get too near it. Be careful asking questions; be careful who you ask. And remember, at least two of those people—the fat one who threatened you, and the man who was with him then—know you by sight."

"Oh, I'll be being very careful."

"Last night, we killed their people—and Dev Rao. Which means it is no longer just business for them; it's personal."

"Yes ... yes, I'll be most extremely careful."

"Careful or dead, Dass. It's just that simple."

"And you on 366, Captain, please remember the same. It may be they understand you now, and so will *expect* you to come to the building again, so immediately soon."

"We'll both be careful. . . ."

As they turned into 42nd Street from the avenue, Dass—who'd been absorbed for blocks watching pedestrians and commenting regarding clothes, bearing, modesty, cheerfulness—suddenly sat up. "Oh, I have no luggage!"

"Dass, you don't need luggage to go to New Jersey."

"I am checking into an hotel."

"Motel."

"It is the same thing, and I have no luggage."

"You have your carpet—"

"Isn't luggage."

"All right. At the Port Authority Terminal, they have gift shops and I think a luggage store. You can buy an airline zipper bag."

"And what do I put into it?"

"Nothing."

"Nothing?"

"For Christ's sake, Dass, put anything in there you want! Get a flashlight. —That's a good idea anyway. Get a book to read. Get a Swiss Army knife—always a good idea. Buy some extra underwear."

"I could do that. I wear Jockey-style, waist thirty-four."

"Well, there you go. Perfect. And a couple of T-shirts and you'll be all set. You'll have luggage."

". . . I would rather stay with you."

The bus pulled out at two-fourteen, Dass in the right front seat across from the driver, his carpet roll slid into the rack above, his blue airline bag under his seat. . . . As the bus backed out onto the ramp, Evan stood on the walkway and waved while Dass, dim through tinted glass, waved back.

The bus paused then, waiting its turn in a line of departing buses, and Evan felt he had to stay, smiling, making little gestures of farewell as Dass did the same.

Then the bus sighed, rumbled into motion, and drove away, Dass still peering back through his window, so Evan smiled and made a thumbs-up gesture remembered from some old film.

It had been agreed he would come in, help with the shopping. . . make sure the ticket was right. See if the bus stopped at the Eastfield exit, or only in the town. —And it hadn't been agreed, but Evan felt it was understood that he would stay until the bus left, to see Dass off.

They'd shopped the terminal's stores—the blue zipper bag purchased first, and then toothpaste, a toothbrush, a blue plastic knife and fork, a small package of paper plates, two pencil flashlights (one for Evan) and extra batteries. A pair of Fruit of the Loom underpants and a T-shirt. A pair of white cotton socks and, at a cutlery outlet, a very expensive Swiss Army knife with a large blade and small blade, three different screwdrivers, a punch, a corkscrew, a can opener, a bottle opener, tiny scissors and a very small magnifying glass.

Dass—happy with the Swiss Army knife, and perfectly willing to pay for it—had refused to pay the much higher price for a pair of 7×35 binoculars, quality uncertain, and Evan had bought those, tucked them in the zipper bag. ". . . If you use these glasses from your room, don't stand at the window; you can be seen. Step back into the room, into shadow, and use them from there."

"That's what I will do." Dass had seemed encouraged after the shopping, and had also picked up two magazines: *Town and Country* and *Sporting Dog.* "I'm thinking of getting a dog," he'd said. "—A little terrier to be at my heel on walks."

Encouraged . . . but slightly unsteady climbing the steep steps into the bus burdened with his rolled carpet, his new airline zipper bag. He'd looked older, and fragile. He'd looked too old to be going where he was going, to do what he was to do. Watching him, Evan had almost stepped up and taken him off the bus. Almost said, "Oh, the hell with it. We'll risk an extra day. Go together tomorrow, and then spend some time looking those people over."

Evan had almost done that, but hadn't.

He walked through the terminal, out the west-side entrance, and down Ninth Avenue, where they'd left the car half a block down from Manganaro's. He stopped at the restaurant, walked through to the back, and stood in line to order a hero sandwich to go—three different cold cuts, marinated red peppers, then slices of three different cheeses topped with red onion on a split Italian loaf. Drenched with peppered vinegar and oil, wrapped in doubled wax paper, and fitted into a narrow brown paper bag. That, and a bottle of Peroni lager.

He carried his dinner back to the car, put it on the passenger seat, and pulled out into traffic to turn east at 36th.

Evan drove down into Soho, parked on Spring Street, and after trying three phones along five blocks, found one that worked and called Ward & Breedon's switchboard, then asked for Peter Talbot.

"Peter, it's Evan."

"Oh ... Evan." Talbot didn't sound happy to hear from him.

"Have you had lunch yet?"

"Well, yes. Matter of fact, I have."

"Why don't you come out for a few minutes anyway, meet me at Jerry Jack's."

". . . OK. Sure, I'll see you in a few minutes, Evan."

"Oh, and Peter—do me a favor, would you? I need the wiring diagram for 366."

"Well, I don't know if I can get my hands on one. . . ."

"Tell Swann I need a wiring diagram for that building, and bring it with you."

"OK. I'll ... give it a try."

Evan had had a double Gibson when Talbot came

out of the afternoon's heat into Jerry Jack's, paused by the bar, then saw Evan and came to the back booth. Talbot looked ill at ease in a seersucker jacket; he had the diagrams under his arm, multiple big sheets of rolled vellum.

"Well ... here we are." Talbot handed the diagrams over, and sat across from Evan. "Abe sends his sympathies. You have had—I have to say, Evan—you have had the most appalling luck."

"Thanks for these—"

"And I want you to know how dreadfully sorry I am. Sue and I are so damned sorry. It's such a tragedy. . . ."

Evan felt himself bracing against the booth's soft leather as if a wind were blowing down the room, and blowing stronger. "What's such a tragedy?"

"Your *house*. . . . Didn't you know? Haven't you been out there?"

"No. I haven't been out there."

"Oh, for God's sake, I thought you knew. . . . Your house burned down last night—or early this morning, I suppose. Some goddamn high school kids apparently had a party down in your backyard; beer cans and girls' panties all over the place. And the young assholes set your house on fire. Your boat too, Evan."

". . . Both gone?"

"Sue drove over this morning and phoned me at work. Your house is gone, Evan. She said the firemen said it was definitely set. Definitely a deliberate thing. . . . And it's such a fucking shame, that wonderful beautiful place—and two hundred years old!"

"Two hundred and sixty, Peter. . . . And it was kids?"

"No doubt about it, apparently. All the signs of a big beer bust. And very noisy; your neighbors heard the music across the cove, that heavy-metal crap—and those idiots thought you and Catherine were having a party."

"No one hurt?"

"Nobody hurt. Oh, your cat bit one of the firemen when he was getting it off the boathouse roof."

". . . And nothing saved from the house."

"No ... I guess not, Evan. Boat, either. —And I can't *tell* you how sorry I am. First, this stuff with Sanchia, poor kid, and now this. And I'll tell you who did it; who did it were some of those back-of-town boys, some of those three-generation welfare wonders. . . . Just human debris pissed off at people who've managed to make something of their lives. It is unbelievable; it is just unbelievable to me that we are taxed for low-income housing, and this sort of shit is the result."

"Beer cans, lost panties, and heavy-metal rock 'n' roll. . . ."

"That's right. . . . Why? What in God's name do you find funny about this, Evan?"

chapter 16

....

Evan drove east, then back up to Central Park . . . not
thinking about his house as he drove. He left the car on
61st Street, and walked over to the park carrying the
wiring diagrams, the paper bag with his sandwich and
beer. He went into the park to the Sheep Meadow,
found clean grass under a tree at its east border, and
lay down.

He studied the wiring diagram for more than two
hours, noticed Sanchia's initials at the bottom of two
sheets, and didn't think of his house all that time.

Then he put the diagrams aside, sat up to eat his
sandwich, enjoying the crusted bread, the complex
sweet and salty layers between (meat, cheese, onions,
meat, peppers, cheese), all drenched with vinegared
oil. Between bites, he sipped the still cool beer . . . and
thought of nothing else.

Finished, he stretched out comfortably on the grass,
not minding occasional people walking past, not concerned he might be threatened by roaming hoodlums as
evening fell. The big bowie and the Colt fenced him at
ease from such casual threats. . . . Evan lay beneath the
tree, and permitted himself to think about his house;
there was more to remember of it than he had time
now to recall. —And that was considering only the

house, not what it had held. That would require a whole other remembering.

He went to sleep at early dark, supposing he'd dream of the house. But he dreamed of rain instead of fire.

Evan woke in starlight. The summer night had cooled.

He got up, stretched to loosen his muscles, and went deeper into the trees to piss. Then he came back, picked up the paper sacks that had held his dinner, and stuffed them in a side pocket of the safari jacket, then rolled the sheets of vellum and tucked them under his arm. He walked east through dark woods—no lamps shining, their bulbs smashed—to a small underpass and through that into soft noises, grunts and moans of intercourse from shadowed brush off to the right. Men.

He saw a lamp standard with an unbroken bulb far down the way, and when he reached its mild yellow light heard someone nearby call softly to him, "You got any money on you, man?"

Evan drew the Colt from his waistband, held it out for a moment, then tucked it away.

"I guess you do." Amused. "An' I guess you're gonna keep it."

After a distance of darkness almost complete under tall trees, Evan came to a path again and saw the lights of occasional traffic moving along Fifth Avenue.

He found a trash barrel just outside the park, put the paper bags in it—then walked several almost deserted blocks over to the car, got in, tossed the vellums into the backseat, then pulled out and drove south through nearly empty streets. The air was warmer here, among the buildings. . . . On 49th Street, he took a right, over to Madison.

. . . 366 rose up into night, faint drifts of stars shining through its skeleton. Evan drove past its southeast corner and a temporary wooden walk-through and found a place to park alongside the chain-link fencing behind a truck's empty flatbed.

He locked the car, and saw through the fencing the distant watchman's shack was lit beside the avenue gate. A figure inside.... Evan walked to the corner, then left along the sidewalk almost a block to the gate. He pushed the night buzzer, and after a while heard the gate bar lifted away on the other side of the heavy plank door.

The watchman was a tall bony man Evan hadn't seen on site before, balding, with remnant rust-colored Irish hair.

"... I'm with Ward & Breedon. Need to go up to check some wiring."

"At this fuckin' time of the night?"

"It's the only time I've got while I'm in town."

"I didn't hear anythin' about this." The tall man's right arm was in a cast from his elbow to the palm of his hand.

"Well, I need to go up, check some wiring placement."

"They should have told me."

"Yes, they should."

"... All right. Hey, you want to go up there? Go."

"Is the work elevator operating?"

"Far as I know...." And walked back to his small shack, sat down under a single bulb's mustard-yellow light, and picked up an open paperback book.

A late moon was rising, still lower than the building's top stories, and frosting the steel latticework soft platinum.

Evan walked around the building's corner to its east side, saw the elevator parked at the ground floor under a worklight, and climbed up the slope of bulldozed gravel to its platform. From there, he could see the office trailers in their rank. The windows in Rao Electric's trailer were dark.

The elevator's open cage jolted at the start, groaned, and heaved faster and faster up along the building's side. Evan looked behind him through the grid of bars shielding the motor and drive wheel. No thug was hanging there tonight, his length of silk streaming from his hand.

The cage rumbled up past the third floor ... the fourth, rising into cooler deeper night and moonlight bright enough to wash out the stars. The elevator's motor sparked as it had before, laboring a little.

Evan was lifted above the avenue's few late-night traffic sounds and headlights, above the streetlights and traffic lights—up to meet distant row on row of lit windows along the cliffsides of other buildings, where nightshift clerks and cleaners worked.

Up this high there was a breeze—the same breeze off the river that had sighed when Josephine Fonsecca fell. The moon, rising with Evan, was almost full, and had the softness, the weight, of summer in its light.

... After a while, the elevator cage clicked ... clacked, and suddenly slowed by itself to the last rigged floor—the seventy-fourth or -fifth—and the control button whined until Evan took his finger off it. The cage settled almost even with the floor's loose plank decking, and hung bumping the building's steel skeleton slightly in the wind.

As he stepped off the elevator—stepping wide over the few inches of shifting space—Evan saw the fat long fishnet roll of safety netting heaped knee-high along the flooring's edge. Furled in to be deployed a floor higher in the morning.

Tonight, in the forests of steel, there was moonlight instead of rain, and Evan, feeling more and more at

home, patrolled the floor from shadow to shadow, the
.45 held casually in his hand. On every floor, a branch
junction box had been located in the diagrams, and he
quartered this floor north, then south, while wind whispered down ranks of massive steel uprights. Then he
cut that quarter to an eighth east to west, and found the
junction box bolted in darkness the moonlight barely
reached. A welding tank leaned against two small motors stacked in crates beside it.

Evan tucked the pistol in his waistband, took the
pencil flash from his jacket's breast pocket, found the
box cover latch by its minor light, and pushed that
open with his thumb. An insulated black rope of the
main—already tagged by the city's inspector—led into
the box from its top. There was a piece of duct tape
stuck to it, with COLD printed on it in black marker.

Evan reached to the small of his back, drew the big
bowie, and by the pencil flash's light slid the great
blade's shallow hook beneath the cable, levered the
knife's handle, and cut half through the line. Then levered hard again, and sliced it through.

Bright copper shone from the cut, and Evan ran a
finger over a perfect multiple wire twist. . . . Then he
slit three smaller lines along their length for several
inches, split them, worried them open, and found again
Class A wire, unmistakable in quality.

The floor breaker box had to be within twelve feet of
the main by code, and Evan found it the next column
over. The box had been sealed by the city's inspector,
and Evan put the point of the bowie into the seal and
twisted it away. Pried the box lid open. A heavy-duty,
multiline box. . . . He levered at the facing plate's edge,
got purchase on it with the knife, pulled the soft metal
out of its screw holes at the top, and popped it free.
Then nicked an incoming line at random, found it cold,

and sliced it in half—fine multiwire copper, and connected as it should have been.

He turned off his small flashlight, put it in his pocket, then stepped sideways ... and sideways again, staying in darkness while his night vision returned. He stood a while, listening for whoever might have seen the small light and come toward it. ... Then he stood a little longer, but heard nothing but the wind, its gentle breeze bringing him only odors of iron, timber ... some asphalt coating. ...

Evan moved to the central elevator shaft—a stretching gulf of blackness, wind droning up through it—found a ladder, set that carefully beside the shaft's edge and climbed it to the next floor. Here, two levels below top-out, the deck was plywood sheeting that shifted, drummed softly beneath Evan's feet. He looked up into a two-story angled geometry of steel, moon-glossed, containing only night and empty air—and hovered over, even higher, by the ponderous mass of the crane that had lifted it all into being, story by story. The crane perched at the building's top like a great metal bird just landed, its block-long beak jutting out into darkness a thousand feet over Madison Avenue. Below and blocks away, a skyscraper's lit capital shone duller than the setting moon.

Here the wind, still gentle, blew more freely, shifting direction from time to time, changing the notes it made through the great lattice of ironwork. It ruffled the hem of Evan's jacket as he walked to the last ladder, set it, and climbed to the first unfloored steel.

Now there was nothing to stand on wider than the width of a beam. No footing firmer than wind-cooled steel. Now there was nothing to hold on to but steel columns rising twelve long steps apart.

Evan stood at an upright for a few moments, cautious of his balance in the breeze—finding balance dif-

ficult with his reference only steel members' perfect
right angles vanishing into shadow under shifting
moonlight. He stood for a few moments, then, keeping
his eyes on the steel, he walked, reached the next column in twelve careful steps.

A story above, steel framework topped the central
elevator shaft—supporting coils of rigging cable, tied
stacks of electrical cable, and twelve huge electric motors, hulking, already bolted home.

There was no ladder leading to it—no safe place to
set a ladder. The way up was the ironworker's way.

Evan faced the column, reached up to grip the
I-beam's thick flanges on either side—and hauled himself up, legs straddling the steel to press his sneakers
along the narrow flanges opposite. Then he climbed as
a boy might climb a tree's wide trunk—clinging, hitch-
ing up, trying for purchase for his feet . . . shifting his
handholds higher, then kicking to find traction against
the steel to lift himself again.

He reached the beam above—stretched up to get a
hand on it . . . heaved, and for a moment hung unsupported but for that hand . . . then drew himself up,
grunting with the effort, got a knee over and wrestled
up onto it as the moon slid behind a cloud. . . . Then he
sat panting, leaning forward clutching the cold steel
with both hands, feeling he was riding through the air,
sailing through the night with no building beneath
him—with nothing beneath him but darkness into
which any fall would be forever.

He rested there until the moon came out again, revealing, frosting more than an acre of air divided by
squared narrow edges of steel, the great crane loom-
ing a hundred feet higher over the northeast corner,
standing on eight immense right-angled legs of yellow-
painted foot-thick steel. . . . Evan rested a few moments more, then slowly got to his feet. To his left,

hirty feet down, the plywood decking lay dull. To his
ight was rectangular emptiness perfectly black, the el-
vator shaft ... only air down seventy-eight stories.
'his central shaft so huge, such vacancy, such nothing-
ess, it called for Evan to step out and into it ... to
earn the rich last secret Jo Fonsecca had learned, but
n darkness.

Evan stood, waiting until that space was only space,
hen he walked to the next upright and the coil of elec-
rical control cable roped to it. Holding the column
vith one hand, he drew the knife, sliced the cable
liagonally—and was able to see, by only moonlight,
hat it was perfect. He sheathed the bowie, swung
around this upright—and noticed as he did an almost
right reflection of moonlight off one of the giant mo-
ors. He paused to look again, and moved his head to
he side to see moonlight striking more of their metal.

The huge curved casings, so black they seemed pur-
ole, took the mild light like mirrors. They glowed with
t, reflecting the moon only slightly blurred in surfaces
erfect as still water.

Evan took a twelve-step walk over to the first motor
n the rank, paused for balance, and stepped out on the
nassive rack that held it above the elevator shaft. He
eaned out carefully ... touched the cold metal.
Smooth ... so smooth, so slippery, it seemed willing to
et his hand suddenly skid off its surface ... leave him
insupported over emptiness. Evan pushed away from
t, reached out to hold onto an upright's rough angle—
and felt the oddest vibration. A sort of humming, a
aint pulsing through the metal as if a huge spider, its
veb disturbed, was coming along the steel. ...

The motors—all of them—had been beautifully
bainted, burnished as richly as lacquerwork. Even in
lear dark, it was the finest finish Evan had seen on any
commercial metal except a Rolls-Royce's. Certainly

he'd never known any motors painted with that car
no routine baked-on finish to equal it.

It was handwork.

He remembered the two small motors stacked i
their crates below, decided to check them, and walke
the twelve balanced steps along a beam to get to th
far corner where he could shinny down from upright t
upright, down two stories to the decking. The win
seemed to be growing stronger.

He had just crossed the beam, focused entirely o
the narrow path of steel beneath his feet . . . carefu
careful in a strengthening wind. He had just crosse
and reached out to hold the upright column when h
felt again that odd throbbing . . . a faint drumbea
through the metal, as if the gigantic gridwork were be
ing softly struck at a distance . . . then slightly neare
Then nearer.

Evan gripped the upright and turned to look.

Something was running toward him over the stee
Huge, oddly shaped, and galloping with a long clot
coat swept back by its speed—looking barely human i
moonlight, its head thrown back in a great grin of plea
sure, long moon-silvered beard, long hair fallen loos
and streaming behind it. This . . . man . . . came run
ning barefoot over the steel as if there were no spaces
no emptiness, as if sparse structures were solid floor
ing all across. There was no sound but the eager pad
ding of his feet, their swift rhythm humming throug
the steel.

*"We think they use a Dond savage . . . for certai
tasks. They are mountain people, not minding height
at all. . . ."*

Evan ran. He fled stumbling down the narrow stee

Terror he hadn't known—even running fro
Chandra Rao and his men—now rose within him as

war wound, swollen with years of infection, had suddenly been struck again so all corruption spurted out.

He felt fear so great that falling, the few moments' safety in the air as he fell, seemed worth the death at the end.

"Where you goin'?" Sergeant Beckwith said to him quite clearly. "—Runnin' don't get it done." The sergeant sat at ease in a ruined uniform on a beam across the way, and seemed amused as Evan scrambled along the steel with no time for careful balancing, trying for what might be shelter among the crane's giant legs. Off to the right along the building's edge, beneath the crane's great boom, there was no decking. Only empty air.

The human creature came loping behind him. Evan knew it without looking back.

Running, he remembered the pistol, but its manufactured threat seemed almost useless to him, as if the pursuer were a werewolf or demon, immune to lead. Only angered by it.

Terrified, nearly tripping off a beam, Evan drew the 45 and forced himself to turn as a cloud obscured the moon. Grinning, great arms outspread, his long coat a cloak behind him, the Dond came running, and Evan shot him—shot at him, shot where he was. Fired three last shots—and for the first the man had faced him smiling, the moonlight on him.

For the other two—the moonlight gone—he was gone. Fallen into darkness. Leaped across into darkness. . . .

Evan ducked left and right, looking, the .45 looking with him—then the fear that gunfire had muffled came pouring back and he turned, swayed an instant on the beam, then ran ... ran under the deeper shadow of the crane as moonlight came flooding back.

He ducked into shade within the massive angle of the

nearest of the crane's supporting legs. He huddled ther
in the corner of steel and stood listening through th
noise of his breathing. He held his breath for better lis
tening, and gripped the .45 so hard his hand ached. . .
Evan imagined he'd hit the man—at least with the firs
shot. He imagined it until it seemed so, and he grev
calmer. "Panic City," he said out loud. "Panic City. . . .
And was glad Beckwith and the others were dead, s
only a dream ghost had seen him run.

The wind seemed colder now, hardly a summer wind
at all.

Evan took a deeper breath, and stood waiting for hi
heart to slow. He remembered his first shot. The mar
had been standing there, smiling. Maybe fifteen fee
away. At most, fifteen feet. Hit, and fallen. . . .

Finally, feeling better—feeling oddly better for hav
ing been so afraid—Evan took another deep breath, re
minded himself to be careful, not to make some stupid
mistake now, getting to a column to climb down . .
and took a cautious step around the crane's huge leg, to
the next beam.

Something bright flashed before him like an electri
arc and he jerked back so quickly he didn't know he'
done it, but felt a numbing blow at his right hand. H
looked down in a dream's slow motion, and saw th
gun was gone. And a long gleaming blade, almost a
sword—having just missed his wrist as he pulled back
having struck the gun instead—moved shining to th
side as the Dond, towering, swung around from th
back of the crane's support to stand on the beam facing
him.

Evan faintly heard the dull thump as the Colt hit th
decking below. There was no expression in the Dond'
dark eyes—eyes as perfectly blank as a shark's. No ex
pression on that long, eagle-beaked face, none of th
glee with which he'd chased. The moonlight shone

silver-gray on the Pathan's beard and the thick hair falling loose below his shoulders. He stood, looking down at Evan for a moment, then said something in an oddly fluting tenor, a language with rattling in it. And when Evan only stood there, staring, the Dond clicked his tongue in disgust, and swung his long blade casually up to disembowel him.

Evan, as if an invisible rope holding him to the tall man had been cut by the blow, jumped far back along the beam as the blade came at him—jumped straight back with nothing to lose, without time to think, with time for nothing but movement.

He jumped back more than three feet, landed almost balanced on the narrow steel, recovered, and reached back under his jacket's cloth to draw the bowie.

The Dond took a stilting barefoot step forward, no longer expressionless. Now he was smiling, very pleased—he stared at the bowie, then grinned down at Evan and nodded his head. Very pleased. . . . And came one two and was there and struck shining first down and across—then backhand too fast to follow.

Too fast for Evan to follow, but the bowie—as though the Dond's long blade was an old friend come to visit from the far side of the earth—did follow, and rose to meet it so the two blades chimed and chimed and rang again as if in celebration, and Evan was cut through cloth along his knife arm, but lightly. The bowie's brass double hilt had caught the Dond's edge.

The Pathan, apparently delighted, stepped back then in again and thrust for Evan's eyes, and Evan brought up the bowie's heavier, slightly shorter blade to guard, knocked the Dond's Khyber knife aside and tried for the man's long arm. A very pleased Pathan, then—joyful, and he did a small dance on the narrow steel, grinning and flicking blood from his forearm before he came again.

Evan took that time to back away to the structure's corner and past it—looked down for an instant and saw he'd backed to a beam along the building's edge. Now, to the right, there was only night.

The Dond was much stronger than Evan. And faster. The blows Evan had blocked, even with the bowie's wonderfully balanced weight, had each struck like the swing of a baseball bat, but swung almost too fast to see.... It was fighting in the ancient warrior way, before gunpowder, before killing from a distance except with bow and arrow. It was history, smiling, that came trotting to Evan again.

The Dond jumped the corner's angle to the edge beam, caught Evan in two long strides, and slashed diagonally across and down—sliced the cloth of Evan's jacket open at his belly—then halted that blow as if it had hit a wall, leaped up into the air and spun full around to strike backhanded from the other direction. —All on a fourteen-inch beam.

Evan was saved by Beckwith's knife and what was left of college fencing, and by twenty years of polo. Born and built for this, the bowie hooked the Pathan's blade as it came, turned it just enough, and carried it clanging away. And Evan's right hand and arm and shoulder—packed with muscle from years of swinging a mallet whipping left and right from a galloping pony—his hand and arm and shoulder parried, and took the shock.

The Dond stood back and relaxed, a bird of prey at ease, and stared at Evan by moonlight, considering, while they both breathed. The two of them were alone in the world; there was no world beside the narrow beam they fought on, nothing beyond the striking circle of their knives. They had become as close as friends, and knew each other.

The Dond nodded to Evan and came in swinging

overhand and striking and striking and striking at
slightly different angles to hack Evan down and give
him no time to strike back.

Evan parried the first blow and the second with the
bowie, caught but couldn't hold his parry of the third.
That cut hissed down as he dodged, hit his left arm
beneath the shoulder, and Evan felt the edge slice
through muscle and snick into bone. The Pathan
grunted to wrench his long blade free as it stuck there
an instant—and Evan had his chance. He turned left
into the Dond as if they were dancing, brought the
bowie around from the right in its classic stroke, and
drove the needle point of its great blade into the Pathan's side.

As the steel went in, the Dond spun away from it, or
tried to—spun and was hooked on the bowie's re-
curved double edge as Evan worked and levered it so
two ribs were sheared like sticks . . . and as if it wished
to, the bowie slid deeper so the Dond had to turn back
again or be opened wide. And he and Evan—locked
together spattering blood—wrestled like lovers, his
long knife slicing across Evan's back as the bowie,
withdrawn, now slid down between them, found a
place, and drove up into the Pathan's groin.

Then the Dond leaped back and away faster than the
bowie could follow. The Dond leaped back and struck
at Evan as he went and cut him hard across the left
side of his face—leaped back and landed lightly
though so badly wounded. Landed lightly on the strip
of steel, and balanced—but landed in a run of blood
they'd left fighting down the beam. Evan's blood. And
the Dond slipped to his right, fell sideways off the
steel—then turned in the air like a great cat as he fell
past, and reached up with an almost casual left hand to
catch the beam's edge, hold it, and begin to draw him-

self up one-handed as if he were being lifted from below.

Then Evan reached him, hacked him hard across the
face as he rose, parried an upthrust so the blades rang
farewell—and bending to the blow, chopped the Pathan's fingers free.

And the Dond fell. At first so slowly it seemed he
still might stretch his long arm up to try a grip. . . .
Then fell faster, his coat bannering out. He fell relaxed,
rolling slowly over in the air, so the Khyber knife
flashed in moonlight.

He fell and fell away in silence, diminished only by
distance as he went.

"Clive?"

"Who the hell is this? It's the goddamned middle of
the night!"

"Morning, actually. It's Evan."

"Evan?"

"Listen to me, Clive—I'm just out of Lenox Hill
emergency and I have curious police officers to avoid
here, and I don't have a lot of time. I've been up on
366, looking for whatever it was that our electrical
friends have been up to—"

"Evan, I will not listen to any more of this—"

"I noticed some very beautifully finished motor casings . . . before I was interrupted. And afterward, I
went down and uncrated two more—little five-horses."

"Evan, for God's sake—"

"They were also very beautifully finished. I've never
seen commercial work so . . . painstaking. So finely
done. Those casings looked like Chinese work, that
sort of wonderfully perfect lacquer painting. Too good
to be true—as the Raos' paperwork was too good to be
true. Motor casings, metal tags, stamps, all beautifully

lone. Perhaps in the last century we used to finish machines that perfectly. Not now."

"What are you saying?"

"They're all used motors, Clive. All secondhand, all
reconditioned motors. I stopped to check three when
I took the elevator down the floors, got the casings
off. . . . My guess is there is not one new electric motor
in 366."

"Oh, you're wrong. I'm sure you're wrong, Evan."

"No, I'm not. I doubt if there's a single new motor
in all those hundreds and hundreds they've mounted,
or have stored on site to be mounted. The few I
checked, the armatures were shot in all of them, Clive.
Worn out, burned out. Some had been rewound, some
not. . . . All beautifully painted junk and must have
saved the Raos at least a couple of million dollars over
the price of new equipment. —And if an elevator were
to fall fifty or sixty floors in a few years, and the safety
braking motors didn't respond—too bad." Evan felt a
mild remoteness settling around him . . . a slight indif-
ference. The young doctor's white tablets.

"My God. Oh dear, oh my God. . . ."

"I'd say our friends must have paid off an inspector
or two, or frightened them off."

"I think I'm going to be ill. . . ."

"Now listen to me, Clive. Listen, and do what I say.
This morning, as soon as possible, call Henry Ward,
call Harris, diNunzio to get men in there to confirm
what I've told you—then call Springman to deal with
the district attorney's office and file a complaint for
fraud. Don't wait, Clive. Make this as public as you
can as fast as you can, or the Raos will kill you to keep
it quiet."

"Oh, Jesus. . . . The banks, the *insurance* people.
Evan, you just don't know—"

"Start phoning, Clive. Do it right now." Evan saw

two policemen come out of the waiting room, look up and down the corridor, then turn away. He hung up the phone as Clive was saying something. Hung up and walked off down the hall toward double glass doors, and what seemed to be one of the hospital's parking lots.

. . . It had taken him time to check the motors on two floors coming down 366, and he'd walked off the elevator nauseated, stumbling from shock. He'd leaned on a cable crate until he felt better, then walked to the watchman's shack—still lit but no one in it—unbarred the gate, and walked out.

When he got to the car, he'd tucked the Colt—found after a considerable search along the decking, and with a deep groove sliced into the slide's steel—tucked the pistol and bowie away under the front seat. Then he'd driven to Lenox Hill with his left side soaked with blood—from the hacked arm, from the cut along his left cheek. A cut down his back, across his left shoulder blade.

Evan had been bloody enough to be gestured almost to the head of the treatment line. Not so bloody that identification and his credit card hadn't been required. . . . He'd thought of trying a false name, trying to pay with cash, but had not felt well enough to bother.

The doctor who came into the small treatment room had been Asian—a weary, plump young man. Chinese, Evan thought. "Oh, wow," he'd said, once Evan's jacket and shirt were off. "Police report on this one."

"Damn right. I already called them. Man can't walk down the street in this town without being robbed."

". . . And what's this neck bandage?"

"That's just an accident, a couple of days ago. I'm lucky I've got any goddamn blood left."

"Um-hmm," the young doctor had said, skeptical but

too tired to press the point. . . . And a very painful later, "You are lucky. The arm isn't good, but no major vessel's severed."

"One of them came up with a knife. . . . I should have just given them my wallet and let it go at that."

"Um-hmm. . . ." It took the doctor a while to finish packing and bandaging the arm. ". . . We're going to let this granulate a little—two, three days—before we close it; bone's nicked pretty deep. Don't get this bandage wet." He'd draped a white cotton sling over Evan's shoulder, and tucked the left arm in it. Then he'd swabbed along Evan's cheek, swabbed again with something stinging, stung it worse with a hypodermic needle, and without waiting began a steady stitching. "Other wrist was a five sutures; this is a seven. Back was a fourteen—all long cuts but fairly superficial. The arm's serious; the others aren't, but you're lucky he missed the trigeminal. . . . Take them all together, if you want me to try for a bed, you could do with staying overnight."

"No, thanks. I'll get right home." The side of Evan's face had slowly numbed. "See my doctor tomorrow morning."

"Um-hmm. . . . Want me to take a look at that neck?"

"No, don't bother. It's nothing."

"Um-hmm. . . . Well, I wouldn't give blood for a while. You're already out a pint or two."

"Right."

"OK. Tell you what, Mr. Scott, I'm going to give you a couple of tablets and another shot, an antibiotic. Then you go back to the waiting room and talk to those police officers on duty out there. They're expecting you, understand?"

"Damn right I will," Evan had said—and out of the treatment room, had looked for a phone. . . .

He reached the double glass doors, heard no policemen calling after him, and went through the doors and out into early-morning sunshine. The light bothered his eyes, and he thought he might have trouble walking to the car, thought he might be sick. The cut on his right wrist hurt more than the left arm. More than his face.

Evan walked three long, long blocks to the Lexus—his clothes so stiff, so maroon with dried blood down his left side, that even New Yorkers noticed.... The car looked odd, and for a moment he couldn't understand why. Then he saw the hubcaps had been taken.

His left arm didn't hurt much, seemed comfortable in the sling—and was even useful driving; he was able to get that hand on the wheel to help him turn out of the parking place.

He drove down to the apartment, found nowhere to park, and went on around the block ... then drove two blocks over, and made that larger circuit. He found a place probably too close to a fire hydrant, maneuvered into it—left hand awkward in the sling, but usable—got out and locked the car.

Evan walked three blocks back toward the apartment, checking phones as he went, found one that worked, and called Clyde Pope in Maine, collect. Clyde's boy answered and accepted the call without his father's hesitation.

"Tommy, this is Evan Scott. Is your dad home?"

"No, Dad's not home, Mr. Scott."

"That's all right, I can ask you. You took my family out to the island?"

"Yep."

"And do you know how they're doing? Everything OK?"

"I guess everything's all right, Mr. Scott. Far as I know, your wife and Beth are still out there, and Pell's on the island, too. Why? Want me to go tell 'em something?"

"No, Tommy, that's all right. Just checking. . . . If you do go out there, or they come in, you might tell my wife that everything's fine. Fine so far. . . . And let your dad know I'll be paying for this call."

Evan crossed the street and walked up the block to the apartment building, feeling slightly nauseated. He went down the steps, unlocked the door, went in and locked it behind him, grateful for the ugly hallway's coolness, the privacy and darkness of the place. He left the lights off, went to his bedroom, and undressed with some difficulty—the sling and bandages awkward. Then he took a shower, and found it wearying trying to keep the bandages dry. They got wet, a little. . . .

Evan had thought of eating, but felt too tired, so only took the milk from the refrigerator, poured a tall glass, and drank it down. . . . He recalled the Dond— not falling, but as he came running to fight, his long hair streaming behind him. So one of Homer's Dorian chieftains must have looked, at Troy. And not a young man, either. Not young. . . .

Evan put the milk back into the refrigerator, walked back to his bedroom, pulled the cot covers back, and lay down, careful of his left arm. His back was sore.

He thought of his house, and saw it very clearly as he went to sleep, but couldn't dream himself into it. Instead, he dreamed of the war—but of no men he knew. His men, he thought, had gone on leave. . . .

Evan woke in late afternoon. His left arm had wakened him; it felt as if the bone were broken, broken edges grating against one another. He woke sweating from the pain, had to get up, and went to look through Dass's first-aid kit in the bathroom. Dass had dumped his own medications in with the army-navy bandages and so forth, and Evan sorted through them one-handed: coated aspirin, eye drops, Chap Stick, vitamin C and vitamin D, a plastic package of some powdered herb that smelled like parsley. Hemorrhoid suppositories, dental floss, and a small plastic bottle of codeine tablets—prescribed by a dentist named P. Mehta.

Evan took two with a large glass of milk, and sat at the kitchen table to see if they would help. He wished Catherine were with him—not Beth. Beth to still stay safe a long way away. But he wished that Catherine were with him—just with him for a few minutes. . . .

He got up and went to his bedroom, got out his pad and drawing pen from his duffel bag, and came back to the kitchen table, sat, and began to draw his house. . . . As he finished the front—just sketching, just quick sketching—the codeine hadn't helped. But as he filled in, recalling window placements more accurately, re-calling window trim . . . and the throw of sunlight across the front door entrance (up three wide stone steps). As he remembered and drew how the roof soffit extended to protect the siding, what sort of shadow it threw . . . as he remembered and drew those things, the codeine seemed to slowly tug the pain a few inches away, leaving only aching. A hard ache, but bearable.

Feeling better, Evan sat drawing his house—though quickly he grew too impatient to stay outside it, and began to sketch the entrance hall and stairs, the den, the dining room, hurriedly, as if he might forget what he didn't draw at once. He wanted to draw it all, but details began more and more to capture him, until he spent a good deal of time on the dining-room clock. He wanted to draw everything—and draw better, draw as beautifully as Dürer. Draw perfectly, so that everything would be as it always had been. . . . And not only surfaces. Evan would have liked to draw just under surfaces, too—the deeper secret grains of wood, the complications of weave through carpets. And colors; he needed colored pencils. . . .

There was more to draw than a lifetime of drawings could accomplish. They would always be incomplete; they could never quite be the house—and the nearer they came, the more clearly they would fail.

Still, Evan drew in step above step of the stairs, each more and more detailed as if, drawn well enough, he might somehow climb them into at least the recent past.

The Lexus smelled of salt, iron, and rot from spoiled blood; the upholstery leather on the driver's side was ruined, but the blood was too dry to stain Evan's clean jeans and canvas zipper jacket.

He drove one-handed—but feeling better for the sleep, feeling much better for his third codeine tablet, had no trouble staying with the traffic going uptown and then across 31st Street to the Lincoln Tunnel entrance.

He'd cleaned the knife before he left the apartment, but had waited too long—some acids in the bloodstains had marked the steel in delicate shades of gray along its edge. The blade would have to be polished to get those stains out. . . . He'd cleaned the knife, stretched his belt out from a nail hammered into the wall by some previous tenant with a picture to put up, then stropped the edge along the leather to keenness.

Heavy rush-hour traffic funneled with him down into the tunnel, rumbled along with him through its gentle decline, then leveled to roar along under lights until the roadway began to rise again, ramped up, and showed him evening light as he drove over the tangle of Weehawken and Union City. . . . It occurred to Evan that near here, before the docks and refineries and chemical plants, Alexander Hamilton had been rowed across on a quiet morning to climb a wooded bank where Burr stood waiting. Hamilton had apparently brought pistols made with secret springs that could lighten either of the flintlocks' heavy trigger pulls—a dishonorable advantage.

Hamilton may have tried that advantage—and fired prematurely as he leveled his pistol, unused to such a sensitive trigger.

Then Burr had shot him through the head.

And what was the reason . . . ? Evan drove south on the New Jersey Turnpike, buffeted by passing tractor trailers. It was still hot on this highway, even at sunset, and the Lexus, its thermostat tripped, turned the air conditioning on. . . . What had the reason been to bring those formidable little men over to New Jersey? At Groton, or Yale, it had been mentioned in an American history class. . . .

Evan passed the Harrison exit.

. . . Hamilton had said something to friends one evening at his home—had said something about Burr's relationship with his daughter. A hint, barely a suggestion of some unwholesome conduct, of closeness beyond fatherly. And Burr had heard of it, and in a series of relentless notes had driven Hamilton at last into that rowboat on a quiet morning. . . .

Evan drove one-handed, feeling pretty well. Right wrist no problem, left arm no problem—comfortable in the sling, and his left hand in a limited way usable. Cut across cheek hurting, codeine or not, while his back felt fine.

He passed the exit for Jersey City, saw the sign for Eastfield, and slid the Lexus into the right lane.

"Oh, *Ram* . . . !" The old man stood at his room door pale as paste.

"I know . . . but it only hurts when I laugh."

"When you laugh?"

"A joke. It looks worse than it is, Dass; just some cuts—and thanks to your dentist, doesn't feel too bad. I borrowed your codeine. . . ."

"Mr. Prakash" had checked into the Oakwood Inn—a two-story plastic-paneled motel on a grassy embankment overlooking the Travelers' Rest. The Travelers' Rest was larger, a rectangular three stories with a long one-story building standing separate behind it. Both buildings presented an unconvincing Southwest stuccoed exterior in weather-streaked white. A tall neon sign, very visible from the turnpike and already lit in twilight, pulsed above its entrance— TRAVELERS' REST—with a small saguaro cactus in green at its corner.

"I should have gone with you. I should have gone with you, and it is your fault I didn't!"

"Dass, can we go down and get some food?" Evan had been fine driving over, but now he felt so hungry it was making him sick, and the bright burnt orange of the room's carpet and bedspreads wasn't helping.

"Sit down, Captain, and rest for a moment. It is a very nice room."

"Food, first."

"In the coffee shop, oh yes." Dass went to the closet, took his jacket out. "I have gone to it four times and had chef's salad, to go, every time, with tuna fish. —What happened?"

"I'll tell you while we eat. I'm not . . . I definitely need something to eat. . . ."

The double cheeseburger ran juice and ketchup together—a sight Evan noticed Dass avoiding. At each bite, the old man looked away. . . . The burger was messy, gripped one-handed, and grew messier each time Evan put it down to fork up some french fries, then picked it up again. He'd forgotten to salt the cheeseburger, and now was reluctant to pry it apart for salting. Should have asked them to toast the bun. If he pulled the burger apart now, it would never recover.

". . . Motors?"

"Motors, Dass—old substituted for new—and a very sweet deal for the Raos. At least a two-million-dollar deal, I'd say."

"And the one man cut you about." Dass was chewing his tuna salad with his mouth open.

"Very well put. That one man did indeed 'cut me about,' and if they had a few more like him, the Raos would own the city. —366 is being pretty well littered with bodies. It's really ... it's really impressive how the Raos manage the housekeeping over there."

"Oh, that's so funny. It's true; that's very funny. We are killing them a great deal. —Captain, they're gone."

"What?"

"Gone. Gone ... gone. I was watching all the day, except for breakfast and lunch—and I brought my food take-out right back to the room—and the Rao men are gone. Five of them came out at two o'clock, fourteen hundred hours, and got into brown German cars. Their *bapu-ji*—"

"Their what?"

"Their daddy. I saw him from my window, I saw that one very clearly. He came out and they escorted him, you know, and put him in the back of a car alone, with his driver in front, and made *namaste*. And the others got in the second car. All together, six men." Dass, some salad left, took a first bite from a large piece of lemon meringue pie.

"Six of them."

"Yes—but not the fat man, the brother who thinks he is so funny. He wasn't coming out, so perhaps he was not there at all. I would know him, and he didn't come out."

"Gone. . . ." Evan finished the last of the cheese-burger and felt much better, even though the arm was beginning to hurt again, the same grinding pain within the bone, as if it were being sawed. "Where would they all be going . . . ?"

"North," Dass said, put his head back and drank some tea. "I watched and they went all around the clo-ver's leaf, and I could follow them through the binoc-ulars coming out and going north."

"See, weren't the glasses useful?" The french fries were good, slightly crisp, some with traces of skin on them.

"Not useful enough to be paying ninety-seven dol-lars and seventy-one cents, Captain. I would have seen without them. I would have seen the two brown cars without them."

"North. . . ."

"North, Captain." Dass ate the last of his salad (two sprigs of parsley), and set the plate aside.

"Then I think they were headed for New York. Prob-ably the matter of the motors is now public, and I think things are getting a little warm for Rao Electric."

" 'The matter of the motors'. . . . Oh, we are causing them such trouble. If they were not *goondas*, I would be sorry for them. As it is, they will be angrier and an-grier and want to kill us even more. —And now to keep us from testifying in the courts, too." He forked a portion of meringue from the top of his pie.

"I'm afraid so. It would have been nice if my family . . . if you and I were safe now, and didn't need to keep going after them. Be a relief if the police would take care of everything."

"Oh, the police are so slow—and they are never tak-ing care of everything."

"No, I suppose not. . . . Well, we'll go for them this one more time. It's possible they might learn to leave

us alone. . . . And by the way, the Raos burned down
my home."

"Oh, damn! They burned your home, out in the
countryside? And it was a beautiful home?"

"Very beautiful."

"And all that they burnt of mine was a silly newsstand—not a beautiful home. But they didn't hurt anyone in the country?"

"There was no one there to hurt."

"Those men . . . those men do nothing but destroy. It
is being their speciality. Do you know, Captain, how
surprising a thing this is . . . for us, for me at any rate,
to be acting against these people? And I am not a
young man; I admit that I am not a young man. It is
not what is usually being done, not the way things are
supposed to be. Do you know *dharma*? This is so very
odd a thing to be doing. They have their place, and the
police have their place, and we people have our place,
do you understand?"

"Yes, I do."

"It seems almost rudeness, what we're doing, except
that they are so cruel, and wishing to kill us, kill your
family." He ate more of the pie's meringue . . . an edge
of crust.

"As if you were standing outside the world. . . ."

"Oh, that is so exactly it! As if I—as if we—were
standing outside the world."

Evan ate his last french fry. "And where do their
families, their women and children, stay?"

"Oh, they are all staying in the main building; behind the office is where they are all staying. I saw the
children come out to play on the back lawn, then their
mothers called them and they went inside to tiffin." As
if prompted by the reference to food, Dass ate two
swift bites of pie.

"And the second building, the one at the back . . ."

"I don't know about that building—perhaps supplies, isn't it?"

"Or something else."

"Yes, or it could be a something else with the Goddess in it. But there is a heavy door at the back I could see every time I went outside, and they have dustbins there, and the door is open all day and night."

"I don't suppose they're much concerned about trespassers, burglars. . . ."

"Captain, these people are not concerned at all about burglars. Other *dacoits,* other people of that sort can smell a tiger—and they are leaving it alone."

"All right, we'll go into the second building, Dass, as soon as it's dark, and we'll see if their goddess is in it."

"We always go in the dark." Dass had another bite of pie. There wasn't much left.

"Damn right. There're only two of us, Dass; we need all the darkness we can get."

"Well . . . I'm frightened and I'm not frightened at the same time."

"You could stand guard at the door, prevent any unpleasant surprises from walking in."

"No, Captain, I will not 'stand guard at the door.' " Dass put his tea glass down with a click. "I stood guard once, and then I didn't accompany you last night and you were cut about. So, I am *not* standing guard at the door; I don't care what you tell me. I'm old enough to be your father."

". . . Thought we'd hear that one again."

"Well, I don't care." Dass ate the last two bites of his lemon meringue pie.

"All right. . . . OK. But once we're inside, you'll do as you're told."

"Yes, once we're in action, I will do as I am told."

"Agreed."

"And since we are fighting side by side, Captain, am I no longer a stranger in your house?"

"That's right, Dass. You are no longer a stranger in my house. . . . In our house."

chapter 17

···

Well after dark, they went down the broad embankment under the deepest shadows of the Oakwood Inn, shadows cast in colors by the tall neon signs and occasional floodlights cutting across the property.

Evan, sidling down the slope's slippery night-damp grass, didn't feel frightened. Felt instead a kind of routine necessity, as if the Pathan, hunting him down such heights by moonlight, had sliced his fear away. Evan found himself, instead, interested in the enormous space they clambered down and into—a great enclosure of buildings and buildings' shadows that carved the grass hillside into territories of various light, filled with the humming vibrations of the turnpike traffic flowing past, constant as a river. . . . Over this sound, Evan heard Dass slip once or twice on the grass behind him, but keep his feet. Evan looked back to see the old man had discarded the narrow roll of carpet, and was using his sheathed saber as a staff.

"Well?" Whispered. "I am tired of going to fight with a rolled-up rug. I am carrying a sword? Very well then, I am carrying a sword."

. . . Seven big garbage cans, brown plastic, stood in a row by an open metal fire door at the back of the lower building behind the Travelers' Rest. There were a few high windows spaced along the structure's side. None lit. Only from the open door bright-yellow light came spilling to fill a neat long rectangle of concrete steps, brown garbage cans, and grass beyond.

The open door was such a convenience, it made Evan uneasy.

"Do you think, Captain," Dass murmuring, "—that this is one of those 'Come into my parlor,' said the spider to the fly'?"

"It may be. We'll pass it by, go in through a window just in case." And went left, away from the open door, to a dark window farther down. It was aluminum-framed, sash-hung, with nothing but darkness behind it.

Evan reached back under his canvas jacket and drew the bowie. "Give me a stirrup hand."

Dass cupped his hands, fingers locked together, and Evan stepped up into them—balanced on that foot as Dass grunted, taking his weight—and reaching up was just able to slide the point of the knife's blade down behind the sash, at the latch. Then he levered out . . . levered again harder, and heard the latch snap as Dass staggered and dropped him.

"I'm sorry. . . ."

"It's done." Evan sheathed the knife, slid the window up—then jumped to get a grip over its sill with his right hand, and with Dass shoving him up from behind, was able to wrestle through the window and slide over and down onto carpeting, his left arm aching from the effort. He stood in darkness, leaned out, took the old man's saber and set it to one side, then leaned out again, caught Dass's hand, and hauled him scrabbling up, helped him through the window—hard work, one-handed.

"Use your light."

Dass tugged his pencil flash out of a jacket pocket,

switched it on, and they saw a room empty of anything but ranks of stored gray metal folding chairs.

Evan took the Colt from his waistband, cocked the hammer, and left the safety on. "Here we go. . . ."

He walked to the room door, opened it awkwardly with his slung left hand, and stepped out into a long empty hallway dimly lit from end to end. . . . Painfully poor construction, the lines ceiling-to-wall untrue even to the eye. Sad, it seemed to Evan, not so much for present ugliness as for its lack of any future but bulldozing. There would be insufficient interior structure to support renovation, let alone any improvement. . . . An ugly rectangular circus tent, frail and temporary, hung on a rack of inferior lumber. . . .

As Dass stepped out into the corridor behind him, Evan heard an odd complicated thudding sound . . . felt that trembling through the building. He stood listening to it, Dass listening beside him.

"Is that machinery?"

"No. . . . That is girls, Captain."

"Girls?"

"Oh, yes. It is Indian dancing for women they are doing. Someone is dancing *Bharata natyam,* classical dancing in the rhythm for ladies."

And now Evan could hear that the thudding involved drums, drumming in very complex rhythms, more complex than in any jazz he'd heard. "Dancing girls. . . . That's all we need."

Dass nodded to the left. "I think they're that way."

"Then we go this way," Evan said, and led off down the hall to the right, past four closed doors—all tried, all locked—and on to the entranceway, the open outside door . . . the row of garbage cans. And Evan saw why the door had been left open. The entranceway and right side of the hall leading from it had been freshly painted, sprayed. The small compressor, its coiled hose, had been left against the wall, and several five-gallon buckets of paint and thinner. The new paint color was a light yellow. . . .

Evan led on down the corridor to its end at a turn to the left. . . . There was no light down that long hall except a small fire-exit bulb at its far end, and Evan stayed to the dark right wall, motioned Dass over to the left, and they went carefully. Dass had drawn his saber, its steel shining even in shadow.

The first door on the left was locked. The second door, farther down on the right, locked. The third, on the left, locked.

"I think the men are all gone." Dass, speaking softly. He ambled on, poked at the carpet with the point of his sword. "They have all gone away."

The door behind him, the last door tried, unlatched and opened, and a very big man in white shirt, white trousers, and a chef's white cap stepped out with a carton under his arm—saw them both in near darkness, and threw the box at Evan's head. As that smacked against the wall and split, dumping canned goods, the big man reached out, hit Dass in the side of the face as the old man turned, then hurled him across the corridor into Evan—and came after him, bronze face expressionless, as if all this motion had nothing to do with him.

Evan tried to level the .45, but Dass was there against him, then fell away as the big man took Evan by the throat with one hand, by his right wrist with the other, and apparently with no effort at all, threw him down the corridor—and was there just after Evan hit the carpet. Evan tried to get up, still had the gun—then didn't; the big man had taken it away from him with an effortless tug and twist that almost broke his wrist.

Evan kicked, kicked and tried to roll away in darkness to get room to draw the bowie, but the big man lifted away from him so the kicks struck nothing. Then, a wrestler and immensely strong, he let Evan roll half over, pinned him, tangled his legs, caught his right arm and doubled it behind his back. . . . Then the grip was changed and Evan, struggling, his slung left arm an agony, was handled like a child—lifted, turned, set down firmly, his back across the giant's bent knee.

Then, with a sigh of satisfaction, the wrestler, his breath smelling sweetly of cloves, bowed in strength, and began to break Evan's back.

The swiftest ache slid through Evan to his spine . . . then along his spine to gather at the small of his back and became a specific place bending obscenely wrong to break. There was, in only a few seconds, no place but that place—no Evan, but in this darkness only those vertebrae about to splinter.

And the sound was a whacking sound. But his back didn't break. The wrestler trembled so Evan felt it through his grip. And the big man slipped sideways and Evan fell, landed on his slung left arm in a jolt of pain, scrambled away and got to his feet.

In shadow, the big man crawled on all fours. Out of shadow the bright curved blade came down again and the big man collapsed on his face . . . then heaved back up, rose to his knees, got one foot under him—and Dass, stepping out of shade, swung his saber two-handed with a grunt and the big man coughed and fell bucking and thrashing on the carpet. Warmth spattered over Evan's right hand, then again, as if he'd stepped into the pattern of a lawn sprinkler, its warm summer water, and he stooped searching for the Colt, found it and stepped away.

He heard Dass hit the man again, and all motion stopped.

". . . So much for the films," Dass said, and the old man's voice wobbled as if he were crying, coming to

Evan down the dark corridor. "In the films anything is possible, Captain. But in real life it is not being possible. His head is still not off, no matter what I did. . . ."

"Are you all right? Are you all right? He hit you hard."

"I am all right. My face is hurting me terribly. I am all right." And as they came into the soft red light of the fire exit, Dass staggered, set his bleeding sword aside, and bent to vomit.

Evan held him, and felt beneath his arm the old man's slightness, the rapid tripping of his heart. . . . And they'd gone the wrong way to avoid the dancing. The drumbeats, wonderfully rapid, complex, were sounding now much louder down this corridor, as if celebrating the big man's death.

Dass tried to stand straight. "I am better now," and wiped his mouth on his jacket sleeve. "*Dirty*. . . . There is not as much Rajput in me as I thought."

"The hell there isn't. That's twice you saved our butts."

" 'Our butts.' . . . Thank you, that is very nice. But still, you know,"—Dass stood erect, looking much older under the fire exit's ruby light—"still I think I do not like going to war. Even a little war like this is surprisingly awful. I will tell you the truth, Captain: if these Raos, these *tugs* had been reasonable even a little bit, I might not have taken my sword out of the closet after all. I did have it hanging on the wall, but my Mandu's wife, who you met, said she didn't care for it. So I was having it in my bedroom, in the closet."

". . . You feeling better?"

"Yes, even though my face hurts there. That *goonda* was an elephant! . . . What did he throw?"

"A box of canned goods, I think—it must have been a supply room."

"Even their mess wallahs are savages. . . ."

"Dass, we have to go on, or get out of here now."

". . . No, I do not want to have to be coming back in here a second time. I would rather stay here than come back in again, even though I have been hurt."

"You sure? You don't have to do this."

"Let's go on, please, Captain."

Evan led again down the corridor, past the fire-exit light into darkness and the tap and rumble of drums. He heard Dass's uneven breathing behind him. . . . "That's an old dude for this shit, man," is what Beckwith would have said if he were with them. "Scrapin' the bottom of the fuckin' barrel. 'Course, Lieutenant, you're no chicken yourself, anymore. . . ."

They passed three more doors in near darkness, and Evan tried each, then knocked softly on each with the Colt ready, Dass standing to the side with his saber swung up and back.

There was no one behind those doors, and they went on to the head of a flight of concrete stairs leading down to a basement level. The sound of drums came rolling and rolling up as if introducing them to the stairs, and what lay beneath the stairs. There were melodies in the drumming.

Evan paused at the head of the staircase. Not frightened, but reluctant, as if what might be beneath would be a burden, and more than he wanted to know.

"I am at your back, Captain," Dass said. And Evan started down shadowed steps, the drums rattling, commenting, welcoming him down. . . .

There were no lights on at the bottom of the stairs except a faint glow behind what seemed a small circular port some distance to the right. Evan stood still in a pool of darkness . . . could see the ghosts of walls to either side only by the soft light of that silver circle fifteen or twenty feet away. He went toward it, walking over some composition-tiled flooring, smooth, its small checkerboard pattern barely distinguishable. The drumming came from the light.

"I can see nothing at all. . . ." Dass whispering, still back by the stairs. Aging eyes. . . .

"Wait. Your eyes will adjust," and Evan came to the circle of light, found a round window cut into a door. And peering through that, he saw a chamber—an immense room two stories high and as wide and long as a basketball court—had probably been built as a basketball court. It was lit by hanging lamps, forty, fifty . . . a hundred flickering hanging lamps that all together glowed as a lower ceiling of small flames that wavered and rippled with currents of air, and lit the room so everything was seen in moving shadow.

Through the door's window, he saw the women dancing—a dance he had never seen before, never imagined. They were dancing facing him—dancing as if for him amid the clatter and thunder of the drums. Four girls, slender in adolescence, and led by a woman, dancing—dancing with knees bent, thighs spread wide as if they were giving birth—and stamping . . . stamping barefooted but hard as if in boots, their anklets jangling. . . . And all in close costumes of gold. All glittering with necklaces, bangles, rings, their fingers drawing angular pictures in the air as they danced together—flashing, sparkling with jewelry. The woman who led them was tall as a man, lean, muscular, and sudden. And all five were obscured in such rich masks of makeup their eyes seemed great animal eyes, their faces the perfection of faces . . . what faces were meant to have been.

They danced in formation away from him, carried away from him on the undertow of the drums. Then the drums brought them back, rolled in with them like surf, and they stamped and stamped down the great room and filled the room with their dancing, and as they came down, came closer and closer, Evan saw the woman's eyes glaring—staring left, then right in counterpoint to her dancing hands, so that there was nothing of her, nothing of the girls that was not dancing.

The pencil flashlight's beam shone over his shoulder, and startled him for an instant before he turned and knocked it down. "Christ!"

"I couldn't see, Captain. . . . I'm sorry."

"Keep that fucking thing out!" He thought he might have seen a swift flare of that light reflected in the dancing woman's eyes—but when he turned to look again, Dass beside him now, she and the girls were sliding away, posturing, gesturing . . . sliding away as if the room's floor was ice. And the drums ushered them that way . . . then persuaded them back, and their jeweled feet hammered, and their heads moved side to side and their eyes gleamed in lamplight.

It looked like the first dancing that was ever danced. . . .

Then the drums stopped.

And standing still was only a tall tired woman dressed in gold, her slender body gleaming with sweat . . . and four tired girls stood still beside her. All fully human now, weary, and only beautiful.

The woman said something abrupt in a language Evan didn't know—the words muffled by the windowed door—then walked over to the left and almost out of sight, bent to a tape player on a folding chair— and pushed a button to turn it off.

"She says they were very bad. Very . . . awkward."

"If that was bad, Dass, then the good must be something to see."

"Well, she is being their *guru*—strict with them. Really, it was pretty good."

The woman said something more, and led the girls

farther to the left and out through a double door at the side of the room.

Then there was nothing left but Kali.

As if the dancers, their movement, their glittering—as if the drums' noise had only been an obscuring curtain—now in silence, in stillness, the Goddess occupied her temple.

The long room was hung in crimson down its walls, crimson rich as blood, and the lamps swung slightly in currents of air and made shadows move in the crimson. At the end of the room, high on her altar of gold, the Goddess poised to dance on garlands of marigolds, but didn't move. In a great space all crimson and lamplight, she was the dark object. Her skin was blue so deep it seemed darker than black. She stood, slightly larger than human, her bare foot lifted . . . waiting for particular music to begin her dance.

She was naked, her breasts looked full of milk—full to hurting her—and she wore a girdle of pale human arms, severed but gripping hand to stump to hand to circle her waist. She had a long necklace of skulls. And four arms almost moving, waiting to move, and so perfect, so balanced, so occupied that having only two arms would have seemed a disfigurement. She gripped in her four hands a short spear . . . a flower, a flame . . and a human head.

Her face was a frozen explosion of fury—held still as she held still, about to dance among her wreaths of marigolds.

"I cannot go in there," Dass said, and in the long room the double doors to the left opened and a girl came back in, still in costume, took a spangled gauze scarf from the back of the folding chair holding the tape player, and went out again.

"We're both going in there, Dass. I need to make

sure those women are getting out of the building." And Evan shoved the door open.

"Wait, wait! Why do we care where they go?"

"Because, Dass, I'm going to burn this motherfucker down."

"Oh, *Ram,* oh my God—burn it down?"

"That's right. Now let's go see the ladies out. Come on. . . ."

And as they went through the door and the door swung shut, the lights came on behind it and a man they couldn't yet see was whistling down the angle of the stairs. He was whistling "Stand By Your Man."

"Move . . . !" Evan shoved Dass, hustled him along to the left, to stand against the wall—then turned and raised the .45. The flames of the temple's hundred lamps reflected dully on the weapon's coated steel . . . the groove the Dond's Khyber knife had made across it.

"Captain—she does not like us here."

"Quiet. . . ."

"Well, she may like you . . . but she isn't liking me."

Something metal clanged out in the hallway. The lights were still on, shining through the door's round window onto the temple floor. Fine-laid narrow hard-wood, a basketball floor.

"Dass, you want to get out of here?"

"Certainly yes!"

"Then get. Go out through that side door, make sure those women are out of the building. Then wait for me over there, in the corridor or whatever. I'll meet you soon as I can."

"And where are you going?"

"God damn it. Can't you the fuck obey an order?"

"I want to know where you're going. . . ."

"Dass, I'm going to keep an eye on whoever just came down those stairs."

"You're not going to do anything?"

"I will not take chances—OK? Now please, mov
out and check on the ladies, make sure they've left . .
because this building is going."

"Oh, all right, all right. . . ." Dass went off, swingin
his saber in lamplight—and didn't look down the roor
where Kali stood poised, waiting for her music.

Evan watched him pause at the double doors . .
then slowly push them open. The hallway beyond wa
dark, and Dass hesitated again and looked back a
Evan, then saluted with his saber, stepped through th
doorway, and was gone.

Evan was oddly pleased to be alone with the Goc
dess. Poised above her altar, her face contorted in furj
long tongue lolling, she glared down—a stare so direc
so personal, it seemed it shouldn't be shared. He felt
kind of affection for her, as if they both possessed th
same sad knowledge to which an immobile rage ha
been the only response.

"But you're not beautiful when you're angry," h
said to her, and walked back out the windowed doc
into the hallway's light.

Across the wide hall, another door stood open. It ha
a steel kickplate, and beyond it a long stainless-stec
table shone under ranks of hanging copper pots an
pans.

He and Dass had heard a man come whistling dow
the stairs, but they hadn't seen him—and perhaps ha
missed a second man, silent, come down with hir
And a second man would make a serious differ
ence. . . . Evan walked across the hall, the .45 by hi
side, and stepped into the kitchen's doorway. A profes
sional kitchen, brightly lit and empty. He heard dishe
rattle in a room beyond. That door was open, too. Per
haps a sort of serving pantry. —A basketball court an
a kitchen. The building must have been planned orig

ally as a health club, or sports club with a cafeteria, before being dedicated to a different service.

If there were two men in the room beyond, they weren't talking. Evan walked into the kitchen, stood alongside the steel table, and listened to the noises of dishes being set out, a refrigerator door opening . . . then closing. Then a pause. A sudden rush of water, the small hollow drumming as a kettle was filled. Probably one man, but Evan felt better waiting. It seemed to him he had done too much in too short a time, and needed to rest a little. . . . His hands were trembling slightly, and he felt as if the wrestler still gripped him, that firm and increasing pressure at the small of his back. . . .

. . . Dass had followed giggles at a distance down a long dark basement corridor, lit only palely on the left by an occasional small high vent window. A long hallway—and two others had branched off from this, and they had been dark.

There was a light in an entranceway, the outside door at the end of the corridor. He had stood and watched as the woman went out, some time ago . . . but now, for the longest while, three of the girls were still waiting there, where a room door was open on the light. —A dressing room possibly, though they hadn't changed their costumes. Or a WC. They were talking in Bengali about a boy named Gopal. Talking, giggling, chirping like birds. . . .

At last the fourth girl came out, still in her costume and carrying a small green canvas bag by the handles—an airline sort of bag, very much like his. And when she came out, she turned off the light there in the entranceway, and all four girls went through the door to outside, and the door slammed shut behind them.

Well, they were gone. If the Captain wished to, he could burn the building down. And why not? The *tugs* had burned his pretty house in the countryside, had

burned an honest man's newsstand. Now let thes
nasty men taste ashes. . . .

Dass turned to go back up the dark corridor to th
temple to wait—not into the temple, but outside. Ther
was no need to be going inside the temple. He turne
and started back . . . reached out to touch the left-sid
wall with his fingers. He could see, but not very wel
and was thinking of using his little flashlight, though
had made the Captain angry before. Probably it wa
bad practice to use a flashlight on patrol. An unprofes
sional practice.

He had gone a distance along the way, a short dis
tance, when he heard the sound. A silvery . . . a swee
sound. A soft, soft chiming sound. It sounded like th
bangle on a dancer's ankle, as she raised her foot t
begin the dance.

Dass stood still where he was. Stopped breathing
and listened. Nothing. . . . Nothing.

He waited, began to breathe again, and still hear
nothing.

Then he took a step—and the pretty chime sounde
once, far up the dark corridor ahead of him.

Dass gripped his saber harder, raised the point. H
could see the blade's gleaming in dim light from a hig
ventilation window many feet away. Light enough t
see the blade, at least.

Carefully, silently, he took another step—and th
bangle chimed from darkness before him, a littl
louder.

And Dass stepped back, and the bangle rang musi
cal. And he stepped back and back—and each step wa
celebrated. Closer.

Another step back. And again someone danced th
step with him. Closer.

Dass stood still, sweating in cool darkness, and de
cided not to move at all. . . .

... In the kitchen's serving pantry, there were no more sounds of dishware being set out. No more opening and closing of a refrigerator. And still no conversation between two men. Whoever was there was alone—and had just whistled the first bars of Patsy Cline's "Crazy," when Evan took a deep breath, felt his hands still trembling a little, snicked off the .45's safety and stepped into the doorway.

The fat man, sitting facing the door, looked up and said, "*Oh, my goodness me. . . .*" Dressed in a rumpled summer suit, the false policeman was sitting on a stool behind the short right angle of a serving counter. "—If it isn't the extraordinary Mr. Scott!"

There was an array of dishes in front of him on the wide countertop. A platter mounded with rice ... four or five other, smaller plates. Another serving platter heaped with sliced pumpernickel. An opened bottle of beer.

"Mr. Scott. And looking as if he'd been to the wars. Wounded hero and so forth. Slight nervous tremor ... ?" The fat man didn't seem to have noticed the .45 in Evan's hand. Didn't seem interested in it.

There were warming bins for hot food down the length of the counter ... and beyond it, a dark and empty dining room of folding tables, folding chairs.

"A person," the fat man said, smiling, "simply cannot be eating a meal in peace these days. A meal I had to serve to myself. You haven't seen our chief cook and bottle-washer, have you? A very large man? —Ah. see. . . . What a busy fellow Mr. Scott has been. You, and I suppose, your old *bapu* of the newsstand." The fat man sighed. "But I don't mean to be inhospitable—will you join me? We could settle our differences after supper."

"I think not." Evan raised the Colt. The weapon's weight seemed to steady his hand.

"No? . . . No. I see your point; you are believing a
certain tension might disturb the digestion, and I suppose you're right." He reached out, scooped a palmful
of rice into his right hand, dipped that neatly into one
of his side dishes, rolled the result into a small ball and
popped it into his mouth. "Mmmm. You are missing
something special." The fat man chewed his bite, relishing, then dipped and rolled another neat portion, and
ate it.

"The others—"

"The 'others,' Mr. Scott—those still left to us after
your brief but really remarkable career—are out attempting to repair the damage you have done. . . . And
speaking of your career, exposing our pretty little motors so now the police are in it and so forth, have you
any idea how rude you've been? And I speak as a person who has done many murders—but always in form,
oh yes. I have never so jumped the tracks as you have
done. I have never been so awkward, so in the way."
He tore a slice of pumpernickel in two, swiftly ate one
half. ". . . I do have one question to be asking before I
put you where the monkey put the pineapple—that is
up the universe's arse. And the question is, how in
God's name did you manage to be killing the Dond? I
had thought our servant was immortal."

"He ran out of luck."

"Such a sinister phrase. . . ." The fat man scooped up
another handful of rice, looked over his sauce dishes,
and chose what looked like chopped green pickles.
"Sure you won't be having something? You're most
welcome to, so long as you don't use your left hand—
and so long as you wash your right. There is blood on
it."

"No, thank you. . . . You shouldn't have tried to kill
my little girl."

"Oh, balls. Easy come and easy go—and in any case

KARMA 415

Our Lady would have taken her into her arms. —Will do, since we intend to finish that business, you bet. . . . No no, you only wanted an excuse to play the hero, to disrupt and spoil things. To show away your so-nasty white man's individuality, no matter the destruction of delicate plans, no matter the cost to other people, though they are more cultured and more aryan than you." The fat man reached beneath the counter into his lap, brought up a starched white linen napkin, and wiped his mouth and right hand.

"—What does a barbarous creature like you, swollen with self-importance, clinging to life like a tick to a dog's neck . . . what can you know of real complication? How could you understand, for example, what it means to have been born into a clown's body, and have the heart of a tiger."

The fat man made a disgusted face, wiped his mouth again. "Face it, Mr. Scott. You have been a bad sport." He put his napkin back into his lap, brought up a snub-nosed revolver and fired one shot that thumped past Evan's ear and cracked into cabinets behind him. Evan dropped as the fat man fired again, starting to rise from his stool in the fastest of slow motion, watching Evan as he rose, his face an amused moon behind the revolver muzzle's small bright circle. —Evan fell to one knee, crouching close against the counter's front, and fired one, two, three, four deliberate shots up through drumming sheet metal.

The fat man seemed to jump, heave up as if he'd been startled by that terrific noise—and fumbled at his belly with his free hand while still standing behind the counter, trying to reach across—and fired again, but high, as Evan triggered three more deliberate rounds up through the countertop and the fat man's dinner dishes smashed and erupted, the food exploding as the slugs came through. . . . Spattered with sauces, but his suit jacket blotched a brighter red, the fat man leaned on the counter, still holding his revolver. His head bent, he braced himself with one hand . . . stood leaning there silent amid thunderous echoes.

Evan stood up, and shot him through the heart.

. . . Then there was only silence and drifting gunsmoke, its smell, the smell of blood and spices.

Evan walked behind the counter, very tired, and found the fat man curled on his side, his dark face a dying baby's, eyes tight shut. And blood crept shining slowly out from beneath him onto white tile, as if wary of the light. . . .

. . . Dass had stood still as long as he could bear it, and after a while thought that perhaps he'd been mistaken in the sounds. Perhaps hadn't heard the sounds at all. He could see three soft pools of ivory light spaced along the dark corridor from the small ventilation windows; and nothing had moved through those places, because he had watched.

He thought he'd been a fool to stand like a frightened child so long. Captain Scott would think he'd been a fool. . . .

Dass took a breath in the silence, then strode out three steps, as if he were marching—and the bangles chimed and rang, the sound shimmering like silver, so loud, so close. And Dass turned and ran and heard a cascade of dancing music sounding down the corridor close behind him.

"No, my lady!" He shouted it in English, and so frightened he felt his urine down his trousers, was too frightened not to see—and found his small flashlight in his jacket pocket as he ran and turned, stumbling, to shine the wavering light behind him into darkness. And there was writhing and dark arms dancing to him; blue breasts shook beneath a swinging necklace of white things amid the arms, two blue arms or more gesturing

d one hand slowly whirling a short spear so Dass
eard it thrumming through the air. Another hand held
omething by the hair that looked as it swung from
de to side. But not as the Goddess looked. The blue
ice, darker than black, bloomed in ferocity in his little
iaking light. Its tongue lolled out. But its eyes, blood-
ed, were still a woman's eyes—lovely, pitiless, and
nused.

Dancing, Kali came to Ram Dass Lal with her chim-
ig music, and what had been true became a dream,
id only she was real.

He ran, dropped his flashlight as if it were too new
thing to keep. But running, still gripped his saber.

He ran to the outside door—and tried it and tried it
nd shook it and it was locked—and he yelled and
ucked into the room to the side of the entrance, and
iought of slowing to slam the door behind him but
ouldn't bear to slow. He ran to the room's far wall
ke a young man, and found only high windows, too
igh, and turned and she was whirling . . . whirling in
ie doorway, changing as she spun, shifting in shadows
iere.

Then she came in.

And Dass, frightened at last beyond fear, called out
RAMA-JIIII!" and went to meet her with his saber.

Then Kali threw her spear.

. . . Evan had heard Dass shout as he came out of the
emple into the side corridor—and he saw Dass, or
omething moving far down at the hallway's end, and
egan to run, awkward, out of balance with his arm in
ie sling. His arm ached and ached worse as he ran
irough darkness and occasional places softly lit by
indows high to the left. And as he ran he remembered
e hadn't reloaded the pistol. Couldn't get it out of his
aistband now, reload it one-handed, running. . . .

Very tired, very tired and breathing hard, he ran t
the long corridor's end, called *"Dass!"* and heard
sound to the right, saw faint window light past a doc
ajar—and ran through it, shoving the door open.

Inside, Evan ducked to the left, trying to control hi
breathing ... listening.

"Captain...."

"I'm here!" Evan reached behind him, fumbled for
light switch,. and found it.

Ram Dass Lal lay in the room's far corner, and th
wall he lay against was red.

"Oh, Jesus, oh my God...." Evan went to kneel be
side him, and saw the old man was gripping a sho
spear in both hands. "I pulled it out," Dass said, an
his jacket was soaked with blood.

"Dass ... Dass, I'm getting you out of here! Please
for Christ's sake, for Christ's sake just hold on—"

"I have been killed by a goddess, Captain. The God
dess has killed me."

"Dass...." Evan pulled his left arm from the sling
He picked the old man up and cradled him. Hugge
him as if to keep the life in him, not let it go. The ol
man was too thin ... too thin. He smelled of salt an
iron.

"I shouldn't have sent her ... wilted flowers...."

"Now God damn it, you listen to me, you hold on
Dass, listen to me, please. I'm going to carry you ou
Just listen to me...." But Ram Dass Lal was payin;
no more attention.

"Kali mata ki!"

Evan turned to the voice as the opened door swun;
back from the wall—and behind it, smiling, stood th
tall woman dancer, naked in blue paint, and drape(
with a necklace of skulls. A human head, long-haire(
withered and preserved, lay on the carpet at her feet

She smiled at Evan as she cupped her left hand to her eye, blinked, and caught a contact lens. The eye revealed was blue, and more savage than the other eye till red.

Evan remembered her, recalled her standing at the elevator door. *"They make the most extraordinary faces. . . ."*

One eye blue, the other red, the tall dancer stopped smiling, lifted Dass's saber, swung it back two-handed, and came at Evan leaping.

He received her on the point of the spear.

Before midnight, Evan climbed very slowly up the grassy bank. He climbed in such fatigue and sorrow that neither seemed as real as the chill of damp clothes against him. He'd found a bathroom, showers, behind what had been the basketball court, and had showered alone in a building of the dead. He'd wet his bandages, had almost fallen asleep under the warm curtain of water. He thought of Dass while he stood in that comfort, and talked out loud to him once or twice, pretending the old man was standing by the sinks, impatient for him to finish so they could go. . . .

Evan had turned the shower off, stepped out, and rinsed the blood from his shirt and trousers and canvas jacket, then wrapped each around a faucet to wring it out one-handed. His left arm was very bad.

When he was dressed, he'd walked through the temple, out the windowed door past the kitchen where the fat man lay with his eyes tight shut . . . then up the stairs and left along the hallway where the big wrestler had died. And after that, a right turn into the painted corridor . . . its buckets of paint, solvent and thinner. . . . There, he'd used Dass's lighter.

Evan climbed very slowly up the grassy bank . . .

climbed, stumbled up through the alternating colors o
the motels' signs. In the building below, behind a rov
of high windows, appeared the first small blossom o
fire.

chapter 18

. . . .

The girl flew relaxed, zipped into gray coveralls and easy in the left-hand seat. By the instrument lights, Evan saw her hands—square and looking strong as a strong boy's—resting comfortable on the yoke.

There had been a long wait at Newark Airport to get a charter pilot for a night run to northeast Maine. Evan had dozed in a waiting-room chair until Joyce Duffin had been called by Busy Bee, had accepted, and had driven in to take the trip. Five hundred and eighty dollars, and an additional hundred and fifty to have the little tower at Rupton manned, the small field's lights turned on. Joyce Duffin, a rawboned girl in glasses, and not good looking—resembling so many young women Evan had seen around horses—had been all business, taken the cash up front, filed her plan ... then led out to the plane to get going. She hadn't seemed much interested in Evan's sling and bandages, the stains on his crumpled clothes.

Now he sat beside her, bumped and jostled occasionally as the aging Aztec met rough air. The Piper drummed in sympathy with its engines, and Evan rode it dreamily on two of Dass's codeines taken at the water fountain before boarding. The pain in his left arm was less important than it had been.

Through the side window's smeared glass was empty
night, and far below it sparkled necklaces and bracelets
of light that stretched and coiled between the treasure
heaps of cities.

"I want to see my wife," Evan said to Joyce Duffin,
and the pilot turned her head, lifted an earphone for
him to repeat it. "I want to see ... my wife."

Joyce understood that, seemed to think it was sensible, and nodded. Then she reached to the dash, set a
small instrument's pointer, turned a switch, and
watched a dial until she was satisfied.

Evan sat back and thought of Catherine, wished to
see her. Had to see her in the most compelling way—
not only out of affection, or love or wanting. It was a
more elemental need. He needed to be in her presence;
she was essential. . . . Beth was not as necessary to
him, didn't seem as absolutely necessary, though he
certainly loved her more in a simple way. He loved
her, but he could do without her. It was Catherine he
couldn't do without. . . . Perhaps only because he was
injured. Perhaps only because he had lost another
man—though this time in winning. Though it would
certainly have been better if he had died instead of
Dass. . . . Dass had died, but perhaps he hadn't been
wasted.

Evan thought of the building he'd burned, and didn't
regret it. He only regretted that Dass's funeral pyre had
been so ugly. . . . He wished he had a notebook and
pen—though there wasn't light enough in the small
plane's cockpit to draw—and instead closed his eyes
and began to imagine a building to replace the one destroyed. . . . This building would welcome the turnpike's traffic, not simply stand beside it. A building
rounded as a river's bend, and built of reinforced concrete faced with polished granite—through which,
room to room, would run a narrow vein of ribboned

silver hammered into the stone. A vein of bright silver to remind passersby of the courage that had run through an old man's veins.

A building like a river's bend to flank a river of traffic never ending, its entrance steps rising as if from shallows into the curving arcade of its first floor ... then a half circle of stone steps lifting to its second floor. And drooping over that, enormous and protective, an umbrella roof—the cast concrete ribbed as umbrellas were ribbed—to provide a place of beauty, of calm and refuge for tired travelers along a hard road.

This building, if built well, floored and trimmed in oak inside, would have been worthy to provide an old Rajput a proper funeral pyre. . . .

Evan slept.

And woke to dawn over the sea, as the Piper banked slowly north to run up along the coast. The sea was a deep slate blue, but its blue uncertain as the sun struck over the horizon's rim. Where that light touched, the sea grew green as pines—and might have been forest tops slowly moving under a forest wind. Sunlight flashed up and gilded the cabin's windows as the plane completed its turn, so Evan was blinded as they came level. He turned away and saw the small pilot, looking weary from half a night's flying, glancing over at him.

"How you doin'?"

"Doing fine," Evan said, loud enough for her to hear him.

"Got some sleep."

"Yes. . . ." And hadn't dreamed. Or had dreamed only of talking with some women on a train. . . . No dream of war. Not the old war, and not this one that had wounded him, and killed his second sergeant—a man old enough, dear enough, to have been his father.

No dream of war, as if this small and vicious fight, so bloody, had burned his old wounds closed.

Evan thought of Dass—of the necessary call now to the State Department and Saudi Arabia to find Dass's son, and speak with him. . . . He thought of Dass and found he missed the old man. Missed him and always would. And perhaps shouldn't have sent him alone to see the women out of the building. Perhaps should have recognized the dancer by her savagery, her cruel and perfect dancing. One blue eye, and one red. She must have performed, danced as their goddess in whatever plays, whatever festivals they'd staged in their basketball-court temple. It seemed to Evan sad in a way—that brutal family, their Pathan killer, their wives and children . . . all come to a country and a time so different from their past that their goddess could be kept alive only by murder.

Now the district attorney's people and the police would be moving against them. A dubious death or two were one thing; a proven multimillion-dollar fraud involving banks and insurance companies would be something else, and treated very directly. —And, of course, the police would want to talk to him. And very odd talking it would be. Disliking private wars, they would find little evidence left of this one, since the Raos, habitually concealing, had cleaned up after him in two encounters. And fire had taken the third.

. . . But all that a day or two—perhaps three or four days—away. For now, for this morning, a ride into Shaddock with the airfield's tower man. Then a climb up Spring Street through sea air and morning sunshine to Jack Micklin's office, to have him take a look at the arm. A very painful look, no doubt. Unbandaging, remarks to be made (wound opened, cleaned), more remarks, "You've got a damaged bone here. . . ."

Then he would go down to Pope's, and have him or Tommy take him out to the island. And the sun would be higher by then and the night lobstermen running into the harbor as the Popes' boat ran out, and the harbor's arms, decorated with pines and summer homes and year-round homes of white clapboard and yellow and light blue and gray clapboard. And the harbor's arms would slowly open as they motored out ... open and open like the embrace of a huge fond woman as she let her loved ones go....

... And there to port, a half mile out, the island rose in evergreen and stone, the first of several standing sentinel into the Atlantic, and Clyde's boy, Tommy, smiled and called, "There she be!" from the tiller, and pushed the button on his air horn so it bleated out loud enough to echo off the island's minor cliffs.

They rode out, rising on the swell, gulls—curious, complaining—sliding through the air above them. They flanked the island's rocks comfortable yards away ... then rounded its wooded headland even wider, and as they swung past the point, Tommy blew his horn again and steered her in toward the landing.... Then Evan saw, high above the cove, a woman and child come running onto the deck of the long cabin, its weathered timbers looking like driftwood cast up to a clearing amid wind-bent pines, and fallen here into perfect order....

In late afternoon, Evan woke and found Beth sitting on the foot of the bed, watching him and unwrapping Hershey's Candy Kiss.

"Daddy, you were snoring."

"... Well, I'm awake now; no more snoring. How are you doing, sweetheart?"

"Now," Beth said, ate the candy, and came on all fours up the bed to curl against him, "now I am just

fine. . . . Mom said you were fighting people, and tha
how you got hurt?"

"Yes."

"Dirty sons of bitches," Beth said, her breath mi
chocolate.

"Don't talk like that. —And besides, they were
goddess's sons. And one of her daughters, too. Th
weren't . . . ordinary."

"They were rats and I'm glad you won."

"I was lucky, and I had a very good man with me.
Do you have any more of that chocolate?"

"One."

"Well . . . ?"

"Well what, Daddy?" Beth said and started to scra
ble off the bed, but Evan caught her with his free han
managed to hold her and inflict enough tickling so s
shouted, "All right . . . !" dug in her jeans pocket for
silver-wrapped candy, and handed it over.

"This is it? Only one?"

"Daddy. . . ." She climbed off the bed. "Anywa
Mom said I was supposed to make you some soup
you woke up. She went shopping. Fred took h
in."

"We'll have to get our boat out; I'll drain the ou
board and gas it up and we'll roll it down tomorro
But I don't want soup."

"Well, what do you want?" Her look, bright-eye
attentive, ready to provide as any grown woman wi
an incompetent to feed, struck Evan like a chord
music so valuable, so directly hers, so certain to be r
peated in infinite variations throughout her life, that
suddenly saw her grown and gone from him. Thou
safe, though alive.

"I want a peanut butter and pickle sandwich."

"All right." Very pleased at that. "But Mom sa
soup."

"She'll forgive us."

"OK. Peanut butter and pickle and mayo." And Beth galloped out of the room, looking taller than Evan had remembered her only a week before.

He lay back then, watching the shifting sea light reflected against the ceiling's white-painted pine boards ... slow coiling waves of different intensity as the sound of slight surf hissed and murmured through the windows. Sound and light, they moved together, and as Evan lay at ease ... at ease ... the slow sea wind, warm with summer, pushed the cotton curtains aside and drifted in with salt scent and pine scent, and slanting sunlight.

They'd both been shocked by the bandages ... his stained and grimy clothes. But Beth was better now. The first hour or so after he'd come she'd clung as if frightened to let him go. Catherine touching him, too—unusual for her—quick soft tentative touches, like a cat's, as he'd explained for Beth a few days of trouble with some people in New York ... all over now. Now the police would be taking care of everything.

Later, Fred Pell had come up—the same weathered stumpy-strong tramp lobsterman, almost toothless now, looking his age after a year or more of adventures wandering God knew where. He'd climbed up the path to the cabin, stood on the deck with one of Catherine's big Remingtons casual over his shoulder.

"How's it goin' for yuh, Mr. Scott?"

"Pretty well, Fred. How's it going for you?"

"I got no complaints. Stayin' down the north end in our shed. Keepin' my boat down there."

"You're welcome to it," Evan had said.

"Pottin' some chickens...." Meaning undersized lobsters, and probably illegal. "With this little lady 'ppose' to come help me."

And Beth, reluctant, had been persuaded to go lob-
stering, since they'd be picking up Cal Thursby's boy,
too. ". . . Barry thinks he's so smart," Beth had said,
and gone in to change her jeans for other jeans.

Fred Pell had waited on deck, smiling and silent.
Had nothing to say about possible trouble . . . no questions to ask—and when Beth came out (pausing by
Evan for another hug) had ambled off down the path
after her, the shotgun across his shoulder swinging
slightly with his stride.

Then Catherine had said, "Come inside," and took
Evan in and up to their bedroom, stood him in the middle of the floor like a child, and undressed him, tender
at the bandages. "Oh, dear God . . . oh, Evan," she'd
said. And he stood finally naked and admiring her as
she took her cotton trousers and T-shirt off—admired
her beauty as she turned and postured, undressing in a
flood of late-morning sunlight. The cabin's room too
simple in its white paint to distract from her moving
light-tan and gold.

"I love you dearly," Evan had said—and naked
she'd taken him by the hand and led him into the bath
room. Then showered with him, gently bathing him—
very careful of his sling, the bandages on his cheek, hi
back, the bandage across his right wrist.

Catherine had said nothing to him under pouring wa
ter, but after a while had knelt and licked him as a ca
might lick a kitten, until he was erect—and her shor
bright hair soaked dark and close, took him in he
mouth as if his cock were all of him, and kissed an
sucked it until she had what she wanted.

. . . She'd dried him, dressed him in pajamas, an
tucked him into bed, then sat on the side of the bed i
her robe, and said, "Tell me."

And the tale was told by noon.

"Jesus," Catherine had said. She'd said it sever

mes, but not when he'd told her about the house,
urned and gone. Then she'd closed her eyes for a mo-
ent, but said nothing.

When he was finished, when he'd told her every-
ing but the smallest worst things about men dying,
atherine said, "Evan, it's a miracle they didn't kill
ou. I knew you'd seen terrible fighting in the war, but
y God. . . ."

"I know, but these people were caught off balance.
hey weren't *used* to anyone coming back at them.
hey had a . . . a sort of religious vocation of mur-
er, I think. And they seemed to assume that would be
espected, in a way. Perhaps in the old days in their
ountry, it had been. —They were surprised by my
aking such violent trouble for them . . . the way
arks are supposed to be disconcerted if you fight
em, stick your thumb in their eye."

"Even so. . . ."

"And I had Dass. He saved both of us once, and di-
ectly saved my life another time."

"And I never met him."

"Not unless you remember him at his newsstand, in
ont of the office."

"No. No, I don't. Evan, I never even bought a mag-
zine from him."

" 'No longer a stranger in your house.' . . ."

"What?"

"Something the old man said."

"And no more trouble now?"

"Oh, there'll be more trouble, sweetheart—certainly
ith the police, trying to clear the mess up. There'll be
ore trouble—but I hope no more danger. The Raos
ave been hit very hard; they should be too busy sav-
g their hides to try to find us now."

"But you said 'a religious vocation.' "

"Yes. . . . Well, we'll spend the summer on the is-

land, be careful of our contacts—I'll go to Bangor t
send letters or make calls—and let the police mo
them up."

"Yes, please 'let the police mop them up.' " An
she'd leaned over to kiss him, and left him to sleep

They ate a late dinner out on the deck by lamplig
and rising moonlight shimmering off the sea. A co
lobster salad with hot buttered rolls, India ale—7U
for Beth—and apple pie with a slice of Mr. Webster
cheddar on it.

Fred Pell hadn't stayed for dinner. "Got drinkin' t
do in town," he'd said earlier, when he brought Be
up to the cabin—tired, suntanned, sun-heated—an
had turned and stumped away down the path.

"Barry Thursby is a real jerk," Beth had said. "H
thinks he's so cute he can say anything. . . ."

After dinner, Evan went in, found the hazelnut l
queur in the cabinet under the sink, and poured a littl
into two teacups. Then they lay before the railing i
battered wood-and-canvas lawn chairs—Evan wit
Beth's warm weight heaped in his lap—and watched a
the last of the lobster boats headed in—slow-runnin
in perfectly black silhouettes against a chain-ma
ocean.

After almost an hour, Beth went to sleep, and Eva
and Catherine rested side by side, occasionally holdin
hands—and so reminding Evan of walking across th
park with Dass, embarrassed by the old man's holdin
his hand. . . .

"We could rebuild the house, Evan. Build it just th
same."

"No, darling, we can't. The timber—chestnut beams
heart of oak, walnut—doesn't exist anymore. Hand
knapped slates, blacksmithed nails and spikes, and th

ld shipwrights who put it together—all gone. You and
'll build a new house, not an old house."

They said nothing more, while the moon rose high-
r—then there were little rattles of explosion barely
eard from the hills above the harbor.

"Today's the Fourth of July," Catherine said, as if he
might have been startled by them.

"Right. . . ."

Soon there was a slow creaming wake around the
oint . . . and a little later moonlight shone off Fred
ell's battered Sea Truck as she turned port into the
ove, running a little too fast.

"Fred's tight," Catherine said.

And Fred, once docked, came shambling up the
ath, proving her right. On the deck, he leaned against
he rail in bright moonlight.

"Sorry, folks—jus' a little drunk."

"That's all right, Fred."

"I'll be goin' down to bed now."

"All right."

"All right?"

"That's all right."

"OK." And left the railing, swayed, caught his bal-
nce and started down the deck steps. "—Oh, an' you
olks got a guest comin' out."

"What guest?" Evan said.

"Some doctor. I was in LeDuc's, an' Jerry Tate—
eal estate guy?—came in an' told me Mrs. Scott's
unt called an' said I was suppose' to rev the place
p."

Evan lifted Beth aside, and stood. "For who, Fred?"

"This doctor. Tate says yesterday this Indian fella
vent to see the old bat—excuse me, old lady—lookin'
o rent someplace real out of the way for summer. So
he told him she had this place an' he could come out

an' look. . . . Must not know you people already came
up."

"Oh, no, oh *no*. . . ."

"Catherine, be quiet. Take Beth inside and get you
shotgun.—Fred!"

"What . . . ?"

"Go down to the shack and get the other shotgun.'

"Uh . . . still on my boat."

"Go get it and get back up here fast. We're in trou
ble."

"Oh, shit. . . ."

"Move!"

Evan heard Pell stumbling, hurrying back down the
path to the cove . . . then turned and walked into the
cabin. Catherine was standing by the stone fireplace
the shotgun in her hands, Beth beside her, still sleepy
and very pale.

"Evan. . . ."

"Turn off the lamps. Now." And he crossed the liv
ing room to the stairs and went up them three at a time
. . . then down the hall to their bedroom and in. Wen
to the bedside table, yanked its drawer open—saw no
.45, no bowie—and crossed the room to the bureau
dragged the top drawer out, and saw a dull glint o
steel by moonlight. He reached in to pick the Colt up
then dug for ammunition and found the magazine
among Catherine's underwear. Searched for the bowie
and didn't find it. Pulled the second drawer out and
saw it sheathed across his socks.

He loaded the pistol, chambered a round (his lef
hand just usable), left the piece cocked and made sure
its safety was on. Then, tucking the sheathed knife into
his belt at the back, he was out of the room, down the
hall and down the stairs, seeming to float through
moonlight, his heart pounding at things so unfair when
all was supposed to be over. . . .

"Daddy. . . ." Beth was standing beside Catherine in moon-shade, crying.

"Beth—shut up, stop crying, and listen to me. You re to stay behind your mother. Do you understand me? *Do you understand me?*"

"Yes. . . ."

"No matter what is happening, you will stay behind your mother and reload that shotgun for her fast when she hands it back to you. Do you understand hat?"

". . . Yes, Daddy."

"Catherine, where are the buckshot shells?"

"On the mantel back here. I've got them on the mantel. . . ."

"Give Beth the box. Beth, open the box and get ready. You can't make a mistake; you can't be slow; you can't pay attention to anything but reloading that gun when your mother hands it back to you."

"I know . . . I know. . . ."

"I said, 'No crying.' We don't have time for it."

". . . All right, Daddy."

"Now, both of you stay back by that fireplace—stay n the shadows there and watch the doors and windows. These people . . . these people are very aggressive infantry. They come right at you, and fast. But we have two things going for us. We know the cabin, and hey have to come to us."

"Evan—"

"And they know about me, what I can do. But I don't think they know about you and that shotgun. Now, I'm going to the kitchen, I'll be right back."

Evan heard Catherine call, "Stay here!" when he was already in the hall. The cabin was mottled in darkness and moonlight, the kitchen darkest of all. He stepped into the room and then to the right and stood listening, smelling the air. . . . Only mayonnaise . . .

faint odor of beer from their unwashed dinner glasses
He crossed to the sink drawer, opened it, and fingered
in among the knives—one slender sharp boning blade
. . . and an old worn-handled butcher knife, edge prickling sharp.

Then he was out of the kitchen and back down the
hall. "Catherine," he said to warn them.

"Yes. . . ." And he was back, relieved to see them
pale in deep shadow, and nothing happened yet.

"Here. . . . Beth, be careful, it's sharp," and handed
her the boning knife. "Put it in your belt, and if anyone
grabs you—and everything will be very noisy, very
scary—but if anyone grabs you or your mother, then
stick this knife into him hard as you can, and keep
sticking. Catherine. . . ." He handed her the butcher
knife.

"But Evan—nobody's even here! There's no one
here, and they may never—"

"They found out yesterday; they should be here to-night."

"But Evan, they're not! We can go into town, to the
police!"

"Catherine, Fred hasn't come back up. I think
they're on the island now—"

"Oh, God. . . . but they'll burn the cabin. They'll
burn us!"

"No. Fire'd be seen on the other islands, and by
fishermen. They'd have a hundred people over here.
They won't start any fires. . . . Now, listen. I'll be up
at the head of the stairs. From there, I can cover the
upstairs hall, and the entrance here. You and Beth stay
right back at the fireplace—and watch the windows. I
wish I had time . . . to tell you how to do this. About
how noisy everything will be and fast and strange.
There isn't time—but listen, combat is like dancing. It
moves back and forth; there's a rhythm to it, changes

in gunfire, movement. Everyone's frightened and everyone's angry, and they want to move together. You'll sense it, you'll sense it—and the secret is to feel those changes coming, and move just a little early. To lead the dance. *Oh, Christ I'm so sorry*—and there's no time!"

"Evan," Catherine said. "We'll do it," and there were light swift footsteps across the deck. "—It's Fred!"

"No, it isn't; Fred was drunk. Get ready!" And Evan started up the stairs as a man came down them so fast Evan only fired once and low before the man slammed into him, knocked him down the steps—and as they fought at the bottom of the stairs, Catherine shouted and fired a blast that blew a front window out. The man snaked behind Evan as he scrambled up, his slung left arm hampering, and snapped a softness around his throat and there was no more air.

For Evan it seemed to make no difference. He felt he moved and acted in a place where air to breathe or no air to breathe—though it might become important soon—was not important yet. He tried, in a ringing silence, to turn the Colt behind him to get a shot into the man. But the strangler turned with him, and there was still no air.... Evan dropped the pistol, wrestled his right hand back to find the bowie's grip, drew the knife and reversed it in his hand so the blade extended down from his fist.

Then, still in a slow, slow world of fast movement but now terrific noise, he suddenly twisted hard to the left—and the man stepped right to stay behind him. He twisted to the left again—and as the strangler again stepped right, Evan turned to the right and into him, struck back along his side, and felt the bowie's blade slide in.

He heard the strangler gasp, but there was still no

air—and Evan turned hard left, then hard right against the band of cloth ... moving, moving, and the strangler kept almost with him. Almost, but not quite. He overstepped to the right again and Evan swung the big knife back and this time it struck in and stayed and the man screamed and his cloth fell away.

Then Evan took a long breath as he turned and sliced the knife free—raised it and brought the big blade down to hack into a dark, tall man's pale summer shirt, split the bone beneath, and sink to the hilt. And the man coughed blood into Evan's face and fell.

Then, scrambling in shadows for his gun, Evan looked for Catherine and Beth and saw them in moonlight first and then gun-flashes and Catherine was crouched with her butcher knife out and Beth, behind her, was reloading.

He found the Colt, looked up, and saw Chandra Rao—tall, his face mournful as if with all the world's grief—standing where the moonlight fell through the open cabin door. He was standing relaxed with a small machine pistol in one hand, aiming down the long room at Catherine to kill her.

Evan shot at him and missed and Rao frowned and turned, fired a burst stuttering at Evan—and a slug smacked him, burned along his hip and sent him staggering into the staircase banister. Still frowning, Chandra Rao gripped the piece two-handed to shoot again—and suddenly, looking astounded, was lifted a little off the floor and slammed sideways and into a bookcase against the wall as if by the shotgun's savage sound alone, though blood was sprayed there with him. Evan got his balance, found he could stand, and saw Catherine, reloaded, ready at port arms by moonlight, looking for another target.

A man fired down at Evan from the top of the stairs, and Catherine and Evan turned and fired back together and Evan limped up the stairs after him, shooting, saw the man silhouetted against the window at the end of the upstairs hall, saw a flash, dimly heard the *crack* of the shot. Evan took his time ... and as the man fired once more, the round snapping past, Evan shot him low center. And when he bowed, shot him through the head.

Silence in the house. Silence that made Evan's ears ache.

Then the shotgun below and a shout. Evan went down the stairs reloading and saw in darkness at the fireplace Catherine whirling ... whirling with a man in and out of moonlight. Both spinning around the shotgun as they wrestled for it.

Evan ran, limping—seemed to move so slowly down and down the long room—and Catherine was off her feet, swung out and off her feet, and as the man twisted the shotgun free, Beth came scooting out of a shadow and stuck him in the back with her knife. He yelled and arched away, then turned on her with the shotgun swinging back over his shoulder like a baseball bat as she stood still, looking up at him amazed at what she'd done.

Evan shot at the man, and he said something, reversed the shotgun and fired back and Evan felt the buckshot slam just past his head, imperious as a passing train, and fired and hit the man so he fell back into the fireplace, dropped the shotgun and tried to struggle up.

Evan shot him once more, and the man, as if glad to rest, settled back into the dark and died.

A humming silence. Evan standing in darkness, Catherine standing in light, her shotgun back in her arms.

And no one came at them.

"... Now! *Now!*" And Evan limped out the moonlit

door onto the deck and down to the deck steps, and
saw no one. Then started back, the .45 ready—and as
if by magic a slender man in dark shirt and trousers
rose up from below the deck, a shining pistol in his
hand, and easy as a great cat vaulted high up and over
the railing—as Catherine settled her shotgun into her
shoulder and took him on the rise.

The shotgun flashed out bright crimson . . . the thin-
nest thread of fire licking toward the vaulting man—
who was held in the air for that instant, then dropped
butchered.

Now the silence was only silence until Evan's hearing cleared, and he heard the sea . . . and a sea wind.
He turned back as Catherine stood watching, the shotgun eased from her shoulder, and hobbled down the
deck steps, then back along the deck's supporting timbers . . . quiet on the clearing's soft carpet of pine needles. The man in dark trousers, looking smaller than
before, lay there in shadow.

Evan went past the deck . . . then out around the corner of the cabin . . . and saw a man standing in the
small clearing. Standing in the moonlight, dressed in
white.

Looking back to be certain there was no one behind
him, Evan racked the pistol's slide halfway, saw the
quick rich glint of a cartridge's brass, and let the slide
snap back into battery.

He limped across the small clearing, and as he came
closer saw the man was wearing a short robe, white in
moonlight. Saw that he was old, and unarmed.

A small man, stocky . . . his skin very dark. He was
barefoot, wore only the white robe. An old man whose
full white beard lifted and softly separated in the sea
wind like white feathers as he stood smiling.

He smiled as if he had made the happiest discovery.

And he was blind; his eyes were silver, lid to lid. He stood in the wind, his beard blowing gently, his silver eyes open as if to watch the sea.

"Isn't it Mr. Scott?" The old man's voice was purring, like a cat's. A soft voice, and Evan took a step nearer to hear it. "Yes, it is Mr. Scott. I smell the blood, and some is old and some is new. Oh, beloved of Kali . . . *beloved* of her, since you have come to her in blood. Though also she loves flowers, being very much a woman, isn't it. . . ." The old man now smiled a sadder smile, and said very softly, "You see, we should not have come across the *kala pani,* your dark ocean. A foolishness." And he looked through Scott with silver eyes. "But now," he said, "—now, you will be my son." And his wonderful smile was smashed at the shotgun's blast.

Evan turned and saw Catherine standing high at the end of the deck as faint gunsmoke drifted, her blond hair frosted white in moonlight, standing with the full moon behind her—a northern goddess, and grim.

The sea was calm in early morning, the tide was in. Fog sifted here and there as Evan rode Fred Pell's Sea Truck in, the ugly boat muttering, rocking its way into the harbor. The water lay like jade, but moved as Evan motored over it, occasional faint fog parting for him. He was weary past weariness, and his bad arm hurt. His hip hurt, too, where Catherine had cleansed a bleeding groove, and run gauze over and taped it.

Beth had slept at last; he'd left her sleeping in Catherine's arms. The left side of Catherine's face bruised blue, where the man had struck her trying for the shotgun.

The others, covered with sheets, spare blankets, lay in a row on soft pine needles, shaded by pines. Fred

Pell, strangled, rested in his shack beneath a countr
quilt.

The fog was fading . . . fading as the sun rose behin
Evan and printed his shadow on the dash.

Beckwith's bowie lay unsheathed on the high sea
beside him. He'd levered and wrenched it out of th
tall man's chest, and brought it away from the islan
and hadn't known why.

Evan took his hand off the wheel and picked the bi
knife up; its blade was badly stained. He wanted to sa
something to it, but could think of no spell to bring
to life to listen. So he lifted it high, drew it back ove
his shoulder, and threw it turning flashing in sunris
out over the sea. And looked away so as not to see
fall. . . .

The Whitcomb brothers were repairing lobster po
on the north dock when Evan brought the big boat ir
and Bud stepped over to a bollard, caught the loop c
line and moored her.

Bud and Henry watched as Evan managed the firs
ladder steps one-handed, then Henry reached down to
help him up. "Looks like you had an accident there
Mr. Scott."

"Several." There was an irregular spatter of fire
crackers back of the hill.

"Come in early." Henry was the talker of the two.

"Yes. Need to make some calls. . . ."

"You hear somebody run off with Jarvis's boat?"
Henry took a mended pot from Bud, stacked it on to;
of others.

"That boat's out at the island, Henry. People who
took it, left it out there on the north side."

"Goddamn kids. . . ." Whitcomb tilted another po
up, shook his head at torn netting. "Well, I'd say yo
Scotts sure had the traditional Fourth out there las

night. Could hear them fireworks poppin' across half a mile of sea."

"Yes," Evan said, and he limped on by. "An old-fashioned Fourth of July."

pilogue

∙∙

ιe house had been growing as a strong young woman
ιght grow, in perfectly supported angles and curves—
raight foot-square timbers for her bones, smooth red-
ood siding for her smooth skin . . . steep cedar-shake
.ingling for the fall of her hair.

Half complete, the house rested as a woman might
st, reclining at ease on a sunny late-autumn afternoon
nong tall oaks and maples. Her windowed eyes
oked south over the Sound.

"Finished by spring," Evan said.

He and Catherine stood on the second floor, looking
wn the lawn over stacked lumber, the scattered
ιilding debris the contractor's men had left over the
eekend.

The house smelled new, the sweep of its decking
Ιlding them high in the air among gold and copper
aves.

Down at the rebuilt dock and boathouse—beams and
ding still pale beneath fresh stain—Beth was sitting
ith Willie lying beside her, both looking out over the
ιve.

"She wants her room painted forest green," Cather-
e said. "I advised against it."

"So, forest green it is."

"Yes. She reminds me more and more of me."

"Lucky the man," Evan said, "—who will get ev an echo of you."

Catherine said nothing. But when they walked insi and down the half spiral of the staircase . . . dov through the house's bright unfinished light, she to his hand as if for balance as they went.

FEAR IS ONLY THE BEGINNING